Praise for *Beautiful Bad*

"Ward writes with the same compelling energy as you get in a blockbuster Netflix series. The original storyline and the expertly drawn minor characters will leave you suspecting everyone—and trusting no one."

—*Daily Mail*

"Readers need to be off-the-charts clever to figure out who's going to kill whom in this disturbing novel." —*Toronto Star*

"Harrowing…. Evocative descriptions and strong senses of time and place complement the intricate, intelligent plot, which shocks and chills."

—*Publishers Weekly*, **starred review**

"Utterly gripping and thrillingly original—I loved the unique settings. Cannot recommend this book highly enough."

—**Karen Hamilton, #1 bestselling author of** *The Perfect Girlfriend*

"One of the most refreshingly international set-ups in contemporary psychological thrillers we've seen in a while." —*CrimeReads*

"A well-constructed thriller… Brilliantly conceived…[*Beautiful Bad*] would do Patricia Highsmith proud." —*Booklist*

"Annie Ward explores a battle-scarred marriage on the brink of disaster in this deft debut. As touching and thought-provoking as it is terrifying, *Beautiful Bad* will leave readers spellbound. A buzzworthy read!"

—**Mary Kubica,** *New York Times* **bestselling author of** *The Good Girl* **and** *When the Lights Go Out*

"*Beautiful Bad* is beautifully written, beautifully twisty—and beautifully twisted. A dark thriller with real psychological depth."

—**JP Delaney,** *New York Times* **bestselling author of** *The Girl Before*

BEAUTIFUL
BAD

ANNIE WARD

PARK
ROW
BOOKS

PARK
ROW
BOOKS™

Recycling programs
for this product may
not exist in your area.

ISBN-13: 978-0-7783-0972-7

Beautiful Bad

First published in 2019. This edition published in 2020.

Copyright © 2019 by Annie Ward

This edition published by arrangement with Harlequin Books S.A.

Park Row Books
22 Adelaide St. West, 40th Floor
Toronto, Ontario M5H 4E3, Canada
ParkRowBooks.com
BookClubbish.com

Printed in U.S.A.

For my family.

BEAUTIFUL
BAD

MADDIE

Twelve weeks before

I type, "Should I see a therapist?"

A popular Google search, it seems. There's a lot of information on the topic. Pages and pages of tests you can take to help you decide if therapy is right for you. If so, what kind of therapy? Psychiatrist versus psychologist? What's your major disorder? There's so much. I could do this all night. Once Ian leaves, maybe I will.

Ian drifts over in my direction, opening and closing drawers. "Have you seen my little phone charger?" he asks, frowning. "The portable one?"

"Nope," I answer, my finger hovering over my laptop, ready to hide my search and switch to Facebook if he comes too close.

He leaves.

Back to business. I start scrolling through the quizzes. Some are straightforward. Tick the box yes or no.

You are anxious or scared about a lot of things in your life. Okay, yes.

You are scared that you are going to lose control, go crazy or die. All three!

You sometimes feel like your mind is possessed by another person or creature. Umm, no. But that sounds fun.

You believe there is something wrong with the way you look. I can't help but chuckle silently. Oh my gosh. They should get a load of me.

Some of the questions verge on the utterly bizarre.

Are you uncomfortable with 1) Singing at a karaoke bar sober? 2) Dancing by yourself in a dimly lit nightclub? 3) Making calls to a stranger from the privacy of your bedroom with no one else listening?

Maybe I'm not nearly as loopy as I thought. I wouldn't be caught dead at a karaoke bar sober.

Ian swoops through again, mumbling. "I've got my watch, my phone, my passport..." He glances at me, but he's elsewhere, deep in thought. I try to smile at him but stop. It hurts my eye too much. My finger is hovering again, just in case he decides to come have a look at what I'm doing. Just in case I need to click on Facebook and show him the video of cute baby goats jumping on each other's backs that one of my friends just posted.

Here's another question. Are you hiding something?

It's so simple. It's so direct. It's almost uncanny. As if someone out there knows I'm not supposed to be thinking the things I'm thinking.

Ian doesn't know about my plan to get some help.

He would not approve. He would say, *They're all quacks, you know. And besides. You're fine. We're fine. Everything's perfect.*

Or then again, he might say what he said two weeks ago. Right before I got hurt.

"You really are a spoiled little bitch."

DAY OF THE KILLING

Meadowlark was a small town an hour and a half south of Kansas City. The emergency call center was located in a claustrophobic back room of the single-story, all-brick police station, which resembled a rest stop bathroom. It was ten at night, and Nick Cooper was alone when he received the call. "Nine-one-one, what's your—" he said nonchalantly into his headset microphone, while opening a packet of sugar for his coffee. He wasn't able to finish his question.

A child was shrieking in frantic bursts, and a woman was whispering, "Go back upstairs, baby, please." Her voice was urgent. "Please! Go! Go now!" And then suddenly she shouted, "Oh my God!"

"What's your emergency, ma'am?" he demanded, knocking over his coffee as he lunged for his computer. He told himself to remain calm, but the sound in his ear of a terrified child was incredibly upsetting. His fingers bordered on useless. An address showed up on his computer screen. "Please, ma'am, can you—"

"Hurry!" she screamed. "Please help us! Hurry!" Eight seconds into the call from the residence at 2240 Lincoln Street, Nick lost contact. The female caller gasped and said "No!" in a desperate voice. Then there was the sound of what he assumed was the phone clattering to the floor. The line went dead. He tried to call back. No luck.

Nick sent out the emergency signal over the radio. "Possible robbery or domestic battery underway at 2240 Lincoln Street," he said, speaking so fast his words ran together. "Female and child in the residence. No further information. Call ended. Unable to reestablish connection. Over."

Officer Diane Varga responded within seconds. "Dispatch, this is 808. I'm headed over now."

Nick grabbed his phone and pressed the speed dial for Barry Shipps. Of Meadowlark's two detectives, Barry was more likely to respond quickly even though he was off duty and probably not near his radio.

"This is Detective Shipps."

"Detective," Nick said. "This is Dispatch. Can you stand by for a possible call-out to 2240 Lincoln Street?"

"I can do better than that," Shipps answered. "I'm filling up my car at Casey's General just down the road." A beat later Shipps was back in his car on his radio. "Dispatch, this is Shipps. I'm en route."

Diane was in Nick's ear again. "And I'm turning off Victory onto 223rd. Almost there."

"Roger 808." Nick almost said be careful. He stopped himself. Every time he ran into Diane in town, he found himself whistling Van Morrison's "Brown Eyed Girl." He took a deep breath and folded his trembling hands in his lap.

★ ★ ★

A mostly white, working-class town, Meadowlark had its fair share of old farm families scattered about the outlying areas. There was one nice place, a beer garden and brewery called The Crooked Crow, which had just enough rural charm to draw people out from the city on sunny weekends. Other than that, there were just two sit-down restaurants. The Wagon Wheel and Gambinos. Last ditch, there was a Subway inside the Walmart.

The words *Sweet Water Creek* were etched into a plaque on a decorative stone wall at the intersection. Officer Varga turned into the neighborhood. It was relatively new, ground broken just six years earlier, with only half the plots sold and a number of uninhabited homes. Moderately priced wooden constructs, they were nevertheless sizable and blandly pleasant, nestled between a couple of small, unimpressive country ponds and some magnificent old elms.

Diane rounded the corner and noticed a red Radio Flyer tricycle overturned on the sidewalk. The silver handlebars gleamed in the cheerful glow from the porch lantern two doors down from her destination.

The house at 2240 Lincoln was one of the larger in the neighborhood, sprawling across a gradually sloping lawn with tasteful landscaping and a terra-cotta stone fountain jutting up from behind a cluster of poorly tended rosebushes. Diane got the feeling that here in Sweet Water Creek, everything was all right. Better than her life, for sure. Her intuition, as she stepped from her car and faced the house, did not say to her, "crime scene."

"Dispatch, I'm on location," she said into the radio mic attached to her uniform chest pocket. Diane walked at a fast clip up the sidewalk toward the front door, framed by two slender evergreen trees on either side. She knocked loudly three times.

"Police!" she called out, but there was no answer. From somewhere close by came the clipped repetition of an upset dog yipping nonstop. She felt her pulse quicken. *This can't be too bad*, she thought. It's Meadowlark. And yet, something was telling her to hurry. She punched her finger on the doorbell, ringing it in frantic succession. The hollow bong of the bell echoed inside. No footsteps on the stairs. Nothing.

The door itself was wooden, framed on either side by decorative windows. Diane peeked inside, trying to focus through the textured glass. The first thing she saw was a pair of tall military-style combat boots sitting just inside the entry. They seemed somehow at odds with the modern home and its vast, shiny floor of polished blond wood. It appeared to be one great room; open plan, like a city loft. Right by the front door was a curved staircase winding up to the second floor. An electronic device, possibly a home phone, lay in smashed plastic pieces on the floor next to the bottom step. Diane moved slightly to get a better angle. Now she could see more of the interior.

She caught her breath.

The beautiful blond wood was stained. There was a red mess in the middle of the room. Her heart commenced hammering in her chest. It was not going to be nothing, as she had hoped. And Nick had mentioned a child.

"Dispatch, I'm looking through a window at what appears to be a lot of fresh blood," she said into her mic, more loudly than intended. "Possible fatality here. I need backup and EMS." With a barely discernible edge of panic, she fumbled to un-holster her semiautomatic Glock pistol and raised it to a tentative ready position.

She rang the bell once more. "Police!" she yelled again, this time in a wilder, louder voice. She tried the door and gave it a hard shove with her shoulder. It was locked and solid.

Diane raced toward the shadowy south side of the home,

looking for another entrance. As she ran, she heard Nick sending out another emergency tone over the radio requesting all
units for backup. She slipped in a patch of mud rounding the
corner and caught herself with her free hand. She could now
tell that the dog barking frantically was in the backyard.

At the end of a row of bushes was a wrought-iron fence
with a gate. Broken and tied shut with a bungee cord. Diane
became frantic in her attempt to wrestle the rusty thing open.

"Come on!" she whispered, frustration mounting. Finally
it gave, the hinges making a horrible scraping noise like claws
dragging down a chalkboard. As she began crossing the backyard, two other officers responded in succession that they were
on their way. Diane said, "Shipps? ETA?"

His voice came over her mic. "Five minutes."

"Roger."

Diane stepped on something that let out a loud squeak.
"Shit," she whispered and looked down to see a duck-shaped
dog toy under her boot. As she progressed farther and her
eyes adjusted to the dark, she saw several partially eaten, old
yellow tennis balls strewn about in the overgrown grass and
weeds. At the edge of the patio was a giant green plastic sandbox in the shape of a turtle. Next to it was a toddler's water
table, just the right size for a small child to stand and splash
and use all the colorful cups to make the water wheel spin.
She thought of the red tricycle near the neighbor's yard and
pictured a child's chubby churning legs. A little three-wheeler
hurtling down the sidewalk and then kicked aside without a
backward glance, forgotten in pursuit of some new adventure.

So Nick had been right. Diane was now sure that her first
priority at the scene was to save a child.

The light seeped through the shutters of the back windows,
and Diane crouched close to the house as she made her way
across the patio toward the door. She saw the barking dog.

There were actually two of them; small, black-and-white Boston terriers. Anxious but sweet creatures, they looked baffled at having been locked out of the house. Their eyes were wide and wet, and both were panting and pacing, completely beside themselves.

Diane turned the handle on the door. "Back door's unlocked," she said into her mic.

Nick was the first to respond. "EMS has been notified. They know you're waiting on a second officer to enter the residence. I've told them to stage at 2218 Lincoln and wait for update."

"Copy," Diane answered. Nick knew the routine. She was, without question, supposed to wait on a second officer to enter. If she went in, she was going against procedure. She'd get in trouble. Diane glanced over her shoulder at the sandbox. The water table. Then she decided. She'd rather lose her job than lose a child.

Diane pushed the door inward and held out her foot to stop the dogs from following her inside. She closed it softly behind her. As she crept into the house, she glanced back. The front paws of both Boston terriers were against the glass, flexing and pleading, coaxing her to return, to come let them in.

The back door opened into a far corner of the lower level next to a round glass breakfast table and four chairs. An empty wine bottle appeared to have rolled to a rest against the wall. On the table was another bottle of wine, and underneath on the floor was an elegant cylinder of Stolichnaya Elit vodka.

Diane was not much of a food snob, but noted that this was no chips-and-dip poker party. In the center of the table was a thick wooden cutting board covered in a semi-eaten array of olives, salami, crackers, cheese and grapes.

Though she tried to focus on the entirety of the scene, the bloodstain was hard to ignore. If she glanced up and across the great room, there it was again. Mesmerizing. Sickening.

Despite the fact that the room was open concept, it was dotted with chairs and a sofa as well as bookcases, end tables and floor lamps. Hiding places everywhere. She moved stealthily, her pistol ready and her eyes flitting back and forth from one quiet corner to another.

As she inched past the breakfast table she had to watch her step. The shattered remains of several glasses were scattered about, big and little shards everywhere. Of the four yellow upholstered chairs surrounding the breakfast table, one was overturned and one was stained a shade darker where there had been a spill. Next to the fallen chair was a wet photograph.

Diane leaned down to get a better look. It pictured two brunette women. That much Diane could tell from all the windswept hair. They were standing in front of an unusual building. The design was vaguely Middle Eastern, almost like a mosque with no minaret. Whatever had pooled on the floor had seeped through the paper and the women's features now bled into one another. Diane imagined someone sitting at this table holding it shortly before. Reminiscing? *Do you remember when we…? Yes, let me just go grab the photo…*

Separating the living area from the kitchen was an island in the shape of a crescent. Several tall chairs ran the length. It was not until Diane passed the breakfast table that she could see over the kitchen bar.

The little puddles varied in size and looked like something left on the sidewalk after a big rain. Except they were crimson. The droplets leading away resembled a beaded necklace, almost like a thin strand of bloody pearls.

The slaughter had happened between the refrigerator and the inside of the bar, where the sink and dishwasher were located. The surrounding walls and appliances were splattered. Diane felt a tightening in the back of her throat. The front of the refrigerator was papered in finger paintings now artistically spotted with tiny red flecks; a nightmarish rain slanting over neat box houses, a stick family of three, fluffy clouds and a happy-face sun.

The trail of bead-like blood moved from the kitchen puddles to the big slick in the middle of the room. It was messy, almost as if mopped, and Diane imagined someone crawling on hands and knees before managing to haul up on his or her feet for one more staggering go at life. She had an irrational urge to start running through the house calling out for the child, but she'd already broken one rule just by entering.

On the wall across the room, an oval wooden African mask with holes carved for the eyes and mouth stared at her with an expression of horror.

Diane looked anxiously over her shoulder at the table laid out as if for an indulgent wine-and-cheese feast among friends. Then she looked ahead, at the nightmarish slop of a human spill beckoning her to come see; come see what unspeakable thing has happened here.

MADDIE

Ten weeks before

Her eyes keep coming back to the top left corner of my face. She looks away toward the window, out over the man-made neighborhood pond visible from her home office, but then it's right back to the place where I've been sewn back together.

I don't know how this is going to work. On her website she says she is "above all a nonjudgmental, compassionate and discreet psychologist accomplished at using writing therapy to address anxiety." For fuck's sake then, stop staring. I've told her I'm here because I'd like to feel less nervous.

She smiles at me. That's better. She says, in a lilting infomercial voice, "There are many, many extremely helpful exercises used in writing therapy. What I love most about it is that you can explore as far and wide and deep as your imagination and inhibitions will allow. We'll try a variety of approaches and see—" she tilts her head to the side in a way that is at once obviously rehearsed and yet strangely attractive "—see what works best for you, Maddie."

I nod, and the hair I wear pulled over the left side of my face must move a little. She's playing it very cool, but her fascination is evident. I'm not surprised. The bruise has faded but the whole mess is still pretty shocking.

I feel discouraged. I need this to work, but this woman is not what I expected. It was important to me that I do writing therapy, and there were not all that many choices in my area. When I chose Dr. Camilla Jones, with her private practice in Overland Park, I pictured a lady in a sophisticated suit and some grandmotherly pumps. Kind eyes. Silver hair.

This woman, this Camilla, has told me that her name rhymes with Pamela. What? Instead of Dr. Jones, she wants me to call her Cami J. She is dressed in a loose, floral off-the-shoulder T-shirt, yoga pants and a baseball cap. I hate to be shallow, but I have to point out that there are rhinestones all over the front of her cap. All over. Everywhere. It's probably as hard for me not to gawk at her cap as it is for her not to gawk at my face. The focal point on this cap is a giant rhinestone fleur-de-lis. This troubles me. She's got be in her early sixties even though she looks fucking great. Honestly, though, I just didn't want my psychologist to remind me of a Zumba instructor.

Finally she is looking me in the eyes. "Maddie?"

"Yes?" I don't know why but I am clenching my fists, then opening them, then clenching them again. I used to get carpal tunnel syndrome from all the writing, and I would do this when my wrists were sore. I stop.

"Let's cut to the chase and start easy. I want you to write down twenty things that set off your anxiety." She passes me a piece of lined notebook paper and a pen. "Try not to think too much about it. Just what scares you or makes you sad or nervous. Write the first things that pop into your head, okay?"

"Okay."

1. When Charlie cries. Anything bad happening to Charlie.

2. When Ian drinks vodka in the basement. Or when he won't wake up.

3. When someone shoots kids in a school, or really when anybody goes and shoots a bunch of people randomly, but especially kids. I don't like the guns in the house either.

4. When someone drives a gigantic eighteen-wheeler through a beach parade in France and mows everyone down.

5. ISIS.

6. It sounds silly but I get scared when I go somewhere to meet new people and they want to sit in a circle and have me tell them about myself. I don't go to the Meadowlark mom's brunch thing anymore.

7. When the angry man with the beard on the treadmill in front of me gets off and walks away and leaves his big backpack sitting there.

8. When I call the dogs and they don't come and I can't find them. (Probably just because this happened last night. They dug under the fence but they didn't get hit by a car. I patched the fence where they got out.)

9. When my parents or Charlie get sick. Deadly new strains of the flu.

10. When Ian goes to dangerous countries to work. All the things that could go wrong.

11. Funerals. Hospitals and lakes.

12. When Ian gets angry at Charlie.

13. That an alligator can lunge out of the Disney lagoon and snatch a little boy right out of his father's arms.

14. When my heart races uncontrollably. This happens usually when I start missing Joanna and thinking about how she probably still hates me.

15. Drowning, especially little Syrian kids that wash up dead on the shore, I can't even cope, sometimes for days, and I dream about Charlie drowning and sometimes I worry about the dogs drowning. Tidal waves.

16. When I take Charlie to the park and then suddenly he's gone and I can't find him.

17. The darkness in some people. Like, that guy in Germany who paid some other guy to cut him up a little bit at a time, cook him and eat him.

18. When Charlie cries.

19. When I have to leave Charlie with Ian.

20. That something is wrong with me.

I slide my paper across to Cami J, who, now that I have gotten a better look at her in very tight seventies-style flared yoga pants, I am tempted to privately think of as "Cami Toe."

She begins to read silently. I say, "I think I repeated myself. I think I wrote 'Charlie crying' twice."

She nods, concentrating on my list. "Repetition can be informative."

After a few minutes she looks up at me, and this time she doesn't even bother with subtlety. Her eyes take a little trip up and down the wrecked and winding road from my lip to my brow. "Does it still hurt?"

"When I smile. A little."

"Is that why you don't smile?"

"I don't? I'm pretty sure I smile." Then I smile, to prove it.

"Have you been to see a plastic surgeon?"

"No. I probably will eventually, though." The truth is, I have always been what my grandmother called *"jolie laide."* Beautiful ugly. My eyes are peculiar and pale gray. My smile is asymmetrical, and there is something fox-like about the shape of my face. I've never lacked for male attention, but I know that whatever appeal I possess lies in my oddity. I have not decided yet if I like my developing scar or not. Sometimes when I look at myself in the mirror I think it is a far more honest cover for the book that is me.

Cami J nods, her eyes moist with motherly empathy. She taps my paper. "You are doing a lot of what we call 'catastrophizing.'"

"That's a new word for me."

"It's more and more common now that we have the constant stream of bad news. The irrational fear of catastrophe. It's easy to overestimate the possibility of an extremely rare tragedy befalling you or a loved one."

I think about telling her about my intimate knowledge of

rare tragedy, but I decide to save it. I say simply, "Accidents happen. Anything at any time."

"Anything? Alligators?" She smiles, leans forward and winks. "German cannibals?"

I shrug and then I can't help it. I laugh. German cannibals.

"There is something else going on here, though," she says, and the whole Zumba vibe is gone, and she is deadly serious. "Would you like to tell me more about your relationship with Ian? Is he Charlie's father?"

I nod, and to be clear, I would love to tell her all about Ian. Really, because it's a great story. But for some reason I suddenly can't speak, and the thought of what's happened to Ian is too much. I find myself paralyzed, my tongue a slimy fish crammed in my mouth, swampy water in my nose. This happens sometimes. I remember being held under, my face just inches under the surface, eyes bulging and air so close and inviting that I opened my mouth to breathe...

The water poured into my mouth and down my throat. It took over and that was that. Everything was different.

"Which way is your bathroom, please?" I manage, standing up. "I'm going to be sick."

MADDIE

2001

Charlie's father. The love of my life. Ian.

Wait. Let me start at the beginning.

I was a "do-gooder." A lot of my friends were do-gooders, too. Back then I lived in a part of the world that most tour guides didn't bother to mention. If they did, they used words like *war-ravaged. Impoverished. Lawless.* All three of those adjectives would have held quite a bit of appeal for me. I found it thrilling to live in, as it was sometimes called, "The darkest, most forgotten corner of Europe." So, I was smack-dab in the middle of my do-gooder phase teaching poor students English in one of the isolated former Soviet Bloc countries known collectively as the Balkans.

I was based in Bulgaria, and my best friend, Joanna, lived one country over from mine, in a little-known but very combustible place called Macedonia.

I first met Ian at a fund-raiser. That sounds boring, doesn't it? He was far from boring.

We were in Ohrid, a touristy resort town a few hours south of Macedonia's capital city of Skopje, not far from the Greek border. Picturesque in a run-down way, its stone villas were stacked on a hill overlooking the sun-dappled lake water. At the highest point, looking out south toward Greece, was the domed, post-card perfect thirteenth-century Church of St. John, so lovely and tranquil that it belied all the discord in the village over which it presided. If it weren't for the tangible tension among the people milling about the twisty alleys and plazas, Ohrid might have been comfortably charming. Instead, it was a holiday destination packed with people of two warring religions, and it seemed to me that everyone was eyeing everyone else with a mixture of bloodlust and suspicion. The country was on the brink of civil war.

The benefit for the Red Cross was "dinner and a show" in a ramshackle tavern perched precariously on waterlogged wooden beams, hanging over the muddy edge of a lake. Joanna worked with women and children in refugee camps around Macedonia. Her boss, Elaine, in Washington, DC, had asked her to attend the charity event and given her two tickets. She'd begged me to come visit for the weekend and go as her "plus one."

Jo had a habit of plaiting her hair when she was bored or nervous. Now she was hunched over her vodka tonic, fingers weaving, her hazel eyes on the handful of mousy intellectuals milling around the communal dinner tables trying to decide where they should sit. "And to think," she said, "we could be somewhere else watching paint dry and having so much more fun."

"Free drinks," I answered. I was indifferent.

"Should we just leave?" she asked, sitting up bright-eyed and suddenly enthusiastic.

"If you won't get in trouble," I answered, openly encouraging a runner.

She wilted. "I might, though. If you help me kiss a few of the more important asses, I think it would be okay to leave in an hour."

At that moment three men walked in, one of whom was very tall and, at least from a distance, shockingly handsome. I leaned in to whisper, "Is he on the list? I might be willing to volunteer."

Jo leaned back and laughed. "Uh, no. I can guarantee you I've never seen that man before in my entire life."

"Wait," I said, noticing the man's companions. "Isn't that your friend Hillbilly Buck? From the American Embassy?"

"Holy shit, yes, it is," Joanna answered, standing up and waving the trio over to our table.

Hillbilly Buck was our name for Mr. Buck Snyder, the whiskery, rabbit-toothed military attaché to the American Embassy who Joanna sometimes called to discuss the security of her refugee camps. We had christened him with the nickname Hillbilly Buck one night after he'd spent a long drunken dinner bragging in his Southern twang that, "All these Balkan women, man, they don't care. You can say anything. Man, you can do whatever. If you're riding with big blue you're still gonna get your dick wet." "Big blue" was Hillbilly Buck's name for his American passport.

As we pretended not to be watching their every move, Joanna and I waited to see if the men would actually come sit with us. Jo reached over, touched my arm and said, "Thank you for coming. I'm so glad I'm not here alone."

I'd been slightly reluctant to get on that horrible bus on this particular occasion. A clash between Macedonia's Christian majority and the growing Muslim minority had resulted in a recent escalation of violence, and like everywhere else in the region, a fog of hatred and fury hovered over the quaint mountain villages like an industrial cloud. Macedonia was no longer safe for anyone.

However, Joanna hadn't exactly twisted my arm to get me to come. I really loved visiting her and felt lucky that we had both ended up living in Eastern Europe after graduate school. It was, however, an uncomfortable five-to eight-hour bus ride for me, depending on how long I was detained at the border separating our two countries. Also, I was tired from work.

I was at the tail end of a fourteen-month Fulbright Scholarship in Bulgaria that involved teaching English classes at the University of Sofia while working on a nonfiction book. My days were comprised of writing, travel and teaching, and I was mostly happy.

I'd met Joanna Jasinski when we were both high school students on a summer exchange program in Spain. We'd had a shared interest in linguistics, making out with Spanish boys at discos, Russian and German philosophers and The Cure. At the time we met, we had both wanted to "grow up" to be interpreters, and we often spoke to one another in a hodgepodge of the various languages we were studying, infuriating and alienating others. For a long time, we were one another's only friend.

She majored in international studies and became an aid worker, and I went into journalism. We were eventually both drawn to work and study in the former Soviet Bloc where we could put our Slavic language training to use, and over the past year we had visited each other more than a dozen times. We kept the wolves of loneliness growling just outside the gate.

After stopping to speak to a few people, Hillbilly Buck and the other two men began crossing the restaurant. I was able to get a better look at them as they moved out of the shadowy entrance and toward our table. Hillbilly Buck was never a handsome man, but next to these two he looked positively rodent-like. They were tall, broad at the top and slim in the hips. One was blond and angelic, with curls and cartoonishly huge blue eyes. The other man was the one Joanna and I had both noticed at once. He was strikingly shaped, with a cleft chin and shoulders like rolling hills. He walked with his eyes on the view of the lake outside, lost in thought or as if he were alone. Unafraid.

His brown hair was short on the sides and tousled on top, and he wore dark, neatly pressed jeans. His chest. I paused there for a second. His chest. It was a showstopper even beneath that horrible apricot-colored dress shirt. There was something boyish about his outfit, like a kid dressed up for his school musical. His classic features were more suited to a black-and-white photo, him seated at an outdoor French café with an espresso. His youthful attire looked wrong on him, and I remember thinking that if he showed up in my hometown of Meadowlark, Kansas, dressed in that apricot getup, he would be beaten to a pastel pulp just for walking in the door.

Hillbilly Buck bellowed introductions so loudly that I concluded he was already drunk. "Ian and Peter, meet Joanna and…"

He snapped his fingers repeatedly in my direction.

"Madeline," I said, pointing to myself helpfully.

"That's right. I remember you now. Ian and Peter work for the British ambassador. Part of his new close-protection team. They've just arrived."

An elderly accordion player in a ragged suit suddenly started making a musical racket on the other side of the restaurant. Joanna said loudly, "I take it your bosses also made you drive down to this nerd-fest on your night off?"

Hillbilly Buck nodded irritably, but curly blond Peter leaned forward and said, in all earnestness, "I was told there's going to be a folk dance show after the food!"

Joanna laughed out loud, her pretty face pink with delight. "Ahh. No one's prepared you for the number of folk dance shows you're going to have to sit through living here. The good news is not all of the singing sounds like a lamb being sacrificed."

Peter looked perplexed. He was adorable. Massive, yet cute. Powerful but pleasant. Not smart.

Joanna touched his arm and said, "Sit down next to me. You're officially my new favorite person."

I sneaked a few glances at Ian, who had taken the seat across from me. He appeared wholly engrossed in his menu, and took no interest in me or Joanna whatsoever. He was reading it like he had eaten poison and on it was written the formula for the antidote. No Macedonian fish tavern menu could be that interesting.

I resolved to appear unimpressed with him as well. A couple of minutes later, Ian had a little chuckle to himself. He leaned back, lit a cigarette and laid his plastic menu down open on the graffiti-scratched wooden table. (The Balkans had nothing against cigarettes, not in a restaurant or even a hospital, for that matter.) After pensively raising his eyebrow, Ian sat up and said, in a charming English accent, "Well, I think I am going to go for the crap."

Jo didn't miss a beat. "In America we say 'go take a crap,' not 'go for the crap,' and what might be even more helpful to you is knowing that we would almost always keep that information to ourselves."

"That is helpful! Thank you. But," Ian said, pointing to his menu, "I was referring to the Lake Ohrid crap. Right here.

"It's either that," he continued in a tone of complete seriousness, "or the house special, which is the Lake Ohrid throat." He leaned forward and fixed his tree-bark eyes on me.

"What do you fancy? The throat or the crap?"

He pushed the menu in front of me. It was immediately obvious to me that whoever had translated *trout* and *carp* for the English menu had made some very unfortunate spelling errors. "Oh I would definitely go for the throat," I answered.

Ian looked amused. Suddenly I saw myself as I supposed he did. I was wearing a conservative beige turtleneck, and I had not taken my hair down after finishing my lecture earlier in the day. I had donned my reading glasses to examine my menu, and I suddenly felt every inch the dowdy librarian I imagined he saw before him.

"Really?" he responded. "I wouldn't have thought so. You seem like a nice young lady."

Heat rose to my cheeks. He gave me a coy smile. I could see it in his eyes. He was teasing me.

"Nice shirt," I said back, annoyed. He didn't know me.

"Thank you," he said, having a quick look down at what he was wearing. He then physically picked up his chair and angled it away from me and toward Joanna. She, though busy tolerating one of Hillbilly Buck's stories, registered this realignment with a glance at Ian and a flicker of a smile.

The toothless octogenarian playing the accordion suddenly fell upon our table like a vampire bat on a herd of cows, and I started digging though my wallet for a tip.

Ian and Peter eventually left with Hillbilly Buck, who announced he wanted to go somewhere "cooler." Joanna and I stayed at the tavern, dancing for hours with the scruffy old accordion player and his equally unkempt grandsons who were in the band that came on after.

That's how we were. Back then.

MADDIE

2001

After a long weekend with Joanna, I made the bus journey back through the mountains from Macedonia to Bulgaria, closing my eyes as we teetered around precipices and trundled along narrow lanes cutting above massive cliffs. Per usual the driver went far too fast, and the road conditions were poor. Yet for some reason, halfway through the nauseating ride, I was already starting to wonder if and when I might be able to return.

Back in the Bulgarian capital of Sofia, it was with a heavy heart that I arrived to teach my very last class at the university a few weeks later. My time was up. My scholarship was ending as were my afternoons with my students. I would have to go home soon, and I didn't want to go home at all.

The urban campus was dominated by a massive baroque revival main hall. The front steps led up to four stately columns, which flanked towering arched windows. The roof was a massive copper dome with a striking jade green patina.

Inside, it was far less impressive. Several floors of classrooms surrounded a small courtyard. The stairwells were covered in graffiti. The coffee shop offered espresso in tiny plastic cups alongside a rack stocked with cigarettes and a variety of pretzels. From the coffee shop you could follow a trail of discarded espresso cups and empty pretzel packages to anywhere in the building. The bins were full. There was no janitor. There was no toilet paper. There was no money.

And it was cold. My classroom was on the top floor. Most of the winter I had taught wearing my coat and gloves, looking out over a sea of stocking caps.

That year in Eastern Europe had been an especially magic time in my life. Just strolling the streets of Sofia, it would have been hard to say what my fascination was with the people and the culture of that maligned country.

Everywhere you looked, there were ghosts. The black-and-white paper death notices featuring photos of the recently deceased were omnipresent in all the Balkan countries; stapled to telephone poles, plastering bus stops, papering walls and nailed to trees. Underneath the gaze of all those dead photocopied eyes the dogs paced, watching the drunk teenagers with their *döner* kebabs. A couple of wrinkly men in old, stained fedoras played backgammon at a plastic table under a Zagorka beer umbrella at a derelict café constructed of metal siding. I breathed in the smells of Sofia. Grilled meat and peppers, smoldering trash, crisp, pungent pine from the mountain, badly masked body odor, flower markets and fresh popcorn. It wasn't for everyone, but I was head over heels for those forlorn and villainous Balkan streets, and my sordid city was about to be wrenched from my desperate embrace. I would have given anything to stay just a little longer.

It was getting dark when I caught the dilapidated tram back to my apartment in the city center. Moments after tossing my keys on the coffee table, my rotary phone—a contraption that looked like it belonged in a silent film or a museum—made its shrill rattle. "Hello?"

It was Caroline, an editor from Fodor's Travel Guides, who had hired me to write a few chapters about Spain when I was fresh out of graduate school. "We're finally breaking down our Eastern European Edition into countries," she said.

It was the best surprise ever.

She offered me the job of covering Bulgaria for their 2003 travel guide. The pay was not good by American standards but in bargain-basement Bulgaria? I'd just been handed the keys to the Kingdom. I was going to travel, all expenses paid, to every corner of my beloved adopted homeland. It was the middle of May and the start of the gorgeous Balkan summer. Bulgaria had vast stretches of unspoiled beaches as well as breathtaking mountains for hiking. Jo could come visit, and we would take weekend drives down to Sozopol, where she would swim while I read on the beach. There would be pic-nic tables laden with succulent lamb chops, salty tomato-and-cucumber salads and crispy french fries covered in crumbly feta. We would go barefoot, and our skin would darken and freckle and we would drink homemade white wine in remote, ancient and tourist-free fishing villages.

I could stay. It was pure happiness. Pure freedom. I called Joanna to tell her the news. "I don't have to go home when my scholarship ends after all," I said. "I'll have lots of time to come see you. I have my laptop. I can write from anywhere. We have the whole summer before I have to leave."

"Yay!" she screamed over the phone. "Oh my God. That is abso-fucking-lutely the best news ever. Congratulations, baby!"

The next night I was standing on the sidewalk in front of my apartment with my ancient, liver-spotted neighbor, Mr. Milov. We were chatting at extreme length about the appalling prices of bread and yogurt, and I was slowly inching away toward the entrance to our building when a black Mercedes pulled up alongside us.

Mr. Milov had impressive eyebrows like silver caterpillars, and they shot up in alarm. The passenger window lowered and a man wearing a cap and sunglasses said with a thick Eastern European accent, "Miss Brandt? I need you to get in the car."

"I'm not getting in your car," I answered, laughing out loud. Then I noticed that Mr. Milov was legitimately terrified and gulping for breath.

I grabbed his arm, but before I could say anything the back door swung open, and there was Joanna, holding a bottle of champagne. "I'm sorry!" she shouted, jumping out. "Is he okay? Are you okay? It was a surprise for Maddie! We're celebrating that she doesn't have to go back home yet! I'm so sorry."

She held up the champagne and said with an embarrassed, guilty smile, "*Iznenada*! Surprise!"

Mr. Milov collected himself and shuffled away, muttering with his hand over his heart.

An hour later Jo and I were huddled at a corner table drinking bellinis and eating beef carpaccio and smoked salmon at the Sheraton's Capitale.

"I owed you a visit," she said, poking her fork at a piece of salmon. "I've been so busy. You've been to see me way more times lately than I've come to see you. It wasn't even that long of a drive. Five hours. Tops. Easy peasy. And honestly? It feels so good to be away from all the rage and hate, having a blast here with you. This salmon is amazing."

She began breathlessly outlining for me the plan she had for us to drive to Montenegro later in the summer and spend a week on the beach at Budva.

"My friend Ana is going to hook us up with a friend of

hers, this guy who rents his flat every summer and goes and lives with his toothless uncle under a bridge or something. But it's got a beautiful view. Ana emailed me a picture, which I'll show you when we get back to your apartment, but honestly, Maddie, it's so awesome and now that you're staying I don't have to go alone! My break is from August sixth to—"

As she was prattling happily along her phone buzzed. She didn't even pause until she had opened it, and then her face changed completely. She had this little vein that ran down her forehead, and when she was upset it would become gorged with blood. It was throbbing. Her hand was shaking. "Oh shit."

"What?"

She closed her phone and lowered her head.

"What's wrong?" I asked.

She looked up and let out a huge sigh. "I have to go back to ball-sack Skopje."

"What!"

"Hold on." She made a quick call to her driver and then motioned to the waiter for the check. "I'm sorry. I can't stay after all."

"What's happened?"

"We have a shipment of baby formula and diapers for the refugees at Stankovac being detained at the Greek border."

"But it's the weekend. Can't it wait until Monday?"

"If I lose this shipment, it's thousands of dollars," she said, rifling through her purse for her wallet. "And apparently the Macedonian police are trying to confiscate it. That would mean we'll never see it again."

"Why would they do that?"

"Because some police officer at the border knows that there's a crazy American lady who will pay to get her shipment released."

"You mean you?"

"Duh."

"You're going to pay off a policeman?"

"Yep," she said nonchalantly, and then knocked back the last sip from her champagne flute.

"Oh my God," I said.

"Oh my God," she said, mimicking me, and then laughed. "It's okay, Maddie. It's just the way things get done."

We grabbed a cab back to my apartment. While she threw her things back into her bag, I packed as well. She noticed and said, "I can't take you back with me."

"Why not?"

"It's not a good idea this time."

"I'm done teaching and my assignment package from Fodor's isn't going to arrive for two weeks. I can't even start working until then. Let me come with you."

"It's getting worse in Macedonia. Massacres. Bombings. All of us Americans are under a travel warning not to enter the country."

"You live there!"

"I have to! Don't be crazy."

"I'm coming."

After a second she reached out and took my hand. "Thank you."

For the first stretch of the drive, Joanna was busy texting her coworkers about the situation. When the border crossing was behind us, my thoughts wandered. My parents would be furious with me for taking the Fodor's job and staying in Eastern Europe. However, I imagined my grandmother Audrey would be quite pleased. She, too, had been frustrated by the inertia of her Midwestern upbringing in a small university town filled with academics and immigrants. But she had learned French in school and German from her grandparents.

When I was thirteen she took me on an architectural tour

of France focusing on the structures of Le Corbusier. On Saturdays she would take me to the Nelson-Atkins Museum of Art and make me repeat after her: "Though Kansas City's Nelson-Atkins museum is primarily distinguished for its extensive collection of Asian art, I have always particularly adored the lovely east wing, which is filled with European paintings by Caravaggio, El Greco, Degas and Monet."

This was one of many rehearsed opinions meant to be shared with the sophisticated and cultured people she introduced me to on our travels. I remember sitting across from her over a light lunch after one such outing to the Nelson-Atkins. We were at her first-choice corner table at the private Carriage Club. I was sipping tea, ignoring the enticing bread basket and picking at my salad as she had taught me to do.

"The problem with Sara," she said, referring to my sexy sister, "is that she has never had her heart broken. And Julia. Well. Julia is brilliant. But book brilliant, if you know what I mean. You, my dear," she said, her small gray eyes boring into mine with fiery ambition, "you are more like me. The type to take on the world. People like us? We don't play by the rules. My grandparents would say you are 'übermensch.' Remarkable."

I took my grandmother's veiny hand in both of mine and leaned toward her to share in her conspiratorial smile. Maybe I was remarkable. She said so and I was game to find out. And unremarkable Kansas played no part in my future whatsoever. My parents had no idea, but I was never going to move back home.

It was partly because of that conversation with Grandmother Audrey that I began to view the rules as guidelines, scoff at danger and flirt with disaster. Like Icarus, I suppose I was giddy and flew too close to the sun.

His wings were fake, constructed of wax and feathers. He

should have known better. They melted and burned. He plummeted from high in the sky into a vast sea where he drowned.

Up front in the driver's seat, Stoyan cracked his window and began to smoke. Only one hand on the wheel. We'd reached a neglected stretch of highway, the road uneven and dark. Trucks coming from the opposite direction barreled by, causing gusts of wind.

Stoyan began to overtake a slow-moving car while headlights from oncoming traffic twinkled ominously in the distance. The radio was loud.

I glanced over at Joanna. She gave me a sleepy smile and then closed her eyes. I did the same.

When we woke, the mountains were behind us.

MADDIE

Nine weeks before

Ian is in Nigeria looking after a small group of firefighters from Boots & Coots who are preparing to extinguish an enormous oil well fire outside Port Harcourt, where there was a suicide bombing last month. These oil fires can take weeks to put out and then there's a massive cleanup. He told me ninety days, but the truth is I don't know when he's coming home.

I'm headed to see Cami J and wondering if part of today's session will be another list of things that scare me. If so, this time I will include Nigeria's Boko Haram jihadists and their fanatic leader. He was on television briefly last night and I rewound it six times. He chomped his gum and gleefully declared, "Guess what? I abducted your girls!"

As I watched the documentary clip again and again I thought about the two hundred girls they took like it was nothing. That's the world now. No consequences. That's where Ian's been for the past three weeks and where he'll be stuck for some time to come.

With Ian out of town and my parents visiting my sister in St. Louis, I need to leave Charlie at the YMCA Kid's Club for the two hours necessary to drive into Overland Park, have my session and drive back. I can't find Charlie's shoes and he can't find his special superhero paracord bracelet Ian made for him. We're running late.

I'm backing out of the driveway like a lunatic, and I nearly run over my neighbor Wayne Randall. Wayne has retired from his job at Heritage Tractor and Trailer and now spends the better part of each day planting trees, trimming his hedges and staging elaborate holiday arrangements around his house and yard about two months too early. He is literally standing behind my car, so that I have to come to a complete stop. Wayne spent three weeks on the English coast forty years ago and is also a fan of Monty Python movies. Without fail, whether Ian is with me or not, Wayne greets me heartily with a horrible British accent.

"Maddie," he says outside my window, moving his hand in frantic circles like he's turning a handle. Charlie leans forward with interest. Wayne may as well be a clown.

I oblige and roll down the window. He pokes his ruddy face in and shouts, "Top o' the mornin', lass. It's been donkey's years!"

I say, "I'm so sorry, Wayne, no time. I'm late for an appointment."

"Okay," he says, not budging. "And how's the wee little lad?" He shows Charlie his big brown teeth.

Charlie frowns and says, "We don't say 'wee' anymore."

"Because you're so big?"

"No. Because I go to the bathroom now. Not wee."

Wayne hits his thigh twice; this is so damn funny. "Isn't that precious?"

"It's true," Charlie says, nodding grimly. He holds up his bare wrist for Wayne to see. "And look. I lost my bracelet."

"Boys don't wear bracelets!" Wayne says teasingly with a wink at me.

Charlie sits straight up and his cheeks flush red. "They do. It's made from parachutes and soldiers wear them and so does my dad."

"Okay, okay," says Wayne apologetically. "I was only—"

"My dad made it for me. You just don't know about it because you're not a soldier."

"All right, Charlie," I say. "That's enough."

A dark cloud passes over Wayne's face and his eye twitches. "Is that what your dad said? Wayne Randall never went to war? Did he say that?"

Wayne starts muttering something about having tried to enlist, and I simply can't wait any longer. "I'm so sorry, Wayne. I should have said straightaway that we're late for a doctor's appointment."

"Well, pardon me. On your way then," he says, retreating. I pull away, and in my rearview mirror I can see him glowering, arms hanging at his sides. I feel a bit bad, but I just can't give our retired neighbor the amount of attention he wants. Charlie and I would spend all of our time in Wayne's garage watching him build birdhouses.

After dropping Charlie off I race north through farmland on the highway that links Meadowlark to the most southern suburbs of Kansas City, the isolated affluence of Overland Park. As the minutes pass, the rotting plywood barns, sheds, sunflowers and junk piles are replaced by rolling manicured lawns bordered by freshly painted white fences.

The houses in Cami J's neighborhood are nicer than the ones in ours. Ian had wanted to buy a house here, but I convinced him that Meadowlark was a safer investment. I didn't want so much of our money tied up. I wanted there to be plenty for vacations and restaurants and fun nights out in the city. Five minutes later, I was pregnant. So much for frivolous intentions. But Charlie...sweet, sticky, apple-cheeked Charlie, his buttery little embraces and spitty kisses, is worth any sacrifice.

I am only two minutes late when I stumble up the steps leading to Cami J's front porch. She swings open the door, looking like a cross between David Lee Roth and a butterfly with her tousled hair, flared pants and diaphanous colorful scarves. She has been waiting for me. "Your appointment was at noon," she says, and I just put my palms over my eyes. I am a mess.

"I've been making a lot of mistakes," I say. "It's embarrassing. I put the bacon in the pantry. I put the electric teakettle on the stove and the house smells like burnt rubber and—"

"Shhhh," she says, and slips one arm around my shoulders. "You've suffered a traumatic brain injury after all. Give yourself a break. I do some of that stuff just because I'm absentminded. You're fine, Maddie, and you're getting better. You're looking after a three-year-old on your own. That's not easy. Come in and let me make you some tea."

I don't cry often, but if I do, it's usually because someone is nice to me. I cry while Cami J makes my tea, and then I feel a lot better. I decide without reservation that I love my Zumba camel-toe hippie psychologist with the rhinestones on her cap. I feel waves of affection for her, and I am pretty sure I can tell that when she looks at me, it is me she sees. Me, Maddie, and not my train wreck of a face.

"So you forgot the photos," she says, once we are seated in her office with our tea.

"I picked them out. I left them on the kitchen table. But then Charlie lost his shoes and we were late and, yeah, I forgot."

"Okay," she says. "No worries. The writing I wanted to start off with today was journaling with photographs, but I have another one that we can try. And, you don't need a thing except your notebook and pen."

She is eyeing me expectantly and I cringe. "You forgot you were supposed to start bringing a notebook and pen?"

"I did."

"Will you be able to find your way home?" she asks archly.

"I hope so. I hope I remember to pick up Charlie."

There is a beat, and then we both say, at the same time, "Not funny."

I laugh really hard, and it does still hurt but also feels great. She stands up and inspects her bookcase, where she has a pile of spiral-ring notebooks. She rifles through them and then turns to me with a playful smile. On the cover of the notebook she has chosen for me is a photo of a happy cat with two different-colored front legs. It says, "Life is too short to worry about matching socks."

"There," she says merrily. "Put your name on it. From now on you'll just use this notebook here in the office. It will be yours and I'll keep it so it's always here, and I'll make you photocopies of your journal entries to take home and look at any time you want. Okay?"

"Thank you, Cami J." I take the notebook.

"So what you do is, you write a letter to someone. Now, it can be someone alive or dead. It could be your grandmother. Or it could be Charlie. It could be Ian. Basically it could be anyone you feel comfortable confiding in. Someone who will understand. Who you write to is not as important to me as the subject of the letter. Okay? The subject I want you to write about is the problem you have been dealing with, particularly the problem that made you think you needed my help. You tell them what's been going on, okay? This letter is never going to be delivered unless you want it to be. No one is going to see it but me, so you can be absolutely as brutally honest as you allow yourself."

"This sounds a lot harder than the last one."

"It's a little harder. Not much."

I close my eyes and think. Mom. Dad. Julia. Sara. No. Ian? No. Someone who will understand, she said.

I pull the notebook close and hunch over it.

Dear Jo,

Well, leave it to you to be above joining Facebook. I literally have no idea what you've been doing for the past four years. Four years ago. That was the last time we spoke.

That really hurt. I called to tell you I was pregnant. I wanted you to come visit. I wanted to put everything behind us and be friends again.

And you hung up on me.

I know how you feel about Ian, and "the terrible things" that you think he did. He tells another story but honestly, I no longer care. The past is the past. You should have come for me. I would have done it for you. I would have. Because you're the best friend I ever had and I know that I will never have another friend like you.

So that brings me to the reason I'm writing you, the one who really understood me. All right. My problems started after I had an accident. I fell. I know that will not surprise you as I have a long history of falling over with you, lol. This time I fell and bashed my head in while Ian and I were camping in Colorado. I was walking to the bathroom and I didn't take my headlamp and I couldn't see where I was going. I had been drinking, as you might have already guessed. Everything from that point on is a little fuzzy. Ian has helped me piece back together what happened.

When I came back to the campsite I was covered in blood and Ian got out the emergency kit and started wiping it away. He was going to use some Steri-Strips to hold me together but then he saw the cut and it was too serious for that. I'm lucky I didn't lose my eye. Ian decided that it was not something he could handle and that he was going to have to call for an ambulance.

I won't bore you with all the details of the rest of the night but Ian couldn't come with me in the ambulance because Charlie was asleep in the tent and we didn't want to scare him with my face. There were lots of nurses and a doctor who stitched me up. He told me I would need a plastic surgeon as soon as I got home. He also said there were two policemen who wanted to speak with me.

The police wanted to know about Ian's background in the military and private security. They wanted to know if we fought. Does he drink and how much? They told me that my injury was inconsistent with a fall and that someone had bludgeoned me with a rock or a branch. I told them they were wrong. Eventually they asked me if "that was my story and I was sticking to it," and I said yes.

I said no to the CT SCAN at the time because our insurance is so bad and I knew we were probably already going to owe thousands of dollars. They gave me a prescription for an antibiotic and hydrocodone and called me a cab. I took a photo of myself with my phone while driving home. I am surprised that they let me walk out of that rural emergency room at three in the morning with half my face mangled and swollen and twenty-two stitches running from my forehead across my eyelid and down my cheek. I am surprised not one person said a word when the front-desk guy sent me back to a campground in the middle of nowhere in a piece-of-shit unlicensed cab with an angry driver.

Since that night, I've been having panic attacks and living with an almost unbearable level of anxiety. I can't watch the news. Every horrible thing that happens—and suddenly it seems like something horrible happens every other day—makes me feel like I need to get Charlie and lie down in bed and take a long nap and not let go of him and make him stay with me in the bed in the dark with the covers and the safety. I know that's not normal. You know I wasn't like that back when we were together. I did have a hard time once before in New York, after you and I went our separate ways. There were a few bad years, but not like this. This is making it hard to function. I need to be a good mom. Something is very, very wrong. My psychologist is trying to help me sort out what is really going on. This letter is part of all that.

The other night, I said to Charlie, "Come sit down to dinner, I'm stuffed. I mean, I'm starved." This has been happening a lot. The words I pick are wrong. Something in my head is off. I keep marking things down on the calendar on the wrong day. It's not enough to make me feel crazy, but I do feel a cloud around me. I can't quite see through it.

About us. Look. I know I did the wrong thing. I know your job had gotten scary and out of hand and also that you'd been sick. You needed me to be a good, reliable friend and what did I do? I took things personally and I left.

Jo, this hurts. I hope you still don't think I chose him over you. I didn't. I swear to God that's not what it was. It was just a mistake is all. I made a mistake and I'm sorry. I would love to see you again.

I MISS YOU.
Maddie

I slide the notebook back to Cami J who makes a photocopy for me. As she reads the letter quietly I think about Jo's house in Skopje, with the stairs leading down to the bad part of the basement which was concrete, frightening and mostly empty. Just the crappy elliptical, the tiny washer and broken dryer, and an old plaid couch. It's where Jo went when she was afraid she might cry.

She said her neighbors hated her. That was the summer of 2001. Things had been about to get so much worse. The second I think about 9/11 my mind goes to the bad things. Every bad thing. All at the same time. Inside my chest a fist clenches around my fluttering heart like it's trying to crush a baby bird, and it feels again almost like when I was held underwater and couldn't breathe.

"This is amazing, Maddie." Cami J and I are on very different pages. Mine is black and sucking me in, and hers has got sparkles and balloons. She is elated and glowing. "You've just told me more about your panic attacks and your accident than you have in any of our previous conversations. I'm so pleased. This is good work. But—"

"Okay," I manage, and fumble for my purse.

Cami J leans toward me, concern causing only the slightest furrow in her smooth, botoxed brow. "I'm worried. This part about your accident? Two policemen thought that you'd been assaulted?"

"Yes," I answer breathlessly, and look at the clock. Our session is only half over, but I suddenly feel the need to leave. I need to pick up Charlie. I need to pick up Charlie. Last week in Gardner a little boy ran out of his day care and into the street and an old man in a truck hit him and killed him. The old man never saw the child. I need to pick up Charlie. A ten-year-old boy was going down a great big waterslide out by the airport, and something went wrong and he lost his head. I mean, they say he literally lost his head, he was decapitated, and the two women who were riding with him were strangers and they ended up covered in his blood, and his family, his mom and dad and brother were standing at the bottom waiting for him to come down after his fun waterslide, and nothing was ever going to be the same again forever and ever and if there is one thing I know it's that life can change in an instant and I don't want to be here I want to be with Charlie. I need to pick up Charlie.

I stand and say, "I need to pick up Charlie," and suddenly I'm wondering how many times I have said this out loud because Cami J is making a weird calm-down gesture with her hands, and her mouth is moving slowly, saying, "It's okay, it's okay."

But it's not okay. I am not okay. I need to be at home with Charlie by my side, curtains closed, Skopie and Sophie chewing store-bought plastic bacon-flavored bones at my feet, watching something for Charlie, like *Jack's Big Music Show*. I really want to be watching *Jack's Big Music Show* or *Yo Gabba Gabba* and to hear Charlie's laughter. The shag multicolored rug in Cami J's office starts to undulate like water weeds.

"Maddie?" I can hear Cami J speaking to me, but I'm looking at the rug. "I'm going to run you to the ER, okay, hon? Maddie?"

I look up at her and say, "I'm fine now."

"You've had a little fit, sweetie. I'm going to run you to the ER."

"No, no," I say. "Not the ER. I'm fine."

"I'm afraid we have to go, Maddie. Let me just grab my purse." She turns her back on me to reach behind her desk.

I take off.

Fall.

Get up.

Start the car. Reverse and hit her recycling bin. Cami J is coming down the front porch steps. I roll down my window and shout, "I'm fine. Really. I'm just late!" I'm not at all late and she knows it.

She is red-cheeked, her wavy hair and layered tunics are all messed up, and her smooth face is knotted up in anger as she dashes toward me. She is fast for her age. "Maddie, please don't drive off when—"

I hit the gas. Book ass to the highway and almost get on going the wrong direction. Fuck!

My eyes are all over the place, back and forth, back and forth. I am going to crash. Then Charlie will be left with Ian. I pull over to the side of the road and tell myself to breathe. My heart is pounding. I rest my head against the steering wheel and ask God if he can help. I turn on the radio and sing along to some Rihanna song about finding love in a hopeless place. After a few minutes I'm better. I breathe. Normal. Charlie isn't expecting me for another hour. It's okay.

I'm even calmed down enough to realize I should probably take this early exit from my session as an opportunity to drive by Premium Stock on the way to the YMCA, hop out and grab one of the largest-sized Stolichnaya vodka. I prefer not to take Charlie to the liquor store with me, even though they do hand out Dum Dum's to kids at the checkout.

Later, I'm finally home in my happy place on the comfy couch. Charlie is snuggled in next to me, and the dogs are asleep at my feet. *House Hunters International* is just starting, and my frozen pizza with "wild" mushrooms is unexpectedly good.

My massive carry-all purse, stuffed with Charlie's snacks, wet wipes, Band-Aids and various crumpled receipts from Walmart, lies partially open on the coffee table. I see my phone, with eight missed calls, four text messages and one voice mail, all from Cami J. The photocopied letter to Jo is in there as well, folded and shoved down the side. I take it out and start reading it again.

"What you reading, Mommy?" Charlie asks, looking up at me with his melty chocolate eyes. God, those lashes. If heaven were real it would be a place where I could always be with Charlie.

"This is a letter I wrote to an old friend."

"Old like Gramma?"

"Not that kind of old, baby. Old as in someone I knew in the past."

He nods as if what I've said is fascinating, and goes back to his puzzle.

Reading the letter gives me a lonely pit in my stomach that eats away at my nice calm safe place. Skopie is twitching and growling as she dreams, probably of unearthing and mauling all the little blind moles with their tiny human fingers. This episode of *House Hunters International* is set in Croatia. I lean against Charlie. His hair smells comfortingly of Johnson's No More Tears. It helps.

I look at my hand. I have a tremor. The letter shakes, insistent. I wonder if I have the courage or the desire to type it up as an email and send it to her. Maybe. Jo and I have unfinished business.

I take Charlie's little fist and raise it to my lips for a quick kiss. "Thank God for you," I say and he looks surprised but pleased, maybe even a little bit smug.

I can't help but wonder. Does Joanna have someone who makes her happy, too?

Probably.

I'm not sure how I feel about that.

MADDIE

2001

Stoyan dropped me and Joanna off at her bungalow-style house on the outskirts of Skopje. I slept and she left before daybreak to head to the Greek border, where she then spent the entire day tracking down her stalled shipment. When she finally got home, I was waiting for her with a big pot of pasta for dinner. She opened a bottle of wine, poured us each a glass and said, "Worst. Fucking. Day. Ever."

"You got everything handled?"

"The babies have diapers tonight, so, yes."

I raised my glass to her. "You're amazing."

She looked around at her living room then. My tea bags and dirty tissues were still on the coffee table. Next to my laptop were three empty beer bottles. "And what did you do today?" she asked.

"Nothing really," I admitted.

"Must be nice," she said, and for a second I thought she was mocking me.

I hesitated and gestured toward the pot of pasta. "Are you hungry?"

She took a huge sip of wine and smiled suddenly. "Famished! Let's eat."

A few nights later I found out Joanna had become "best friends" with Ian, Peter and the four other men who had swooped into Macedonia to protect the British ambassador as the country grew increasingly violent. She affectionately called them "the British bodyguards" and swore up and down that, despite appearances, they were witty, funny, gentle giants. I assumed this patently delusional conclusion must have been the result of the fact that she so rarely spent time with anyone who could even speak our language.

The ambassador had been called back to London, and the off-duty bodyguards had invited me and Joanna out for drinks in grimy central Skopje, at an ex-patriot hangout called the Irish Pub.

Ian was dressed in a rather whimsical boy-band style outfit with stylishly windswept gelled hair, but he was scowling out the window. He was the first man I had ever met who really owned his own resting bitch face. I revised my initial conclusion that his pop fashion sense would have gotten him beaten up in Kansas. You would have to be extremely confident, extremely stupid or maybe on steroids to take on this moody rake.

I was shocked to see Joanna ignore Ian's obviously miserable disposition and wrap her arms around him in a very playful hug. His darkness seemed to lift, and he gave her a kiss on the crown of her shiny brown hair.

I walked to the bar and ordered a shot of vodka.

"Oh let me get that for you," Ian said pleasantly over my shoulder. It was another thing Joanna had told me she liked about the British bodyguards. They would not let you buy your own drinks. Such gentlemen.

"I'm fine, thanks," I answered, seeing again that image of him lowering those perfect lips to her hair. Our conversation played again in my head: *What did you do today? Nothing really. Must be nice.*

After a few rounds and several orders of a mayonnaise-laden Eastern European version of loaded potato skins, Joanna said, "Oh look! Eddie's here."

"Who's Eddie?" Ian asked, looking sideways.

"He's my Albanian connection for pillowcases and sanitary napkins. I'll be right back." She blew us a little kiss as she grabbed her wine and scurried into the back, yelling, "Eddieeee!"

"She knows bloody everyone, doesn't she?" Ian asked, his eyes following her as she hugged a swarthy man at the far end of the bar.

"It's called networking."

Ian looked at me and asked, point-blank, "Are they just friends, do you think?"

"None of your business! For God's sake!"

He appeared to disapprove of my answer. He looked down at his phone and began to text. This didn't stop him from continuing to talk. "She's buying stuff off the black market and she's offering bribes to police officers. Doesn't that sound dangerous to you?"

"She's taking care of refugees who have nothing."

"Okay. So I'm the only one concerned for her." He gave me a very frank and challenging look.

"I'm her best friend," I said. "I think she's fine."

"Forget it," he said, treating me to one last dismissive frown.

The other bodyguards had dispersed around the pub, and I was left alone with Ian, who from then on ignored me and texted at manic speed under the table. I, in turn, treated him to my own extreme nonchalance. Until ten minutes later when his fingers were still flying and I could no longer help myself.

I cleared my throat. "Are you texting someone instructions on how to dismantle a ticking bomb?" I asked.

"No," he answered immediately, as if I'd asked a perfectly reasonable question. "That was yesterday." Then he broke into a grin.

He went back to his phone. "Bollocks," he said, shaking his head and finally slipping it away into his pocket. He glanced over at Joanna, who was now doing shots with a group of men dressed mainly in leather. After a moment he turned to me and looked me squarely in the eyes for what seemed like a long time. I looked back.

Eventually he broke the silence by saying politely, "I don't believe I know where you're from."

"The United States. Kansas."

"Kansas?" he repeated loudly. He looked taken aback, as if I had just told him my daddy was also my grandfather and that I had been raised in a giant prairie dog den.

"Yes. Kansas."

"Isn't that the place with the tornadoes and the wicked witch?"

"The Wizard of Oz."

"That's it! And the pretty girl. With the little white socks and the braids?"

"Dorothy."

"You and Joanna always wear those trousers and clunky boots. I'm not saying it's bad. Not at all. But you'd look awfully nice in a smart little dress like Dorothy's."

Not sure how to respond, I started walking away toward Jo, who seemed to be having a much better time with the Albanian black market sanitary napkin king in the back.

"Wait!" he called after me. "I'm sorry! Look, I saw *The Wizard of Oz* when I was, like, seven, so it was completely age appropriate for me to have had a crush on Dorothy. And you certainly don't need a blue dress or little socks."

"Thank you."

"Maybe just the braids."

I stopped and turned back, gaping at him. He was giggling and smiling that lopsided smile. There was something about him. The dimple. The wink. "Sit back down," he said, patting the seat I had just vacated. "I'm going to buy you a nice big glass of that awful Macedonian wine you like, and you're going to tell me a little bit about where you're from. This *Wizard of Oz* place. Okay?"

Two glasses of wine later, I leaned forward and admitted, "To tell you the truth, I was dying to get out of Meadowlark."

"Were you?"

"Dying. I'd done some traveling with my grandmother so I knew what I was missing out on. I actually founded our school's international exchange club so that I could spend six months in Spain."

Ian laughed loudly, and I caught Joanna's head spin swiftly from her conversation in the back toward us. "We lived really far south of Kansas City way out in the sticks. At a certain point you just wake up one day and realize you're tired of all the same faces at school year after year, 4-H, cow-tipping, field parties and the four-step."

Ian tapped his chin. "I know what a field party is and I am vaguely acquainted with the idea of school, but the rest is just baffling."

"Four-H is an agricultural, livestock, folk and crafts club with annual membership perks such as the 4-H fair. The fair is advertised as this wholesome, family-themed carnival, but it is really a very smelly gathering of all types of livestock eating and crapping for days on end in their stalls."

"What's not to like?"

"Right? And inside these toxic tents, boys and girls dressed in Stetson hats, Lee jeans, cowboy boots and plaid shirts hose the crap off each other's animals."

"Kinky! Was this festival entirely crap-themed then?"

"Not entirely, no. There are contests, too. Most outstanding ear of corn. Biggest turnip. Heifer of the Year."

"Oh. I feel quite bad for the girl who won that."

"A heifer is a cow."

"I know," he said. "I was teasing."

"I can assure you, it was taken very seriously."

"I apologize for my earlier comments. I had no idea Kansas was so sophisticated. If I'd known from the get-go that you were so posh, I probably would never have taken a fancy to you at all."

"Ha," I replied flippantly. "As opposed to now?"

"Yes," Ian said gently, reaching over to take the clasp of my necklace and move it back behind my neck. I shivered and instinctively bent my head toward his hand. "As opposed to now."

Joanna startled us by clapping her hand down on Ian's shoulder. "I'm bored. Why don't we all go back to my place?"

This idea was greeted by the other bodyguards with unanimous approval. Jo and I walked ahead of the men as we followed the winding, climbing road that led from the city to her little white bungalow. I glanced back at Ian, who was trailing behind us. He was busy. I couldn't believe it. He was texting again.

We were already pouring wine into glasses in Jo's kitchen when Ian appeared in the hallway.

"You left your front door wide open," he barked at Jo, pointing toward the foyer accusingly. "Wide open. An invitation to get murdered."

"Sorry!"

"Jo!" he shouted, and I cringed. "What are you thinking?

Isn't it dangerous enough for you here already? Christ!" He then marched through the room and scowled as Jo walked breezily past him. "Is it just wine then?" he called after her. "Or do you have any vodka?"

"Hmm. I'm torn between, 'Go help yourself' and, 'Go fuck yourself.'"

"I'm a bodyguard, Jo. I can't help it."

"Your bottle of vodka is in the freezer."

Your? Your bottle of vodka? I gave Joanna a questioning look, which she completely ignored. Certainly I'd misheard.

Panda, Jo's black-and-white former street cat, came to greet me in the kitchen and did figure eights between my legs. I scratched all around her neck and back for a minute as Joanna and the other men settled on the patio off the living room. Ian and I were the last ones in the house and as I walked out of the kitchen with my wine to join the others, he was silently pouring his vodka.

Twenty minutes later I went inside to the pantry to get some chips. Jo's bungalow had a second, tiny outdoor area behind the kitchen. Through the window I could see the burning ash at the tip of Ian's cigarette. I hesitated, but then knocked on the glass before sliding open the door and stepping outside. He was sitting in one of Joanna's rickety white plastic patio chairs.

"Hey," I said.

"Hey."

"So do you have, like, your own drawer now? A place to put your toothbrush?"

He looked up at me sharply. "What do you mean?"

"You've got your own bottle of vodka in the freezer."

"Oh that," he said, going back to his phone. "She had a party. I left it."

"Oh."

He quickly slipped his cell phone into his pocket. He looked sad.

"Are you all right?" I asked. It was the wrong thing to say.

"I want five minutes of peace and quiet and there's something wrong with me?"

"Never mind. I'm going."

"No. I'm an arse. Don't mind me. You don't have to leave."

"No, no. Take your five minutes."

"Stay, will you?"

I stood there awkwardly for a moment until finally I laughed and sat in the patio chair across from him.

"What?" he said.

"You seem, I don't know. Tightly wound."

"You might be right about that."

"It's okay. Anyone who does what you do would have to be a little on edge."

Ian looked to the side and made a tsk noise.

"What? You disagree?"

"No. I'm a far more miserable twat than most."

"Exactly. Even though you clearly have a pleasant side, there's definitely a sort of sinister bastard brooding in the background."

Ian feigned surprise. "Really? Is he here now? Maybe the moody sod can fetch me another vodka if he's not up to anything else?"

"At least you still have a sense of humor."

"I try." He held up his empty cup. "Seriously, though. Are you making drinks, elf-lady?"

"Elf-lady?"

"Yeah. You've got those Leeloo eyes. Noticed them the night we met. The feast of crap and throat."

I smiled. "From the *The Fifth Element*? Thank you."

"Christ, woman, you're full of surprises, aren't you? Come here."

I got up, walked over slowly and stood in front of him. He looked at my lips and bit his own. His phone vibrated in his pocket, but neither of us moved. I exhaled.

A shadow passed over his face. Someone had moved into the window frame, blocking the light. I glanced toward the house. Jo was watching us, her eyes bright, the vein in her forehead visible like a divining rod. My stomach did a little flip and I started to raise my hand, but she'd already turned her back on us.

I stood there for a second, and then without a word I left Ian and went back inside the house. The other bodyguards were all on the other patio, but Joanna wasn't with them.

I waited. I played hostess. Eventually I sent them all home. As it turned out, she'd gone up to bed without saying good-night.

MADDIE

2001

Home in Sofia, my glass-enclosed balcony in the city center faced north, looking out over gray apartment blocks dripping in urban vegetation. The dirty, white, splayed petals of satellite dishes clung to every balcony. Cables like climbing vines traversed the dingy concrete facades. Antennas poked from nooks and crannies facing the sky. Below me was a depressing square where children from the ground-floor nursery played. An iron fence protected them from the feral dogs pacing the perimeter, panting greedily as they gaped at the children as if they were potential meals.

My horizon, however, was breathtaking. When I paused in my writing, I kept my eyes lifted to the mountain in the distance that towered over Sofia. Quaint red-roofed villas meandered this way and that up the side of Vitosha until the mountain gave way to solid, verdant green. I knew from many hikes that at this time of year Vitosha's wide sloping lawns would be covered in alpine flowers.

I felt satisfied. I had completed a quarter of my work in a month. It was too easy. I even had free time to visit Jo. And Ian, a little voice whispered. I tried to silence it but my imagination had always been torturously active. I pictured them running into one another at the Irish Pub and him bringing her a drink. I saw her thanking him with a hug. Maybe even a kiss. The nights were getting hotter. Joanna's shoulders and arms were always bare. If Ian so much as touched her, it was likely to be her warm skin.

In the weeks I'd been away, the tension between the Muslim rebels and the Macedonian military had escalated even further. There'd been several bombings in the city center, not just in the mountain villages. My parents had made me promise them I wouldn't visit Joanna. But they were far away, and they would never know. In any case, I couldn't stand it anymore. I had to go.

By this point, the border guards were beyond baffled by my repeated visits to the pit of hell.

"Why now you come in Macedonia?" the potbellied border guard asked me angrily, as he unzipped my backpack and began to scrounge around in the pockets. "Why so many times? Don't you know it's not safe here?"

I had grown accustomed to a long and tedious customs clearance when crossing the border, but this trip was the worst. Previously, the customs officials had been looking for illegal liquor, cigarettes and fuel. Now they were expecting something more sinister, like weapons from the Middle East bound for the Muslim rebel camps.

Normally, I rode the bus from Bulgaria with a chattering gaggle of female smugglers who were busy trafficking black-market perfume, cigarettes and brassieres between the two countries. This time, the heavily made-up, gum-chewing gossips with their frosted hair and penciled-in eyebrows were nowhere to be seen. It was just me and a few shifty-eyed young men in wash-worn tracksuits.

He handed my passport to his skeletal colleague with hollow eyes who flipped through my pages of Macedonian, Bulgarian, Turkish and Greek stamps. He shrugged and sneered as he handed it back. The two of them bickered for a moment, and I interrupted them.

"Mnogo mi haresva Makedonia," I said loudly, feeling stupid as I looked around at several heaps of fuming garbage and a gang of slobbering, starving, black-toothed stray dogs. *I like Macedonia very much.*

Potbelly narrowed his eyes and nodded, sucking on a candy that popped in and out from the inside of his lip while he looked me up and down. "Where you stay?"

"In Skopje. With my friend."

"Good friend?"

"Yes," I said, returning his salacious smile. "Very good friend."

"Ahh," he said, rolling his eyes and shrugging as in, *Why not tell me sooner about this Balkan lover and save all this interrogation?* "Okay then." He winked.

From the bus station I took a taxi into the center and met Jo after her nightly swim at the municipal pool.

She and I walked to dinner at Pizza Maria. The pizzeria overlooked the main square in Skopje, which was unparalleled for people-watching. Jo and I usually split a salad, a pizza, a bottle of wine and her favorite dessert, the strawberry crepe with fresh cream but no walnuts due to her tree-nut allergy. Our check was always less than fifteen dollars. We had begun to lose interest in cooking at home.

I looked up from the menu to find Peter and Ian standing next to our table.

"Fancy seeing you here!" said Peter, by far the most agreeable of all the bodyguards, with his soft farm-boy curls and devotion to his wife and little daughter back home.

Ian looked slightly uncomfortable. I mumbled a greeting and tried to smile. My heart was racing, and I didn't trust myself to speak. Joanna was also uncharacteristically silent. Eventually Peter said, "Shall we join you then?"

Joanna answered, "Why, but of course!" in a sarcastic way that suggested she was a member of the British royal family.

Ian frowned, but Peter happily pulled out a chair and sat. "Simon will be joining us shortly," he said brightly. "You know Simon."

"Yes, I do," Joanna replied, terse yet polite.

"So!" Ian awkwardly scooted his chair closer to Peter. "We were told that this place has excellent food and waitresses in very short skirts." Joanna looked at him. "But I doubt that's what brought you ladies here tonight."

"We like the toilets," said Jo, deadpan.

Ian nodded. "I hear they're spotless."

I noticed that underneath the table, one of her legs was in a spasm, jittering up and down on her toes. Concerned, I touched her knee.

She mouthed, "I'm fine," and began to massage her calf with one hand.

At that moment, big bald Simon showed up and shouted his hellos. The first thing he did was order a bottle of vodka for the table.

Two hours later I tumbled out of an illegally over-packed cab behind Jo, Simon, Peter, Ian and Nina, one of the Pizza Maria waitresses. We were at Club Lipstick. During the ride from the restaurant to the disco I discovered a few interesting things: Simon had a yin and yang tattoo on the inside of his lower lip where I did not even realize you could have a tattoo, and Peter had been a hairdresser before he joined the military. Lastly, Nina was wearing faux-leather crotchless panties of which she was quite proud.

Nina motioned us to a VIP entrance where, by paying the Macedonian equivalent of a few dollars, we were all allowed to enter before the surging horde of Macedonian night-clubbers pushing one another around in the velvet rope line that ran along a trash-strewn street crawling with shadows and, of course, dogs. Our preferential treatment did not go unnoticed, and the biggest out of a trio of muscular men in Diesel shirts, distressed jeans and bling shouted after us in a thick accent, "Go home, fuckeen Yankees, go fuck off and go home! You not wanted here!"

Nina gave him the finger and said to all of us, "Ignore him. Come on, let's go now."

Inside, it was a low-rent version of Ibiza, with pedestals, balconies, cages and trippy cartoons playing on an old-school film projector against walls splashed by strobes and lasers. Jo pointed toward a couple of men hunched over the bar in deep conversation and yelled above the music, "There's Stoyan." I looked over and saw her driver, who I recognized by the long black leather trench coat that seemed to be his permanent attire. She patted my shoulder. "I'm going to go say hi."

Nina had joined a couple of her friends on a pedestal to dance and give everyone the occasional glimpse of her unusual undergarment, and I made my way to the bar.

Ian and Peter waylaid me before I could buy my own drink. "It's on us, Maddie!" Peter shouted with a wink. "Vodka and Red Bull tonight."

The DJ started bleeding into the current song with a remix of "Storm Animal," and Ian, Peter and I headed for the dance floor. Within seconds Jo had joined us, bouncing up and down like a pogo stick. She and I broke off from the guys and flew around the floor like we were the only ones there because we didn't care if we looked crazy or like sluts—it wasn't our

country on the brink of war, we had the money and the pass-
ports that could take us anywhere, and we were at the same
time deep and incredibly shallow. We could do whatever we
wanted and we did things that others wouldn't do and we
owned it like bitches. No wonder they hated us and we loved
each other.

A half hour later we found Ian, Peter and Simon at a table
in the corner. Our hair was sweaty and matted to our faces
and necks. We slumped into the remaining two seats with
our bottles of water.

Jo noticed it first. "What the hell happened?"

Then I saw it. Simon's nose was swollen, and his lower face
was ruddy from wiped-away blood. Ian had a fat lip.

"Not to worry," Simon shouted over the loud, thumping
bass.

"A little disagreement," yelled Ian.

"These two decided to have a word with the three stooges
from outside," said Peter, his big blue eyes wide. He was clearly
upset.

Simon leaned forward. "We were insulted. They thought
we were Yankees! Hell no. Had to correct that."

Ian said, "No, no, no. That's not what happened."

"Well, then, what was it?" I asked.

"It was nothing," Ian answered.

Simon laughed. "They were calling you names!"

Joanna finally looked up. "What? Who? Us?"

Ian said, "Shhhhh. Simon, it doesn't matter."

"What did they call us?" Joanna persisted.

"American whores," Peter answered, and I swear I think his
voice cracked. "And Ian grabbed one of them. The other came
at me with a knife!" Peter motioned toward the table, and
sure enough, there sat a medium-sized knife with a wooden
handle that I hadn't noticed. "Ian and Simon started fighting with them, and it was me they pulled the knife on. Me!"

"He wasn't going to hurt you, Peter," said Ian, laughing. "He stabbed like this." He grabbed the knife and made a poking motion with his hand while pulling a goofy face, much like a dainty fencer. Simon joined him laughing.

"None of the rest of you have children, do you?" Peter asked, rather disdainfully, crossing his arms over his chest. "It's not funny."

"Good grief, Peter," said Simon. "Might be you're in the wrong line of work, mate."

"Where are they now?" I asked, glancing at the knife and then around the crowded club.

"They probably went home," said Simon. "They weren't pleased when we took away their butter spreader." This caused more laughter from Ian and Simon. Peter stood up and walked away.

"You guys are a bag of dicks," Jo said. "Scaring him like that 'to defend our honor.' That was dumb."

"You see that, Ian?" asked Simon. "That's why chivalry is dead."

"Joanna," Ian said, "they weren't dangerous, okay? The guy with the knife didn't even know how to use it. You've got to hold it like this," he explained, tilting the blade down, "if you want to hurt someone, if you want to get the blade between their ribs and puncture the lungs. This guy was going to poke our pretty Peter Pan like a schoolboy with his pencil."

"Oh my God, you fucking pervert!" yelled Simon, and they both practically fell out of their chairs.

"Cretins," Jo said dismissively. "Psychos."

"Certifiable, actually," Ian said affably, recovering.

"Umm-hmm. Good for you."

"Really. I was told by a doctor that I was crazy. By an army psychologist," Ian went on, arms crossed over his chest, nodding toward Jo.

"Wow!"

"I was."

"I believe you!" she said, as if he were a child.

"Maddie, would you care to hear my story?"

"Go on," I said, scooting my chair in close to hear him over the new song, which had a bass beat slightly less alarming than the previous.

"On my first assignment to Africa, I'd been chosen to be deployed to Uganda to be part of a six-man team to look after British Ambassador Edward Davis."

"Ed-vard Davis," said Simon with a touch of fanfare. "Ooh la la!"

"Yes, indeedy. I was looking forward to it. I did my predeployment training, and then my team had to be examined and approved by a psychologist. He gave us a test. Have you ever wet the bed? Are you afraid of the dark? Have you read *Alice in Wonderland*? Write an essay about your family.

"Afterward, the doctor showed up and said, 'I'd like to interview Corporal Wilson.' The rest of my team instantly went, 'Ooohh.'

"The doctor was very polite. I sat down and he said to me, 'I'm happy with your answers. It's your family that I'd like to talk about. I see you are the youngest of ten. Now, there has been a study done on chimpanzees. The dominant male and the dominant female have a baby and they love it and they play with it. Then they have another baby, and the second baby doesn't get as much love and attention. By the time they have their last baby, they're not interested whatsoever in it. They never feed it. They allow it to be bullied and beaten by the other chimpanzees. Did this happen to you, being the last child?'"

Suddenly Ian stood up. I instinctively leaned back. I was uncomfortably aware of the knife still lying on the table. He held up a fist. "And I said, 'Are you trying to say that my mother is a bloody chimpanzee?' Apparently, I'm a sociopath because my mum didn't love me enough? 'My mum loved me, okay? You want to see some sociopathic behavior, I'll treat you to some if you say one more fucking word about my mum! Where I come from we don't talk about women like that!'"

I took a deep breath and glanced at Joanna, who was staring at him with such naked hatred that I suddenly felt nervous. On my last visit it was hugs and laughter between them. Something had gone rotten.

And then Ian's face went back to its normal color. He smiled amiably and sat back down in his chair and started toying with the knife with his left hand. He sipped almost daintily on his vodka Red Bull. "What a cheeky fucking bastard, that arsehole. The guy was like ninety years old and believed everything that he read. He was a fucking loon and I hope he dropped dead."

Joanna was no longer looking at him. She slumped there in her metal chair, moving her bracelets up and down her arm. When had she become so withdrawn and remote? So tight and coiled, like a tiny, poisonous, gorgeous snake. Oh and her eyes. Olives and almonds. Reptilian.

Suddenly I was very unhappy. We'd been so close. We knew everything about each other. It was starting to seem like that was no longer the case.

Joanna's eyes rolled up and took in the table. Me, hunched and looking grief stricken for no apparent reason. The men, bloodied, pleased and preening. And then she was back. She stood and said, "I'm going to go dance." It was clear that she was not asking me to come with her.

And dance she did, by herself, while everyone watched.

MADDIE

Eight weeks before

Cami J is at the door.

She is punching the buzzer like she wants her finger to break.

Now she is backing up into the front yard and making the gesture for "call me" up toward the windows. This is way beyond unprofessional. This is ridiculous. Go away.

I can't deal with this right now. I'm officially not home.

Charlie and I are sort of hiding behind the Yucca tree that basks in the light let in by the balcony while I watch and he plays. Cami J is a force of nature, honestly. I admire her. I really do. And, I love our sessions. I find them invigorating, challenging and even sometimes amusing. But I can't go back to see her until I've done some serious thinking, so I've had to cancel this week's session. She's not happy. She's in a frenzy over her newfound fear for my well-being.

I'm not happy either. I'm looking at the latest emails from Ian's ex-girlfriend, Fiona. She's the woman who was on the other end of Ian's frantic text messages years ago in Macedonia, and believe it or not, she's still in our lives. In those days, she was always threatening to kill herself in order to make him stay. Now she's got some new strategies for trying to get him back. This has been going on for quite a while now, and honestly, I'm sick of it.

I've always known that Ian has two computers. One strictly for work, and another far more powerful one for his graphically intense video games. I've also always known that he has two email addresses. Again, one strictly for work. The other one is very old, from back in his newbie army days.

Spartanwarrior69@yahoo.com.

I laugh every time I see it. Every time.

However, it was only while he was away on the assignment before this one, after a few mysterious and somewhat troubling letters had arrived in the mail, that I decided to try to hack into his messages.

In the tiny space on the other side of the Yucca tree Charlie is rifling through the plastic bags of all kinds of paracord that Ian has had delivered. He can't make a bracelet yet, but he's not terrible at a simple braid and he would rather play with all the colored rope than any expensive normal toy I've ever gotten for him. He particularly loves to pull the cords open to unravel and inspect the magic threads inside.

Through the palm fronds and the French doors to the Juliet balcony I am watching Cami J march across the street to Wayne's front door. No answer. Big surprise. She is wearing her usual combination of yoga pants, sandals and scarves. Wayne is going to think she's a drug-addicted prostitute, no doubt; he has so little interaction with anyone who doesn't own a truck and a shotgun.

Eventually I go back to my task. I am scrolling through the most recent arrivals at Spartanwarior69@yahoo.com.

It took me a while to get access to Ian's old army email. First

I tried his two desktop computers. It was easy to open his work email on those, but I'm not the least bit interested in lengthy reports for big oil companies on whether or not it's safe to lay a pipeline across the tribal desert in Yemen. (Hint: It isn't.)

Ian puts his gaming laptop in its case under his desk when he leaves on assignment. It was pass code protected. Luckily Ian is a sentimental old soldier who uses his army regimental number as the password for half his devices. I didn't know what his army number had been, but I did remember him telling me that it was stamped on his war medals, which he'd thrown into a drawer in the basement where they were gathering dust. It wasn't long before I was privy to his online antics. And his old email.

So now I am looking at photos of Fiona's pierced clitoris and silver-studded shaved outer labia. My favorite, though, would have to be the one where she is on all fours. She is looking back at me with a sweet and sunshiny smile as she uses one hand to pull back and reveal her creamy bleached butt crack. These are all new improvements apparently, designed to lure Ian away from his wife and child. I have to admit, I would find it hard to compete with this.

I mark the email as unread. Oh fuck you, Fiona.

Then Charlie is at my side and I have to slam the laptop closed. He is pointing across the street at Wayne's front door swinging open. "Look, Mommy. Wayne Randall is letting in the lady you don't like."

"I like her," I say. I watch, rapt, as Wayne ushers Cami J into his house. "I just don't want to see her right now." I wonder what Wayne's disabled wife will make of this heavenly peacock-colored lady songbird who has just fluttered into her hospital and vomit-flavored home. "I'm trying to figure some things out right now, Charlie. I need to make some important decisions, and I need time to think."

He blinks. What the heck am I doing? This is all way too

much information for Charlie. I sigh. Aside from my mom and dad I've got no one really to talk to, and sometimes I suppose I treat him as more of an equal than I should. At least I didn't tell him all the truth. I didn't tell him that the message underneath Fiona's bare bottom was, "It's not too late to get rid of that boring bitch and choose me."

"Okay," he says finally, and then returns to his paracord braiding project. I pull up his shirt and tickle his back.

How long will Cami J stay inside Wayne's smelly house?

Could she get in trouble for coming here? For speaking to my neighbor?

I think she could.

I picture the two of them huddled together in his garage, examining all the birdhouses he's built and whispering things about me and Ian.

MADDIE

2001

Joanna first told me about Fiona that night in Skopje at Club Lipstick. While Simon and Ian prattled on boastfully about their knife fight, Jo returned from the dance floor and touched my arm. She leaned down and whispered in my ear, "Come to the bathroom with me."

I got up and followed her. As we walked we saw a surge of agitated clubbers shouting and pushing as they headed to the outdoor patio. We cut through them and continued on into a bathroom with six hole-in-the-ground toilets separated by thin plywood barriers. It was crowded with drunk teenage girls, but Joanna barged through them to the last stall and slipped in as a girl slipped out. She handed me her purse and didn't bother with the door. After throwing up twice she said, "I have some tissues in my bag. Could you grab them?"

I handed her the packet of Kleenex and put my hand on her back. "Are you okay?"

"I did some shots with Stoyan at the bar. They were horrible. I'm fine now."

She leaned her butt against the filthy bathroom sink, her hands plunged into the front pockets of her orange corduroys. Jo was dressed like a backpacker who shopped at Goodwill, in a retro button-up shirt with layers of necklaces and bracelets stacked thick. She looked about sixteen. "So, I did something dumb."

"What?"

"Right after your last visit I went out with these guys, and we went to see some horseshit heavy-metal band and I got wasted. At the end of the night I asked Ian if he wanted to come back to my place."

"Just the two of you?"

"Yeah."

"Oh my God, okay."

"I know, crazy, right?"

"What did he say?"

Jo looked down and spun one of her silver rings around her finger. She cleared her throat and shook her hair back. "He said no. Let's just say I didn't take it like a lady."

She laughed, and I managed something fake that sounded almost like I was laughing with her.

"Turns out he has a girlfriend. Her name is Fiona. That's who he's always texting. She was in the army with them, military police also."

"He has a girlfriend?"

"Yes."

Military police also? "Kind of out of nowhere," I said.

"That's funny, because guess what? She showed up out of nowhere, and that's how we all found out."

"You're kidding."

"No. We were hanging out at the Irish Pub. Me, Hillbilly Buck, Stoyan and the other British bodyguards. And this woman walks up."

"And it was her?" I asked, spellbound.

"Ian nearly fell out of his chair."

"What did she look like?"

"Exactly like you and me, crossed with Juliette Lewis in *Natural Born Killers*, except with giant tits and if we had 'bat-shit crazy' tattooed on our foreheads."

"Shut up," I said. "Seriously?"

"Yeah," said Jo, nodding emphatically. "The bitch tried to trip me."

"What?"

"Yeah. She did. She sat down with all of us and was being really cute, excited about how she had managed to surprise Ian, and when I got up to go to the bathroom she tried to trip me! I'm telling you, she put out her leg at the last minute while I was walking by. Like a ten-year-old in the lunchroom."

"God! Why would she do that?"

Joanna studied me in a weird way, as if trying to figure out where she knew me from. "No idea," she answered.

"So she flew into Skopje? Without telling him?" Despite the fact that I came and went from this dangerous country as I wanted, the realization that there was another woman who dared do the same filled me with an inexplicable fury.

"Yeah. And he had to work! Hillbilly Buck told me Ian let her spend the night with him."

"At the ambassador's residence?" My voice actually squeaked. Trouble.

"I know," she said, shaking her head. "I mean, Ian's boss would be none too pleased."

I whistled. I myself was also none too pleased. I even felt sick.

"Anyway," she went on, "I wanted you to know. Even

though nothing happened. I think it's best for us to take a breather from the British bodyguards for a while."

I stared at the shoe-scuffed muck below my feet. "Yeah," I managed, focusing on the filthy floor. "Maybe we should call it a night."

She put her arm through mine. "Read my thoughts."

That's when the cavernous club began to shake. One of the bathroom-stall hook-locks started making a rat-a-tat noise. A ferocious metallic whirr could be heard above us and we all looked up at the water-stained ceiling. A sagging remnant of drywall came loose, danced and fell. Like sheep, the drunk and high girls emerged from the bathroom stalls, rearranging clothes and stumbling in their platforms. Jo and I grabbed hands and followed the others out to the patio, where a crowd had already gathered.

They were all looking west. A few miles away the woods of Mount Vodno were on fire. Military helicopters were stampeding over our heads like immense dark buffalo, massive and blotting out the stars.

The mountain was only a slightly darker shade of black than the world behind it, and it loomed like a pyramid over the city center, a frightening but almost identical twin to Sofia's Mount Vitosha. There were many small fires and one large one, and it looked as if they were all growing. The glassy-eyed clientele of Lipstick stood in awe, staring at the throbbing sky and the burning forest. Rockets from the lower part of the mountain were visible arcing up and into the area below the summit.

"The military is shelling the rebels," said Jo with an unmistakable note of terror as she fumbled for her phone. "They better stay the fuck away from the camps."

I felt a hand on my shoulder and looked up. Ian had approached behind us and, without taking his eyes off the sky, started to steer us away. One hand around Jo, the other around me. "Let's go, girls," he said softly, pulling us back. "Let's go home."

As Jo and I allowed ourselves to be backed away from the others still staring into the sky and up at the mountain, I looked back and forth—at her, at him and back at her. Neither one could tear their eyes away from the destruction. Suddenly, Jo brushed Ian's hand away from her shoulder with a sound of utter disgust. She pulled me away from him and whispered in my ear, "I just want him to leave us both alone."

MADDIE

2001

I was at my apartment in Bulgaria working on the travel guide, and I had no plans to visit Joanna again anytime soon. I told myself that I was being responsible and focusing on my career, but the truth was, now that we had decided to "take a breather from the British bodyguards," the thought of running around the squalid streets of Skopje had lost some of its allure. I pictured being in that city, walking down sidewalks, entering restaurants and sitting in the park, constantly on the lookout for a glimpse of his face. It seemed excruciating.

Eventually, however, I had no more excuses. The reality of returning to America was again on my mind. My time was dwindling, and I'd been in denial. Joanna missed me. She'd been telling me that she was lonely and her work made her depressed. "I don't know how much longer I can do this," she said. "I don't even want to be here anymore."

Finally I went.

★ ★ ★

The buses in Eastern Europe never arrived on time. Sometimes they were detained at the border. Sometimes the driver stopped at a restaurant for a sandwich and several beers. They broke down. They ran out of gas. Anything could happen, but somehow Jo was always waiting for me. I didn't mind taking taxis from the bus station during the day, but at night we both thought it best for her to pick me up. This time I arrived long after dark.

This time she wasn't there.

I paid an illegal taxi driver far too much to take me up to Joanna's bungalow on the hill. I rang the doorbell three or four times before she finally answered, looking colorless and shocked.

"I'm sorry, Maddie!" she said, grabbing my arm and pulling me in for a hug. "I'm so sorry. I set my alarm, but I must not have heard it."

"You were asleep?" She usually burned the midnight oil.

"I've been sick," she said, with a dismissive wave of her hand. "I'm fine now. The worst was a few days ago. Let me make you some tea."

She was feeling better the next day.

It turned out that while I'd been working on the travel guide not much had changed in Skopje, except the men in Jo's life. She'd ditched the company of the British bodyguards for "the horseshit heavy-metal band." Her new friends were four Macedonian guys in their early twenties who played in a band called Vengeant, which they insisted (inaccurately) was an actual word in English. The thing I liked best about these disgruntled musicians was the way they treated Joanna's adopted street cat, Panda. They doted on her and brought her little tins of smelly fish. It didn't matter how mangy she was, they scratched and stroked her matted black-and-white fur like she was a fluffy Persian princess.

They would gather often, the unemployed quartet, on Jo's patio to smoke and drink when it was time for her to get home from work. This would infallibly incense the tiny, vile, ancient neighbor lady who they called "the old witch." She would give us the evil eye over the rock wall while she grilled peppers or beat rugs or simply stewed in outrage, all the while working on something in her mouth with that powerful, old, spotted-hyena jaw.

"What's she so angry about?" I asked the boys of Vengeant. One of them shrugged and said, "Life. War. Cats."

Another pointed to Panda, who sat there, fat and pleased with herself. "She's going to have kittens. More damn dirty animals all over the place."

"She's pregnant?" I asked happily and knelt down and stroked her until she purred. For some reason this made them laugh.

Sometimes I would politely offer the four of them tea, pausing by their outdoor naked-torso jam sessions, and they would say, "Yes, please, thank you. Cool." I could see why Joanna might find it helpful to have such young disaffected nationalists as friends, since they were usually the sort of people who protested the refugee camps and made her job hard.

On the Friday after my arrival, she came home from work and said, "There's a party tonight. Locals. Students, rock climbers, musicians—locals instead of just ex-pats for a change." She smiled. "Okay?"

I was genuinely surprised by the feeling of disappointment that washed over me. I realized that I'd been hoping, in the worst way, to head down to the Irish Pub for a chance encounter with Ian. What I said was, "Of course."

Jo and I drank vodka tonics until Bogdan, the drummer for Vengeant, and Dragan, the bassist, finally picked us up in a Russian Lada that was missing so many parts we were doubtful it would make it up the street, much less to the party. Dragan drove and Jo sat on Bogdan's lap. The good news was that the Russian Lada did, in fact, transport us to the parking lot of a graffiti-covered high-rise block on the west side of the city.

The entire block appeared to be inhabited by students having parties, and most of the doors were swung wide. We took the stairs to the ninth floor because the lift was broken, lugging up with us several bags of some sort of pirated rakia, which I had no plans to go near, and a few massive glass bottles of brown beer.

Jo entered the party with a sideways whisper, "I might leave and go back to Bogdan's place, but you can grab a cab at the corner and you know where the key is."

"Okay," I said indifferently, though I was annoyed.

She immediately joined the sweaty drummer of Vengeant, who was lounging on the dirty sofa, bare-chested again. He was playing the guitar and leading a Macedonian heavy-metal ballad sing-along with a handful of people strewn about the couches.

I pushed my way through a group of rowdy, young, handsome and dirty men with impressive dreadlocks who I guessed were the rock climbers. I opened the door to the balcony and stepped outside into yet another braying group of drunks. I had just achieved the respite of the railing when I felt a tug on my ponytail.

I whirled around, furious, and there was Ian; wobbly, happy, grinning from ear to ear.

Butterflies went wild in my stomach, and it was all I could do not to jump up and down clapping my hands.

"My God, woman," he said, looking astonished and elated. "It is you! I said it once and I'll say it again. You are full of fucking surprises. What the hell are you doing here?"

"Joanna knows the band guys!" I yelled over the clamor. "The guys from Vengeant."

"Oh? Of course she does. Follow me," he said. "I know where it's quieter."

He beckoned me to come with him as he made his way to the back of the balcony, where a metal fire escape ladder led the way up to the balcony above. He started climbing. "Come on."

"Where are you going?"

"I know the girl who lives in this one," he said, pointing.

"But I don't know her."

"It's fine. She's dating Jason. She's nice. She's a veterinarian who runs an animal shelter. Come on."

I followed him up the ladder, and from the balcony I could see into this other apartment, much homier than the one below. Jason, the bodyguard, whom I had come to think of as "the quiet one," and a handful of people sat around a kitchen table talking. Ian said, "Wait here a sec, would you?"

I stood out there eavesdropping on the wild scene down below, and a minute later Ian showed up with a glass of wine. He handed it to me and proposed a toast. "Here's to random encounters," he said, smiling. "And American girls who don't have the slightest idea what's good for them."

"I don't think I'll toast to that."

"What is it?" he said, leaning in and peering at me. "Did you do something you shouldn't have done? Or is it a family thing? Some horrible skeleton in your closet? Maybe you didn't do anything. Maybe something bad happened to you."

"I told you, Joanna knows the guys from Vengeant—"

"No! What are you doing here? Here! In this country that is on the brink of civil war? Do you have any idea how—" he searched for a word "—unreasonable it seems to me that I keep running into you here? A few hours away from a recent genocide? I see you and I'm so happy. But then I'm angry because you shouldn't be here. Happy. Angry. Happy. Angry. You've got me all worked up, young lady."

A part of me wanted to say, *I'm here because you're here.* I held back. "It's nothing dark or crazy or scandalous. I'm sorry to disappoint you. I got a Fulbright scholarship to write a book about life under Communism, and then I got hired to write a travel guide to Bulgaria."

"Oh my God, you're the tortured artist with a death wish."

"No. I'm the journalist and the teacher. I wish I was half as interesting as you imagine."

"Okay," he said finally. "So you're normal."

"I didn't say that either."

"But you're not crazy. You're just a good writer."

"I'm all right."

"You've written two bloody books?"

"They're not, like, *Harry Potter*, you know. But when this one is done, yes, I will have written two bloody books."

"Are you allowed to do that at your age?"

"I am not sure what the writing age is in England, but in America I can assure you I am completely legal."

"Well, now I am really surprised that you graced us with your presence at this pikey circus." He looked up and through the window into the apartment, which was now more crowded, as if scanning for Jason or anybody else.

"Why's that?"

He continued avoiding my eyes. "Because Fulbright scholars and book authors don't usually hang out with metal heads, rock climbers and bodyguards."

"That's fucking ridiculous. Of course they do." I rolled my eyes. "Everybody wants to hang out with those guys."

"Well. In England that would never happen. We have the class system." When he said "the class system" he gave me a mischievous look as if I was naughty for ignoring this important age-old institution.

The thought of him thinking I was naughty made me blush.

I was much happier with that, though, than the night I'd met him and he'd said I seemed like a "nice young lady."

I glanced in the window and saw Jo enter the apartment via the front door. She made her way across the room and then joined us on the balcony. "Hello," she said, handing me a napkin piled with slices of lukanka, a dried sausage that smelled like feet. "How's your girlfriend, Ian?"

"She's fine, thank you. You're so kind to ask."

Jo glared at Ian, and he ignored it.

"The class system exists, Maddie," Ian went on. "I left school when I was sixteen. And I barely went even before that. You can't imagine the shit that went down in that schoolyard, and my mum said, 'You're done with that. You're coming to work with me cleaning the pubs.'"

Jo looked him over with a raised eyebrow. "What? Really? That's a shame. You strike me as more of an Artful Dodger than an Oliver Twist, though, Ian. I hope you're not waiting for Maddie to fall over infatuated with you just because she's never met anyone from the wrong side of the tracks before."

"Wow. And if I concede that while my taste tends more toward *X-Men* and *Star Wars*, I have in fact heard of Charles Dickens, then—"

"Then your sob story about your lack of education is just, how do you put it? 'A load of bollocks'?"

"Hmm." He examined a burn mark on the side of his finger for a moment and then looked up. "You know, Joanna? One of the things I first liked about you? Your sense of humor. It's a bit like British sarcasm. If only you had any idea when to stop. But...you don't know when to stop, do you?"

She held his eye but eventually lost and looked away.

Stoyan the driver sidled up beside us in his usual costume of black leather and bad-guy trench coat, his eyes as dark as his clothes and unhinged from some dirty Eastern European amphetamine. "We are off to Seksi," he said, sounding like a dog growling. "Room in the car if you want to join."

Ian seemed to be watching for my reaction, and I could tell this irritated Jo. "It's a strip club, Mad," she said. "I've been there a bunch of times with these guys. It's no big deal. You don't want to go."

I looked right at Ian. At first he offered a restrained half smile, a curious look in his eyes. There was something boyish in his anticipation to see what my answer would be. Then he winked, as if daring me. There was a curling in my stomach. It was hard to breathe. Something clicked and I wanted him. I wanted to be against him or underneath him, my hands in his hair or on the low-slung back pockets of his jeans, pulling him into me. I hate to think how I must have looked as my eyes traveled over him at that moment, lingering on the dark hollow under his bottom lip, at the corded muscles linking his neck to those broad shoulders. His T-shirt loosely clung to the bottom of his square pectoral muscles, tattoos peeking out from under the sleeves. His big hands rested on his hips in a cavalier fashion. As he waited, his eyes lowered, taking in all of me in return, and then he met my eyes again. This gave me a dizzy feeling; something ugly, desperate and embarrassingly carnal. He was smiling at me like he knew what I was thinking and like he would know exactly what to do with me. My cheeks were aflame for the second time in so many minutes.

I said, "I'll go."

Jo was shocked. "Oh?"

"Sure. I'll go."

"Seriously?" Her mouth was hanging open. "I take it you're staying somewhere else tonight then?"

"Why?"

"Never mind. You know what? I don't care what you do."

"Why are you being like this just because I want to go and

you don't? You already made it clear that I was on my own to get home if you got a better offer."

"How did you get so drunk, Maddie?"

"How did you get so transparent, Jo?"

"Please. What?"

"Come on! This is about him!"

Ian shoved his hands in his pockets and stood up straighter.

Her shock turned quickly to fury, and she glanced at Ian. "About him? Sure. When pigs sprout wings and fly, babe. Whatever. Have fun." She started to turn away and then looked back with a wicked little smile. "Let me know if you finally get that gang bang you've been fantasizing about tonight. Maddie's a secret crowd-pleaser. Believe me, that's something I'd like to hear all about."

I'd had enough. "Honestly, Jo. Go to hell."

Ian and I walked in silence down the last few flights of stairs until we reached the gravel parking lot of the block. There was a wooden bench at the bus stop, and Ian motioned for me to have a seat.

I sat. "Where is everybody?" I asked, fumbling in my bag for my lipstick. "Who's driving us to the strip club?"

"Let's not go," he said. "I'm not in the mood. Do you mind?"

"No," I answered, secretly relieved. It had all been about spending time with him. "Of course not."

It was a perfect summer night, but there was a cool breeze. "Are you cold?" he asked.

"No," I said, even though I felt a chill running up my back.

"So my first impression of you wasn't quite correct," he said with an appreciative grin.

"How so?"

"You're very sweet. But you can be fierce."

"I'm sorry about all that."

"Don't be. Friendship isn't all clean and pretty. Neither is family. I find honesty more appealing than naivete."

I nodded. "Me, too."

"Look at that," he said, pointing to the concrete entrance to the next block over. A pack of dogs were curled up sleeping by the buzzers. "Comfy as houses they are. God. Between the dogs and the fires and the bloody simmering hate, I could be back in Africa."

"I take it you weren't there on safari."

He shook his head with a rueful smile. "No, I wish. I would have loved to see a rhino or a cheetah. I did see about three thousand gazelles. They're beautiful animals," he said, suddenly looking thoughtful. "You're a bit like a gazelle."

"That's one I've never heard before."

"Graceful. Doe-eyed. Skittish. They bolt the second you get too close."

"I'm not running."

He laughed out loud. "No, not now. But that night early on, I scared you off. With my comments about *The Wizard of Oz* and Dorothy's little white socks. My God, what you must have thought. I had to lure you back."

I couldn't help but smile.

"There's that smile." He paused, looking pained. "But I wasn't there on safari." He rubbed his face, and I only barely caught the fact that he was embarrassed and clearing away a mere glimmer of a tear.

His phone beeped, and he pulled it out. He received a text message and quickly responded, his thumb flying across the buttons. "Bloody Fiona," he whispered. "She's going to get herself killed."

"That's your girlfriend, I take it?"

"Yes," he said somberly. "Back in London."

"If you need to speak with her now, it's okay. I can go."

"No, no," he said, slipping his phone back in his pocket. "Where were we?"

"You weren't there on safari."

"No, during that first assignment I was transferred over to Rwanda to look after a woman by the name of Helena Rowley, a British doctor working in Kigali. It was just after the genocide."

"Just you? Not a team like here?"

"Just me. Dr. Rowley's 'official' job was to help the British government provide things for the locals that would improve their quality of life. She ordered books for the schools, things like that. But really she was there to secretly document what had just happened during the genocide. The massacres. It was the worst assignment I ever had." He cringed suddenly, his chin jerking to the side.

"What?"

"Hold on." He massaged the back of his neck while he looked down. He stayed like that for a long time. "Helena stepped in front of a lorry back in London and died the year after we returned. She was a wonderful, kind person who wanted to help. A bit like Joanna but not as strong. She couldn't get over it. I remember one night after a day trip to a grave site, I walked her to her door, and she turned and said to me, 'So it's true, Ian. God is dead.'"

I looked down for a moment and gathered my courage. "If God is dead, then everything is permissible."

"Something tells me you've read some of the same books as Helena. You are such a bloody nerd. I love that about you."

He said love. He said you.

"So fuck Fiona." I waited.

He slipped his hand around to the back of my neck and took hold of my ponytail again. "She's not who I want to fuck right now, and you know it."

I waited. I could barely breathe. Had I been able to talk

I'm afraid I may have begged. He was still holding me, and staring down at my mouth. "You have the prettiest lips I've ever seen. You've been a huge surprise, you know that? Here's this extraordinary flower growing up through a crack in my concrete nightmare. What am I supposed to do?" In an agonizing gesture, he touched the center of my bottom lip while looking in my eyes. "Like a petal," he said softly. "Blowing through all this. You'll be gone before I know it."

It was too much. "Ian, please." I pulled him toward me.

"No," he said, letting go. "That would be a mistake, believe me. I want to handle this properly."

I swallowed and looked away.

Neither of us spoke for a while after that. He walked me to the main road, and just as Jo said, there were several taxis on the corner. Ian climbed into the back with me, and we rode the five minutes up to Jo's house with his arm around my shoulders. I could barely stand it. I was spinning and yet it was all innocent. Then it was over. The taxi stopped.

"Thanks for bringing me home."

"My pleasure." He paid the cabdriver and got out as well. His house was a short walk away.

He waited for me to retrieve the spare key and wave from Jo's well-lit front foyer. As he walked away down the street he called back once to say, "From now on it's only the funny stories, okay?"

After closing the door I turned around. There, by the staircase, were Joanna's big black platform boots, almost identical to mine. She was home. I sat down right there on the white tiles and took off my shoes. I tiptoed into the living room. The light was on at the bottom of the basement stairs. She must have gone down to the plaid couch to sleep to avoid seeing me. Our bedrooms were next to each other, and anyway, she had been sleeping down there more and more often recently.

Quickly, I grabbed a glass of water and ran up to my room. I closed the door, and for the first time ever, I locked it. As I undressed for bed I discovered that my period had arrived early. After running through various ineffective plans to try to deal with it, I decided to brave a trip to Joanna's bathroom.

I unlocked my door quietly, checked to make sure her bedroom still appeared empty and dashed down the hall. I left her bedroom dark and only turned on the light in the bathroom. Per usual, it was a mess. Joanna had a thing for lacy lingerie, and her colorful bras and panties were drying and dangling from every rod and hook.

I knelt down and opened up the cabinet underneath the sink. I actually rocked back on my heels; I was so startled by the stench. It was both rusty and sweet and for no reason at all it made me think of the lake water and then I was choking. I closed the cabinet on one of Joanna's big white towels, now almost completely brown with old and crusted blood.

My eyes jerked back and forth from the tub to the floor. The grooves between the white octagonal tiles were delicately lined with brown. Left over after a cleanup. Strangely my first thought was not what happened, but what have you done? The troubling distance between us was crumbling into a chasm, and her silence to me about all these secrets was like static, increasing in volume, turning into a shriek in my head.

I switched off the light and ran back to my bedroom. I was struggling to catch my breath, and like a child, I got into bed, curled up in a ball and hid under the covers. I had forgotten to lock myself in. I threw off the comforter and swung my legs out and that was when the door flew open, hitting the wall with a bang. Jo flipped on the light.

She was not asleep.

Joanna stood there, chin lowered, eyes sullied with black makeup and her torrential hair spilling around her slumped shoulders. "What the hell were you doing in my room?"

IAN

2001

Joanna lived just ten minutes up the road from the house that had been provided to the British close-protection team.

The neighborhood was quiet and the windows dark. The moon emerged from behind a cluster of clouds, and suddenly the modest white houses with their red-tiled roofs looked quaint and comfortable. Safe. Nevertheless Ian didn't slow his pace to enjoy the night air and the solitude. His eyes roamed over the alleyways between buildings, and he paid particular attention to the wooded areas.

It wasn't until he could see the driveway leading up to the team's rental villa that he allowed his thoughts to drift back to earlier in the evening.

Joanna's behavior toward her best friend had shocked him. He could understand her anger toward him, but to go after Maddie like that? What had she done?

She'd shown a brief interest in spending time with him, that's what.

He fished out his keys. Neither he nor any of his roommates would make the same mistake as Joanna and leave their door unlocked or open. Inside, music was playing. Ian checked his watch.

Two thirty in the morning. Still early.

He walked into the kitchen where Peter, wearing honest-to-goodness real pajama pants with a drawstring waist, was building what appeared to be a tower of toast. "Hiya, mate," Ian said.

"Hello! Just you, is it?"

"The others went on to that strip club out on the motorway."

Peter pursed his lips and said, "Seksi."

"That's the one. You should have come out. The party was a good laugh."

"I promised Ashley I'd have a long chat with her and Polly," he said, licking some butter off his finger. "I wish I hadn't, honestly. Ashley's gone and gotten her ears pierced!"

"Didn't she have pierced ears already?" Ian asked, taking a bottle of orange juice out of the fridge.

"Not Ashley, mate. Polly! She pierced Polly's ears. She's not even five yet."

Ian nodded sympathetically though it wasn't a subject that interested or incensed him in the least. "Vodka orange for you?" he asked, opening the glass cabinet.

"Go on," Peter answered. "Thanks. I'm going to have plenty of cheese on toast here in a minute."

"Sounds good." Ian made the drinks and then went to stand beside Peter. There were crumbs everywhere. A stick of butter was melting on the counter. "I don't think I realized you were such a slob."

Peter laughed. "Such a chef, you mean! You didn't realize I was such a chef." He placed the bread on a tray and then started topping each with slices of yellow cheese.

Ian sat down at the kitchen table and took a long drink. His phone beeped, and he lowered his elbows to his knees and looked at the floor.

Peter glanced over. "That'll be Fiona, I suppose?"

"Yes, it will."

"Is she all right, is she?" he asked, bent over the oven with his tray.

No. She's violent, suicidal, homicidal and a self-destructive sex addict. "To tell you the truth, Pete," Ian said slowly. "I don't know if she's all right. I don't think she's ever really been all right."

"Is that so?" Peter grabbed the drink Ian had made for him and came over to lean against the counter. "Can't say I'm all that surprised. Jason and I, we both got the impression maybe you fancied Joanna."

Ian looked up, curious. "Why's that?"

"I don't know. If I didn't have Ashley, I'd fancy Joanna."

"Well," said Ian sitting up straight. "That does surprise me. I would have taken you for more of a 'Baby Spice' type of bloke."

Peter made a horrible face. "No! Baby Spice looks just like my sister. Nah, me? I'd go for Posh."

"Ahh," Ian said, leaning back and waggling a finger. "So that's your deal with Joanna. You like the legs."

"Guilty as charged, sir," Peter answered, raising his glass. "But it's not just that. She takes care of all those mothers and babies. And don't forget, she told me that I was 'officially her new favorite person' the night at the fund-raiser."

"My God, man," Ian said, rocking backward in his chair and laughing out loud. "She said that like ten seconds after she met you. She was teasing you because you were all giddy about the fucking folk dance show." After a second he said, "Anyway. I quite like Maddie as it turns out."

"I don't really know her," Peter said, donning two big oven mitts. "She's got a pretty smile, though."

"She does, doesn't she?" Ian sniffed the air. "I think the chef is about to burn the toast."

"Shit. Thanks." Peter turned his attention back to the oven.

"There's something about her. You're right about that smile. It makes me..." Ian trailed off.

As Peter plated the toast, he said, "Sorry, mate, what was that? Her smile makes you...what? Horny?"

"No! Jesus, Peter. No. Her smile makes me happy." Ian paused dramatically. "Her tits make me horny."

Peter laughed uproariously, and his cheeks turned even pinker. "All right. Time to eat." He slid a plate over to Ian and then sat across from him.

"Don't you think," Ian said quietly, looking down at his food, "that it would be a waste of time to pursue someone like Maddie or Joanna? I mean to seriously pursue them?"

"Why's that?"

"I mean, do they really like us? Or is it just fun to, you know, go slumming from time to time?"

Peter slapped the table. "I've never been so offended in my life!" Then he smirked. "I don't know, mate. I can't help you there. Ashley didn't have much growing up. We were always on the same page, if you know what I mean."

"I never had to worry about that with Fiona either. I had plenty of other shit to worry about, believe me, but never that she was too good for me."

They chewed in satisfied silence for a minute, their massive shoulders hunched, the bread tiny in their hands. Finally Ian said, "They got in a fight over me. Maddie and Joanna."

Peter grinned, keeping his lips together. His mouth was full. "Was it awesome?" he managed to mumble.

"Kind of," Ian answered, looking a little ashamed. "I'll admit it felt sort of nice."

At that moment the front door slammed open. After a few seconds Simon staggered into the kitchen yelling, "Do I smell cheese on toast?"

Peter winked at Ian and got up to start a second batch.

DAY OF THE KILLING

There was something surreal about this quiet house, Diane thought, silently skirting the bloodstain. Sinister and surreal, with its gruesome little Hansel and Gretel trail of clues. Follow the toys and find the boy, for it was likely a boy. There, a plastic yellow toolbox. And there, a Tupperware bowl filled with Legos. A Nerf gun and a floor puzzle. Matchbox cars and a broken track.

A boy who refused to tidy up. A boy who got in trouble?

Shipps would be angry at her for not waiting. It wasn't that she disrespected her boss. In fact, Diane liked him quite a lot. But if a child was going to be carried out of this house she wanted to make sure it was by her and not the coroner.

A light flashed through the front window, and she knew it was Detective Shipps arriving in his SUV and she was no longer alone.

"This is Shipps," he said over her radio. "I'm here."

Diane inclined her head toward the mic. "I'm inside."

"What?" He was angry.

She'd known he would be. "I just came in."

"Are you okay?"

"Yes. Only found a missing bleeder so far."

"Nick mentioned a kid. You haven't found a kid?"

Barry Shipps and his wife, Megan, had twelve-year-old twin boys. It didn't surprise Diane that his first thought was for the child.

"No," she whispered. "It's a quiet scene. A lot of blood but that's it."

Skirting the middle of the room and the bulk of the evidence, she could see several bloody smudges in the basement stairwell. Handprints. She could also see that the item smashed at the bottom of the main staircase was, as she'd suspected, a phone. Not a cell phone but a bulkier cordless landline. The plastic back had come off, and the batteries had rolled away. The clear plastic from the display was cracked.

Again Diane noticed the tall combat boots by the door. They were enormous. *A big man lives here*, she thought. Her father had worn boots like those and sometimes left them by the door when he came home. Her father had been a soldier.

The smell, though. It was something summery. Sunshine. Diane recognized it as the smell of her own childhood swimming lessons at the same moment that she saw the Puddle Jumper swim vest and damp trunks in a pile on the other side of the door.

A child had played at the pool today.

Diane suddenly felt a shiver at the back of her neck, like someone whispering in her ear. Something compelled her eyes to travel up, up.

There, hanging on the wall above the staircase, was a large decorative mirror in a carved wooden frame. In the upper third of the mirror, she could see the reflection of the iron spindles that formed the upstairs railing, identical to the ones climbing up the staircase in front of her. They were thin and black and yet, in the reflection, there were two places where the area between the spindles was solid.

Diane raised her pistol. She realized that she was looking at a pair of legs. A person was standing directly above her at the upstairs railing, very still, watching and waiting to see what she would do next.

Outside in the distance, racing through tranquil, hilly fields, an ambulance announced its approach, startling the neighborhood awake. The dogs in the backyard continued thier protest. Diane kept her eyes on the mirror, breathing in the last lingering scent of childhood and coconut sunblock. The coppery smell of blood was slowly taking over.

Diane took a deep breath. She whirled around to face the upstairs railing. "Police! Hands up!" she shouted, her Glock pointing at shadows. A heartbeat, and the vague figure was gone, slipping back into the hallway.

Diane fumbled to pull out her flashlight. A second later she trained it over the area where she'd seen the legs. She knew she was too late. "Don't run!" she shouted, though no one was there. She was about to start up the stairs herself when there was a loud rap over her shoulder. She jumped.

Behind the frosted glass of the front door was the indistinct, bulky outline of Detective Shipps. Diane let him in. His gun was ready, and he was already breathing fast. "You should have waited for me."

"I'm sorry."

She wasn't. Adrenaline coursed through her, and she wanted to take the stairs two at a time. Perspiration was gathering at her hairline. Her words tumbled out awkwardly. "Bleeder downstairs. I've just seen someone upstairs. I need to go after them."

"Slow down, Di. Who did you see?"

"Just a glimpse. Someone small. A woman or a child."

"Okay then. You take the upstairs, and I'll take the basement. Bill and CJ should be here any minute." Shipps left then, following the path of blood through the basement doorway and down.

As badly as she wanted to race, Diane forced herself to proceed with caution. With one wrist resting on the other, she was able to point both the flashlight and the muzzle of her gun at the darkness above. She was sweating more now, and a small drop rolled along her nose and fell to the hardwood floor. She glanced down as she took her first step onto the stairs and suddenly realized that though Shipps had followed the biggest blood trail, he had not followed the only one.

Her flashlight illuminated a few tiny red droplets. There was something in the middle of the staircase. Maybe a pile of dirty clothes? Diane moved her flashlight up to reveal a fluffy yellow blanket with a satiny border, wadded up and tossed aside. It was smeared with blood.

Diane paused. Depending on who was upstairs, they might try to jump from a window. "Arriving officers? Secure the perimeter."

CJ responded first. "Copy that. I'll take the northeast."

Bill came over her mic a split second later. "Copy. I'll be southwest."

Diane advanced against the wall, gun ready and flashlight creating a circle of light to follow. She could see that there were three doors and a turn at the end of the hall. The first door was on her left. It was open. She shone her light through the crack between the door hinge and the wall. There was no one hiding behind. She lit up the room. It appeared to be a spare. Three places to hide. She checked underneath and on the other side of the bed, and then the closet. Empty.

Diane moved out of the room and continued down the hall to the next open door on the right. Again, she looked for someone in the darkness between the door hinge and the wall. No one.

Someone was crying. Diane swallowed and waited. Was that crying? Or night sounds? This damn lurid house, breathing. No, it was crying. It was coming from behind a closed door. She crept nearer. In a very small voice, a boy was repeating a phrase over and over. It was a mumbled accusation said with devastated disbelief. "You hurted me! You hurted me!"

MADDIE

Seven weeks before

"Charlie, you cut that out!" I shout, but he knows me too well. He knows I'm not really mad at him, and he and his new little friend will continue wrestling and throwing their Happy Meal toys down the slide. I make the "I'm watching you" hand gesture, and this sends him into giggles. I return to my phone and iced coffee.

There's a six-hour time difference between here and Nigeria. That, along with the fact that Ian can't text when he's out in the oil field, means I usually only hear from him once a day. Today, however, a vehicle has broken down, and he's stuck at the hotel. He's suddenly being very chatty.

My phone beeps again.

More than halfway through this assignment now, he writes.

I type, Yay!

Is Charlie being good?

I look up, and there he is with his hands splayed in the window of the little airplane at the top of the McDonald's PlayPlace climbing structure. He is making fish faces against the clear plastic and probably licking it, too. Nice, Charlie. Schedule in strep throat for next week.

Yes, I type. He's being perfect. He even ate most of his Happy Meal.

Well, I'm jealous you two are at McDonald's. That tells you a bit about the quality of the food here. I miss you, Petal. Give Charlie a hug from me. X

I stir my watery McCafé iced coffee and frown at the brown apples left on Charlie's tray.

Ian, I type. Please don't act like everything is normal. We are not okay. I know what's going on with Fiona. And there's the night of my accident, and the argument we were having just before. You are keeping too much from me and I am not happy living like this. I love you but look how damaged we have become. Something has to change. I am scared for Charlie.

I stare at my text and my finger hovers over Send. Will this help us? Will it change anything? Perhaps.

I delete it all.

"Charlie?" I call, standing up. "Come down and get your shoes. Let's get out of here."

MADDIE

2001

I'd never seen Joanna act like this.

I hadn't yet caught my breath when she burst into my room, and the sight of her standing there staring at me so malevolently didn't help. I was in the grip of terror. Helpless, I could only think that to use my incapacitated state to my advantage was the best way of defusing the situation.

"I'm sorry," I managed to whisper. "You scared the shit out of me."

She rolled her eyes, which I found somehow comforting. Suddenly I very much wanted to remember her as the boy-crazy sixteen-year-old I'd taken advanced language classes with in Spain. My nerdy BFF.

"No, really," I went on, using the time to pull my thoughts together. "You did."

"Sorry. But seriously. What the fuck were you up to in my room?"

My first impulse was to tell her the truth. There was no

harm in what I'd done, only harm in what I'd found. But if I told her the truth, she would immediately surmise that I had opened the cabinet and seen the blood-soaked towel. And what of it? Surely there was a reasonable explanation and it didn't matter.

But for me suddenly, it was not just a towel soaked with more blood than what would come from an ordinary wound. It was her recent strange behavior. It was her defensive and aggressive attitude about participating in shady deals with corrupt policemen and criminals for the sake of the greater good. It was, more than anything, this growing nastiness fed by the very existence of Ian. Plus, I hated the way she was staring at me. She was still pale from her illness. Pale with dark half-moons dragging down her beautiful eyes. Those eyes. Now cold, motionless and accusatory.

I said, "I went in to see you. So I could say I was sorry. I was going to say good-night, but you weren't there, so I decided to just go to bed."

She stepped into the room, crossed her arms and leaned back against the dresser. I was suddenly able to swallow and breathe. The fear was fading. I could see that she believed me, and that we were going to be okay.

"Well," she said, suddenly inspecting her nails in a bourgeois way that did not suit her. Instead of addressing any part of the actual argument, she said nonchalantly, "We both had too much to drink."

"Yes," I said, nodding vigorously. "Too much to drink and we said things we didn't mean."

"Except…"

"Except what?"

She looked up at the ceiling, and for a split second I thought I saw her lower lip tremble. And then she was fine. "I don't want you to think I'm just jealous. I liked Ian at first. A lot. That's true. But, Maddie, he's not a nice guy. He just isn't.

He's a crazy, heartless fuckwit. I wouldn't wish him on you. On my worst enemy? Maybe. But not on you. Okay?"

"Okay."

"I mean it. He's different than us. He'll only hurt you."

"He's not going to hurt me if I don't let him."

She gave me a questioning look with a slight smile. "All right, Maddie. Good night."

She switched off my light and started to slip out the door. "Jo?"

"Yeah?"

"Are we good? I don't want us to be mad at each other anymore. I don't think I'll be able to sleep unless I know that we're good."

"It's still you and me, Mad," she said, sounding like the Joanna I remembered. Warm. Loyal. It was pitch-dark, so I couldn't see her when she whispered one last thing before shutting the door. I think she was crying. "Just us. Us against the world."

Jo and I made up, but something had changed. We were not so easy to laugh, and when we spoke, one or both of us averted our eyes. A selfish, weak voice in my head told me to stay despite the awkward aftermath of the fight, just stay and hope to see Ian again. I might have listened to that voice, had it not been clear that Joanna had no intention of running into the British bodyguards out and about in Skopje. After a couple of days, I told Jo I needed to go back to Sofia and work.

I kept busy finishing my project for Fodor's. I traveled and researched for two weeks and then went home to my apartment to write. Back in Sofia, sitting on my little balcony with my laptop, I was suddenly very aware that I was almost completely alone. I thought about Joanna and Ian constantly.

When Joanna and I first met, it was as if we both contained a seed of anarchy inside us lying dormant, waiting to be watered by the other. We'd had ten good years. Lovers. Adventures. Success. Devotion. Chaos. And then that thing inside us that had made us gravitate to one another changed its course. We became two helpless skittering magnets, and Ian a dark heavy block of iron.

I started to call Jo twice but changed my mind, and I didn't have Ian's number. Just when I thought I couldn't bear Jo's silence a minute more, she called.

"Hey, it's me." Her voice had a flat effect that scared me. Had she called to argue?

"Hey."

"Panda had her kittens." She tried to sound upbeat, but I wasn't fooled. She wasn't happy.

"Yay! When?"

"Two weeks ago. They're just starting to open their eyes and crawl. They're so cute. You have to come see them."

Kittens. The excuses we come up with to swallow our pride.

I think it took me under an hour to shower, pack, catch a taxi, buy a ticket and board the bus. This time Potbelly at the border was not surprised to see me. He stamped my passport with a lecherous grin and a wink that implicitly wished me many mind-altering Balkan orgasms. "Enjoy your visit, miss."

As if nothing had ever gone wrong between us, Jo had bought two bottles of red wine, cheese and crackers and set it out on the back patio. We fussed over Panda and her six tiny babies in the patio cat-birthing palace that Joanna had constructed out of a giant cardboard box and blankets. Eventually Panda started transitioning from pride to agitation. We left her alone and moved to the patio off the kitchen.

"How is your work going?" she asked me, looking into her wineglass instead of at me. She seemed a subdued version of herself. I wondered if maybe she'd started smoking weed with the Vengeant quartet.

"Pretty well," I answered. "I'll meet my deadline."

She swirled her wine around in her glass and didn't look up. "And I suppose after that you'll be packing up and heading home?"

"I'm in no rush. My mom is, but not me."

"Good," she said, but her voice was robotic. I realized that even when we were playing with the cat and the kittens, she hadn't smiled once since I'd arrived.

"What about you? I know how hard you're working and what you're up against. Are you doing okay?"

I will never forget the expression on her face when she answered. There was defeat, hopelessness and confusion. "No. Not really. I think we're losing, Maddie."

She took a big drink of wine. "I'm sorry. I forgot that I have to check on something." Then she got up and walked away.

Looking back, I think I know the last moment when Joanna seemed herself, seemed the outrageously outspoken and confident teenager I'd met in Spain. It was a brief glimpse of who she used to be and would never be again. She told me she had a business meeting with someone important in Greece. Someone who might be able to help her get a large batch of first-aid kits to the families that would soon be leaving the Macedonian refugee camps and returning to an apocalyptic reality in their old villages across Bosnia. She had to drive to Neos Marmaras over the weekend, and she would love it if I would come with her to the little beach town for one night.

We drank iced coffee from the gas station as we drove toward the Greek border in her SUV, windows down, singing over one another and the wind.

We stopped at a rustic tavern overlooking the Aegean outside Kalamaria for a late lunch and sat at a wooden picnic table on the terrace. Greek music played over a speaker in the garden and a group of Polish tourists were dancing the horo in a circle with some locals and restaurant employees. It felt briefly like a real holiday.

We ate tzatziki and char-grilled octopus with chickpea salad and shared a bottle of rosé. Joanna laughed at my imitation of Potbelly at the border checking my passport, and we retold each other a bunch of old stories about Spanish boyfriends we had back when we first met. Our bedroom-eyed, long-haired Greek server who was named of all things Earl, brought us a complimentary shot of ouzo and after we drank it, Jo looked at me with regret.

"I'm sorry about what happened the last time you came to visit."

"Me, too. Really sorry."

"He won't come between us anymore."

"Ian?"

She made a noise like pfft and drank from her shot glass again even though there was nothing left. "Yeah, Ian."

"Of course he won't," I said. "Anyway, we never see him anymore. It's been almost a month." Three weeks and four days.

She was tan already. She crossed her arms and rested her chin on one pretty, thin, bangled wrist. Her smile was enigmatic. "I heard something the other day. I think Ian might be sent home to England."

"What? Why?"

"The team leader found out about him letting Fiona spend the night with him at work. Hillbilly Buck told me. That's a big deal. I imagine they'll have to let him go."

I nodded silently. She stood up and said, "I'm going to the ladies." I watched her walk through the garden, where she invited herself to join the horo and linked arms with the Polish tourists. She danced with them to their delight for a full circle before extricating herself and disappearing down the path.

Waves crashed down below, and the Polish tour bus began boarding. I stared at the water, remembering how it had nearly finished me all those years ago. I couldn't help but wonder who it was who'd told Ian's boss about his indiscretion with Fiona.

That evening Jo had dinner with "someone" at the Miramare Hotel. When she came back to our little rental where I was reading in bed, she went into the bathroom saying, "I'm so tired. Aren't you?"

She ran a bath with the door closed. I knocked after an hour, and she said, "I'm okay, Maddie. You go to sleep."

I tried. Twice I slipped off, and twice I jerked awake from a nightmare in which Joanna emerged from the bathroom, walked over to me and covered my face with a blood-soaked towel. I finally drifted off with the light on. I have no idea if she ever came to bed.

I had no reason to go back to Bulgaria. Joanna seemed happy to have me, and I could do my work on my laptop sitting on her couch. She left at half past eight every morning and came home at five, and we always stayed up talking, walking or watching television until midnight. We rarely went into town. Sometimes the thought flickered through my mind, *I'm not leaving until I see him.*

Even with the beautiful summer weather, Jo showed little interest in socializing around Skopje the way we had previously. I cooked pounds of pasta. We took after-dinner walks through the parks. I napped sometimes during the days when she was at work, the hum of the air conditioner softening the sound of the helicopters coming and going overhead.

I was asleep in my room on the second Saturday of my visit

when I woke up to voices coming from downstairs. Someone started yelling. A man.

"Crap," I whispered, scrambling for my clothes. I cursed more as I tripped pulling on my jeans. I opened my bedroom door slowly and quietly. I crept across to the balcony overlooking the living room, and down below I saw Joanna and Ian. His jaw was clenched, and her hand was out as if to push him back.

I was just above them and could hear the words they spat back and forth. "I know it was you," Ian was saying.

"No way."

"But I also know what you're dealing with. And I do feel for you."

"Bullshit. Stop it."

"Look. It didn't work. I'm still here. My team leader values me enough to know it wasn't worth it to sack me."

I ran down the hall and halfway down the stairs. "What's going on?"

Joanna looked up at me and said, "Go back to your room, Maddie," as if she were my mother.

"She tried to get me fired," Ian said, looking startled to see me. "Tried to ruin my whole life."

"Oh my God," she said, her hands on her hips. "Ruin your whole life? Please."

This made Ian go wild. "I've got no education! What else am I supposed to do? The only thing I've ever been good at is close protection, and it's the only way I've got to make a decent wage. I pay for my mum's nursing home. If you'd gotten me fired it would have been the end of my career. No more deployments. That would have been it for me and my seventy-six-year-old mum!"

I walked down the last six steps to the foyer and turned toward Joanna, who was standing in the doorway to the living room, now ashen and slouching. "It's not true, is it?" I asked.

A storm passed through what was already anguish. "Of course you would believe him!"

"No, I—"

The next second, a Greek vase was hurling toward me. She lost several of her bracelets along with the throw. The vase broke against the wall behind me. Ian grabbed me and shoved me toward the front door and stood between the two of us.

Joanna was crying for real now. The way she was standing made her look broken. "How could you believe him? You know me!"

"Jo," I said, trying to get around Ian so I could go to her. He was not having it, and blocked me with his arm.

"Get out of here," she said, her smudged, shiny eyes turning to the floor. In a trembling voice she went on, "I was getting sick of seeing you sleeping in for days on end while I work my ass off 24/7 anyway."

"What?" I held my hands out, stunned. "I thought—"

"Get out!" She stabbed at the door with her long, purple fingernail. "Both of you, get the fuck out of my house, right the fuck now."

"I need my—"

She reached down, picked up my boots and hurled them at me. "Go!"

We went.

MADDIE

2001

Ian and I walked out of Joanna's house like children who had been punished. Heads down, arms at our sides, staring at the ground. My bottom lip was shaking, but Ian was, I think, just fuming.

Neither one of us actually made the decision to walk to the Irish Pub, we just started out silently in that direction. We passed through the woods and reached the graffiti-splattered footbridge that crossed a branch of the River Vardar. Without a word we followed the sidewalk that led to the center. The downtown was mostly neglected and dirty, but also had the occasional clean, modern block where the shop owners had valiantly managed to keep cheery displays in sparkling windows.

Behind the shopping mall and across the river, in between the mosque and the mountains, I could see the prominent and striking Skopsko Kale, a tenth-century Roman fortress that looked out over the city. Lit by dozens of little lamps dotting the hillside below, the long stone wall meandered across the high ridge, ending in a medieval tower with three black windows that looked like keyholes in the amber stone which shone like gold.

We carried on in silence into the center, him smoking and me looking at the death notices stapled to telephone poles and the cork public-announcement boards. There were dozens. The eyes of the Balkan dead were everywhere. They watched constantly.

The Irish Pub was just like it always was: bright, loud and full of ex-pats. It felt like entering a Christmas party, but there was no special occasion. Ian and I were greeted upon entering with back slaps and hellos.

We ordered drinks and sat down. I fought back tears.

"It's okay," he said. He put his hand gently on the back of my head and pulled me toward him until my cheek was on his shoulder. He hugged me and stroked the back of my hair. After a while he sat up and smiled at me with bright eyes. "I'm sorry about what just happened up there. But I'll admit that I'm thrilled to be alone with you."

Maybe something good might come out of all this pain between me and Jo. "Me, too," I said, meaning it.

"I've been wanting to ask you something. That quote that you knew, the same one as Helena, about God being dead?"

"It's Nietzsche," I answered quietly.

"It seems like such a strange coincidence to me, that two of my favorite people read the same obscure book."

After a second I said, "Well, Nietzsche's not that obscure. Not if your dad's an atheist like mine."

He looked appropriately shocked. "Really?"

"Yeah. One of his favorite quotes was, 'A man's ethical behavior should be based effectually on sympathy, education, and social ties and needs; no religious basis is necessary. Man would indeed be in a poor way if he had to be restrained by fear of punishment and hopes of reward after death.'"

"Your dad's like you then. Unconventional."

"But I'm not an atheist," I said. "I nearly died when I was ten. I felt different afterward. Protected. I felt like I'd been chosen. I always said my prayers to myself under the covers because I didn't want my dad to know. I was afraid he would think I was just another one of the flock. I suppose I am, really."

"You could never be just another one of the flock," Ian said, leaning close to me and looking into my eyes. One of his fingers batted at my hair. "Your wool is far too dark."

He was finally going to kiss me. He stayed like that, looking in my eyes, as if he was reading something written in tiny letters. After a few seconds he said, "I wonder, are you as authentic as you seem? I've never met someone so unafraid to wear their heart on their sleeve."

"I don't know how to be any other way."

"I'm not a trusting person."

"I can see that. Maybe I can help."

He shook his head.

I reached out and placed my hand on his arm while returning his gaze. I could hear my own breath coming in and going out. "Ian. Come on."

He looked down. "I don't want to mess this up. I'm sorry. I need some time to sort things out."

It was like a slap. I nodded and said okay. I think that's what I said. I can't actually remember. I stood up to excuse myself and the room was spinning.

I know I stumbled. He caught me. I pulled loose and I left.

Later that night at Joanna's, I slipped inside quietly, locking the door behind me. It was close to midnight, and I hoped Jo would be asleep, preferably in the basement. I was not in the mood for either an interrogation or an argument.

Dammit!

She was awake.

I saw her from across the living room, shoulders hunched, sobbing over the kitchen sink. She was out of control, and all my anger was gone then and there. I ran to her.

"I'm sorry, Jo. I wouldn't have gone with him if you hadn't started throwing things. Jo. Please! Look at me?"

I tried to put my arms around her, and she shoved me away. Then she pointed to the patio, at the little palace she had built for Panda and the kittens. The overhead light was on outside and I could see Panda on her blanket. Like usual, she lay on her side, nursing the kittens. I turned back to Jo and looked at her helplessly.

"She's dead."

"What?"

"I was checking on them before bed. I opened the glass door, and that's when I saw that the kittens were crying. They didn't know what was going on. Their mom is dead. There is…" She fumbled over her words and clasped her fingers together in a tight knot to control the trembling, and I suddenly loved her even more. "I found… Someone put poison in her bowl."

"Someone. Who?"

She threw her hands in the air and looked at me with such malice it was as if I were responsible for the death. *"Starata vešterka sosed, koj drug?"* she shouted, telling me, "The old witch next door, who else?" At that moment it crossed my mind, with bizarre clarity and brevity, that I had begun dreaming in Bulgarian, and she was shouting at me in Macedonian. We were going native, as it was called by the senior ex-pats, and it was probably time for a long visit home.

"It could have been her, but it could have been anyone. They hate us. They don't want us here. They hate the Americans, all the aid workers and the other Westerners, and especially the refugees. They hate us!

"What do we do about the kittens?" I whispered, horror mounting.

Jo made a choking noise. "How the fuck do I know?"

"We can take care of them," I said, standing directly in front of her and forcing her to look at me. "When I was growing up one of our cats died when the kittens were little and we saved two of them. I'll look it up on the internet. I'll find out what to do. I'll stay and help."

"Oh you want to stay for another couple of weeks? Get in some quality time with Ian? Awesome. I must admit I envy your schedule. The artist. No. You can take your laptop and go write your little travel guide somewhere else. Find another sponsor."

"Joanna, stop acting this way. We can fix this."

"We," she said, emphasizing the word and stepping away from me, "are not doing anything together. You need to leave in the morning. If you're going to believe Ian over me after all this time, all we have been through together, then I was wrong about you."

"I never said I believed him. You threw my boots at me and told me to get the fuck out."

"You believe him. Just say so."

I sighed. "You said to me a week ago, 'He's going to be sent home to England.' You knew. You said it. At that restaurant in Greece."

She laughed. "I did know! I knew you thought it was me who told. It wasn't, but that doesn't matter now. You know what? I thought you were the one real thing, Maddie. In all of this. In my life. But I was wrong. You have no idea how much you've hurt me. But good luck with Ian. Ian with the brown English teeth and the bad tattoos and no education. Oh and with the bipolar girlfriend in London. Good luck with all that. You made your choice."

When I left for the bus station before dawn the next morning, I walked down the drive past a plastic bag that obviously contained Panda's body. I could not bear to think about the kittens.

I was back in Sofia, but my beautiful city, my beloved home was suddenly lusterless. The once perfect plummy tomatoes were a blight on my tongue. The smell of the flowers in the park was that of a saccharine soap. The trees were twisted and the sound of the children's laughter below my balcony was a jeering series of taunts. *You'll never have him. You'll never get what you want.*

Time dragged. I began to search the internet for cheap plane tickets home. Sofia was no longer my paradise. The colors had faded. I walked with my eyes on the ground.

After several hours of writing in the coffee and pastry shop around the corner, I stopped into the tiny grocery kiosk beneath my apartment. I was startled at the sight of the usually rosy-cheeked lady who sold me my bottled water, chocolates and wine. That afternoon, she was addled, aghast and stammering. Her bright-red permed hair with the gray roots looked as if she had just raked her fingers through it backward and then forward.

As usual she was watching her ancient black-and-white television with the bent coat hanger antennae. She'd always been so nice to me, so pleased to chat with the friendly American woman with the funny accent who taught at the university. Now she looked as if she was choking on something. Her plump finger waved again and again in the direction of the television.

"Kakvo stava?" I asked. "What's going on?" I looked at the television and a plane was flying into the World Trade Cen-

ter. Clearly the woman was watching a science-fiction film. I smiled at her. *"Kakvo gledate?"* What are you watching?

"Milichka," she said, her voice shaking. She often called me little dear, but today she was looking at me with sad, world-weary eyes, as if I were actually a child. *"Triyabva da se kachish i da se obadish na tvoite roditeli. Vednaga."* You need to go upstairs and call your family. At once.

MADDIE

Six weeks before

"I've brought you something, chicken!" Wayne says merrily, when I open the door.

Oh God, not again, I think. In the past year he's arrived on our doorstep a number of times with baffling presents. For Charlie he's gift-wrapped a pair of matching Harley-Davidson socks and underpants, a kid-sized shovel and the world's largest disgusting gummy snake. He's also brought me two bottles of perfume that he claims he bought for his seventy-year-old wife but that she didn't like. Red Sin and Midnight Heat. Ian politely told him that I was stocked for scents. And then added, "But, Wayne, feel free to bring me something nice for a change!"

Wayne didn't laugh.

Now he's holding out a Crock-Pot.

"My wife was just saying how knackered you must be, all on your own. 'Take her some of that chili you made,' she told me. 'She and Charlie will love it!' she said. And you will,

Maddie. I promise. Not to toot my own horn too much, but I only make this twice a year and everyone says it's the bee's knees."

Apparently Wayne's son has killed a deer, so Wayne has made a big pot of venison chili. Mmm-mmm. I take the Bambi stew over to my parents' house and tell them to eat it.

My mom transfers the contents of Wayne's Crock-Pot into Tupperware and chats to me all the while. "Are you cooking for Charlie?"

"I am," I answer. "We actually don't just stop eating completely when the man of the house goes away."

"But not just Lunchables. Not just frozen pizza."

"No. Just broccoli and tofu."

She laughs and spills a plop of red stew on the floor. "I'm serious! You need to take care of yourself. You look pasty. You need to eat more meat."

"Pasty?" I repeat, or rather stammer. "Pasty?"

"Yes. Pasty."

"Seriously, Mom?" I say, using my hands to frame my disaster face. "I think you're missing the five car pile-up because you're fixated on a ding in the door."

She drops down with a handful of paper towel to address the mess she's made. She would rather not talk about the mess that is looking at her, waiting for a reaction.

I let it go.

My mom and dad have offered to watch Charlie this afternoon while I see Cami J. Skopie and Sophie have come along with him to the farm, to chase squirrels and dig for moles. Charlie is adorably ecstatic about each and every visit we make to my parents' house, as if it is a special occasion rather than a weekly event. My mom spoils him with packaged ice-cream bars, and my dad helps him hunt for frogs and toads with a fishing net. Charlie's shoes are always covered in mud when

I come to pick him up, and he is always red-cheeked from being outdoors and so happy.

It's time for me to leave.

I wave out the window to Charlie and my parents as I pull away and head down the long winding driveway. Charlie is on the front steps, and my mom is behind him, arms over his shoulders hugging him into her. My dad is already standing by the swing that hangs from the giant walnut tree in the front yard, calling for Charlie to join him.

I am wearing my *Breakfast at Tiffany's* oversize sunglasses and a sundress. My scar is all but completely covered. When I get to Hometown Liquor and Video there is a brand-new young man working who doesn't know I've come in a few times in the last month, so I feel pretty good about just going for it and buying not one but two half-gallon Stolichnaya vodkas. He doesn't bat an eye except to look me up and down. He smiles as if he would like to be invited to my vodka party.

Ian Skyped me earlier and said he expects to be headed home from Nigeria by the end of next month. I'm in a good mood.

That is, until Cami J, who I've really started to look forward to seeing, suggests that I get a new doctor. "I understand that you're angry with me about dashing off last time," I say, sounding as if I'm the doctor and she the patient.

Today Cami J is dressed in holey jeans and a Rolling Stones tank top with an eighties grunge-rock plaid shirt tied around her waist. She wears her signature rhinestone cap over her long, wavy, graying hair. She is watering her ferns and looking at me with sadness and affection. "I'm not angry with you. I'm worried about you. For more reasons than one, as I think you're aware."

I ignore this. She has been trying to get me to talk about Ian and the night I got my injury at the campground, but I refuse to go there. "I don't want to see anyone else," I say, promptly appalled that I sound pouty, as if I am addressing a reluctant lover.

"Maddie, I don't want to stop working with you. But if I'm right, and what I saw happening with you at the end of our last session was a partial seizure—"

"Seizure!" I practically shout. "You said, 'You've had a little fit, sweetie.'"

"Okay. I get it. It sounds scary, I'm sure, but it may be nothing. But if it's not nothing, then you need to know! You need to have an electroencephalogram."

"Is that a tongue twister? What is that?"

"An EEG is a procedure used to monitor the electrical activity in the brain."

"To find out what?"

"To find out if there's something off in there. Something that could be causing this sudden onset of crippling anxiety. There could be bruising or bleeding. Brain injury is one reason people develop seizures, and there are different kinds, Maddie. One type is called a psychic seizure, and it can cause all sorts of disorienting and frightening feelings. I'm not the right person to diagnose this, hon. Look, I'm a psychologist. I'm a certified journal therapist. But for this type of thing you need a neurologist."

"They told me that I had a mild traumatic brain injury. A concussion. Nobody said anything about seeing a neurologist."

"Nobody could have predicted you might have a seizure. I'm not even sure you had a seizure. But the other day when you kept repeating, 'I need to get Charlie, I need to get Charlie'? It made me remember that in our first session you were clenching and unclenching your hands."

"What does that mean?"

"I don't know! That's exactly what I'm trying to tell you!

I don't know. You need to see a neurologist. You need to get your head checked."

"I can't believe you just said I need to get my head checked." I burst out laughing. "Okay," I say finally. "If I find a neurologist and get this EEG done, can I still keep coming to you to do my writing?"

"Of course you can, Maddie. Of course."

"Good." I sit there for a second, processing these new upsetting developments, and then I remember. "Oh! I brought my homework and my photos for the photo exercise. Are we still doing that one?"

"Absolutely."

My assignment was to choose three photographs and bring them to our session. They didn't necessarily have to be the best photographs in the world. It made no difference if they were photographs of people or places. What was important, Cami J had said, was that they be photographs that, when I looked at them, "impacted me emotionally and made me really feel."

The first one I pass to her makes her smile. She taps a glossy fingernail on Charlie's face and then raises her eyes to mine. "Now there's a cute kid."

It's a piece of paper with a red Chuck E. Cheese border and a black-and-white sketch of the two of us in the center. The photo booth had cost two dollars, and it was the best two dollars I ever spent. He's on my lap, looking up at me with wide eyes and an open mouth as if I have just told the most hilarious joke ever. I'm grinning so big I have a dimple.

Cami J passes me my kitty cat notebook and a pen and says, "What made you choose this picture?"

I chose this picture because this was the first of many amazing moments with Charlie. I did want a child. I wanted him in the worst way.

But...

He was a hard baby. He was loud and angry and not sweet like we'd thought he'd be. Ian and I fought a lot about him. I was always tired and Ian didn't help me much—if at all. Charlie was not a happy camper. He cried if I put him down. He cried if I stopped singing. He cried if I stopped bouncing him or swinging him or God forbid, what if I closed my eyes for just one second? He cried, he cried, you know what, he SCREAMED. I didn't feel like he really loved me, just that he needed me to do things for him. Ian never wanted to go out anywhere when Charlie was a baby. The few times we did, Charlie would throw a tantrum and Ian would stand up and say, "Let's just go home. I don't know why we bother."

But when Ian took the really long assignment in Afghanistan when Charlie was two, it started to feel like we were totally on our own. Charlie and I just started going everywhere. We went to McDonald's PlayPlace. We went to Oak Park Shopping Mall and rode the carousel. All the baby things that moms figure out to do. Jumpin' Jaxx and Little Monkey Business. The park. The playgrounds. Chuck E. Cheese. And that day, when we took this picture, I knew that we had fallen in love with each other. It was the most important day of my life, discovering that my child was my soul mate. It had taken almost three years to get all the way to where we needed to be but we had clicked and it was perfect and I was officially the mom I had always wanted to be. Smiling and loving and so happy that Charlie and I had each other. It was a day that changed everything *because I felt that we were safe and normal and fine, and that life would only get better.*

"You have two more minutes if you want to keep going," Cami J says.

"No. I'm good with that."

She reads for a second and says, "Very sweet. That's a special bond. We'll talk more about it next week after I read it more carefully."

I nod.

Cami J makes a copy with her printer and hands it to me. "All right," she says. "May I see the next photo?"

This is one of my favorite photographs. Black and white, eight by ten, with the stunning Orthodox Church of Sveta Nedelya behind us, Jo and I look, quite honestly, beautiful. Neither one of us is model material, but this photo is flattering to the point of being almost an outright lie. Back in the day we both dressed in the same sort of Eastern European Urban Outfitters shoddiness; wide-leg corduroys, tiny strappy tanks, gobs of cheap jewelry and big black boots. We wore our wavy brown hair the same way also, in un-styled cascades around our shoulders. We could have been sisters. I had the fuller lips and better cheekbones (thanks to my mom, who is a quarter Comanche), but Jo was tall and rail-thin with striking wide-set eyes. In the photo our hair is whipping around our faces as if we'd hired a wind machine for a photo shoot. Plus, we were young, reckless and ready for anything, and that kind of fearlessness is irresistible.

I put my pen to paper and say, "Do you want me to write why I chose this?"

"Let's do something different with this one," she answers. "I want you to tell me about the person in the photo with you."

This is Joanna. She's the old friend who I wrote the letter to in our last writing-therapy session. When I look at her I feel loss. I feel sadness because I went home and she was left there all by herself. I feel shame. Guilt.

Also, I feel anger. She was wrong. I was the real thing. It wasn't just about him, it was about us. She always was better than me at everything and the one time when it seemed like I had won, when Ian liked me better, she completely turned on me. She wasn't able to step back and see that she was the successful one, the funny one. She was smarter and more interesting and she had the great body and she was always the first choice. She had the amazing job and she'd always been better at languages without even trying. She had it all. Why begrudge me one little triumph?

I don't know why Ian didn't fall for her. Every other guy did. I can't explain it, there was just something unusual between Ian and me. If she had just let me have that one thing for myself rather than lashing out about it, we would still be friends. If she had been able to do the right thing instead of bursting into tears and hanging up on me when I told her I was going to have a baby and I wanted her to come visit.

But she was furious with me.

I push the notebook away.

"You didn't write for very long."

"I'm done."

"Can you write for another minute?" Cami J asks, and I shake my head no.

"Are you all right, Maddie?"

"Yes. I am. But I feel…"

In my head I have images and thoughts circling. The bats and the blood and the lake and the lies.

"What? You feel what?"

"Just like I want to finish and go home."

"Okay," she says kindly. "If you feel like it later, write about your last photo and email it to me, okay?"

"All right," I say standing. "I'm sorry."

"Don't be sorry, Maddie. Don't be sorry for anything."

I promise to try.

MADDIE

2001

I took the bare concrete stairs up to my apartment two at a time, and at one point I stumbled and fell. I could barely make the numbers on my rotary phone go around with my finger. The shopkeeper had told me to call my family immediately, and I was calling Jo. I was not thinking of the horrible things she'd said to me or even that she might hang up. My only thought was to call the person who mattered the most. I knew that for Joanna, this would be unfathomable news. It would be for anyone. But she was in a hostile, lonely, dismal place already.

To my relief, she answered straightaway. "Maddie, oh my God, Maddie! What is going on?"

I knew without a doubt that this was something that transcended and bridged the rift between us. I started crying. She was being nice.

"I'm going home, Jo," I said. "Home home. Back to the

States. Can I come and say goodbye? I want to see you before I leave, if it's okay. Please. I want to apologize."

"I'm sorry, too," she said and I knew she was crashing. "Of course you can come. I don't want you to go without us seeing each other, okay? Please come. I'm falling apart."

Everyone was.

I arrived in Skopje on the twelfth, the day after. That night, some kind Macedonians held a candlelight vigil outside the American Embassy. It didn't last long because the vigil was interrupted by other, less kind Macedonians, throwing rocks and screaming that we'd gotten what we deserved. Those with the candles ran for their lives, and the others, the enraged ones, smashed windows with bricks and threw trash and Molotov cocktails over the security fence.

Islamic terrorists had just attacked America, and the radical nationalists in the Balkans were attacking us because we sided with the Muslims in Bosnia, but apparently that alliance made no difference to the Middle East. As Ian said to me afterward, "You know, I don't think the Middle East and the Balkans are talking." It was confusing, but one thing was clear. We were damned.

I was supposed to visit for four days before returning to Bulgaria to pack up and fly home, but in the end I stayed two weeks. Not a word was spoken about me overstaying my welcome. The deadline for the travel guide had been pushed back, and I planned to finish it in the States. I thought about Ian constantly but didn't try to get in touch with him. He'd made it clear that he was going to stay with his girlfriend, and I wanted no further problems with Jo anyway. The sky had just fallen. So I'd had a crush. Maybe it had felt like love, but it had been unrequited. It was depressing and painful and hopeless. In what way did that differ from everything else at that moment? I persuaded myself that I didn't care. I fed my seed of anarchy. Grief. Scorn. Indifference. Fury. Total and complete disillusion. Ian was nothing. What did he really matter?

Jo and I spent most of that time slumped in front of the news, trying to make sense of our changed world. At one point she called in sick to work four days in a row. This was unheard of for Jo, who was notorious for calling Stoyan in the middle of the night and having him drive her to the camps when there was an emergency. She'd stopped going down to curl up on the plaid couch in the basement to cry. Now we cried silently together, watching desperate people jump to their death from the top of the towers. The news showed it over and over, and it never stopped feeling like the end of everything.

It was late on my last night, and Joanna and I had decided it was time to walk home from the Irish Pub. As I was paying the bill a bald man wearing faded army fatigues brushed up against me and grabbed my ass. I swung and missed. "Fucking bitch," he said, loud enough to grab Joanna's attention. She stormed over.

"What happened?" she demanded. The man and I stared at each other.

"Nothing," I said. Things in this part of the world went very wrong very quickly, and the best thing to do was leave.

I told Joanna I was just going to use the bathroom, and I'd be right back. When I came out Ian was there pacing furtively in the corridor, looking distraught.

"Peter just told me you were here," he said angrily.

I didn't know what to say.

"How long are you staying?"

"I'm going home tomorrow."

"Christ!" he said, looking shocked. "Can you stay a little longer?"

"I can't, actually. I've got a flight to catch in Sofia."

"Where are you going?"

"Home," I said, feeling a lump rising in my throat. "I'm going home."

"What do you mean? The States? Are you coming back?"

My eyes filled, and I shook my head no.

"Oh hey there." That was Joanna, who had walked up behind us. "Sorry, Ian," she said, almost sweetly. "Are we leaving?"

"Yes," I answered, and I sounded dutiful even to myself.

Joanna turned to walk away, taking my arm.

"Maddie?" he said, imploring.

Joanna responded by giving him her middle finger.

Outside the Irish Pub, we turned up the main road and headed home. I looked down the alleyway and saw the silhouettes of two men. One had the other by the throat. He wore a long coat. A long coat like the one Stoyan, Joanna's friend and driver, always wore.

"Jo," I said, clutching her sleeve. "I think that's—"

"The guy who grabbed you? Yeah, it's him. Don't stop," she said. "That douchebag deserves it. He needs to learn to keep his hands to himself. Stoyan's only going to scare him."

"Okay," I said, cringing at the tiny squeak of my voice. Was it fear? I wondered. No, I decided. It was an uncomfortable awe.

When we were almost to her house Joanna suddenly asked, "It doesn't bother you? Going back to the States?"

"No," I said truthfully. "I finally want to go home."

"What will you do?"

"Get my apartment back from my subletter. Eat some decent Mexican food. Sleep. Get a job."

We walked in silence until I finally said, "What about you?"

"There will be a few months of inventory and paperwork after we get the tents down. And then… I'll continue to work for Elaine, I suppose. It will probably be in Africa somewhere."

"I thought," I said carefully, "that you told me you don't want to do this anymore."

"I did say that. But…"

"But what?"

"Then I realized that this job is all I have."

I started to respond and she cut me off. "Something happened, Maddie. Something happened that would have meant I had to leave my job. I tried to make myself believe it was all for the best. But it didn't really happen after all. And it's okay. I'm good at what I do."

She took a giant hitching breath. I hugged her, and I was much shorter than her, so when she spoke it was into the top of my shoulder. "It's okay. I'm okay."

"What was it? What happened?"

"I promise to tell you. One day I will. I'm just not ready to talk about it quite yet."

It was ten the next morning. Joanna had long been at work, and I was preparing to leave for the bus station. The doorbell rang. I expected it to be the taxi driver I had called some time before. When I opened the door, there stood Ian, in the suit he had told me he wore while working but which I had never seen. He looked so serious, and so handsome, that I was kicked in the stomach with that now-familiar flutter that made me helplessly want to reach up and pull him down.

He nodded hello, his lips pressed together, his eyes downcast. After a second he tried to smile. Suddenly I was afraid I might come completely unglued and grab him by the jacket and yank him into me. I was out of my comfort zone, and felt light-headed. I needed a sign that I was not alone in this, that I was not imagining how we felt about each other.

Neither one of us moved or spoke. After a long, steady, regretful gaze that traveled across every part of my face, he touched my cheek and then trailed his fingers back to tuck my hair behind my ear. I shivered and felt the onset of the emptiness that was sure to be agony. I almost said out loud, *God no. This can't really be the end.*

"I came to say a proper goodbye, Petal."

"Is that all?"

"And to get your phone number in the States."

I told him, and he typed the numbers into his mobile. I blinked and felt paralyzed. I waited stiffly, holding my breath.

"I'll call you."

I'll call you? I covered my mouth with my hand and must have looked like I was about to be sick. I'd known this was coming, but I hadn't anticipated what it would feel like to have him standing there, so close, knowing that whatever it was that we'd had was over. He spun around and then walked away.

I watched him, trying not to scream, waiting for him to pull out his cigarettes and look up as he made his way down the street, past the Roma house where children, dogs and broken appliances blanketed the yard. Trying not to throw a tantrum like a two-year-old. His steps were slow and measured, his face turned down. *Turn around*, I thought. *Stop and make this okay. You motherfucker, turn around and make this okay. Don't leave me. Don't leave this way! Will I ever see you again? Say something. Turn around!*

I stood there, my eyes locked on his stooped shoulders until he disappeared around the corner at the bottom of the street, into the woods and the winding path that would take him to the city. He never once looked up, and though I held my breath and willed it, though I stood on tiptoe, craned my neck and prayed for it, neither did he ever once look back.

As I was waiting in line to board the bus back to Sofia, Jo called me. I didn't pick up. In my seat and waiting for the bus to depart, I leaned my cheek against the dirty glass and looked out at that bleak place, wondering if and when I would return.

My eyes strayed to the stone wall outside the broken door of the café where the corkboard was papered in obituaries, the edges and corners of the photocopies rustling in the breeze. There were so many little black crosses next to the cherished portraits and beautiful Cyrillic writing, all to honor and remember the deceased. One set of eyes seemed particularly familiar, and I wondered where I might have seen that oddly beautiful middle-aged woman with the full lips and Roman nose. There was something predatory and hawkish in her eyes; a startling and familiar intensity that made me sit up. She looked a bit like me.

I was dead after the encounter with Ian. Dead and angry and done. Ian had been right when he'd said I was just a petal blowing through his nightmare. "You'll be gone before I know it."

Joanna's call went unreturned. I never even listened to her message.

A few weeks later, at my parents' house in Kansas, I got a text message from Jo in the middle of the night. It said, So that's it? Okay then. You'll regret this.

Years would pass.

MADDIE

2002

After deciding I wanted to return to America after the 9/11 attacks, I visited my family in Kansas for a few quiet, solemn, restful weeks.

Then I returned to New York and took back my apartment from the subletter. It was a tiny studio on West Fourth Street right on the corner of Jane, over a popular burger bar called The Corner Bistro. On most nights my entire building smelled of blood, beef and grease from their kitchen. It was a combination that never failed to take me back to Joanna's house in Skopje and the smell of the towel under the sink.

I found a job. Print journalism was slowly suffocating, and dirty, dog-eared, handheld travel guides were being replaced by the internet. Instead of writing, I went to work at a high-end tutoring company called Unique U. Wealthy Manhattan families wanted "mentors" with degrees from Ivy League institutions to dispense advice and wisdom to their wayward teenagers.

My schedule was erratic. Sometimes I worked an hour in the morning, an hour over lunch, two hours after school and three hours before bed. I tutored in the family homes—dark, huge and twisty old-money apartments off Central Park West, airy, arty lofts in Tribeca and bohemian brownstones in Brooklyn filled with antiques, candles, pillows and pets. Sometimes there was not enough time to go home between students. I began to drink during the day.

I had used my Eastern European contacts to introduce me to a couple of seedy hangouts for Balkan transplants and a variety of other ne'er-do-wells. Trakia Bar was, without a doubt, the shittiest little run-down roach-infested hole-in-the-wall in all of Greenwich Village. It had become the only place I wanted to be. I felt comforted by the lack of judgment and end-of-the-road acceptance that emanated from the people who drank there on sunny afternoons.

I walked up to the entrance at three o'clock on a Tuesday. I'd just come from tutoring a teenage pharmaceutical heir, and I had a bulimic ballerina later in the day. I had decided to pass the time in between with my friend Stefan the bartender, who I sometimes covered for if he wanted to take one of the "patrons" into the basement to smoke a bowl or have sex.

"Hey, Stefan," I said, walking in and placing my computer and briefcase on the bar. "What do you think we would be doing right now if we were back in Bulgaria?"

Stefan killed a fly with his towel. "I would be wondering how best to end my life if I don't escape that pant-crap country." Not everyone shared my ridiculous fondness for the pant crappiness of Bulgaria.

He brought me a glass of wine, and I had a look around to see which kooks were in attendance today. The usuals. I nodded hello to bad-wig lady with her tattered pile of old

People magazines and gave a friendly wave to seventies-mustache-drug-casualty guy slouched in the corner itching his sad, skinny ankles.

"There's a cookie tray with coke lines in the oven today," said Stefan, as if he were telling me about a drink special. "Help yourself."

Trakia was foul-smelling and corrupt, mismanaged by shady Bulgarians and frequented by scoundrels, drug dealers and vagrants. Outside people were walking dogs, making dinner reservations, looking forward to first dates and buying flowers for anniversaries. Shiny happy people, who looked, for all intents and purposes, more or less like me, were managing to do all the normal things, like lunching with parents and playing with children.

I, on the other hand, sat with my back to all that, behind the dirty, shattered window. More often than not, I was thinking about Ian. Reliving our conversations. Remembering his arm around me in an illegal taxi. The taste of the bad wine at the Irish Pub and the smell of his aftershave when he pulled my head down to his shoulder and stroked my hair. I might as well have never left the Balkans. And the thing was, I wished I never had.

Seven hours later, I walked into my apartment with a plastic container of buffet food from the deli at my Eighth Avenue subway stop. I sat down on my futon, turned on the television and began to shovel tasteless crap into my mouth. When my phone rang, I considered not answering because it said Unknown. I picked it up.

"Hello?"

"Hiya, Petal."

It was him. I can't even begin to describe the shock and delirium at hearing his voice. My elbow hit my plastic wine cup, and the contents spilled onto my comforter. It had been well over a year. "Hi! Oh my God. Hi!" I told myself to calm down.

"Where are you?"

"I'm fine. How are you?"

"I said, 'Where are you?' Not, 'How are you?'"

"I'm in New York."

"I thought maybe I might catch you in Kansas, you know, maybe catch you between feeding the chickens and shearing the sheep."

"No. I'm in New York. You've caught me eating a late deli buffet dinner of tuna salad and a soggy egg roll. At least I thought it was an egg roll. Now I'm not so sure."

"Good God, no wonder you were always fawning over the crappy food in the Balkans."

"It wasn't crappy at all. I miss it."

"You should see the shit I'm being fed in Bosnia. Everything is stuffed inside a pepper. Meat inside a pepper. Rice inside a pepper. Cheese inside a pepper. I don't ever want to see another bloody pepper."

"You're in Bosnia?"

"I am. Would you like to hear what I've been doing since we went our separate ways?"

"Please."

"Okay, so, yes, I'm in Bosnia at the moment. But the biggest news I've got is that I'm no longer in the military."

"What? Seriously?"

"Retired. A free agent. A soldier of fortune, actually. I hadn't been long back in London working as a training officer when my brother John phoned me up."

Ian used to talk about his older brother John quite a bit back in Skopje. He was, apparently, Ian's idol. A badass with an incorruptible moral compass, he'd been the head of the Wilson clan since the death of their father despite the fact that he was the third youngest of ten. He'd been in the British military for twentysomething years and had left to do private security work while we were all in Macedonia.

"John got me a close-protection job in Bosnia with the American company Dynamics. So, I went to my unit and put in my papers for voluntary release. Two weeks later and two hundred quid lighter, I was out of the army. And here I am."

"Congratulations!"

"Thank you! I'm looking after the top guy in the Office of High Representatives in Brčko, so it's a bit of a feather in my cap."

"What's Bosnia like?"

"It's a lot like Macedonia, really, except there are no fun American girls around."

I laughed and felt warm. He still made me blush.

"Maddie, you wouldn't believe it. The money is great. For the first time in my life I've been thinking about life after being a bodyguard. It's a long way off, but I might actually be able to buy a house. My own house, which I can decorate or defile in whatever way I see fit, you know? A nice tub. Not a metal trough but a nice tub. A place to put all my junk."

"That's awesome, Ian."

He let out a sigh. "I can hear you smiling. I miss your smile."

"Thank you. And on that note. How's Fiona?"

"Cheeky! I like it."

"Well?"

"We broke up, actually." A rush of adrenaline surged through me and I waited. After a pause, during which I could hear him exhaling smoke, he added, "She was jealous of you, as it turns out."

"She was?"

"She had this idea that I had cheated on her with you."

"My God, you were a saint. Why would she think that?"

"Because I talked about you, I guess. I talked about Joanna, too. She had this idea I was having sex with the pair of you."

"Wow. Like, at the same time or just in general?"

"Not sure on that one." He cleared his throat. I imagined him in some dismal little Balkan flat with bad, peeling, floral wallpaper overlaid with trashy, enticing posters of half-naked Serbian pop stars. I figured the other bodyguards were nearby, mixing protein shakes, doing push-ups or watching music videos on the television. I pictured Ian cupping his hand around the phone and turning toward the wall. There was a very long pause. "Petal," he said quietly. "Here's the thing."

"What?"

"I want to see you."

I tried to sleep that night, but the euphoria was intoxicating. My skin was tingling. My head was swimming. I became Ian and I was touching myself and he was finally kissing me and pushing me back on my futon and finally. Finally. Bliss.

When I couldn't take any more of my fantasies I went and opened up the little white window facing the Hudson River. I ducked through it and crouched on my wrought-iron fire escape, looking out at the blurry blend of night city colors and the squares of warmth lit in the high-rises and brownstones. I listened to cars honking and a girl below laughing. It was a symphony and an awakening. Life was happening, here and to me. I stood up and felt the wind blowing my hair back, blowing the long T-shirt that just barely covered the tops of my thighs. I was floating, and I felt like I could fall and smash and still be happy because…

Ian wanted to see me. I loved him and I believed that he loved me.

It was like drowning all over again. It was the most magical little death of all.

MADDIE

Five weeks before

As I unload my groceries and vodka, Mary from the YMCA Kids Club phones to tell me that Charlie has pushed a jelly bean up his nose. I'm standing in my garage with the door open, and I can see Wayne weed-eating around the "guardian angel garden statue" that he gifted his wife last Christmas. I wave, but he turns his back to me and makes a shifty retreat into his own garage and disappears. I frown. I really should be nicer to him.

Mary is overexcited about this jelly bean thing. She wants me to know two things. Personally she thought it was a bad idea to give the kids jelly beans, and Charlie appears to be in a lot of pain. They recommend picking him up right away and visiting Urgent Care.

Seriously?

I check the time. It's noon, and I don't have Cami J for two and a half hours. I can handle it. How big a deal can it be?

Huge. Before I can even walk out of the door of the YMCA

with Charlie, the director is trotting behind me droning on about all the forms that need signing. Charlie is wailing like he is being tortured. It turns out the jelly beans were part of some "gross out" new kids game, and the flavor that is stuck up his nose could be anything from spoiled milk and rotten eggs to canned dog food or dead fish. I gag into my mouth as I drive him to Urgent Care.

The room is full of frazzled parents and listless children waiting and by the time Charlie sees the doctor, the jelly bean has melted into a sugary slime and slid down his throat. There is no need for any treatment; no need for anything in fact, other than for me to pay them 115 dollars for looking up his nose.

My parents agree to meet me at McDonald's for a quick hand-off. They will play at the PlayPlace, have probably two ice-cream cones and then take him back to their house to let him eat more crap and win a few times at Hungry Hungry Hippos.

It's for these reasons that I'm again not prepared for my appointment with Cami J. It's almost comical at this point. Today I was supposed to have with me a gift from Ian. Any gift from Ian. It's obvious how badly she wants to dig up some shit on Ian.

I am sitting outside Cami J's house rummaging around in my car like a cokehead who has dropped a bag. I'm on my knees in the back, finding prehistoric french fries, super balls and fake gold jewelry won with the claw at Chuck E. Cheese. Wet wipes, old gloves and the wrappers and paper backings from at least twenty Band-Aids. A muddy sock, some gum wadded up in a tissue and a broken pair of sunglasses. I am literally trying to come up with some sweet, sappy story about Ian presenting me with old gloves or broken sunglasses when I open the console.

There is Charlie's missing paracord superhero bracelet. I snatch it up. I can lie. I can say Ian made it for me.

This is my paracord bracelet, I write in my kitty notebook, hunched over the big antique desk. **Ian made it for me last year.**

I sneak a glance up at Cami J, who is smiling slightly and looking out the window in a happy way. I wonder if she has a boyfriend.

I had never heard of a paracord bracelet before Ian told me about them. They are actually really cool. This one means a lot to me because Ian made it using my favorite colors. It was really thoughtful of him and it took him quite a while to make it.

I glance up at Cami J again. She is looking at me. Oddly. I take a deep breath and am about to start writing again when I stand up and say, "Bathroom break!"

In her flowery scented bathroom with the seashell soaps and the trio of tiny paintings of fairies, I realize that I can't do this. I can easily do my assignments when I know I'm doing it for my own well-being; for my future with Charlie. This is ridiculous. Perhaps I should just be honest.

Cami J is in the kitchen making tea. I sit down at the desk and grab my kitty notebook.

I was lying before. Ian didn't give me this bracelet. He gave it to Charlie. Here are a few things Ian has given to me: a Breitling watch. A Crock-Pot. A house. Charlie.

But this bracelet that Ian gave to Charlie really is meaningful. I made fun of Ian for sitting down

in the basement and weaving these bracelets but maybe I was just jealous. I would have rather he made me one of these than give me a fancy watch.

Here's the thing. Every bracelet is woven out of paracord. Inside every paracord are a number of smaller threads, all with their own special use.

I find I am writing faster and faster.

I watched as Ian made it while explaining the purpose of each thread. Charlie hung on his every word. "This one is for if you're hurt and you need stitches. This bracelet can heal you. And see this one?" Ian held out a very fine wire. "This one is copper. It can be used as a trip wire around your camp while you're sleeping. This bracelet can protect you from your enemies." He told Charlie the next time we go camping he will show him how to use the waxed jute thread in his bracelet to start a fire. "This bracelet can keep you warm."

Charlie calls them his superhero bracelets. Ian makes him feel safe. He's convinced his son that if the worst comes to pass, he will save us with a bit of string. He was always a great protector. It is one of the reasons I fell so much in love with him.

But then...

Ian said, "It can be used to kill as well, Charlie."

Charlie wasn't sure what to make of this and neither was I. And then Ian went on. He pulled out a particular thread and said to our son, "This is the one you use to make a snare. I'll teach you to feed yourself in the wild! We'll catch a rabbit."

I thought to myself, Charlie loves the bunnies at the petting zoo.

And then Ian said, "Once we've snared it, we just pinch a bit of skin on its back. Rabbit skin is quite thin so the knife will go in easily."

I said, "He's too young," but too softly.

"Then, Charlie, you hook your fingers into the hole you've created and you pull it open, like you're pulling open the drapes to see who is hiding outside." As he demonstrated this, I felt a ripple of revulsion.

"And then, matey, what you do is you work the hide down until you can free the little legs. You pull very hard and you tear the skin away from the body from both sides."

Charlie was horrified.

"The rabbit will be left with two little furry shoes, a bit like Mummy in her slippers."

I stop writing and stare at the ceiling, remembering what I did. "Charlie," I'd said brightly with a smile. "It's bath time."

It was not bath time. It was two o'clock on a Sunday afternoon. "Charlie, come with me. Charlie, come with me. Charlie come with me now!"

Cami J shouts, "Shit, Maddie!" and I look back down from the ceiling. She's right here lunging for the desk to set down the tea. One of the cups teeters on the edge. It falls and shatters. The other sloshes scalding water onto her hand. I feel terrible. She is going to miss her rainbow unicorn teacup so much and that burn is going to hurt.

"Are you okay?" I ask, standing.

She holds her red hand close to her chest and looks at me as if she's just found me having a pee in the corner of her office. I actually check to make sure I'm fully clothed.

"Are you?" she asks carefully, coming toward me, but hesitantly.

I don't know. There's nothing to do really, but wait and see.

MADDIE

2003

We planned for months, speaking on the phone every week. I was on cloud nine. Until the day I left New York and started heading across the world to meet Ian.

I arrived in Zagreb on one of the most frightening flights of my entire life. While we plummeted toward the ground at what felt like a ninety-degree angle, a Croatian flight attendant with the stature and face of a supermodel casually handed me a shiny wrapped chocolate as she made her way down the aisle, clinging to the back of each seat in her struggle to fight gravity in six-inch heels. *"Dobar tek,"* she said repeatedly, which meant, "Bon appétit." She was elegant and polite as she smiled down upon us passengers looking up at her with eyes like eggs, our mouths hidden inside our vomit bags.

The flight from New York to Zagreb had been fifteen hours, including the four-hour layover in Paris. The bus ride that would take me from Zagreb to Ian in Brc̆ko was four hours long. I could have left that night at 10:00 p.m. on the last route of the day, but Ian and I agreed it was both too dangerous and too exhausting. I would spend the night in Zagreb and take the second bus out in the morning.

Ian had booked me a room at the Zagreb Double Tree Hilton. It was a hot evening in downtown Zagreb when my taxi dropped me off in front of the Double Tree. I was desperate to lie down in a quiet, cool, dark room and try to forget the flight from hell. When the jackhammers started up literally on the sidewalk in front of the hotel entrance, I simply walked away.

I had my travel-battered carry-on with me, and I didn't want to have to hunt down another taxi, so I started down the sidewalk away from the construction. Once the jackhammering was a light buzz in the distance, I chose the first hotel I came across. It was called, "Hotel." I didn't care. I was only there for one night.

Ian had asked me to call him when I arrived, so that he would know I was safe. I tried my phone and it didn't work. There was a teenage girl sitting at the front desk.

"Dobra večer," I said.

"Dobra večer."

"Do you speak English?"

"Yes, I do," she said, with a friendly smile.

"Can you help me? I don't have any cell phone reception and I'm wondering what the best place—"

She interrupted me. "What? Let me see."

I handed her my American cell phone, a device which incited a thorough and baffled inspection. "Europe has started using global satellite mobiles. I don't think this is a global satellite phone. It has nothing to do with reception." She handed it back to me and rather haughtily added, "Croatia has excellent service."

"Where's the closest internet café?"

It was only a few blocks away. I wanted to hug the boy

who took my money and gave me a beer and access to a computer. It was with a mixture of triumph and anticipation that I started to type in my email details. I would send Ian a message to confirm that I had arrived safely and would be on the bus he had asked me to take tomorrow morning.

My password was incorrect.

I tried it again. Incorrect.

I approached the boy at the front with a rapidly rising level of frustration. His English was not nearly as good as the girl's back at my hotel. "My password isn't working!"

"Maybe you forget?"

"No, I didn't forget. I didn't forget! I'm one of those morons who uses the same easy password for everything. So I don't forget!"

"Let me see." He came over to the computer I was using and tapped away at it for a second. He smiled at me. "No worry. It was with Croatian keyboard. Now it's with English. Working now, okay?"

"Thank you."

Not unpredictably, when I tried to log in, I was told yet again that my password was incorrect. This time, however, it also told me that because I had failed to log in three times at a computer other than my laptop, they would be texting me a security question to confirm my identity. Of course they would be texting it to my useless, shitty, third-world, American, not-remotely-global-satellite-fuckety-fuck-phone. I fought the urge to stand up and push the computer monitor over backward.

Washing over me was the very unsettling and superstitious feeling that I had cursed myself with my optimistic thoughts of a future with Ian. Why on earth had I allowed myself to imagine Sunday-morning sleep-ins with him spooned behind me? I should have known better than to hope. I should have known something would go wrong.

★ ★ ★

The next morning the kiosk in front of "Hotel" was open, and I bought a Croatian prepaid card for a public phone. There was a phone booth inside the bus station, and its discovery filled me with elation and a new faith in this reunion. I slid my card into the slot and dialed, feeling weak in the knees. I hoped I wasn't going to throw up.

"Hello?" Ian answered almost before the first ring had finished, and I wasn't ready. I was still inhaling to calm myself.

"Hi," I managed. "It's me."

"Hello?" he said again.

"It's me, Maddie. Can you hear me?"

"Hello?" he yelled again, and this time I knew. His voice was different. Cold. Something was wrong.

"It's me, Ian. Maddie. It's me!" I was screaming at the top of my lungs and people were staring.

The line didn't go dead. It just started making a hollow, horrible beep. Like someone flatlining.

Take the second bus in the morning. Take the second bus in the morning. I repeated this in my head as I walked across the station to the man in the window and bought my ticket...for the second bus in the morning. It was hypnotic and reassuring. Ian knew what bus I was taking. Everything would be fine. He would be waiting for me.

I curled into a ball in the very back seat just like I used to do on the trip between Sofia and Skopje. I tried to reassure myself. He just couldn't hear me. Why was I overreacting? This was ridiculous. The public phone wasn't working, but that meant nothing and he would be there when I arrived. A voice in my head hissed, *Don't be stupid and naive. This is going to end badly.*

The bus station in Brčko was nothing more than a metal shed in the middle of a parking lot. I was the last one off the bus, but I'd been looking out the window searching for Ian ever since we'd arrived.

He wasn't there.

I barely had enough energy to get myself down the bus stairs and collect my little case from the undercarriage. I hadn't even begun to think of what I would do next. Try to call him again, I supposed.

And then, there was a man. He had sandy blond hair, and he was handsome. Handsome in the same way as Ian. Strong and sure of himself. He was on the other side of the lot, walking toward me. "Madeline?" he called.

"Yes?"

Then he broke into a jog. As he came closer, I knew who he was. Ian's brother. He grabbed one of my hands in both of his. My hand disappeared. John was a big man, even bigger than Ian.

"I'm John, Ian's brother. There's been a problem," he said, and I was impressed by his sincerity. His green eyes were gorgeous and sad. He looked absolutely wretched with worry, and he didn't even know me.

"Is Ian okay?"

"Yes and no," he answered, and I felt the blood rush from my head.

"What's happened?"

"He wants to talk to you." He handed me his phone. I looked at it with apprehension. Apparently Ian was waiting on the line.

My voice shook. I'd been hoping that wouldn't happen. "Hello?"

He said, "Oh thank God. Oh thank God."

"Ian, what's going on?"

"You're safe. You're good. You're with my brother."

"I'm not good! I'm scared to death! Are you okay?"

"I've been going out of my mind trying to reach you."

"My phone isn't working."

"I figured that out. I left you three messages at the hotel."

"I had to stay somewhere different. I'm sorry. Please tell me what's going on." I glanced up at John, who was studying me with such concern that I thought I must look like I was about to spontaneously combust.

"God, Maddie," Ian said, infuriatingly.

"Stop saying God and tell me something real."

"I'm so sorry. I want you to know, I never ever intended to disappoint you. Or hurt you."

"You're making my stomach hurt right now."

"I am afraid you're going to hate me. Please don't hate me."

"Is it... Don't you want to see me anymore?"

"I want to see you more than ever, Petal."

"Then what?"

"I got an offer I couldn't refuse. They gave me an ultimatum. I had no choice."

"Who is 'they'? What kind of offer?"

"Money. I'm sorry. I know it sounds bad, but, Maddie, I've got to go. They need someone immediately. If I say no they'll hire someone else, and this opportunity will be gone."

"Go where?" Now I was yelling. John began to pace and look at me warily.

"I didn't want to do this to you and I tried to work it out, but in the end there was just no other way. I couldn't turn it down."

"Can't you just come and get me so we can have this conversation in person? Please? This is crazy! I'm right here. If you have to go, then go, but come see me first. Even if it's for five minutes. I want to touch you. Please, Ian. I've been thinking about you constantly. I need to see you. This means everything to me."

John began walking away. Giving my desperation some privacy.

When Ian spoke next, I knew it was over. "I'm already gone, Maddie. I'm sitting at the airport in Sarajevo waiting on a flight. I've accepted a job in Iraq. I had to do what's best for—"

Red descended, and I roared in a voice I didn't even know I owned, "You selfish prick! Of course! Do what's best for you!"

I hung up.

John was standing about ten paces from me. He shook his head sadly and said, "I'm so sorry." Then he started walking toward me, arms out, as if to give me a hug.

A hug.

He seemed like a nice man and it was the wrong thing to do, but I did it anyway. I threw his phone at him, and while my aim was terrible, I managed to hit him in the shin. He bent over and grimaced, and I felt a stab of satisfaction pierce through the haze of disbelief and disappointment.

I grabbed my crappy carry-on and stomped away, pulling it behind me, to go and hail an illegal taxi. When in Rome. I was in Bosnia, and I was going to go find some soldiers and drink some fucking bootleg beer.

MADDIE

Four weeks before

I still owe Cami J a writing assignment. I never wrote down why that last photo was important to me. Instead I'd left early. One of many times. I'm not so good at this therapy thing. I have no idea why she seems to like me so much.

I sit at my computer while Charlie works on making a messy "sculpture" out of marshmallows and toothpicks at the breakfast table. The dogs are happily snoozing in the sun in the backyard.

I touch the photograph. It's me in front of my apartment in New York. Where I lived while I was a tutor. I miss that version of myself. A whole person. I miss my pretty eye and the unlined face. I've aged. And changed in other ways as well.

I start to write.

This is where I lived when Ian called me and asked me to come meet him in Bosnia. This is where I lived when I came home from that trip. I had a lot of good times in this apartment before I got on that plane to Croatia. I know I did. It was too small to have even a little dinner party but I had Stefan over sometimes for a glass of wine before we went down the street to the Art Bar. It had seemed like a good-luck place. I'd been living with a crazy model before that. Her name was Shayna and she rented me her walk-in closet for eight-fifty a month. She was mean and I wanted out of there and I stumbled onto the studio just walking around. I was the first person to see it and the landlord liked me and I felt like everything fell into place so perfectly. It wasn't a good-luck place, though. Not in the end. When I flew back from Croatia it became a dark home, a place to hide.

I slept and drank whenever I wasn't working. Like a lot of women after 9/11 I pretty much brought home every police officer or firefighter I stumbled across in the street. When I was lonely I would go down to the Corner Bistro around ten and sit at the bar and hook up. I dreamed about Ian a lot. Sometimes I yelled at him for leaving me, and I'd wake up shaking and sweaty. Sometimes, though, the dream was our first kiss, the one that never happened, the one that I'd been waiting for. The one I still wanted more than anything. Lying on my stomach, pressing my nose into the wine-stained sheets, the smell of his memory would come back to me. Like a cookout in the forest. Smoke. Vodka, orange juice and sugary coffee mixed with butterscotch candies.

I'd hung up on him that day in Bosnia. I would have given anything to take back my words, change my actions, to do everything all over again from the very beginning and make it right. The past was the past, I thought. I didn't know I'd get another chance.

I tried Match.com and met a really scary guy and then I completely stopped wanting to get together with anyone at all.

This is the apartment where, when I got home from tutoring, I just lay on the futon. It was in this apartment on my futon that I saw a horrible photo on the internet. Ian's blackened body hacked to pieces and strung from a bridge with a laughing teenage boy dancing underneath, celebrating. It was not Ian but for a chilling, breathless second in my mind, it was.

I still remember their names. Scott, Wes and Mike. Bodyguards. After their cars were blown up by a roadside IED in Fallujah, their corpses were pulled out, beaten, jumped on and torn apart. They were burned, dragged behind cars and carts, and strung up for everyone to appreciate. These guys had been, as Ian would have put it, "looking after" the drivers of a convoy of catering trucks.

This was the apartment where I fought the nightmares. Crouching men in orange jumpsuits kneeling before men with giant knives in black hoods. Centipedes and rats. Sometimes I left to go buy coke from Stefan's friend JT. I just climbed into his van and rode around with whoever was inside until I got what I wanted and they dropped me off back at home. This is the apartment where I gave up hope. Much later, when Ian came, he hated this apartment. I guess maybe it turns out that this photo impacts me emotionally in a really negative way. This was not a good photo to bring after all.

This is too revealing, I think. This is too much information.

But somewhere deep inside, part of me wants her to know. To really know. Something real about me.

I press Send.

A few minutes go by and I get an email back from her. She is truly there for me.

It says, What the hell was Ian doing the whole time this was going on?

I reply. Well. From what little I know, he was making shitloads of money, watching all the people around him die and trying not to completely lose his mind.

Her response is, I'm so sorry Maddie.

Aren't we all.

IAN

2003

Ian had arrived at the US military base in Kirkuk after a nauseating descent on a Hercules transport aircraft. He'd been escorted from the aircraft to the hangar. There was an overall air of alarm as soldiers scattered pell-mell, talking nonstop into various devices. Ian wondered what the Americans knew that they weren't sharing. Ten minutes into his new job and he wasn't very happy.

The passengers from the Hercules were asked to wait in the hangar, presumably for any information on their five-minute drive across the base to their overnight accommodation.

An American soldier with big ears and a cheek ballooning to one side from a giant wad of chewing tobacco ambled past Ian. He looked to be in his early twenties, and he carried his spit cup lodged in his trousers. He spotted Ian, and his eyes traveled over his civilian clothes and gear with envy. Ian immediately pretended to be busy with his iPod, and managed to pop the headphones into his ears before the soldier could approach.

"How you doin'?"

The voice came from behind him, and he turned slowly to face the young soldier. "Not bad. Yourself?"

"Bored to tears waiting for my ride, but other than that I can't complain. I'm Ben."

"Nice to meet you, Ben. Ian."

"You look like a contractor."

"Do I?"

"You got all the Gucci equipment."

"Believe me, I jumped through some fiery hoops to get the stuff you see me with now."

"Uh-huh. So then like, what? You are one?"

"I work for a private military company."

"Fuck, man. That's awesome. You're the boss."

Ian looked away from Ben and across the room. His expression changed from boredom to curiosity. A huge blond man with close-cropped curly hair and a reddish beard was digging through a duffel bag in the middle of the waiting area.

Ian stood suddenly, his mouth dropping open. "Peter?"

Ben was surprised and looked over his shoulder.

"No fucking way!" Ian ran to Peter and practically knocked him over.

Peter got a look at Ian's face and burst into laughter. "My God, Ian, you're worse than a puppy!"

Ian grinned. "It's nice to see you, too."

The American soldier skulked away as Ian and Peter hugged.

"Fancy meeting you here!" Peter said.

"Where are you headed?" Ian asked.

"Baghdad."

"Me, too!" Ian responded, shaking his head. "What are the odds, mate?"

"How was Bosnia?" Peter asked.

"It was shite. How was Afghanistan?"

"Fubar."

They both erupted into laughter.

Ian said, "Go out for a smoke?"

"I quit!" Peter said. "Can you believe it? I did!" He patted his jacket pocket. "I've got one in here. Worst-case scenario."

"Good on you, mate," Ian said nodding. "I've not been able to do it."

"Yeah. You think this will be the worst then? Baghdad?"

"Better than Africa. Not as nice as Macedonia."

Peter paused. "You still in touch with Joanna?"

Ian went silent for a second. Then, "No. I'm not."

Peter shrugged. "I'm sorry, mate. I know you two were close."

Ian nodded. "Yeah, it's complicated. I actually got a bit involved with Maddie as it happened. It was crazy but—"

"Hold on, Ian," Peter said. His phone was buzzing. "That's Ashley calling."

"Tell her I said hello!" Ian said, pointing at the phone. "Tell her I want a rematch at darts."

"Will do, but you don't stand a chance." Peter gave Ian a quick wave before walking toward the windows. "I'll find you later."

Ian was woken some time later by one of the air force guys speaking over the Tannoy system. "Transports have arrived," he announced in a monotone. "Gather just outside the hangar and you'll be escorted to your vehicles."

Ian looked around, but Peter wasn't there. He stepped out of the building into the enveloping black sky over the huge US base. Moving away from the hangar, he looked up and down the wide grassy field that faded into a wall of darkness. Two balls of red light were moving erratically up and down, back and forth. The escorts were approaching with flashlights.

Little by little, figures emerged from the darkness, and eventually he could make out their faces. *You've got to be kidding me*, thought Ian. *I wonder if these boys even have hair on their privates yet, for fuck's sake. They made the American kid Ben look like a hoary old vet.*

"We're ready to escort you out to the trucks," said the breathless taller of the two. "They're five hundred meters from here."

Ian picked up his bag and again scanned the crowd for Peter. He wanted to at least say goodbye. The boys began to lead them out into the field, and the passengers all scrambled to get their gear and follow. Ian did as well. They were approaching the 250-meter mark, almost directly between the hangar and the vehicles, when the fiery star came sailing in, landed and rocked the desert. When the sirens sounded, the civilians panicked and looked to the air force escorts for direction. Somewhere over behind the hangars, they saw a swelling red sphere, followed by a heart-stopping explosion. The sirens continued their frenzied wailing, and a couple of people from the group began crawling across the ground, no longer waiting for instructions from the boys who'd been leading the way. A flashlight played quickly over the group, and Ian could see their scared, clean-shaven baby faces.

Bollocks, Ian thought. *I've met many a sergeant in the British military who couldn't arrange a piss-up in a brewery, but at least they were old enough to drink. These spotty American sergeants leading us across the desert don't have a clue.*

He was on his own. At best this bombing was going to delay his transport, and at worst it was going to blow him to bits. One by one, the rest of the group were going down, lying on their stomachs.

Off to his right, he saw a rectangular shadow. He crouched down and ran closer. It was an abandoned military jeep. He heard another explosion in the distance. Glancing again at the jeep, he thought, *If I'm going to die, I'm having a smoke.*

He sprinted for it, sliding to a stop in the dust. He brushed himself off and rolled over. Hunkering down next to the jeep, he positioned himself with his back against a wheel and pulled out his cigarettes. In the grand scheme of things, taking cover next to the vehicle was stupid because it might get hit. On the other hand, if a bomb landed anywhere close by, it might be good, because he had some protection from the shrapnel. Six of one, half a dozen of the other. Fuck it.

He lit his cigarette and cupped his hand to hide the speck of orange, just in case. The sirens continued the earsplitting falsetto performance, punctuated by explosive cymbal clashes in the distance. Soldiers from the base began to return fire to the southern hills, and their intermittent tracer rounds glowed like staccato lasers.

Ian sat and smoked and listened. Now that the tracer fire had indicated which direction the assault was coming from, someone shot up a flare to locate the attackers. Suddenly, Ian was startled by a massive shadow loping toward him. It was Peter. What? He knew better. Ian sat up in shock. What was he doing?

The flare spread, and Peter was illuminated as he ran.

And just like that, Peter crashed to the ground.

Hit by a sniper.

"Pete!" Ian yelled frantically as he sprung into a crouch and bear-crawled to his friend. He grabbed Peter's wrists and pulled him backward until they reached the jeep.

Peter said, "What happened?"

"Sniper," Ian answered. "What were you doing?"

"I saw you. I saw you'd found cover. I thought I could make it."

"You should have made it, mate. That bastard got lucky."

"How the hell..." He struggled with something in his throat. "Did that just happen?" He blinked rapidly and gasped. "Ashley's having another...another..."

"Baby?" Ian asked, sitting Peter up against the wheel. He grabbed him by the chin, and tried to get him to make eye contact. "Pete. You're okay! I've got you, mate. I've got you. Remember the numbers. Fifteen percent instant kill, everything else can be fixed or replaced. If you aren't already dead, you're not going to be. Look at me. Pete."

Peter's eyes couldn't focus, and the lower part of his shirt around his waist was turning red. "Pete?" Ian asked. "It's going to be okay."

Ian had a personal first-aid kit strapped to his thigh. He fumbled in his pouch and tore open a package containing a field dressing. He pressed the pad against Peter's stomach and said, "I've got a field dressing right here. You'll be good. This thing will stop the bleeding. Just lean forward so I can wrap it around you. You'll be fine."

Peter did as Ian asked and leaned forward. Ian checked to make sure there was no exit wound. But when he lifted Peter's shirt, it was apparent the bullet had tumbled inside his body and exited underneath his shoulder blade, leaving a hole the size of his fist.

Ian's field dressing could absorb up to a pint of blood. If the bullet was still in Peter's body he would have had a chance. Not now.

Peter tried to say something. It was incomprehensible.

"Ashley's having another baby?" Ian asked desperately, continuing to bandage Peter, though it was useless. "That's great, mate. I'm so happy for you. Let's get you fixed up." The feeling of helplessness was unbearable. "You've got such a nice family. I always thought you were so lucky."

Peter's hand was flapping like a fish at his side.

"You're going to be fine."

Ian flashed back to the night he met Maddie at that dorky fund-raiser and how Peter had actually been looking forward to the folk dance show. Ian and the other guys had teased him about it relentlessly. Ian wished he could go back in time. See Peter laugh again.

There was a spark of presence in Peter's eyes. "Ashley," he managed.

"Yes, Pete. I'll tell her, mate. Don't worry. She'll know."

Peter's flapping fingers made it to his pocket and pulled out the cigarette. He folded his hand over Ian's and passed it to him, securing the handoff just before his body convulsed.

Ian struggled to light it, but as he finally slipped it between Peter's lips, he was gone.

Ian sat there, arms wrapped protectively around his dead friend and listening to the exchange of fire. Peter was not going home to his pregnant wife. Hit with grief so hard it took his breath away, Ian couldn't help but picture Maddie.

And think, *I'll probably never see that girl again.*

MADDIE

Three weeks before

My mom and dad tell me to take my time. "Go," they say, shooing me toward the front door with a chirpiness that strikes me as fake. Through the kitchen window I can see Skopie and Sophie trotting toward the back of the property on the trail of some poor doomed rodent. Charlie has already seated himself at the kitchen table for a snack. He is playing with that horrible squeezy cheese that comes out of the can in little yellow worms on the cracker. I used to love it when I was a kid, too. My mom has never been a gourmet. Grandmother Audrey used to turn her nose up at anything my mom ever tried to serve to her.

"Goodbye, Charlie." I wave.

He doesn't look up but he says, "Bye bye, Mommy. I hope you don't get shot."

I'm startled and for a second, suddenly and senselessly picturing Ian's pistol. Why would Charlie say such a thing? And then I realize. He must be remembering his last vaccination and the dreadful sight of that long needle.

We all start laughing. "Are you afraid your mom is going to have to get a shot?" my dad asks.

"Well, she is going to the doctor. Doctors give shots."

My mom grabs my hand and folds a wad of cash into it. "Go shopping, okay? You're driving all the way to the Plaza. You need something new and cute to cheer you up," she says, fussing with the buttons on my shirt because she doesn't like to look at my eye. "And maybe this new doctor will have some ideas. You know, about how to get back to normal. Fix things."

Back to normal. What an amazing, beautiful and inconceivable dream. "Mom, you don't have to do that. I have money."

"I know. I like to. Take it. You should have some fun. Treat yourself. I used to shop at the Talbots down there. They used to have a very nice petite section."

"Don't hurry back," my dad says. "Charlie and I are going to do some fishing later on, right, kiddo?"

"No, don't hurry back. Find a nice outdoor café and sit and get a glass of wine. Live a little," my mom says, touching the ends of my hair. The portion by my shoulders, not by my face. I'm sorry for my mom. I think this is harder for her than it is for me.

I get in my car to drive the forty-five minutes it will take me to get to the downtown St. Luke's Neurological Consultants office, which was Cami J's suggestion. They have a clinic closer to me, but I would have had to wait six weeks to be seen there, and I am obviously very eager to have this over with before Ian returns from Africa.

The office is close to the hospital, which, as my mom pointed out, is just a few minutes away from the Plaza. This luxurious little hamlet of Kansas City is where my grandmother Audrey squandered her husband's natural gas inheritance on charities and private clubs while presiding over phony lackeys and admirers. Driving slowly past the boutiques, fountains, flowers and cafés, I realize how long it's been since I have been anywhere more adult or cosmopolitan than Applebee's. I decide that maybe I will walk around after my appointment. Window shop. Get a bite to eat. Never remove my hat and sunglasses.

As instructed, I arrive thirty minutes early for my appointment with neurologist Dr. Stephen Roberts, and fill out my paperwork surrounded by a handful of other patients, none of whom appear to be younger than seventy-five. I am reminded of my days spent at Trakia Bar back in New York, where the crowd I hung out with had looked only marginally less depraved than these poor, slack-jawed and vacant-eyed patients. I am suddenly tremendously relieved. I do not have Parkinson's. I have not suffered a stroke. I don't know what's wrong with me, but I feel sure that whatever it is, everything is going to be fine.

Dr. Roberts turns out to be a very thin, beautiful and gentle African man in loose taupe trousers with an accent. He wears expensive-looking eyeglasses and leather shoes. When he shakes my hand, I make the bizarre observation that he has the longest and softest fingers I have ever seen in my life. I like his gummy smile right away. He has chocolatey eyes like Charlie, but not the amazing lashes.

"Please have a seat on the end of the exam table, Madeline," he says. I rustle as I walk, wearing my paper patient polka-dot dress.

He pulls up a chair and folds his hands together. "This may seem a little odd, but I usually start my examinations by asking you if you know what day today is."

"Tuesday."

"And what did you have for breakfast this morning?"

This one throws me for a second. "Coffee. A couple bites of waffle and two of my son's string-cheese thingies."

He laughs. "A busy-mom meal. My wife eats horrible stuff like that, too. Okay. If you'll just give me a minute here." He flips through my paperwork for a long time. "So," he says finally, looking up. He gestures vaguely toward my scar. "You've suffered a head injury recently."

"Yes."

"I see there is very little illness in your past. Your only hospitalizations are an appendectomy at eighteen and a boating accident when you were ten?"

"Yes."

"Six days in the ICU, it says."

"I nearly died."

"But you made a full recovery."

"I did."

"Did you have a head injury then as well?"

"No."

"And these episodes of panic, what you are experiencing now, these are brand-new?"

"Yes."

"Tell me about the cause of your injury."

"I fell. From what I understand I fell very hard, umm, at an angle, over a rock and into more rocks. I was kind of high up, because I was walking from our tent toward the road and there was, probably, like a three-foot drop-off. It was dark and I tripped."

"Okay. And then what?"

"I think I blacked out for a while. Not passed out, but blacked out, because I was walking around. I didn't even know I was hurt. I had been going to the bathroom, but I guess I got confused and eventually I found my way back to the campsite and my husband. And he looked up and saw me coming, and my head was covered in blood."

"But you don't remember any of this?"

"To be honest I don't even remember falling. I don't remember anything clearly until the ambulance arrived. You should know—it's not amnesia. I hit my head very hard, but I'd also just had too much wine. I'd probably had a bottle, but I can't say for sure because it was in a box."

"What was in a box?"

"The wine."

"You know, I've heard of that. Wine in a box. Very funny." He pauses. "I'm not much of a drinker."

I shrug and smile.

"Okay. Now we start the examination, mmm?"

He begins to examine me in a way that I can only describe as tender. He holds my hands and tells me to squeeze. He tickles my arms one at a time and asks if I can feel it. We make funny faces at each other, and he watches me walk around the room. When he turns out the lights and leans in to look in my eyes I can smell his aftershave. It reminds me of the clove-poked orange I made in Girl Scouts and hung in my closet to make my clothes smell nice. My thirty-minute physical exam is more tactile and emotionally pleasing than several of the relationships I'd had in my twenties.

When he is done, he crosses his arms over his chest and looks at me with a stern expression. "I want to make sure I understand completely. You went to Dr. Jones because of a sudden onset of severe anxiety following your head injury."

"Right."

"And while working with you she observed something she believed to be a partial seizure."

"To be honest, I don't know what she saw. I began repeating myself, I guess. I just thought maybe it was the beginning of a panic attack."

"But you didn't go to the emergency room?"

"No."

"You should have."

"That's what Cami J said."

"Cami J?"

"Dr. Jones. She wanted to take me. But I just panicked and left. I wanted to go pick up my son. She chased after me, but I just wanted to go."

"Interesting. Suggests some impulsive behavior as well as anxiety."

"You have to understand, I didn't think I'd even had a seizure. To be honest, I still don't. To me it seemed, you know, that I was dizzy for a second like when I get really nervous."

"You did not lose consciousness, even for a second?"

"No."

"So not a complex seizure. Did you smell anything unusual while this was happening?"

"Smell something?"

"Like a chemical. Or something burning. Maybe perfume or flowers?"

I think about saying sewage and blood, but I answer, "No."

"And you didn't experience any profound feelings at that moment? Euphoria? Anger?"

"Panic. Just panic and fear and wanting to leave."

"Okay." He looks at me for a long time, thinking. "I suppose it could be an absence seizure," he says finally.

"Pardon me?"

"Absence seizure. But they are more common in children." His forehead furrows. "There are dozens of types of partial seizures. I will order a full blood screen, of course, okay? Rule things out. And we can do some tests on your brain, yes?"

"Now?"

"No. no. There is quite a queue for these procedures, I'm afraid. There are some good options, Madeline. There is more than one way to look for problems, if you will, in the brain. I would suggest we schedule an MRI, which will tell me about the structure of your brain. In addition, I suggest we schedule an EEG, which will tell me about the way your brain is functioning by looking at its electrical activity. The MRI is perhaps better when looking for damage from injuries. I must tell you, though, we often end up doing both exams without a definitive answer."

"Can I think about it? My husband is a private contractor, and I'm not working right now. I'm staying at home with my little son at the moment, so we have a huge insurance deductible. I'll probably have to pay the full cost of whatever I choose, and with no guarantee…"

"I completely understand, Madeline." He offers me his willowy handshake again. "Before you go?"

"Yes?"

"I'm always interested in how certain areas of damage affect behavior." He reaches out and softly lays his hand along the side of my cheek, just beside the scar, and squints down at me with fascination. "It would not surprise me if we find you have suffered a frontal lobe injury."

"Is that really bad?"

"Not always. But it can be. Especially in the case of repetitive injury, which is fortunately not the situation with you. In rare instances, people have woken up from a brain injury with a new ability. One man in New Jersey hit his head diving into a pool and when he emerged from his coma he could suddenly play the piano."

"Wow," I say loudly, impressed.

Dr. Roberts is so thrilled by my reaction that he claps his hands together and says, "It's true. But that is the exception, not the rule. More often we find that traumatic brain injuries result in more common everyday ailments and problems. Aggression, negativity, intolerance. And like with you, anxiety."

"Interesting."

"It's very interesting, Madeline, how the disruption of impulse control in the frontal lobe can affect all kinds of behavior. Gambling. Promiscuity. Substance abuse. Violence. It's always fascinated me." He turns and reaches for the door handle, but stops.

"Do you feel…a lack of restraint at all? Any difference from before the fall?"

"I don't think so."

"What about your refusal to go to the ER, even though Dr. Jones insisted? Was that unusual for you?"

"Not really. After going to the ER for my accident in Colorado I would quite happily never step foot in another ER again."

"So you feel confident your impulses are ordinary?"

"I'm not sure my impulses were ever ordinary."

He finds this very witty and treats me to a wide white smile as he opens the door. "Just call Betty when you decide how you want to proceed regarding the tests. Best of luck to you, Madeline."

"Thank you, Dr. Roberts."

After driving to the Plaza I sit at a wrought-iron table on the back patio of the Classic Cup with a glass of Far Niente chardonnay. The little courtyard is surrounded on all sides by hanging baskets dripping with lavender trailing petunias. With my enormous black sunglasses covering most of my face and my hair pulled forward around my cheeks under a pretty white sunhat, I feel anonymous and content. I decide that I will, after all, go shopping.

My grandmother had often called her Plaza home "The City of Fountains," and as I walk down Forty-Seventh Street toward Anthropologie I pass several. I stop at a small sculpture embedded in the stone wall on the corner at Broadway. A bronze piece called Quiet Talk, it is a kneeling mother holding her son close as they seem to search each other's eyes. I think of Dr. Roberts. Maybe I should have told him about yesterday.

Charlie had spilled his Goldfish on the shag rug under the dining room table. It wouldn't have been so bad if he had not decided to use the heel of his sneaker to crush all the bits and pieces down into the carpet until it was just a dusty orange stain. He'd said he thought if he "smashed it good" I wouldn't notice. I'd pulled him over and made him lean down with me, both our noses nearly to the floor and shouted, "I can see it, Charlie? Can you see it?" Negativity. Intolerance. I turn away from the beautiful, sensitive mother with the kind eyes and continue walking.

In the window of Anthropologie there's a gauzy, black patchwork peasant dress that catches my eye. It's the kind of thing Ian likes for me to wear. My mom said to get something cute to cheer me up. I take it back to the dressing room and have just finished tying the sash when a young salesgirl parts the curtain and pokes her spiky white-blonde head into my room. "How's the—"

She has the wrong room, but it's her expression when I spin around that makes me want to punch her. My hat, glasses, purse and clothes are littered across the floor. She sees my startled, naked face and says, "Oww. Fuck!" before looking horrified by her own outburst and letting the curtain fall back into place.

I turn back to the mirror. I pull my hair back and bend toward the glass. The morning after the fall, the entire left side of my face had been a combination of green and purple with a raw red scrape across the whole discolored mess. The black stitches stuck out like tiny housefly legs from where they were knotted in several places. My eye was swollen completely shut under a bump the size of a golf ball on my eyebrow. My cheek puffed out like a grotesque chipmunk, cleaved into two sides by the deep wound. It had been repulsive, and Charlie had cried uncontrollably until he could barely breathe when he woke up and saw me. I rocked him and whispered, "It's okay, shh, it's okay, shh." It went on like that forever.

I've been healing for a while now, and I've stopped noticing it every time I look in the mirror. But I'd seen her shock. And disgust. I saw it through the salesgirl's eyes. The middle of my eyebrow is missing, as if singed. The lightning-shaped zigzag between the two halves is a motley combination of varying skin colors ranging from purple to white. The corner of my eye is the worst part. It is pinched together, with a thumb and finger-like web in between where it was sewn just a tad too tight, making my left eye a quarter smaller than my right. Down my cheek, like an afterthought, the scar casually strolls this way and that, until it stops a half inch above the corner of my mouth.

The patchwork peasant dress is a wisp of a garment, priced at $275. It is beautiful and I no longer am. I rip it off over my head, and it tears and that feels good.

My phone keeps ringing inside my purse, and I ignore it until it hits me that someone needs to reach me. How do I have four missed calls? What if it's my parents? My heart races. I have two voice mails. My thoughts crumble into little pieces of meaning. Charlie. Something has happened to Charlie. Something big, my intuition tells me. Something huge has happened.

It's Joanna.

I sent the email after all. The letter I wrote to her in Cami J's office. I got up the courage to send it. Now she wants to talk.

IAN

2003

Ian sat in his cubicle in the opulent conference room of Saddam Hussein's Baghdad palace. Surrounding him was glitz and its antithesis. There were molded ceilings, chandeliers, polished wood, marble and mosaic. There was also body odor. Sand on the floor. Soldiers with dirt-stained faces and the general beleaguered atmosphere of an overtired office filled with worker bees, stress and barely concealed anger.

Ian tried to tune it all out with his headphones as he bent over his laptop, frowning, sweating and typing.

From: Ian Wilson
To: Madeline Brandt
Sent: Friday, 8 August 2003
Subject: Hi Petal

Hiya, Maddie, it's Ian.

I know I have a lot to explain. The day before you were due to arrive in Croatia, my brother John got a call from an American company called Atlas. They wanted to hire John for a very important role in Iraq. He was chosen to be the head of security for the transitional government in northern Iraq. He got me hired as well. The problem was that they needed my position filled immediately. That's why I had to leave. Had I not gone when I did, they would have simply hired someone else in my place.

I had to go, Maddie. But it wasn't what you think. On the phone that day, you thought I was going to say, "I have to do what's best for me." That's not it at all. I was going to say, "I have to do what's best for us."

I wanted to see you so badly. I never wanted to hurt you. My feelings for you in Macedonia have never changed.

You think it was about money. Yes, it was. I won't lie because it's true. I never had any. When I realized that I really wanted to be with you the first thing I thought was that I was not good enough for you. I didn't go to university. I couldn't give you the life you were used to and that you deserve.

I'm not daft. I know you liked me. But back then as a soldier, was I the sort of person you would have taken seriously for the long haul?

Maybe now I can be. That's what's keeping me going.

The job is not exactly what I expected. The company is not very good and I'm guarding a VIP General who doesn't seem to give a shit about his bodyguards. He keeps eating night after bloody night at this downtown hangout of Westerners and it's just a matter of time before a teenager strapped with explosives comes barging through the door shouting "Allah Akbar!"

I've started daydreaming about shooting the General myself, ha ha.

But the money is good.

John arrives next week or I would have quit by now. Once he's here I'll leave Baghdad and become his partner in charge of security for the coalition in the north.

That will be much better, I think.

For a while I gave up on us. But I can't live that way. I'm going to get through this. I'm going to find you and make up for what I did to you. I'm going to tell you how I feel and we will make this work.

I just need a little time.

Ian never sent his message to Maddie.

Two weeks later, Ian joined his brother John in northern Iraq to become his right-hand man and second in command of the security of the regional coalition.

The heat slithered in waves over an undulating hillside. Looking ahead was dizzying, like squinting at the bottom of a swimming pool through gently lapping water. The wind stunk of burning tires, and there was the occasional drone of helicopters, which appeared in twos and threes on the horizon, buzzing like bugs, and then dipping out of eyesight.

The brothers drove at a treacherous speed past the monotony of cardboard-colored countryside, and the occasional charred remains of a battered car or warning sign for minefields. Along this road they also passed palm trees, mud huts, starving sheep and cattle, and three of Saddam's former prisons, huge, nightmarish and lonely brick constructions in the middle of a sea of dead, sand-colored grass.

Ian had been quiet for a long time. Eventually he tipped his head to the side. "We don't have to keep working for these wankers. We could work for ourselves."

John made a noise. "That again."

"What?"

"I told you in Bosnia," John said brusquely. "I'm not starting a company."

"Makes more sense now than ever. You think we couldn't run a better operation than these guys?"

"It's not that. I'll accept that a bunch of monkeys could probably do a better job. But where would we get the money? How would we get our first contract? Who would we employ?"

"We know tons of guys from our time in the military."

"Yeah, we do. Now name five guys you would want working for our company that you could trust with your life and a multimillion-dollar contract."

"Okay. Andy Fremont. Vick Davies. Brent Halifax." Ian paused, his fingers raised as he ticked off names. He had been throwing out the idea of working for themselves on and off for two years. Each time they talked about it, John reminded him of how huge an undertaking it would be.

Nevertheless, Ian daydreamed about becoming the CEO or vice president of a successful international private security company. He had a vision of himself with a Breitling watch sparkling on one wrist and olive-tinted Cartier sunglasses holding back his hair. Wearing a fitted Armani suit, he pictured himself stepping out of a Mercedes SL convertible. The transformation from military bodyguard to international businessman would be complete. He would no longer be just a soldier. He would be good enough to shake Maddie's father's hand and feel confident as he smiled and said, "Nice to meet you, sir."

Out loud he said, "Did I say Andy Fremont?"

"Yes. You said him first."

"Okay. I'm still thinking."

"You've got three so far."

"I know. Give me a second."

"You can't come up with five. Neither can I. Three trust-worthy guys? That's hardly a company."

Ian dropped his hands, defeated. "Okay. Maybe you're right. It wouldn't be easy." John nodded knowingly, and they drifted into silence.

After five minutes of monotonous desert and sweltering heat, Ian cleared his throat and spoke suddenly. "For fuck's sake, man. Whether I'm in Rwanda, Northern Ireland, Bos-nia, Iraq, it doesn't matter. This job is ninety-nine percent mind-numbing nothing. Sitting around waiting for something to happen. Then the other one percent is chaos and anarchy. Cats and dogs living together."

"Yep."

"I hate this place."

"You're talkative today."

"I just want to get away from people sometimes. You know? Completely away. A cabin in the woods somewhere."

With Maddie, he thought. Under a quilt with snow-tipped mountains visible through a little wooden-framed window. "If I could find a place where I could be alone with some vodka, cigarettes and my computer I wouldn't fucking care if I never saw another human being again. Seriously," he lied. Except for Maddie.

"You know what I think you should do?"

"Shut up?"

"No. I think you should get back in touch with the Amer-ican girl."

The American Girl. Ian felt the hair on the back of his neck bristle. Had he spoken out loud? Did his brother know him so well? It felt almost like an invasion of privacy, like John had been reading his mind. "As if things didn't go badly enough last time. You think maybe I should invite her to Iraq? This time she might throw a rock at your head instead of a phone at your leg."

"She struck me as being worth a second try."

Ian went serious. "Yeah. She is."

"Have her meet you in Cyprus."

Ian stewed on this. "She's a journalist. I gather her family may have some money. Both her sisters are doctors. Just look at it from my point of view. The fact that things didn't work out in Bosnia simply sped up the inevitable. You think a girl like that would really go for me?"

"No, I don't. But what do I know about women? Monica says anyone would be lucky to have you, and I think she's got pretty good taste."

"Let's not forget that your wife is seriously biased and secretly in love with me. Anyway, it's not that easy."

In a separate car accompanying the Wilson brothers were an ex-Gurkha captain and his driver. Soldiers from Nepal who had fought for the British army since the turn of the century, many former Gurkhas had offered their services to private security companies. The Gurkha Captain Rai was in his early sixties, and had probably not been in a wartime deployment since the Falkland Islands in 1982.

Offhand, Ian said, "I like Captain Rai. Nice guy."

"Yeah. He's all right, isn't he?" John said, nodding.

"Far too old to be here, though. He needs to go home and retire while he still has some limbs."

"You know how far Rai's pay probably goes in Nepal?" John asked and then whistled. "Jesus."

"I bet. It's just that he's so polite and friendly and little. He's someone's granddad. I'd like to see him at the park, smoking a pipe and scowling at the young folk. Or at trivia night at the pub with his buddies."

"There's a car overtaking us on the left," John said.

"Yeah. I see it." Ian leaned forward to check the right-hand mirror. "Will you look at that?" he asked, watching the dusty

Volkswagen Passat speeding unapologetically forward. "What the hell is he doing?"

"Who's in the car?"

Ian looked back. "Driver's a man. Someone small in the passenger seat. It's not four young thugs with 'we hate the co-alition' flags hanging out their car."

"Imagine that!"

"I know. Some cell leader somewhere is slacking off."

"Ha!"

Ian turned around in his seat and squinted as the car drew even nearer. The driver was grizzled, bearded and gray, and the small passenger had two little hands on the dash, as if he or she were leaning forward curiously to get a better look at Ian and John.

"Let 'em pass," said Ian, continuing to observe the car through his mirror. "I might be losing my mind, but I'm not quite ready to run a grandfather and a little girl off the road in the name of the Queen."

"Blasphemer," John said as he pulled over slightly to allow for the car to pass. Just as it pulled up level with the brothers, a deafening explosion rocked the desert. A geyser of dirt shot into the air from the median, where a roadside bomb had been buried. Ian and John were both whipped sideways as the explosion blew the safety glass out of their windows. Pieces of the civilian car rained down on their hood and windshield in chunks and shards.

John slammed his foot on the accelerator, anticipating small arms fire to follow. He looked in his wing mirror and saw what was left of the Volkswagen, a grayish-black frame consumed by flames, careen off the road and into a ditch. Ian ran his hand down the side of his face and neck. His skin was bubbled and bleeding. Was he alive? Yes. He looked at John and saw there were tiny pieces of safety glass stuck in his brother's arm, cheek and temple.

Ian contacted Captain Rai to make sure he was all right and the Gurkha's absurd response was, "We okay! Car go bang! Drive, drive, drive!"

"Okay," Ian said. "Okay, Captain Rai. I'm here. We're all good." But it wasn't true. Like the flying debris following the bomb, he was untethered, sailing, losing precious little pieces of himself as he tumbled across Iraq.

After that it was a blur. Ian's memory kicked back in miles down the highway when John stopped the car, stumbled out onto the roadside to throw up repeatedly and then got back in and drove, drove, drove.

MADDIE

Two weeks before

Cami J has filled the pockets of her black Aerosmith hoodie with fish pellets and we are standing at the muddy edge of the man-made pond out in the back of her house.

She throws some food into the water and the carp come and eat it up with their giant blow-job mouths. *Look at those giant blow-job mouths*, I almost say but I stop myself. I don't just say whatever pops into my head. I may be glitchy, but I'm mostly in control.

Except for yesterday at the gym. That was weird. Of course, it's annoying when you drive all the way into Overland Park from Meadowlark to show up thirty minutes early at Lifetime Fitness for a Cardio Kickboxing class. It's annoying to take the time to calm your inconsolable three-year-old before leaving him in the day care that smells of poop and bleach, get your bench and mat and weights and towel and water, only for some arrogant, entitled woman who walks around with her back arched to show up two minutes into the class. It's annoying when she sets up an inch from you and leaves her Fabletics bag and vitamin water right where you are supposed to be doing your goddamn grapevine. Everyone would agree. Fucking annoying.

She was too damn close. She came late, and she was too damn close so it happened. I said it was an accident. I said it to the crying arched-back woman, and I said it to the gym trainer who ushered her away with an ice pack, and I even said it to the unhappy instructor who shouldn't have allowed her class to get overcrowded in the first place. Sorry.

"Do you want to throw some food for the fish?" Cami J asks, and I shake my head.

"Did you follow up with the neurologist about getting in for that EEG?"

I nod.

"And?"

"No openings until August."

"Shut the front door. What about the MRI?"

"Same."

"You're awfully quiet today."

"I didn't sleep well. I had a really sad nightmare. About Jo's old cat Panda."

"You told me about her. The cat who was poisoned. With all the kittens. I suppose they died?"

"They didn't actually," I say, remembering what Ian had told me. "Turns out Ian took the kittens to a shelter. A couple of them lived."

Cami J looks perplexed. "Ian did that for Joanna? Why? After everything you've written, I thought they hated each other?"

The answer to that question would likely blow her mind, as it had mine, but it wasn't her business. "Also, I had another panic attack this morning."

"Why didn't you tell me?"

"I was going to. When we started our session."

Cami J tosses the remainder of the fish pellets from her pockets into the pond, causing a slimy riot. "Come on then. I'm sorry. Let's get to work."

We enter the back door of the house, and we both slip our shoes off. I suppose I've gotten very comfortable here. As she makes chamomile tea, she asks me over her shoulder, "What brought on the panic attack?"

"I went snooping."

"You did?" she asks, turning around to look at me.

"Yeah. Ian has two laptops. One for work and one for his superspecial graphic intense games. He also has two emails. A new one for work and an old one that he started years ago. A few months ago, I had opened a letter addressed to him that made it sound like he'd bought some property that he hadn't told me about, so I went looking around in his piles of papers since he was out of town. Eventually I got out his gaming laptop, hacked the password and looked at his old email account."

"And?"

"His ex has been sending him sexy selfies."

"Eww. My daughter told me never to do that. There's an app for your phone that erases them after a minute or so."

So she does have a boyfriend. Or boyfriends. I grin at her. You go, Granny.

"I mean, that's obviously not the issue," she says, backpedaling and straightening a pen and a pack of Post-its on the kitchen counter.

She makes me laugh. God I love her. "I kind of doubt this woman still has his phone number," I say, unable to hide my amusement. "Also, try as I might, I could find no evidence that he's reciprocating with dick pics to her. I did see one very PG rated digital card wishing her and her parents a Happy New Year."

"But he hasn't deleted the dirty photos."

"No. At least not all of them. And he saves some of them in a folder he calls, 'Bunny Boiler.'"

"Hmm. And how does all this make you feel?"

"Ech," I say, making a face. "But not really angry. I mean, he's a man. They're very visual, aren't they? That's what everyone says. It doesn't mean he's cheating on me."

"Very evolved of you," she says and motions for me to follow. She carries our tea into her office. "Get comfy."

I cross my feet underneath me in the big plump armchair. "Honestly, though, that's not what triggered the panic attack."

"So what was it?" she asks.

"To look through his stuff I had to spend time in the basement. I never go down there. That weird letter I was talking about? It was from a company that builds bunkers. Acting like he was interested in having them build him one. They're expensive!"

Cami J narrows her eyes suspiciously and taps the end of her pen against her temple. "Bunkers? You mean, like, secret bunkers?"

"Yeah, I guess. So I just thought, I'm going to see what he's been up to. I came across the pictures of Fiona by accident. He hadn't tried really, to hide them. But what happened then was, I looked up and saw the door to the bad part of the basement. And I got a very weird feeling. I've only been in there a few times, right after we moved into the house. Suddenly I was incredibly interested to know what he keeps—"

Cami J holds up a hand and says, "Hold on. You should be writing this, don't you think?"

"Okay."

She hands me my kitty notebook, and as I am putting the pen to the paper, I have second thoughts. This is important. I need to think clearly. I look up at Cami J and say, "I'm kind of tired of writing, and it's so easy to talk to you. Maybe we could just talk today?"

She is flattered. "Sure. Just two gals chatting away today."

"So, suddenly I was very interested to see this bad part of the basement. He acts like it's nothing. I thought he calls it the bad part of the basement because it's dirty and scary. I thought there was nothing much back there. Just the furnace, the sump pump, the plastic tub with the fake Christmas tree in it and all the ornaments, and a bunch of spiders and mice. But I went in. I opened the door and... He has a wall of water."

"A wall of what?" This is obviously not what she was expecting.

"Bricks of water. Plastic containers that stack on top of one another and you fill each one up with water and you can build a wall of water. He has enough water for months. And there were barrels of freeze-dried food. Enough dehydrated eggs and potatoes for a year if not more. Hundreds of cans of food. When I say hundreds it could be thousands. Soup, chili, tinned meat and bags of rice and crates of bug spray and batteries, knives, flashlights, solar panels, headlamps, three sets of bows and arrows, emergency liners for sleeping bags used only for snow camping...and traps. Animal traps. I was shocked. Does he know something I don't know? Then I thought, No. He doesn't know anything. He's crazy. What's going to happen to Charlie with a doomsday Dad? And then I was mad at myself. Because I should have been more careful. I knew he wasn't—" I pause "—an ideal person to choose to be a father. I knew there might be...issues. And... And... I decided..."

Cami J's eyes are glistening, and she is finally getting what she's been wanting. When she speaks, she sounds like a breathy character in a soap opera. She draws out her whisper. "Yeeessss?"

I sit here trembling. I can't speak. I am certain, absolutely certain, that something sad and painful is going to happen, and there is nothing Charlie or I can do to stop it. "I can't tell you."

"Yes you can, Maddie. You knew what he was and you chose him anyway. You chose to have a child with him knowing that he's unstable. You can tell me. What did you decide?"

The tears are running down my face, and I can't meet her eyes. I don't want anyone to know the truth, but I need to say it. "You will think so much less of me."

"No, I won't."

"I loved him. But I knew he was damaged. And I just thought, if I marry him, maybe I'll have a baby. I know it sounds terrible, to bring a baby into a world where there's an angry, troubled man, but I told myself that if Ian didn't get better, then what happened after would be…negotiable."

"Oh, Maddie."

"I know. God help me if he ever finds out I've thought of leaving him and taking Charlie away with me. I don't know what he would do to us."

"Does he know?"

"I don't think so."

"Does anyone know?"

I bury my head in my hands and answer, "Yes."

"Who?"

"My sister Sara."

"And that's it?" she asks, leaning toward me like I'm whispering and she can't hear.

"That's it," I say. "Just Sara. And a few days ago I told Joanna."

I'd decided to call her. In the morning.

I lay in bed with Charlie for a long time the night before, tickling his back. I didn't want to go into my room and stare at the ceiling, thinking about my idea to invite Joanna to come visit me again, wondering if I was making a mistake.

What I didn't want was a repeat of what happened the one and only time I'd spoken to her since we last saw each other. It was four years ago now. Maybe more. I was hugely pregnant and hormonal. That was my excuse. That's why I was so naive and thought maybe she would be happy for me, maybe she'd come to see me and I could hug her again.

"Hello?" she'd snapped after the first ring all those years ago. I could hear tap tap tapping in the background and I knew that Joanna was an efficient multitasker. She'd answered the phone while typing on her computer.

"Jo?" I said, and there it was again. That timid, dutiful voice that wasn't me at all. That small, scared part of me that only ever emerged around Jo.

"Maddie!" she shouted, her voice as loud as if she'd just won the lottery. "I was just thinking about you!"

"What?" I was shocked. "You were? Why?" This was not at all how I thought the conversation was going to go.

"I swear to God I was. I was just sitting here in Mississippi—"

"Mississippi!" Joanna had always wondered out loud how I managed to visit my mom and dad in Kansas every year without slitting my wrists, and now she was in Mississippi?

"Yeah!" she said enthusiastically. "I'm working for a refugee resettlement organization and guess where our first Syrian family is going next year? Kansas City! Woot woot! Isn't that wild? I was just telling this guy in our office that I used to spend time there with my old friend Maddie. Best barbecue in the world! I was literally just talking about you. Were you tingling?"

I was still tingling. I couldn't find my voice. I was unable to respond like a normal person. "What?" I asked, nonsensically. "How are you?" I asked, looking down at my enormous pregnant belly and touching the terrain. Lumps and volcanic activity.

"I'm okay," she said. I could hear her still typing. Prioritizing. This conversation wasn't as important to her as it was to me. Typical. "How are you? What's new? This is such a crazy nice surprise!"

There was only one thing that was new. There was only one earth-shattering development in my life. "I'm going to have a baby, Jo. A boy. I was wondering if maybe you could come and see me. I was thinking…"

I paused. What was I thinking? I could hear that she had stopped typing. Perhaps she'd even stopped breathing. It was that quiet.

Her voice was soft. Restrained. "So you and Ian got married after all? You really did?"

"Yes. Jo, listen, please. I'm a little scared, and I miss you—"

She hung up, but not before I could hear the start of a furious sob escape her throat. When the line went dead I sat there, cringing, hearing the continuation of her sorrow even though it was silent.

My baby kicked.

And a few days ago, there I was lying spooned around that same baby, now a little boy who was growing up so fast and was almost four and again I was terrified of calling my best friend, Joanna.

I got up and went downstairs and poured a glass of wine. *Fuck it*, I thought. *I'm getting this over with.* I dialed.

She was not at work. She was not typing or busy or even a little bit awkward, after all this time. "I've been waiting for your call," she said. "Tell me everything."

IAN

2006

Ian was actually shivering. Nobody could tell, he hoped. No one knew that when he walked, he heard snapping beneath his boots. It was all the time now. Every night, more dreams about the church in Africa. The one he went to with Dr. Rowley. He was careful now. He talked less. He didn't want anyone to worry.

In the lobby of the Khanzard Hotel Ian sat with his laptop composing his goodbye email to Maddie. He was back to thinking that he wasn't going to make it home alive. It was a roller coaster. *I'm coming to get you. I will survive this. I'll never see you again. I'm sorry.* He had good days and bad days.

John sat down beside him.

"The colonel's just phoned me asking for a favor."

"Yeah? What favor?" Ian spoke almost normally. His voice barely shook.

"He'd like us to do an assessment on a coalition compound. They've been getting hit, and he wants to improve the security."

Ian sat up. Work settled him and gave him a focus. "Seems only right to go down and check it out if we've been asked."

"How about tomorrow?"

"Tomorrow?" asked Ian, making a face.

"Sorry. Were you going to work on your tan by the pool tomorrow?"

"Ugh. We'll have to leave at daybreak."

"It's not as if I've asked you to pop around to Mum's house for gin rummy with Helen and Lynn now, is it? I know it's last minute, but it's important."

"Yeah, yeah." Ian stood up and stretched. "All right then. I'll see you at zero five hundred."

John pointed sideways at a clear iced drink on the table next to the chair. "Zero five hundred."

"That's what I just said."

"Is that vodka?"

"Is it?" asked Ian, recoiling dramatically. "Blech! For God's sake, remove it from my sight!"

"I'm counting on you. I don't want any more problems. Don't make me have to haul your arse out of bed."

"Fuck off, Mum. I'm good. Christ! As if I'm a baby." He walked away breezily, pulling out his cigarettes and approaching the group of reservists talking by the front desk.

"You are the baby!" shouted John, attracting the attention of pretty much everyone in the room. "And I'll be up in fifteen minutes to change your nappy and tuck you in."

Ian flipped John off to a chorus of laughter from the American troops.

From: Ian Wilson
To: Madeline Brandt
Sent: Friday, 11 August 2006
Subject: Bye Petal

Dear Maddie,

I said I was going to make loads of money and come find you. I said I was going to go back to school and get a degree so I wouldn't have to do this anymore and we could live a normal life. I said so many things. I'm sorry. At least I never sent you any of those messages.

Turns out I lied and I couldn't bear to have you think I'd lied to you again.

I'm not coming. I am so far from being on a white stallion headed your way with flowers like some savior prince that it's untrue.

Someone shot the pregnant dog I was feeding. I went to Halabjah and a woman told me that first the birds stopped singing and then the children started dying.

And before all that, there was Rwanda and the church and the story I wasn't able to tell you. Helena and I, we took a shortcut from our car to the church and halfway through this meadow we realized we were walking on bones. There was a baby-gro. I think you call them footie pajamas. And a sippy cup. And a toy car. And bones.

I'm afraid that after all this even if I don't die I will still be dead.

Some people made fun of us, did you know that? Used to call us bodyguards "human sandbags." Good for nothing but blocking bullets. You made me feel important and wanted. You saw me. That meant more to me than you can ever imagine. One bright unexpected flower. I say it at night to myself. Petal.

I will always remember Skopje, that hate-filled place and the amazing gift of you showing up and making me feel alive. Thank you.

What I had hoped for was naive and unrealistic. I'm not letting you go. I'm accepting the fact that you were never within my grasp…

★ ★ ★

He didn't send the email.

Neither did he die.

Instead, three weeks after the brothers had done the favor for the colonel and assessed the compound, the colonel called them while they were cleaning their weapons on their hotel balcony. He told them the compound had been rocketed, and if not for the improvements Ian and John had advised making, dozens would be dead. He also said he had heard they wanted to start their own company. He thought it was a brilliant idea, and he had an idea where they might get their first contract.

Two months later, the brothers had founded their own private security company called Bastion Defense and won their first bid with the help of the colonel. It was an eleven-thousand-dollar deal off which they made a profit of four hundred dollars. But, after another six months of maxing out their credit cards, bidding on contracts and losing, they won a multimillion-dollar deal with an American construction company that needed protection as it made its way across Iraq rebuilding power stations.

Years passed, and in the "Drafts" folder of Ian's email, the number of unsent letters to Maddie grew and grew.

DAY OF THE KILLING

It was a heartbreaking chant. "You hurted me. You hurted me."

The boy in the bathroom sounded so surprised, so broken, so betrayed. As hard as it was to hear his pain and terror, there was also a silent, internal rejoicing. He was alive. Diane put her hand on the doorknob and started to turn it, gambling on him being alone. "Shh. Don't be scared..."

She swung the door in on the bathroom, and there he was. Brown eyes and a mop of curly hair. He stared at her, wide-eyed and inert, huddled in the corner. After a second she realized he was literally paralyzed with terror.

She started to softly close the door behind her, and that's when he bolted. It was a Jack and Jill bathroom, and he made a run for the opposite exit. She was able to catch his arm.

He jerked it away and screamed.

"I'm sorry," she whispered, placing her finger to her lips.

"Shh! I'm so sorry! But we have to be quiet, okay? Whispers only."

His howling subsided, and he stared into Diane's eyes, as dark brown as his own.

"Is your mommy in the house?"

He nodded.

"Is she hurt?"

He shrugged.

"Can you tell me what happened?"

The boy looked down at the bathroom floor and picked up a plastic bathtub toy. "This is Dolphin," he said.

"I love dolphins," she whispered. "I swam with a dolphin when I was a little bit older than you. In Mexico."

The boy gave her the tiniest hint of a smile.

"Can you tell me what happened tonight?"

He thought about it, turning the dolphin this way and that in his small hands. "Mommy had a friend over, and Daddy came home."

His little belly was poking out over the top of his nighttime Easy Ups, and he had sleep in his eyes. Now he looked traumatized, but she recognized him from the hallway gallery of blissful family moments. Child with the delighted eyes at the petting zoo. Child laughing with Santa. Child playing at the beach.

Alone in that bathroom with the boy, Diane suddenly felt very claustrophobic and vulnerable. "Do you have any brothers or sisters?"

He shook his head.

"Can I carry you, sweetie? Would that be all right? I think maybe we should go outside now."

He nodded.

Diane picked the boy up and pulled his legs astride her hips. With her Glock down by her side where it wouldn't frighten him, she moved warily into the hall. Diane could hear sirens outside, and there were flashing red lights pulsing in the windows. To one side of the hall, she saw an alcove and a handrail. "Is that stairs?" she asked, gesturing with her chin.

He nodded.

She carried the boy silently down the dark, narrow wooden back staircase. At the bottom, before stepping into the great room, she said to the boy, "Have you ever been blindfolded? Maybe at a birthday party where there was a piñata?"

"One time," he answered.

"Can I cover your eyes with my hand just for a few seconds? Like a blindfold. Would that be okay?"

He nodded. She had to holster her gun in order to place her palm and fingers over his upper face as she darted past the kitchen area toward the back entrance. She didn't want him to see the blood.

Diane was holding the boy with one hand under his bottom. There was movement on the back patio. The dogs? Then there was a faint scraping noise. Diane glanced to the side, where there was a window. Had a tree branch scratched the glass in the wind? She didn't remember so much as a breeze when she'd arrived. The kitchen lights were on, and it was deep night outside. The glass door was a composite of reflections from inside the house and the opaque outlines of trees and bushes edging the patio. Diane cupped her free hand to the side of her eyes and pressed it against the glass, searching.

The dogs sat panting outside the door where she'd left them, still waiting patiently to be let in. She saw the sandbox. The water table. The bushes.

And a man's profile, standing a few feet away in the yard, next to the tree that had scratched the window. There was the full dome and bill of a baseball cap, and underneath that a jutting chin and long neck. The man, who looked as if he'd been trying to back his body into the trees and shrubs circling the house, turned his face toward Diane.

"There's a man in the backyard!" Diane yelled at the top of her lungs. She put the boy down and cracked the back door. The man in the baseball cap took off racing through the backyard of the house, tripping over the sandbox and falling, flailing, through a prehistoric growth of Pampas grass.

"Runner in the back!" Diane shouted into the yard before slamming the door shut. There was a switch by the door which she hit, luckily throwing on the backyard spotlight. "Bill!" she said breathlessly into her mic. "We have a runner. I just saw some guy outside. He's headed to the south side."

Bill replied over his mic, "I see him!"

Shipps, who was standing in the foyer, shouted, "I'll cut him off at the front!" He went barreling out the front door, leaving it open behind him.

The boy was shaking and gulping.

Diane picked him back up again and said, "I'm going to carry you again. We'll play the blindfold game for just one more second, all right?"

She covered his eyes again with her hand and made for the front door. By the time they got there, Bill was on her mic. "We got him! Shipps and I got him! He's handcuffed."

"Copy," Diane answered. "CJ, can you meet me at the front?"

CJ showed up a few seconds later, and Diane handed the boy over into his arms. "Can you take him to the ambulance and get him checked out? I need to finish clearing the upstairs."

"Of course."

She turned to go and then looked back. The boy was staring at her as if she'd just betrayed him. "You'll be okay," she said, and had to leave.

Diane went back into the house, bounded up the stairs and retraced her steps until she reached the master suite. First she cleared the walk-in closet, and then she moved on to the sitting room. Finally she climbed the three steps that led up to the big bedroom. With her flashlight and gun in position, she had a look around.

She could see a comfy, stuffed chair. A pile of laundry. A bench at the foot of the bed. There were two end tables on either side of the bed, one of which was stacked with books. Diane shone her flashlight into the space between the night-stand and the wall. The first thing she saw were the two bare, thin, cadaverous calves. Skinny, long shins, pressed together, the feet bare. A woman was wedged in the cramped space, knees drawn against her body and arms wrapped around them. Her eyes were closed despite the bright light from the flash-light, and her head hung to the side. She wore a tank top and shorts, and her lank, wavy hair looked like black worms crawl-ing over her pale shoulders.

Diane said softly, "Police."

The woman didn't flinch.

Diane knelt before her and placed her fingers against her carotid artery. There was a pulse.

As Diane registered this, the woman's eyes sprang open, a monstrous red, and she grabbed at Diane's hand. Her mouth opened and out came a guttural, bloodcurdling scream that threw Diane backward. She aimed her gun at the woman, who responded by snapping her mouth closed like a puppet.

A light turned on in the hallway outside, and a shadow formed a dark blot on the pale cream wall. A thud on the stairs. And another. The doorway filled with a hunched figure, a bat raised over its head. It lumbered forward. Diane turned on it with her weapon, prepared to shoot.

"Drop your weapon," she shouted. "Drop it now or you're dead."

Outside the bedroom window, the yard pulsed with red-and-blue lights, playing rhythmically over Diane's face and the whites of her unblinking eyes.

MADDIE

Twelve days before

I didn't feel like writing during my last session with Cami J, and she let me get away with it. Sort of. She did give me a homework assignment. She wants me to write about a time when I got mad.

Oh boy.

Where to start? Our cable service. Health insurance. There's that little boy Blake who picks on Charlie at Kids Club. The teenagers who drive through our neighborhood at breakneck speed. The news. Politicians. People who hurt animals. Ian. Ian has made me mad many times. Probably the worst was when he stood me up in Bosnia. I remember being furious.

No, that was not the worst. I remember now.

Homework for Dr. Camilla Jones
A Time When I Was Very Angry
By Madeline Wilson

We were playing.

That's how the story starts. That's what I remember. We were playing. Charlie and me. I can't even remember where Ian was. Kazakhstan? South Korea? Honestly I have no idea. Maybe he wasn't even gone. Maybe he was in the basement and we hadn't seen him in a while.

I was chasing Charlie. I was saying, "I'm going to get you!"

He was laughing and running and I was a little worried because he kept looking back at me over his shoulder and I was afraid he was going to bump into the wall or something and hurt himself. I said, "That's enough, Charlie. Let's just calm down for a little bit. Come and let me cut you up an apple."

But he didn't calm down. He went running up the stairs, still making that funny heavy breathing noise he makes when he's excited and having fun.

He wanted to be chased. He didn't want the game to end. I crept over into the foyer and I could see his legs reflected in the mirror at the top of the stairs. He was waiting for me, standing at the railing at the top, watching.

I started up the staircase after him. I said, "I'm coming for you!"

He giggled and took off.

When I reached the top of the staircase, he jumped out at the other end. He had his gun.

"Oh no!" I yelled, throwing my hands in the air. "Don't shoot me!"

But he shot me anyway. His Nerf dart hit me in the arm.

"Oww!" I cried and fell to the floor. "You killed me! I'm dead."

Charlie walked down the length of the hallway with his gun hanging at his side, looking quite a bit like a small bounty hunter. He looked at me lying there holding my arm and he wasn't laughing. He was thinking about something. "You're not dead," he said. "I didn't get you in the X."

I sat up. "What's the X?"

He drew an X across his torso, from shoulder to opposite hip and then again on the other side. "This is the X. You only win if you hit the X."

I looked him in the eyes. "Who told you that?"

"Daddy," he answered.

"When?" I asked.

"When he was showing me how to shoot properly."

"I didn't know Daddy showed you how to shoot."

"You were at the store. It was a secret."

He had my attention. "You and Daddy are keeping secrets from me?"

"No."

"But you just said it. You said it was a secret. Did Daddy say, 'Don't tell Mom'?"

"He said you might not like it."

"Why would I care about the two of you playing with a Nerf—" And then I got it. "Oh," I said.

Charlie shifted back and forth on his chubby legs. Nervous.

"Was Daddy showing you how to shoot this gun?" I asked, smacking the Nerf gun so hard he had to scramble to catch it.

"No."

"Then which gun, Charlie? Which gun did he show you how to shoot?"

"His gun."

"His gun?" My voice was shaking. Charlie was scared. "Which gun? The big one or the little one?"

Charlie's chest was heaving in and out. He didn't want to answer.

"Which one?" I screamed.

"The rifle!" he answered finally. "The rifle like the one I'm going to get when I turn eight!"

And that, Cami J, made me very fucking angry.

IAN

2009

From: Ian Wilson
To: Madeline Brandt
Sent: Sunday, 11 January 2009
Subject: Hello

Hi Maddie,

I've written you a number of letters. None of which I've sent. I've been a bit afraid of not hearing back from you, or of hearing back from a distant, indifferent you, or finding out that you were married, or worst of all just having you tell me to go fuck myself.

I'm still very sorry for what happened when I left you in Bosnia but the truth is, I made the right decision.

John and I started our own company. We made loads of money, Maddie. I won't have to go back to school. I have enough money now. We are handing over the operations to our employees and taking a long, long leave. We might be closing down the company altogether.

We've only just transferred some of the money from the company into our own accounts and so far all I've bought are a couple of antique swords and a new therapeutic walk-in bath for my mum back in Birkenhead that I've asked my brother Robbie to install. What I'd really like to do is buy something nice for you.

I'm sorry I've been out of touch for so long. I went back and forth, thinking I'd come sweep you off your feet and then, for a while, I didn't think I would ever come home at all. It made no sense to keep harassing you.

I've got some time off. Maybe you'd like to come visit me? I've got a nice house in Cyprus. Maybe I could come to see you? I've always wanted to see Kansas. Or New York. Wherever you are.

I'm a bit nervous, Maddie. There's something I should tell you. It's something I've known for a very long time. I love you.

Had it not been for those last three words, Ian might have sent that email to Maddie.

He didn't.

Instead, Fiona pulled one of her bizarre surprise arrivals at Ian's new house in Cyprus. He was headed to his pool in flip-flops when she showed up.

"Surprise," she shouted, a glossy-haired minx in tiny jean shorts and heels, waving to him from the street as she paid the taxi driver. "Fergus and I broke up!"

The last time Ian had seen Fiona she'd gotten drunk and accused him of trying to have sex with his pregnant sister-in-law. Then she'd bitten him. Ian had long suspected she was bipolar and had broken up with her for the tenth time. Each time he broke up with her, she threatened to kill herself and sent him lengthy text messages detailing what she was doing to herself to achieve that end, sometimes with photos. He'd once tried to get a restraining order against her but, not having saved any evidence, had failed.

He wasn't happy to see her, though he had to admit she was more beautiful now in her thirties than she'd ever been before. After so many close brushes with death she seemed to pose a far more minor threat. And he'd not touched a woman in a very long time. He allowed her to come in his house, feeling darkly delighted and terribly ashamed. He fucked her over the table just inside the front door. Then she made drinks.

A week later, they were still going.

Ian's scarred hand was wrapped around a giant plastic tumbler filled with vodka and ice, and in the other hand a cigarette hung down, dipping in and out of the water. The cigarette was soaked and ruined and still he clenched it between his fingers as he slipped in and out of consciousness.

The plastic floatie had a pink horse's head, which popped up between his muscular legs. As the pool water moved gently with the motion of the roving filter, he looked like a drunk cowboy struggling to stay perched on top of his doddering old mare.

Music blared from inside the villa, but he could still make out the sudden sound of glass breaking. He dropped his cigarette into the pool and fell face-first into the shallow end. After a second he stood up, shook the water from his hair and crawled out of the pool. He took a few lurching steps toward the kitchen before he stubbed his toe on a chaise longue. While he stopped to silently scream, he looked in through the half-open kitchen window.

A pile of silver cutlery shimmered in the middle of the linoleum floor. Fiona, with her cat teeth and blood-red gums revealed in a snarl, was wrenching a third drawer free from the cabinets. When she got it loose she held it over her head and smashed it against the counter.

He slipped on wet tiles and nearly fell running to the kitchen door. "What's wrong with you?" he shouted.

She said nothing, but her kohl-lined eyes were frightening. She staggered to the adjacent living room and used her whole arm to swipe a lamp from an end table to the floor. It smashed.

"Stop it!" he shouted, but she continued in silence.

She threw an ashtray against the wall. She kicked a chair. Just as she was about to pry a glass-framed photo from the wall, Ian was there, grabbing and pinning her arms to her sides. "Let go of me," she spat, trying to wrench her arms free. "You make me sick. You're pathetic and crazy."

"You're the one destroying the house!"

"You lied to me."

"About what?"

"You said you weren't sleeping with Maddie."

He took his hands off her and said, "I wasn't."

"Liar!" Fiona ran back into the kitchen and threw the giant steel frying pan toward the window. It was too heavy and hit the counter before thudding to the floor.

"That's it. You need to leave."

"I don't have anywhere to go!" Suddenly Fiona collapsed on the floor and rolled onto her side. She started sobbing and curled up in the fetal position. "I don't have anywhere to go."

"Fiona..." Ian leaned down and gently stroked the dark hair out of her wet green eyes. Her face was blotchy and her whole body was trembling. "You're acting like a bloody lunatic, and I want you to go to bed. Tomorrow I'm booking you a flight back to Scotland."

"I'm going to kill myself and it will be your fault."

"You know what? You've been threatening me with that since our third date. At this point, if that's how you want to resolve this relationship, fine. I'm out."

"I hate her. I hate her so much."

"You need to go to bed." Ian helped Fiona up and slung one of her arms over his shoulders. Like that, he half carried her up the winding staircase to their room and dropped her into the pile of dirty clothes heaped on the bed.

He switched off the light and went downstairs and back out to the pool. The sun had gone down while they were arguing, and he lit a mosquito candle. He thought about going for the vodka, but already the lights of the fishing village down below were bleeding into one another, something like cars moving on a highway.

It was almost completely quiet, but it was not a cabin nestled in a bucolic valley between forested mountains. It was not the sanctuary Ian wanted. While it was isolated, perched amid empty buildings and unfinished construction projects, the villa still had neighbors. Tala, the closest town, was a fifteen-minute drive away, but there were Cypriot families scattered across the hillside. Down the winding road that traversed the dry, dusty mountain, unfinished white adobe villas baked in the Mediterranean heat. Far below, where the parched hills gave way to the turquoise blue water, there was festive Paphos, a bustling vacation spot popular with Brits and Germans. Though Fiona had pleaded with him to take her into town for a meal or a drink at one of the holiday pubs, Ian refused to go anywhere near the crowds. He sat on his hill alone and looked down at the town teeming with people and their speedboats, jet skis, sandals and sunburns. He wanted nothing to do with them.

When he and John decided to start delegating the majority of Bastion's administrative work, they moved their base of operations to Cyprus. Ian had just signed the lease on the cookie-cutter villa oddly placed in a graveyard of half-finished holiday housing projects on a derelict plot of land overrun by cats and lizards.

Shortly before Fiona's surprise arrival, he had driven down

to the Tala supermarket and filled a shopping cart with alcohol and meat.

Looking down on the Mediterranean below, and out toward the mainland where Syria separated him from his men and his work in Iraq, he marveled at the fact that he was alive at all. Time for another vodka.

Plodding through the kitchen toward the liquor cabinet, he glanced at his computer and noticed that his email was open. When he looked closer, he saw that it was his "Drafts" folder. It was a folder he didn't use. He had never saved his emails as drafts but simply closed them without finishing them and forgotten them. But there they were. Over a hundred unfinished letters to Madeline. No wonder Fiona had told him he was pathetic and crazy. Quite honestly, he agreed. He wondered how far Fiona had gotten with his seemingly endless cache of love letters to Maddie before she'd started doing shots and trashing the house.

He stood up and walked outside to the shallow end of the pool. He nearly fell in, trying to lower himself to a seat at the edge.

Of all the outcomes he had imagined, this was not one of them. When his school counselor had asked him years ago how he saw the future, he would never have answered, "I plan to protect the supposedly good people from the supposedly bad people, and then I plan to make a lot of money off of a tragic war. The coalition will never coalesce and the countries that refused to help will be angry that they weren't given any spoils of war. After none of it is over, none of it, I will just go and sit by my pool with a woman who I have stuck by for years for no other reason except I didn't want another person to die. So I will be with her, instead of with the woman I love. And then I will spend most of my time drunk, wondering if tomorrow will be the day I don't wake up."

The first time he nearly died had been when he'd just

turned twenty. He hadn't exactly laughed it off, but neither did he mull it over with the morbid curiosity that he felt now. Since then the close calls had been getting more frequent and more serious, and it was harder to brush them off with a soldier's sense of humor.

On a pitch-black night on a lonely road outside an army barracks in Bielefeld, Germany, there had been the wild-eyed, drunk giant whom Ian had been chasing down in his police car. Pumped full of alcohol and adrenaline, the man propelled himself through the driver's-side open window and wrapped both meaty hands around Ian's neck. Ian had no choice but to step on the gas and go careening down the street with the man's lower body hanging out of the window. He smashed the man's legs against a row of cars parked on the side of the road, setting off alarm after alarm. Eventually the man fell off and rolled like a log until he came to rest facedown.

Not long after, there was that unusually quiet night working in Burundi. Normally, Ian read his book while trying to ignore the sporadic gunshots of yet another attempted coup. The team had eaten their evening meal together and discussed what was happening in the country with a modicum of hope. Afterward, Ian stepped outside for his last cigarette before bed. Seconds later a huge blast shook the ground. Smoke curled in front of the moon from behind the palm trees lining the driveway. Ian stared toward the explosion, his hand on his gun, waiting and breathing hard.

It had been a land mine just outside the ambassador's residence, and it had been meant for the first car on the road the next morning. Some unlucky, unknown person had made the fatal and arbitrary decision to drive that road past curfew. The first car on the road the next morning would have been Ian with the ambassador, and that unlucky person had just saved Ian's life by swapping it for his own.

Ian waded out to the pink plastic horse bobbing up and

down in his pool. "Why am I still here?" he asked. "Me? I'm nothing."

The horse looked at him with giant, white uncomprehending eyes.

Ian was quiet for a long time. Finally he climbed out of the pool and trailed water through the kitchen and up the wooden stairs. He needed to check and make sure Fiona was okay.

At the top of the stairs he could see that the bedside lamp had been turned back on, casting a long path of dim light through the door and across a section of the hallway. He could not hear anything. He walked quietly to the door and looked inside.

Fiona had propped herself up against the headboard and she was slumped over, hair hanging down, her arms to the sides, palms up on top of the covers.

Ian felt an icy gush down his spine. "Fiona?"

She didn't move.

He threw up in his mouth and swallowed it down. He took a step forward. "Fiona?"

She raised her head and looked at him from underneath her hair. "If it weren't for her, you and I would be married by now. With a little baby."

Ian let out a great gasp and felt his legs nearly buckle. He grabbed on to the doorjamb and began mumbling under his breath.

"What?" she asked. "What? I can't hear you."

"Just that I dodged a bullet there, didn't I?"

Fiona laughed. A barking sound. "You better pray to God that I never get my hands on her."

"Yeah. I'll do that. And while I'm at it, I'll thank him for telling me to kick your arse out of my house and never speak to you again."

"Nice, Ian. You know what? You can both go rot in hell."

MADDIE

2010

Eventually I found my way back to my former cheerful self. I stopped tutoring spoiled jerks who had been expelled or suspended and started tutoring regular, bashful, silly kids. My focus had changed and I had enrolled at Hunter College to get my master's in education so that I could apply for a full-time job at the Upper East Side school most of my students attended. Finally, I had wholeheartedly embraced the role I believed I was destined for in the world, that rare single friend of married people, who is popular with and kind to their kids.

I was visiting an old college friend upstate, and the exhausted single mom had fallen asleep while reading a bedtime story to her young daughter. I sat with a glass of wine on the chaise longue by the window. Alone.

The apartment was in an old mansion which had been quartered to create four three-bedroom apartments, and my friend had the back-patio view of the lake. It was breathtaking. Rows of warm spheres of light around each streetlight reflected off the water, and the tree branches drooped toward the ground, heavy with the last of the fall colors. Above everything was the crisp, clear black sky. It was a night when anything could happen, and the unexpected did.

I walked across the living room and sat down at the desk to use my friend's computer. I had five emails. Suddenly disbelief and a feeling of frantic joy rushed through my body. One of the emails was from Ian. Years of heartache welled up in me and caught in my throat. The screen blurred in front of me as my eyes filled.

I wasn't able to read it right away. I went to the kitchen and splashed water on my face. I hugged my stomach and said, "I'm good, I'm good." After a few minutes I stood up and walked back to the computer. I didn't sit down. I read it from a distance, my arm outstretched to scroll down, in case I needed to get away quickly from how it made me feel.

From: Ian Wilson
To: Madeline Brandt
Sent: Friday, 19 November 2010
Subject: Sorry

Hiya, Petal,

I hope this message finds you well and happy. I can't apologize enough for the fact that I have been out of touch for so long. Suffice it to say, my life has flown by me these past years and I don't know where the time has gone, except down my throat in the form of vodka. My brother and I started our own business in Iraq and it became my whole life, but it's time to close it down. My mum passed away and I haven't seen my family in a long time so I'm going home for the holidays, but I've got some free time after that. I don't know

where you are or what your situation is, but if you'd like to
see me, I'll have my minions make the arrangements.

Love, Ian

p.s. I am so, so sorry for not writing. If you will see me, I
can explain. I wanted to write you the perfect email when
really all I should have done was write you to tell you I was
thinking of you.
    Maddie, I was thinking of you. All these years. X

I stood up, walked to the window overlooking the lake
and laced my hands together. He had been thinking of me all
these years, even though he'd left me. Twice.

I was angry. But I was also over the moon. He was alive. If
I wanted to berate him for what he'd done, I could…and then
I could forgive him. I could love him, be with him, I could do
anything because everything was possible. I whispered, "Thank
you," to the beautiful starry night over and over, probably fifty
times, until I collapsed on the chaise longue again, smiling so
big my face hurt. I might have my happy ending after all.

Two days after Christmas, I exited the subway at Columbus Circle and walked hesitantly, nervously up Fifty-Eighth
Street toward the Hudson Hotel. I wondered if I would even
recognize him. I was frozen with fear as I rode the escalator
from the street up to the lanai lobby. I walked underneath
hanging ivy and sparkling chandeliers to the east wing of the
hotel. Ahead to my right was the Library Lounge. It was a
bar, but it was a quiet, grown-up place where I'd met friends
before. You could sip a glass of wine and enjoy a book. There
was a chessboard in the back and a billiards table to one side,
and many plush comfortable chairs in a living-room-type setting. This was where I had said I would meet him. I was try-

ing to send a message. I was a woman now. Not a brash and hot-tempered girl.

I stopped in the long hallway, halfway between the lobby and the lounge next to the elevators. I needed to take a deep breath. Then another.

I entered the lounge with what I hoped was a bright, excited look on my face. I turned this way and that, expecting to meet his familiar flashing eyes, see his smirking grin or hear him greeting me with, "Hiya, Petal." The atmosphere was austere and alarmingly quiet.

A middle-aged couple played chess, a stunning woman read a newspaper and a shaggy-haired young man sipped a beer while texting on his phone. Also, a very drawn-faced man sat in the corner on a bench with his elbows resting on his knees staring down at the floor. His hair was badly dyed, with random spots of blond sticking out of the brown. I looked away from him and scanned the room again. When my eyes traveled back in the direction of the tired man, he was looking up at me. He had circles under his sunken eyes, and his mouth was tightly turned down in a frown. Between his knees he played with a Zippo lighter, but his hands looked lonely and helpless without his cigarettes. It was Ian. Suddenly his lips parted, and his eyes widened with recognition. He raised one hand slightly, unsure.

I stood up straighter. I waved and forced a smile. His eyes searched my face with trepidation, and I hoped he could not read what I was thinking. The years apart had been too many. Our experiences in those years had changed us too much.

Then he stood slowly, his long, powerful body unfurling to his full height. His features passed out of the shadow into the light, and I could see that, yes, he was older and careworn, but the gaunt hollows under his cheekbones had given him a strange and rugged elegance. He faced me in that rigid military stance of his. His shoulders were immense. Both the bartender and the shaggy-haired young man gave Ian a glance, looking away quickly in some animal vestige of urban male deference. At fortysomething now, Ian still had that British bad boy, *Trainspotting* gleam in his eye. Then, there was that smirk that I remembered. It felt like I was walking through water as I went to him.

"Hiya, Petal," he said, tucking my hair back behind my ear just like he used to do at the Irish Pub. "It's been a while."

I was back in Macedonia, at Jo's door, the last time I saw him, the day he walked up from the city to say a proper goodbye before I got on my bus to Bulgaria. Neither one of us had made a move to touch the other. I had rewritten that moment in my mind a thousand times. Now, my arms moved without my permission. They reached up and my hands rested on the backs of his shoulders. I pulled him to me and leaned my head into his chest. His heart was beating as fast as mine.

We walked in awkward silence across the street to the Time Warner building with its plate glass wall of windows looking out over Central Park. I led him to a bar called the Stone Rose on the fourth floor with a view out over the tops of the trees, and at two in the afternoon there were only a handful of people sprawled about on the banquettes.

Ian took a seat at the bar rather than at one of the more intimate tables, and I sat stiffly next to him, trying not to run off at the mouth like a nervous teenager. He cleared his throat. "My room actually isn't all that large," he said. "Or I would have invited you up for a drink."

"That's okay," I said. "New York isn't known for the size of its hotel rooms. They're all tiny."

"It's supposed to be a bloody suite," he said, looking at me apologetically. "I was quite shocked to open the door and find myself practically staring down at my own bed."

"It's a very jam-packed island. Lots of competition for real estate."

"I'll admit I don't like crowds much anymore."

"I promise not to take you to Times Square." I laughed but he didn't get my joke.

Ian gazed out the window, considering the Columbus traffic circle and its buses, honking taxis and shuffling pedestrians with confusion and disapproval. "Why do so many people want to live here?"

I gestured at the panoramic window framing the maze of trails, snow-covered hills and glistening ice-coated trees of Central Park opposite. "Isn't it obvious?"

He considered this and said, "Well, no, actually. I've seen parks before. They all have trees and benches. I've still booked a deluxe suite and wound up in a room the size of a shoebox. So far this city is just like London, and I'm not too keen on London either. Would you not rather be somewhere beautiful, peaceful and safe? With lots of space and trees and privacy?"

"I grew up in a place like that." I looked down at my hands and resisted the urge to start picking at my nails.

He touched my chin and tilted my head up. "Are you all right?"

"I think so. Yes."

"Would you like some champagne?"

"That would be nice. We're celebrating, aren't we?"

"We are," he confirmed although without the slightest trace of merriment. He leaned forward to chat quietly with the waitress.

She beamed at him and nodded. "Absolutely, sir. I'll be right back with a bottle of Cristal." She glanced at me in a curious way and gave me a little "well done" wink.

"Are you crazy?" I said. "That bottle is as much as the suite you were just complaining about."

"Not nearly as much, actually."

"That's two weeks' rent right there."

"Really! Well, thank God, I don't drink champagne."

"What do you mean you don't drink champagne?"

"I don't drink it. I don't like champagne. I'm having a vodka orange."

"So I'm about to have my first taste, I mean bottle, of Cristal—by myself?"

"I've been wanting to buy you something nice, and now I've had the opportunity. Are you complaining?" He smiled, but the question still stung.

"No. I'm not complaining."

"What's wrong then?" he asked. Not smiling this time.

"Nothing."

He stared at me. I stared back. "You seem angry," I said. "You don't like your room and you don't like New York and you don't seem too thrilled with me either."

The waitress mumbled an apology as she awkwardly served us his screwdriver and my four-hundred-dollar bottle of champagne.

"How is it?" Ian asked, after I'd had my first taste.

"It's lovely. Thank you."

"Good," he said. "That's better."

I put down my glass. "Why are you being so mean?"

"Mean?" he asked, taken aback. "Is that what you think? Nervous, maybe, okay. Listen. If you don't like this, if you don't like me, there's nothing I can do about it, can I? I told myself, life is short, just go see her. Here I am, and it is what it is. I can't take away the last nine years. I can't go back to Macedonia and tell you how I feel about you instead of walking away. I can't go back to Bosnia and meet you at the bus station with flowers as I'd planned. I certainly can't take back all the fucking awful things I've seen that have turned my hair gray. I never thought you would want to be with me and I still don't, and there you have it. I'm sick of worrying about it one way or another. Whatever is going to happen is going to happen whether I like it or not. I'm not being mean, Maddie. I'm waiting for you to have your little visit with me and then walk out of here with no intention of ever seeing me again, at which point in time I'll go up to my room and get drunk."

The blanket of self-doubt that settled over his face made him look vulnerable, like the younger man he'd been when we met. He wanted something. It was the same thing that I wanted. He just didn't know it yet.

I grabbed him by the sides of his stubbled face and pulled him toward me, covering his lips with mine, inhaling tobacco and orange, inhaling who we were once. Time hadn't changed anything. The room spun. Something sparkled and tickled in my head like feathers and firecrackers, and I swear I nearly fell off the bar stool. He caught me and passed his thumb over my lips, staring at them. Then he raised his eyes to mine. "We'll go back to my tiny suite then?"

I nodded, unable to speak. He drained his screwdriver and slapped a credit card down on the bar. Within minutes we were staggering up West Fifty-Eighth with an open bottle of Cristal, not because we were drunk but because we couldn't keep our hands off each other.

Inside the Hudson, waiting for the elevator, he held the bottle with one hand, and the hair at the back of my neck with the other. His kiss was aggressive and demanding, and once we were inside the room, his lower body pushed into mine until I was dizzy and sliding down the carpeted wall. He was relentless. There was no small talk. He gave short, gruff, easy orders, and I did what he asked. *Take these off. Oh my God. You are so fucking sexy. So beautiful. Come here. That's it. Look at me. That's it.* I came when he told me to. *Look at me. Look at me, Maddie, look at me now.*

I did. Again and again and again.

We put on the robes and sat on top of each other on the tiny couch in the tiny suite looking over the room-service menu. We fed each other. We took long, decadent showers and used way too much soap. There were always more desserts or cheese boards, endless horror movies and inane comedies on demand, bottles of pricey wine, and hours in bed. The sheets were wet. Our lips were chapped and I ached all over. I limped between the bed and the bathroom. I was never far enough away from the bed that he couldn't reach out and pull me down.

We didn't leave the tiny suite in the hotel he despised for days.

MADDIE

2010

The curtains on our hotel window were drawn so that the lit skyline would not keep him awake. The sounds of Columbus Circle were varied and intense. Garbage trucks backed up beeping, and Ian caught his breath, held it, made a rasping noise in the back of his throat for far too long and then noisily coughed out air. In the bowels of the hotel a nightclub was going strong, and I could feel the slight vibration of the bass through the walls and the halls. Room-service plates and a sparkling pile of expensive bottles gave our suite the ambiance of an after-party. Wine, as well as the overflowing ashtray, had spilled onto the crisp white bedsheets, giving our lair a smell of excess and sick.

He slept while I watched movies. All of my students were away with their families, and I had no work to worry about until well after New Year's.

I should have been lying next to him. I should have stroked his forehead when it suddenly creased and kissed his cheek when his jaw ground down with the nighttime explosions and gunfire. He had a pinkish, rough patch of skin where the safety glass from the IED in Iraq had scarred his cheek. I wondered if it was why he was never now clean-shaven.

A couple arguing in the hallway outside approached our room, and Ian sat up, groggy, sleepy-eyed and appealing.

"Come here," he said, stretching his hand out toward me.

I joined him in between layers of ash, night sweat and wine-stained white linen.

During those days at the Hudson, I started to question how well I had known Ian back in Macedonia. Had he taken off his cloak of darkness to smile and entertain me at the Irish Pub? Or had it been there all along, tossed over his shoulder or tucked under his arm, and I just never noticed?

Ultimately our marathon conversations would reach the bottom of a bottle, and Ian would pass out. Sometimes I would, too. Other times I sat and watched him, snoring, twitching and gasping, his closed eyes seeing an Iraqi highway, his hands curled around the butt of his rifle.

Ian refused to leave the hotel room. I suggested we go downtown to some of my favorite restaurants and bars close by my Village studio. He would rather not. I pointed out that Central Park was just a five-minute walk away and that it was romantic at sunset. He was "not bothered." I told him I was feeling claustrophobic and shut in and that we should just go down to the lobby for a drink. Still, politely, no.

He did not like to go to sleep, but it was nearly impossible to wake him once he passed out. Sometimes in the middle of the night he would suddenly swing from prone position to sitting, like he was possessed.

Waking to Ian sitting on the edge of the bed was an experience I came to dread. I felt helpless but protective, along with a touch of pity. There was something unnatural about the sight of such a powerful man so collapsed, inconsequential and inert. His hands would be clasped together, his elbows resting on his knees and his head lowered almost to his lap. Sometimes when he assumed this position he would mumble incoherently for long periods of time before he would finally lie back down.

Draped around our room was a gray shroud of soft quiet. There was the hum of steady air, the drone of "Snow Patrol" from Ian's computer and the eerie sensation that we were hiding. I wondered suddenly, how long does he expect this strange chapter in life to last?

I poured myself a drink from our twelve-dollar cylinder of designer water, took two Advil to ward off the morning hangover and snuggled down into the blankets behind him. His hand took mine and he whispered, "Are you warm enough?" Then he covered me with all of his heat, and I told him yes.

The next day I woke up before Ian. I showered, shaved my legs, put on makeup and actually got dressed in something other than the white hotel robe. When I walked out of the bathroom, he was going about the usual morning business of thumbing through the room-service menu, preparing to order a decadent breakfast along with Bloody Marys and mimosas. The curtains were slightly parted, and I again noticed the strange leopard-like yellow spots in his otherwise salt-and-pepper hair.

"You're dressed," he remarked brightly. "You look very nice."

"Thank you," I answered. "As do you, in your birthday suit."

"I must say, I'm relieved you seem to like it."

I walked over to him, combed my fingers through his bizarrely colored hair and said, "Don't be offended, but I can't keep it to myself any longer. What's up with the dye job?"

Ian sat up and examined himself in the mirror adjacent to the bed. "What? You don't like my trendy new look?"

I laughed. He was now forty-three years old. "It might have been more appropriate when I first met you, back in your boy-band days. It's not that I don't like it. I just find it…curious."

"It's the hot new thing in Liverpool."

"Is it now?"

"No," he said, lying back with his hands laced behind his head, displaying muscular definition like an anatomical drawing. "It was my sister-in-law's idea. One of the many reasons I was nervous about coming here was because I've gone quite gray since I saw you last. I didn't even know if you would recognize me. I thought you'd see me and think I'd become an old man. So my sister-in-law told me that if I got some nice blond highlights, it would hide the gray. Apparently that's what she does to her hair, only her results were never nearly as freakish as mine. So a day or two before I was scheduled to fly I went to downtown Birkenhead, which is not a place to ever get your hair done, by the way, and had some bleach-blonde Scouser proceed to smother my head in something that smelled like ammonia."

"Oh no."

"Oh yes. And all the while I was sitting there getting my head wrapped in foil like it was a giant baked potato, these girls kept bringing me drinks. In retrospect I see very clearly that I should have been suspicious of a salon that felt the need to get you drunk before you see the results of their handiwork. But when they unveiled my new youthful head of highlights and I saw that my head resembled a mangy leopard, I was already half cut, so I just said cheers to the girl. 'Well done. I certainly doubt anybody is going to notice the gray when they have this mess to feast their eyes on!'"

"It is a feast," I said, straddling him.

He smacked both hands heartily on my hips. "And on that

note, what will it be this morning? Eggs Benedict? Waffles with cream and jam? Hmm?"

"Listen," I said, extricating myself and grabbing my purse. "You know what it should be this morning? The New York special. Bagels, cream cheese, lox, the works. And deli coffee."

"I don't believe that's on the menu."

I laughed. "I know."

"No mimosas or Bloody Marys?"

"I'm going to have to detox soon. I have to go back to work in a few days."

"You don't have to go back to work."

"I do, Ian."

"I love this. I love you. Just stay and let's keep doing what we're doing."

"There's still some time. I'll pick up some champagne and orange juice while I'm out. There's a liquor store around the corner. It will save us a bundle of money."

"What do you mean? Really? You're actually going out?"

"Yeah. To the deli for bagels and a newspaper. I'll be quick, okay?"

"No. Not okay."

Something in his voice stopped me, and I turned to face him. I knew he had no interest in leaving the hotel room. He'd made that clear from the start. But it had never occurred to me that he might actually try to stop me from leaving. He was staring at me with a confused, mounting rage.

"Not okay?" I asked, trying to keep my tone light.

"No. I don't want you to leave."

"It's just for thirty minutes."

"No."

"We're wasting so much money, Ian!"

"It's my money, and I'll waste it if I want to. Why the hell do you want to go out there when we have everything we need right here?"

"I was just trying to be helpful."

"Really? Try harder then! Be helpful by keeping your arse right here in this hotel room with me."

"Ian!"

"What?" he asked, sitting up straight. "I don't want you to go out there. Why would you want to go out there when there's no reason we can't stay right here, just the two of us, and have them come to us?"

"I just—"

"There must be some reason why you'd want to get dressed and hike around in the snow in New York City where anything can happen to you. You want to get shot or robbed or raped? Which is it?"

"I used to go anywhere I wanted at any time of the day."

"Well, that was bloody stupid of you, now wasn't it? Maybe you're not as smart as I thought you were. You're acting like Joanna used to! Taking unnecessary risks and thinking you're invincible. It makes me crazy. You're not going out in the snow in the city to buy some goddamn sandwiches when I'm offering to get us a real breakfast from room service. Now sit down!"

I stood there, trying to decide whether I should sit down on the edge of the bed as he had asked or grab my coat and go and never look back. I glared at him. "You're scaring me."

He stared at me for a few more seconds, and then suddenly he looked down. "I'm sorry. What if something happens to you and I'm not there? That would be my fault and I can't lose you."

Time stood still for me as I wavered. I had limits. I had pride. But in the end, he was more important. Finally I sat down beside him and put my arm around his shoulder. "Okay. No problem. We'll get room service. I'm in the mood for an omelet."

"Thank God," he said, clearly relieved. "With potatoes or salad?"

"Potatoes. I didn't mean to upset you."

"I didn't mean to yell at you, Maddie. I really am sorry."

"It's all right," I said, thankful that whatever it was that had taken control of him had passed. I didn't want to see that look on his face ever again. "But seriously. I was raised in the Midwest. My mom and dad were comfortable, yes, but very frugal. They felt strongly that spoiled children don't do well in the real world. It's hard for me to just bask in all this luxury."

Ian held out his arms and pulled me down beside him. He turned me around so that he was hugging me from behind, and he set his chin down on my shoulder.

"Here's what I haven't told you. I can pay for this. We can stay in this suite as long as we want. We can get room service day and night. I never really explained it all to you, but that company my brother and I started? We made a lot of money. And now I'm done with that. All I want to do now is be with you. And we can do anything you want. We can live anywhere you want. You don't have to work anymore."

I was stunned. I had to go back to tutoring in a few days. I couldn't stay shut up in that room any longer. My decadent bender with Ian was supposed to be coming to an end, with the return to real life just around the corner. "Are you being serious?"

"Completely."

"You don't have to go back to Iraq at all?"

"John and I, we made a deal at the start. When it seemed to us that the only way forward in our business in Iraq was going to involve bribery, backhanded deals, and exploiting and endangering our teams, we were going to bail out. We would have had to be both disgustingly greedy and complete idiots to continue. We made some money and we got out.

Alive. And now that I'm here with you I truly have every-thing I could want."

"I thought when our time here was up that you would be headed off to Chechnya or Somalia or who knows where. I was going to visit you all over the globe, waiting for you in some godforsaken fleabag hotel room in the nearest safe zone to where you were working." I had actually been looking forward to this.

"Yeah. That's not going to happen. I'm going to stay with you until they kick me out of this country. I know what hap-pens when you and I get separated. I am not letting you out of my sight. Not ever again. And you're going to have to get used to flying first class and drinking the best champagne without regressing to your frugal Midwestern upbringing and causing problems. Running out in the snow for sandwiches, for fuck's sake. Please."

"What's going to happen to your company?"

"I just want it to be over. I just want to shut the business down. We're up for a big contract that would make us mil-lions, but you know, I hope we don't get it. I just want to shut the business down."

"Why?"

"It's complicated," he answered in a spasm of motion. Within seconds he had lit a cigarette. "I don't want to go into it. I just don't ever want to go back to Iraq. Not even for a meeting. Not even for a minute. Not ever."

The day before I was due to return to my tutoring job, Ian and I packed up our stuff and checked out of the Hudson. We hailed a taxi and headed downtown toward Greenwich Village. Hurtling down raucous Seventh Avenue, the Middle Eastern cabdriver fishtailed in and out of pedestrians while shouting into his cell phone, stomped on the gas after each green light and braked to a squealing stop at every crosswalk.

Ian looked ahead with narrowed eyes and squeezed the strap of his duffel bag with both hands.

"You'll like the West Village," I said. "It's very pretty and quiet. Not like this, with all the lights and horns and hustle bustle."

He said nothing.

"My apartment is actually on a cobblestone street. Can you imagine that in New York? There aren't very many of those left. The apartment is small but it's cute. It's the attic apartment, with a skylight."

"Right," he said.

"Are you okay?" I asked.

"Could we please not talk right now?" he responded.

And we were off.

Ian was dumbfounded by the size of my apartment. For me, it was a quaint alcove. For him it was a roomy coffin. When we entered, the door swung inward and hit the back of the futon. A few inches away from the futon was a little coffee table where the old television sat against the far wall. Ian looked at the space and then looked at me. "I imagined being a writer and all that you would have quite a nice flat."

"I'm mostly a teacher now. This is what I can afford. It's a thousand dollars a month."

"What?"

"Yeah. To have a 'quite nice flat' you have to be a hedge-fund manager or a dot-com millionaire."

"What is it about these big bloody cities?" he asked, throwing down his duffel bag and his computer case.

I took a deep breath, hugged myself and looked down at my feet. "Ian," I said softly. "If you aren't happy here, it's okay. You can leave."

He spun around. I looked up and met his eyes, hoping I wouldn't cry.

Ian took me into his arms. I realized I was physically shaking. "What's important," he whispered, "is that I'm happy with you. I've been to some really bad places and seen some really bad things, and, yes, I'm a bit of a shut-in. But I'll change. You'll see. I'll come around. I know I will. If that's what it will take for us to be together, I'll do it. Just give me a little time. That's all I ask. I won't try to stop you from going out again, I promise. Do the things you like to do. Take walks, go to work, see your friends. One of these days soon I'll be able to join you. But for now, is it so bad to come home and find me here, waiting? Waiting just to be with you and be happy?"

I thought of the many days and nights I'd climbed those dingy, meat-scented stairs with a six-pack of Corona and a plastic carton of some horrible pasta salad from the corner deli. Watching box sets of DVDs one after another with my computer sitting on my lap. Never forgetting the birthdays of my friends' and families' children because I wanted to be invited around and to have children in my life. Being alone and living with the expectation of long lonely years to come.

I loved him for better or for worse. The tears finally came, and he kissed them away.

He stayed and I was grateful.

MADDIE

Ten days before

Skopie and Sophie are traumatized. On and off for three days it's as if a train has been rumbling past the house, reminding me of the night the helicopters blanketed the sky in Skopje. Kansas storms are legend and for good reason. They're some of the most beautiful and terrifying I've ever seen. The sky becomes fissured with roping, coiling clouds. Spiraling funnels dip down, and then the electric cracks and booms begin, coming from all directions, shaking the shutters. Our storms throw everything at you; rain, sleet, lightning, wind and swirling black tornado clouds more evil than those over Sauron's Dark Tower.

It's stormed for three days, and these little dogs, they can't stop trembling. They follow me everywhere. If I'm dressing in my closet and Charlie is in the connecting room watching television, they curl up in the piles of clothes that Ian has left on his side. I suppose the underwear, T-shirts and socks must smell comfortingly like Ian. Yesterday Skopie found an especially appealing spot on one of Ian's favorite fleece camping jackets. Maybe he has been waiting all this time for me to sort through his shit. Iron it, too, no doubt—you know, with all the free time I have when I'm not looking after Charlie. Let his clothes be a dog bed then.

I suppose he'll be angry when he gets home.

Today, the torrential rains are slowing down. The yard is mud. The ponds are full. The gutters are gushing, but it's almost over. Skopie and Sophie seem less afraid, and Cami J has agreed to see me today since I canceled yesterday, not wanting to leave the dogs frightened at home alone during the storms.

"Charlie, come get dressed, sugar booger! I've got to drop you by Kids Club for a few hours."

He comes running to me on his slightly bowed legs with his round tummy leading the way. One of the million things I love about having him to myself is that I don't have to worry about Ian calling him a "Mama's Boy." Charlie will run and hug me every time I summon him, as if that's just what all children do.

As we are backing out of the driveway, I can see that Wayne is in his driveway with his wheelbarrow, contemplating his miniature fortress comprised of fiftysomething bags of mulch. He's stayed in the last three days of rain, but now he's back at it. He's wearing overalls, a baseball cap and work gloves. It occurs to me that I have not seen his wife come or go, nor roll her chair to the window or porch, in a very, very long time.

I stop the car and lower the window. I put on my biggest, friendliest smile. "Hey, Wayne! How's my favorite neighbor?"

He trots over gleefully. "G'day, you two." He peeks in my window and grins at Charlie. "And how's the little cheeky monkey, eh? Y'all right, lad? You been mindin' yer mum?"

Charlie regards him suspiciously, and I wonder if he can even understand a word Wayne says in his trailer-park English accent.

"We're fine, Wayne. How're you and Linda?"

"Linda could be better, but I'm all right. I need to get a new layer of mulch down, though." He glances toward the weeds that run rampant around our rosebushes and trees. "If you need anything, Maddie, you just call. I can help you with the yard or what have you. You know that, right?"

"I do! Thank you. There is something, actually."

"What, doll?"

"My dad just called and said there's another flood warning and asked if my sump pump is working. I don't know about sump pumps."

"Oh that's easy. I'll come have a look and sort it out some-time this week. Call me."

"Thank you, Wayne."

"That's all right, doll." He switches back into his accent and removes his cap with a flourish. "Wayne Randall, handyman extraordinaire, at your service, milady."

Cami J's assignments are becoming more focused. Despite her unconventional demeanor and approach, I can see that she is smarter, more perceptive and altogether more demanding than I originally thought. I suppose I should have expected this.

I'm having trouble.
I don't like this one. I don't know if I can do this.
It's just that, I really can't remember.

I put my pen down and look up at Cami J helplessly. "Cami J," I say. "This is the one subject you keep asking me to work on, and it's the one that I feel I can't do and it's getting frus-trating. Like maybe you don't believe me."

Cami J is not hiding her irritation very well. It's been build-ing for a long time, and she wants to know exactly what happened that night in Colorado. "I'm sorry," she says, obviously exasperated. "Okay. Look. I'm after something here. If you can't write about it, let's talk."

"All right."

"Tell me about the camping trip. Can you do that?"

"Up until the accident, I guess. Sure."

"Where did you go?"

"Estes Park. I used to go to a sleepover camp there when I was a teenager, so I knew I really liked it. I chose Jellystone Campground because Charlie's still so little, and those kinds of places are fun. There are other kids. There's a pool and miniature golf, normal bathrooms, stuff like that. Ian wanted to go a little more hard core but—"

"When you say hard core, what do you mean?"

We both have a little nervous laugh, but we are not in our safe, naughty humor, everything-is-okay place anymore. Not that kind of hard core. She wants answers.

"Just farther into the woods, away from the RVs and all the people."

Her mouth drops open for a split second before she snaps it shut. Her eyes are snarky and inquisitive, as if she'd like to ask, *So he could punish you for planning to leave him by bashing your head in with a rock with no one around to see?*

What she actually says is, "So he could do his whole survivalist thing."

"So it would be real camping, I guess."

"But you didn't know the extent of his obsession with the doomsday prepping until much later. When you found out about the bunker."

"Yes. But..." I laugh. "I'm not sure I agree with the use of words like *obsession* and *doomsday*."

"You don't?"

"The more I think about it, the more I realize I should have seen that whole thing coming. A lot was going wrong in the world all of a sudden last year. North Korea, ISIS, Ebola, Syria was getting worse, and Ian was very worried about what NA-TO's response would be to Russia going into the Ukraine. He had worries about the looting after Hurricane Katrina. He had his reasons. He believed that World War III was a real possibility. He did what he thought was…was…prudent."

"Prudent?" Cami J is staring at me.

"Okay, it's a weird word. Why are you looking at me like that?"

"You've never really been willing to talk very openly about your relationship with Ian."

"Well, he's been out of the country the entire time I've been seeing you, so."

"How would you characterize it, though?"

"Strained, but functioning. I love him. Obviously I'm upset about the 'Fiona porn from the past' but—"

She shoots up from her slouch. "See! It concerns me that you might be trivializing something disturbing by referring to it in that sarcastic way."

I'm starting to feel defensive and I don't like it. "Look. He's a man, and he has some pornography on his computer. Obviously I'm not thrilled about it. But what I'm trying to convey here is that it's possible I overreacted when I found the wall of water and all the food and supplies. I don't know. He's not necessarily a nut job because he has some canned food and water set aside in a corner of the basement."

I laugh and Cami J does not. She's playing with her pen. "So you're good with the bunker now."

"I'm going to ask Ian about it when he gets home. But I'm better with it now than I was when I found it."

"So you're no longer considering leaving with Charlie?"

"It's something I think about from time to time. That's all it's ever been and that's still where I am."

"Okay fine. Back to the camping. Do you actually like it?"

"Yes. Ian does it well. It's almost glamping with him. Our tent is huge and we sleep on cots, and he hangs colored lanterns in the trees. We make a fire and have a nice dinner, and Charlie and I take the dogs on walks. Ian always brings some of those glow-in-the-dark necklaces and torches and the other kids from the campground run around with them. We play music. We drink wine. He's at his best when he is away from crowds and the hustle bustle. He's fun."

"And that's what you were doing right before you fell. Drinking wine and having fun."

There is something I don't like about the way she asks this question. I want my warm and cuddly Cami J back. Today she actually seems angry. Today she won't stop fucking around with her damn pen and looking at me sideways.

I glance at the clock, and for the first time since I have been coming to see her, I am relieved that my time with Cami J is up. "Gosh," I say. "That went by fast today."

"Wait," she says, as I start to stand. "Can we try something different?"

"Sadly, our time is up." She blinks and I must admit, I sounded a bit like a game show announcer.

"I'll be quick. I understand that you can't write about a frightening accident if you can't remember it. I'm trying to do something here, Maddie. Trust me. I'm trying to understand how you, as an individual, process a traumatic experience. The more insight I have into your thoughts and feelings when confronted with danger or pain, the better I can address the ensuing anxiety and denial—"

"But what am I denying?" I ask, involuntarily throwing my arms out in exasperation. I hear the unintended confrontation in my own voice.

"Okay." She uses her open hand to shush me. "Okay. Maybe you aren't denying anything, and all this anxiety you're feeling is directly related to the accident and not to your overall circumstances. In that event, what I want you to do will be even more helpful. Listen."

"I'm listening."

"If you can't write about your fall, can you write about another time in your life when you were very scared? When something bad happened and you had to deal with it and then with the aftermath? Could you do that for me?"

"I had that bad boating accident when I was a kid. I've mentioned it."

"That sounds like that would work. I'd like to experience that with you, through your words. What happened before, during and after, and how you felt about it."

I look at the clock again. "The only problem is, that might take me a while."

"This is another homework assignment, Maddie. Write about your experience at home and bring it to me next week."

"Okay," I say, relieved to be excused, and also relieved at the prospect of finally being forced to write this story. I had been involuntarily reliving it pretty much every day of my entire life.

MADDIE

2011–2012

Ian was nocturnal. It took only that first month of sitting quietly next to me on the futon watching television at low volume all night while I slept for him to insist that we move into a bigger apartment. We packed up my little studio, said goodbye to the pretty, tree-lined, cobblestoned streets of the Village and relocated to a large two-bedroom on the Upper East Side.

Ian liked the wide even streets, tall buildings and clean, cold steel of uptown. The location was close to the school most of my tutoring kids attended, as well as to Hunter College, where I was taking evening classes toward my master's in education so that I could teach full-time. Ian was happy that I would no longer be traveling by subway, which he had flatly refused to ever enter for any reason.

I missed the Village, but the new apartment was spacious, bright and even had a kitchen. And, yes, Ian was paying for it. He could stay up at night in the living room and drink, smoke and laugh out loud at the ongoing chat with his brothers back home and his World of Warcraft guild, and I could sleep peacefully in a quiet, dark room of my own. Though I wished he would come to bed with me, I understood that I was working and he was not. Ian was essentially on vacation, and it wasn't as if I could bug him to get out and find a job. He took care of everything. He provided all that I could possibly want without lifting a finger. I sometimes had to remind myself that he had made enormous sacrifices for the comfortable life that he enabled us to lead.

I adored him, as damaged as he was. I found him all the more fascinating for the chunks that had been torn out of him. I told myself that even if I could never change him, I would never abandon him.

Ian had been going home for a week or two every ninety days to keep his visa legal. He'd been with me in the States for over a year, and he was due for his fifth visit to England. He made arrangements to split his time between brothers and sisters in Birkenhead for two weeks. He promised to call me every night.

Ten days into his absence, I woke up and saw that it was three o'clock in the morning. I'd been expecting his call five hours earlier.

That night I tossed and turned with a pit in my stomach. Early Saturday morning when he still hadn't called I decided to track him down. I knew that he'd gone to the horse races in Chester with some of his brothers and brothers-in-law, and I decided that Robbie was the most likely to answer my questions truthfully if I were able to get ahold of him.

"Alo?" Robbie was a prison guard at one of the worst jails in Northern England, and he had a Scouse accent that I could not always understand.

"Robbie, it's Madeline."

"Ah, love," he said, and it was as though he'd already told me the whole story. Whatever it was, it was bad.

"So? Has something happened with Ian?"

"Yeah, love, he's okay, but he's been arrested and is in the nick overnight. I would've rung you, but I thought it was the middle of the night over there. Listen. There was a bit of trouble after the race."

"Oh no." My stomach cramped.

"It wasn't our Ian's fault. All the streets in Chester town center were closed down to cars after the race, and the bunch of us were just walking around and hitting the pubs. Anyway, like I said, the streets were closed down to cars, but all of a sudden some git comes up behind us and revs his engine. So we ignore him, Ian, Barry, our Chris and I do. And the next thing you know he bumped us."

That was all I needed to know. For over a year I had seen the effect the city had on Ian. He recoiled from the horns, the sirens and the blinking lights. He tried to stay away from the crowds, and he did his best to stay out of trouble. He knew he was volatile, and he wanted to be careful to keep himself under control. He tried to be responsible. I could only imagine what dark fury had passed through his body when he heard the car's revving engine behind him.

"What did he do?"

Robbie laughed. "Shat his pants like the rest of us. But then Ian walked over to the driver's window and put his fist straight through it."

"You're kidding."

"No. Safety glass it was. If I'd not seen it I'd have said it was impossible. And there he was reaching through all that broken glass for the guy's neck when all of a sudden he just pulled his hand out and walked over to a police officer and turned himself in."

"Is he okay?"

"Yes, love, he's fine. A few stitches. The only thing he's worried about now is if this is going to keep him from coming back to you. He doesn't know how he let such a stupid thing happen. Ah, love, he's miserable, he is. Awful sorry, love."

Ian was in the nick. Cute word, *nick*. I call it *jail*. My boyfriend was in jail.

Because Ian turned himself in, paid immediately and in full for the damage to the driver's window, and made a counter complaint against the driver, the charges against him were eventually dropped.

A week later, the night before his flight back to New York, he was unusually cheerful when he called. He said to me, "This has been a wake-up call. I realize it, Maddie. I've got to calm down, sort myself out and cut back on the drinking. Yeah?"

"I'm on board with that."

"I thought for a second I might not be able to return to you. Depending on if they charged me and with what, it might have been bad, but we're okay. It made me realize that losing you would be the stupidest thing I could ever do. You've saved my life, Petal. I don't know where I'd be without you."

This was all very nice, but he was the one into saving lives, not me. I didn't say this, but apparently I didn't have to.

"And to prove to you that I'm not going to be a pain in the bum anymore, I think we should take a little trip."

I started picturing topless beaches in Spain or Greece.

"Let's go to Kansas!" he said.

"Kansas?"

"When do your students have spring break?" he asked.

"April twelfth. So, in just a week."

"Let's rent a car and drive cross-country to Kansas. It would be fun. You can show me some of your country. Plus, I want to meet your family."

This was not what I'd been expecting. But I missed my mom and dad, and it was time for them to meet the man I'd been living with for more than a year. It took me so long to respond that he finally asked if I was still on the line.

"I am, Ian," I said. "I'm still here."

Two weeks later, he and I woke up together in my old bedroom in my parents' farmhouse in Meadowlark.

When I opened my eyes I was tangled up with him in the bed where I had once spent long hours dreaming about distant countries, castles, nightclubs, foreign boys and various means of escape from the countryside.

Ian's body was curled into me comfortably, his dark, scratchy beard pressed into a demure lacy pillow, his tattoos oddly vibrant and beautiful against my mom's eggshell sheets. I felt a pure, deep love for him as I watched him snore surrounded by the quaintness of my mother's interior decorating scheme, which included many a ceramic vase filled with colorful fake flowers, not one without its own useless little china saucer centered atop an antique doily. I'd always wanted something different. I'd brought home someone who fit the bill.

I slipped out of bed without waking him. I went quietly downstairs hoping to get a cup of coffee with my dad before he left for his morning run, but I was too late. There was a light fog hovering over the ground toward the back of the property, and three deer were grazing just down the hill, where the lawn turned into forest. Blue jays and cardinals swarmed the bird feeder over by the rope hammock, and the older pair of my parents' four Irish setters were sleeping in dog beds in the kitchen while the other two rooted around in the yard for the ever-elusive moles.

I took my coffee out to the screened-in porch and stood, looking out at the land where I had played tag when I was little, and where all four of my grandparents' ashes had been spread. This was where my sisters and I had chased lightning bugs and set off fireworks, camped out with a stolen stash of beer from the garage, and brought our dates home for long X-rated romps in the woods.

My parents had sold about twenty-five acres, but the farm was still big enough that you couldn't see anything but trees and hills and fence and sky.

I jumped when Ian appeared behind me and slipped his arm around my waist. He had helped himself to coffee, and he was already smoking his first cigarette of the day. He looked happy and relaxed, as calm and content as I had ever seen him. The weariness seemed to have lifted. His eyes were brighter and clearer, and his skin had some color, like back when I first met him.

"How did you sleep?" I asked.

"It was so quiet," he said. "No bloody bin trucks beeping and honking, no drunks shouting at three in the morning."

"Good," I said, leaning into him.

He ran a hand though his hair. "This morning I could hear birds singing. In Iraq where I lived, Saddam had all the trees cut down so the Kurds had nowhere to hide other than the mountains. It's been a long time since I heard songbirds."

"And crickets, too, right? Did you hear the crickets?"

"Yeah. I wasn't sure at first, but wait—look there." His arm around me had tightened and his mouth hung open. He jabbed his finger against the screen, gaping out at the fog. "What is that? Holy shit!"

"What?"

"Are those deer? Those are deer!"

"Yes!" I was caught up in his enthusiasm.

"Right there. Eating your mum's tree!"

"I know! She hates it."

The dogs finally spotted the deer as well and began growling. The deer were far too fast to be in danger, but the dogs took a celebratory prance around the property after the deer had loped lazily into the woods.

"And they're gone. A mum and two little babies!" Ian exclaimed. At that point I had to turn and study him to make sure that all the vodka and cigarettes had not caused him to suffer some sort of personality-altering stroke in the night. "Do you think?" he asked me cheerfully. "Do you think it was a mum and two babies?"

"I do."

Ian pulled me in for a long hug against his chest. Eventually he leaned back so that he could see my face. I was startled to see that his eyes were glistening. "This is such a pretty, peaceful place."

"It is peaceful," I answered. "Nice and quiet."

He laughed suddenly, and surveyed the backyard appreciatively. "It's very relaxing," he continued, turning his head from left to right and looking out over the acres of my parents' land. "It's so green. And hilly. I never imagined Kansas being so green and hilly. That's a motherfucking hummingbird, isn't it?"

"Yes. That's a motherfucking hummingbird."

"I prefer this to any place I've ever been," he said, crossing his arms over his chest and looking royally around as if he had just discovered Kansas and planted his British Empire flag.

My jaw dropped. "Any place?"

"Granted, I've been mostly to war-torn, terrorist-ridden, third-world countries."

"Right. Well, I can see how this is better than that."

"Maddie." The glistening eyes were back. He looked almost overcome. He took my hand. "We would be happy here."

"Here? What do you mean, here?"

"It would be so much cheaper than New York. Think of how much money we could save and use to travel."

I was quiet. He plunged ahead.

"I've told you that I want us to be together and I've told you that I love you. But what I've never said is that I want this to be forever. Our whole lives, you and me. I want to give you a complete life. All the things that normal people do, the things that make them happy. A home. Kids. Maddie, let's come here to this quiet, safe place and get married and be a family."

I couldn't breathe.

Suddenly he dropped to one knee and said, "I'm so sorry, I haven't got a ring. That all just hit me like a ton of bricks, and I had to say it."

"No, that's not it," I managed to say. I didn't care about a ring. I'd suddenly realized that all this time I had been afraid. He walked away from me in Macedonia. He wasn't there when I went to be with him in Bosnia. All this time I had secretly, deeply known somehow that I would end up alone, but here he was saying the word I needed to hear: *forever*. He said forever. He was going to stay and make pancakes and fall asleep on the couch and tinker in the garage and we would take lovely vacations to the beach and we were going to be normal. I pictured Ian with a child hoisted up on his strong, broad shoulders, the two of them watching fireworks out over my parents' front field. When I left the farm, it had been a lonely place. My sisters had cleared out years before me. But before, when we were a big family, it had been the scene of picnics and parties, hayrides and Easter-egg hunts.

He was offering me permanence. Though I'd known that I loved him, I hadn't had a clue how magnificent it would be to feel safe in that love.

I said yes.

We kissed like it was the first time and ended up tiptoeing back up to my bedroom, where we fell on one another like wolves. Ian dozed afterward.

It was wonderful just to lie in my bed. The sheets smelled of my mother's lavender fabric softener. I kept my eyes closed and pretended to be asleep for over an hour. I would have to leave Hunter College and my students, but I could always go back and work on my master's in education elsewhere. Why not try this tranquil place where songbirds sang and Ian slept and smiled real smiles? As I lay there next to the man I loved, I came to terms with moving back to where I had vowed never to return. I had what I had wanted for so long—unconditional love and an ally in the long fight. I was bringing the great wide world home with me. Ian had been through enough. I would do whatever was necessary to help him heal.

MADDIE

2012–2017

That autumn, a little less than two years after he and I found each other again in New York, Ian and I were married on my parents' screened-in porch, facing out over the sloping farmland that I had left and that Ian had instantly loved. My mom and dad held hands like teenagers as the justice of the peace pronounced us man and wife, and my sister Sara laughed and wiped tears from under each eye with her thumb.

It was a last-minute event designed to gain him residency, and the airfares had been too expensive for most of Ian's family to attend. My other sister Julia was there with her husband and two children, as was Ian's brother Jimmy. John was doing a security assessment for ExxonMobil in some sweltering and dodgy desert, and Robbie couldn't get out of work, but Jimmy had come from England at the last minute, and he fidgeted in the suit we had bought him at Oak Park Mall a few days before.

Ian's charm, sense of humor, lack of pretension, good looks

and "better than Sean Connery" accent won my mom over immediately. At the rehearsal dinner, under fire from my mom and sisters with questions about Princess Diana's lovers and Kate Middleton's marriage to Prince William, Ian said, "You know, ladies? You want to know who's really the best of the bunch? I will tell you who's a lovely person, and that's Prince Charles!"

I had not yet heard this story. "I'm sure I'd know if you had guarded Prince Charles!"

My mom and sisters looked like a trio of statues, all leaning into Ian with their chins on their fists. We were in a private room at the Capital Grille, an upscale steakhouse on the Plaza. Ian got up from the table, ambled around to the other end, and plucked himself a fresh slice of bread from a basket. "I was guarding the royal family's doctor, and following him around with this giant red rucksack with all the medical supplies inside. It was a long day and Prince Charles had been to a number of different events and ceremonies, and there was food and champagne and lots of people."

Ian walked back to his seat, grabbed his vodka and leaned toward my mom and sisters. "Now, at some stage Prince Charles must have noticed me and wondered what the hell I was up to. Eventually we finished his schedule and pulled up at his castle. The doctor and I went into a small side room by ourselves and began to relax. Not thirty seconds had gone by when the door to this little room opens and Prince Charles walks in, totally by himself." Ian went on in a more royal, nasal accent, 'I'm sorry to bother you, but I noticed you have been following me around whilst carrying a huge—red—rucksack!'

"Well," Ian said, "the doctor straightened up and said, 'I'm Captain So-and-So. I'm the army doctor, and this is Corporal Wilson. It's his job to assist me and carry around the medical equipment that may be needed in an emergency.'"

Ian took a long sip of his drink. "Prince Charles said,

'Ooohhhh! How fascinating! Do you mind if I have a look at what kind of equipment you have in there?'

"The doctor went awfully pale and kept looking from side to side as if he wanted to make a run for it. He opened up the rucksack so slowly that Prince Charles and I couldn't help but dart a glance at one another. And then, there nestled neatly on top of all the supplies were two bottles of very expensive champagne that the good old Doctor Klepto had nicked from an earlier engagement."

Ian reached into his pocket to whisk out his cigarettes. "The doctor blushed! And I thought my military career was over. Right? We'd bloody nicked the Royal champers! But no!"

Ian wagged his finger at us all. "Prince Charles looked in, like so, and then looked back up at us. His hands were clasped behind his back. After a second he nodded and said, 'Well, then. Gentlemen. I can imagine that would come in very handy in a medical emergency. Thank you and good night.'"

My sisters erupted in a middle-aged version of girlish giggles, and my mom couldn't stop dabbing at her eyes with her napkin, mopping up tears of sheer hilarity.

Ian said to my mom, "Judy. Would you care to pop outside for a ciggie with me?" As she accompanied him away from the table, she looked back at me over her shoulder with such pride and smiled at me as if I was the luckiest woman on earth.

My dad, Jack, a former air force pilot, accepted Ian with the warmth and gravity of a new son, and the two of them often rambled off together on walks about the farm to discuss ancient battles, famous military commanders, foreign wars, guns and the business of being a bodyguard. Once a month they went to the range for a friendly comparison of shooting skills and later to Panera, where my dad regularly insisted on treating Ian to a soup-in-a-bread-bowl lunch. For Ian, who'd lost his own dad when he was so young and whose mother had passed away just before he left Iraq, it was as if he'd gained another set of parents as well as a wife.

It was with ease that Ian staged his coup. He pronounced our neck of the woods in Kansas to be the greatest place on earth with a finality and devotion that most people reserved for their birthplace. Everyone who met him in Meadowlark, everyone who sweltered and froze through the extreme seasons and who had been told all their lives that they lived in a place reputed to be one of the most boring anywhere, all these people were able to walk away from meeting Ian feeling good about their life. This witty British chap who had been all over the globe just declared their hometown of Meadowlark, which they had always been secretly a little ashamed of, the very best place he'd ever been in his many travels.

Eventually Ian and I moved into a house ten minutes west of my parents' farm, in a brand-new subdivision in Meadowlark called Sweet Water Creek, built in the middle of a former pasture where I once went to isolated field keg parties in high school. We'd seen probably thirty houses at that point, but he knew which one he wanted. He chose the unusual house with the huge open lower level because it reminded him of a renovated old English barn he'd once dreamed of buying. From the upstairs window we could see herds of Angus cows and an algae-covered farm pond where a heron regularly swooped in to perch on one leg and rest in the shadow of a giant sycamore tree. Behind all that were some large but lackluster wooden houses that looked more or less like ours, along with a stable, a grain silo, unfurling modest hills and the western horizon. This space and privacy is what Ian needed.

For Ian it was love at first sight.

He was especially happy with the fact that all houses in tornado alley had basements, which are mostly unheard of in

England. He had ours finished with his own little pub built in the back, a movie screen and projector, a pool table, and an L-shaped desk in the corner for all his computers. Down there it was always dark, cool, quiet and safe. It smelled of cigarettes, licorice, Coke and liquor, spilled and soaked into the chairs.

Ian told me that things would be different here. He would have his own house to work on and care for, and that the quaintness and calmness would draw him out into the world, for walks and talks and dinners and dates, away from the recurring thoughts and memories that made him need his time alone.

Things didn't change in the way that he told me they would. He outfitted our four-bedroom house with security befitting a Beverly Hills palace. It was truly a fortified sanctuary, one that made Ian comfortable and content. He spent most of his time blissfully in his basement, surrounded by machinery, technology, man-toys and distractions.

He purchased six hundred "Warhammer" miniature models to paint. I cringed with too much love and a mixture of regret and fury as I watched him hunched over his worktable. With trembling hands and squinting eyes, he gathered up the tiny parts of those dismembered soldiers and carefully glued them together. Hours and days and nights crawled by as he put his gray plastic pieces of warriors together and painted them with bright colors to bring them to life.

And then splattered them with blood.

I'll give him this. He tried. He tried very hard.

As that first year slowly rolled in and out, we had some blissful times. As long as I was content to stay home and cook meat-centric meals and watch movies and make love, he was happy. One of his very favorite things to do was to drive over to my parents' farm and have fried chicken and potato salad on their enclosed back patio at twilight as the fireflies started flickering. His initial delight at discovering the deer never seemed to diminish, and my mom and dad never grew tired of his war stories, opinions on the European Union, global terrorism and of course, the offspring of the royal family.

We would sit on the patio for hours talking with them. The Irish setters visited us often, begging for treats. Then they trotted off to play and hunt moles down the hill. One night I turned to him and said, "We're settled enough, don't you think? We should get a dog."

He reached over and took my hand. He smiled and said, "Let's get two. So they're never lonely."

There had been a raid at a puppy mill in Missouri a few days earlier, and our local shelter had taken in a lot of the rescues. I knew that Ian particularly liked big dogs, but again, I could see him trying. He immediately spotted the girl siblings that would steal my heart and we took our tiny black-and-white big-eyed babies home with us then and there. We named our puppies Skopie and Sophie in honor of the lives we were living when we first met. I adored them, and it was me who walked and fed them, but I suspect Ian may have loved them just as much or even more. He would lie down on the couch and let them climb all over his body as if it were a giant play structure. He let them lick his face and fall asleep with their bellies stretched over his neck or with their tiny heads nestled in the crook of each shoulder.

Ian called that the year we "lived in one another's pockets." We had been in tight quarters in New York, but I had left every day to go to work. In Kansas, I was free to spend my time with Ian. My parents invited us to use their spare tent and camp with them at their favorite spot outside Eureka Springs, Arkansas. Ian absolutely loved the quiet of the lush forest, the footpaths, stone bridges and glassy water. He said to my dad, "One day I'd like to have a cabin in a beautiful place like this."

In the meantime, he had been transformed into an outdoorsman and spent a small fortune at REI to jump-start his new life's hobby with top-quality gear. "I didn't realize," he said, "that camping in the forest would be such a great escape." He spent hours looking at websites and images of America's national parks. We packed up the car and hit the road whenever the mood struck him, which was often. We had no jobs or children. It was la-la land.

Until one night in the fall, when we'd been married for about a year. I was woken by loud wind and thunder. It had been one of those long days that should never have started the way that it did. One of my old high-school friends had a Sunday brunch with tons of delicious food and an entire table covered with the fixings for mimosas and Bloody Marys. Ian had started mixing his first vodka orange at eleven. I persuaded him to come home with me about four, but when I suggested a sobering walk with the dogs, he waved me off and poured a drink.

I watched him happily dancing around in the kitchen to a song that was only in his head, and I knew that I didn't want to be around when his private party turned in on itself. In recent months he'd started to occasionally mock me for having grown up in such a sheltered, privileged place. It was as if he was angry at me for having grown up where he wanted to have grown up. Sometimes when he drank he ridiculed me for being pampered and naive.

When the storm woke me, I found myself upright in the recliner in my bedroom. I had fallen asleep while reading. I glanced at the clock and saw that it was a little after ten at night. I got up and walked down the hall and then the stairs. I could see Ian across the house in the kitchen, rifling through the pantry. I walked over quietly. I watched as he wrestled with the plastic packaging on some candies as if the packaging were fighting back.

"Hey, baby," I said softly. I was hoping to entice him up to bed.

When he turned and I saw his eyes, I knew that wasn't going to happen. I had the distinct feeling when he looked at me, that I wasn't there at all. "Are you okay?" I asked.

"I thought you'd gone to bed ages ago," he said in a way that insinuated I had become old, boring and an altogether puritanical party pooper.

"Never mind," I said. "I can see you're not okay."

"Why? Because I didn't want to go on a walk with you and the dogs earlier?"

"I just wanted your company," I said, backing away. "The neighbors never see us together. They never see you."

"Who cares? You and your bloody walks! You don't have a clue. I can't just 'go for walks.' I can't 'chat' with the neighbors. I can't watch my feet taking step after step when I'm not trying to get somewhere. I can hear the bones snapping beneath my boots. Those poor people. They had shitty lives and then they were fucking massacred and then what did I do? I trampled over their bones. Helena and I both did."

"What are you talking about?"

"I'm talking about Rwanda. I'm talking about the church we were told to visit."

"What happened there?" I asked, feeling spooked. I had a very distant vague memory of him starting to tell me this story in Skopje. He hadn't been able to finish it.

"We took a shortcut through the woods. We didn't realize we were walking over bodies until we were in the middle of the meadow. We were standing on top of a family. There was a baby. His footie pajamas and his sippy cup." Ian's eyes appeared more lost and unfocused than before. "It's the reason she killed herself and the reason I can't bloody sleep! You can't even imagine it! How could you know?"

"Ian." I took another step backward, my flannel pajama pants tripping me as I stumbled away from him. "Please calm down. It's all right."

"It's not all right and don't tell me to calm down. Calm down? Calm down! Tell that to the people in Belfast, in Bosnia, in Rwanda and in Iraq," he shouted, counting on his fingers. "Just before they were slaughtered. I suppose you never heard of World War II either. You think it can't happen here? It can happen anywhere! Even to you, princess. Fuck walks, fuck the neighbors and fuck you."

Aside from Wayne and his reclusive disabled wife, our neighbors were the widowed mother of one of my former schoolmates and some newlyweds with a cat. I tried to stop myself, but I couldn't. "I should have listened to Joanna."

"What?" Those unhinged eyes were boring into me now.

My voice trembled when I said, "Maybe...maybe Joanna was right about you."

"Really? In what way?"

"She said you were different from us. That you'd hurt me."

"I'd like to hurt you right now."

I started crying and retreating toward the stairs. "She called you crazy and heartless."

He was usually unshakable but this threw him. "Heartless?" he singled out, apparently oblivious to crazy. He crossed the room in a few large strides. "What? She said I'm heartless?"

"Yes."

"That bitch. I should've let her kittens die."

"What?" I stopped crying. I stopped backing away.

"I saved those fucking kittens. I took them to Jason's girlfriend. Joanna had already tried to get me fired, and still I took her dead cat's babies away so she wouldn't have to watch them die after what she'd been through. Me, heartless!"

It was dawning on me then. "And what had she been through?"

"Aww! She didn't tell you? Her best friend in the whole wide world? I thought she told you everything."

"Just tell me. What had she been through?"

"Joanna lost a child there, in Skopje. She had a miscarriage."

I was gritting my teeth. "And she told you. And not me."

Ian's drunken eyes seemed to slide sideways, and he suddenly looked disturbed. "You'd already gone home," he slurred, turning away. I think he realized he'd crossed a line.

"No, I hadn't." I was only sure because now I finally understood why there'd been a blood-soaked towel underneath her bathroom sink. I finally understood why she'd failed to meet me at the bus station that one and only time. She'd been home sick for days. Oh my God. Joanna.

Ian was trying to think. "Okay. Maybe not. Then I guess you must have been in Sofia working."

"Still, I find it very hard to believe she confided in you of all people."

"Don't forget that Joanna and I were close once. It's not like she had a lot of people to turn to, what with her being practically on her own out there. And the two of you had already fallen out."

"Over you. We only ever fought over you."

"Should I be sorry or honored?"

"It's true. We'd never had anything more than an argument. In ten years. Then you came along and she tried to tell me things about you, and I wouldn't listen."

"Thank God you didn't listen! We wouldn't even be together if you had. Anyway, she's a liar. She was then, and she probably still is. An angry, selfish liar."

"Why would she lie?"

"She wanted you to hate me."

"Why?"

"She had her reasons."

"What?"

"You want to keep talking about this, do you?"

"Yes. What reasons?"

"Maybe she didn't want you to know that we'd been fucking."

And there it was, and I was suddenly aware of how blind I'd been. But I was not blind any longer, and now my vision warped and bent, and I could see every angle and implication of this drunk confession. He was the father of Joanna's baby. He was the reason she'd said, "Something happened that would have meant I had to leave my job. I tried to make myself believe it was all for the best. But it didn't really happen after all."

What must it have been like, to have Ian go back to Fiona, when Joanna was pregnant with his child? I was so ashamed of the way I'd behaved toward her. And embarrassed. Blood rushed through my head. I'd tried so hard to seduce him.

"You wouldn't touch me back then, and you said it was because of Fiona."

"I didn't want to fuck it up with you! I never wanted you to think I was a cheater. I didn't give a damn what Joanna thought."

"But you are a cheater."

"Christ!"

"And you had an affair with a woman you say you despised! Which makes me think you're a liar, too."

"See, this is why I never told you before. You never struck me as the type to really get the whole hate-fucking thing."

"You're actually sicker than I ever realized."

"Really? I thought you had already diagnosed me. You think I haven't found your little PTSD library?"

It was true. I had read book after book on PTSD, look-

ing for cures and finding only warnings and tragedies, ac-
cusations and injustices. There were no fairy-tale endings.
Just horror.

"I'm sick. Right? Aren't I?" he said, smacking his chest. "I
meet the criteria, don't I? Yes, I lost friends. Tick. Yes, I almost
died. Tick. Not just once but a number of times. How many
of those close calls took someone else's life and left me to walk
away? All of them! Tick, tick. Yes, I felt betrayed. And, yes, I
feel like I deserve to be dead. Tick, tick, tick."

Despite my anger I reached for him. He batted my hand
away.

"You're always asking me what's wrong." He began imitat-
ing me. Speaking in a clownish version of my voice. "'Oh! Are
you in a bad mood? Not again! You're no fun.'" He laughed
suddenly. "You want to know the reason I shut down a company that was making me millions? I'll tell you. Those six
guys? Where was I when they were executed? You want to
know?"

This was the first I had ever heard about six murdered men.
I covered my mouth with my hands and waited.

"Ask me. I was in Cyprus. In the pool. Paddling around
on a floatie with a vodka orange in the cup holder, smoking
a cigarette, listening to my music. I was waiting for the barbecue to get hot. And I never returned John's or Abbi's calls
because I didn't even bother to check my phone. I should have
been the one to go to the families and tell them and apologize. I should have been there, grieving with them over the
death of their sons and husbands and fathers. It should have
been me who told them, me who knocked on the door and
said how sorry I was. But I was by the pool! Can you imagine how outraged their wives and children would have been
if they saw me there? Lying in the sun while my guys were
pulled over and executed?"

"Ian," I said, again trying to touch him and again him having none of it. "Why didn't you tell me?"

He leaned against the wall and slid to a sitting position. "There's so much I haven't told you, Maddie. So much."

Ian and I didn't speak for days. I crept around the house like a mouse, walking on eggshells, trying to avoid him. I scuttled to our bedroom when I heard his footsteps coming up the basement stairs. I spent long stretches of time at my mom and dad's house. At last he appeared at my bedside in the early morning. He said, "I'm going back to work."

Atlas had offered him a position as an independent contractor, carrying out security assessments on business compounds around the world. Within weeks he was given a two-month overseas position reviewing the security at several oil-processing facilities in Kazakhstan.

Ian came to me a few nights before he left and put his arms around my waist. He kissed the top of my head. "Petal," he said. "We can get past this. We got past me walking away in Macedonia and standing you up in Bosnia, didn't we? This is no big deal."

I thought about saying, *Yes, look at how I let you treat me, and still, here I am. Look at how many times I've forgiven you.* But I didn't. I loved him still, and we'd only been married a year. It was too early to fail.

We stayed up late the night before he left. He liked to tell me again and again how he had fallen for me at once, but believed I was too good for him. I would always respond with my own story of wanting him desperately all those years we were apart. This was our routine and we strutted about our own private stage reenacting our parts in the magical romance for one another. That night we re-created those initial days at the Hudson with a marathon binge of *Game of Thrones* broken up by wine, vodka, cigarettes and bouts of circus sex on the couch. I would find out that I was pregnant before I saw him again.

And then…

Charlie was born.

I fell into an exhausted sleep for a while after the delivery. When I woke, Ian and a nurse were shouting at one another nose to nose, and I remember thinking, *Oh my God, Ian's fighting with her!*

I tried to sit up, and it felt as if the stitches in my Caesarean incision had ripped open. I must have made a horrible noise because Ian and the nurse both froze and turned to look at me. I could see what they were fighting over. It was a tiny white card, the kind that accompanies a delivery of flowers.

No one was handing me a bouquet.

Ian grabbed for the card again and said softly yet firmly, "I don't want to upset her."

The nurse, a formidable red-haired lady who looked like she'd be willing to meet Ian outside on the street to set-tle things, replied, "She deserves to know that someone has threatened her baby. We should call the police!"

My pain was severe. I saw little floating spots of white be-fore my eyes. It felt as if I'd been stabbed. The floor was a mess. It was confusing. Everywhere I looked I saw shards of glass, fake moss and black petals. Ian was clinging to the nurse's hand. For a second, through the twinkling stars and agony, it sounded like he was crying.

No. Ian doesn't cry.

After waking up in my hospital room and discovering Ian and a nurse wrestling over a card that had been stuck in a smashed black floral arrangement addressed to me, I felt very ill and sad and afraid. I was heavily medicated and weak, and I honestly lacked the will to argue with him over that damn card. I saved my voice on the way home. I alternated between squinting out the window at the cornfields and glancing back every few seconds to look at the frustratingly uninformative gray back of the rear-facing child seat. I desperately wanted to get home and see my baby's face.

Ian chattered incessantly. "It's nothing to worry about, Maddie. That card. Honestly, Maddie, I'm telling you. It was someone's idea of a joke. Probably someone who doesn't like me and wanted to ruin our special moment. We won't let it, though, will we, Petal? We won't let someone do that to us."

"What did it say?"

"The card?"

"Yes, the fucking card!"

"Oh it said something like, 'I hope your stupid baby keeps you up at night.' Something like that."

I hope your stupid baby keeps you up at night. I shook my head. "You're lying. That's ridiculous."

"No, I'm not. It was something like that."

"It was Fiona," I said, while wondering, Was it Joanna?

"No, it wasn't. It was someone's idea of a joke. Forget it."

But the card? It had gotten to him, too. I could tell.

Ian had turned down an offer of ninety days' work in Saudi Arabia to be with me for Charlie's arrival. It was a good thing, too, because after the incident in the hospital room I didn't get better. Three days after leaving the hospital I was running a temperature, and alternating Tylenol and Advil. I assumed my incision had gone from being infected to being badly infected. I had an appointment to see my doctor the following morning. I wasn't sure I would be able to wait.

I woke up to reach for Ian knowing he would not be there. My hand ran across the sheets where he had tried fleetingly to stay put, feeling the sweat left behind after his stunted rest by my side. My fever had spiked. Charlie was not in the little bassinet by my bed. They were both gone. I felt a surge of adrenaline and jumped up in a panic. I tried to reason with myself. Surely Charlie was with Ian. And yet this thought gave me no comfort at all.

In the past, before Charlie arrived, I would sometimes get out of bed and go look for Ian. Usually I found him sitting alone in the basement, cigarette between his lips, eyes on the ceiling, just staring. Every once in a while, I would go and place my chin over his shoulder to kiss the roughness of his scarred jaw. Other times I would decide to let him be, quietly turn around, and head back up to bed without disturbing him.

That night, burning up and feeling an awful, overwhelming need to find Charlie, I tiptoed halfway down the stairs. I could hear Ian in the kitchen humming. I heard the light whistle of the teakettle. I continued down to the bottom, and I could see Ian at the refrigerator. Charlie was in his basket on the couch making wah wah noises, one little clenched fist waving back and forth in the air. Relief flooded through me. Ian was making Charlie a bottle.

My head hurt so badly that suddenly all I wanted was to be back in bed. I leaned on the railing a second before pulling myself together and retracing my way up the steps. A wave of nausea and vertigo nearly toppled me, and I put my hands down on the stairs. I crouched like a cat, all paws on the ground, bowing my head. I stayed like that, trembling on all fours, until the dizziness passed. When I stood back up in that fog of fever, I remember something like a lucid dream, or a vivid hallucination. As I walked back to the burning, vacant spot in my bed, the house around me shimmered, as if I was looking through a dappled glass. For those ephemeral few minutes as I walked up the stairs and down the long hall, I could see through Ian's eyes.

This beautiful place of ours was also a house of horrors. How could it not be? Look who had followed my husband home. There, in the alcove by the Juliet balcony, I saw a bowed figure. A Rwandan boy soldier in tattered clothes was hunched down hiding in the corner, tossing a grenade up and down, up and down, meeting my eyes with a menacing, lopsided smile.

Through the French doors, under the streetlight where the shadows were bunched and monstrous from the overhanging trees, a car was parked in front of Wayne's house. I could just make out the soft outline of two bodies resting against one another. The heart-shaped form of the Iraqi grandfather and the little girl were melted together in an unintended but intimate ashen embrace and were intertwined and asleep for always.

The silence loomed as large as the great golden moon outside. This endless house was both labyrinthine and dead end. It took forever to walk from one side to the other. There was a sliver of light at the end of the hall. Down the far end of the upstairs corridor, off the unused bedroom in the untouched bath, there would be a mess. If I were to reach out and touch the door, swing it open just an inch, I knew what I would find inside. A tiled floor stained with bloody circles like clouds in a toddler's finger painting. The towel used to mop up the mess. And somewhere hidden to the eye, whatever remained of the child.

Before returning to my room, I stopped beside the door to the upstairs laundry. I saw a pair of Charlie's tiny footie pajamas. They lay there, light blue and fuzzy, and I was glad that I found them first, because if Ian were to see this he would likely collapse. Mumble. Pace. The church, the sippy cup, the toy car. Helena and the meadow of bones.

I slipped back into bed, took two more Advil, and wondered about his six murdered employees. I could only guess that they were down there in Ian's basement. I imagined their hands were tied behind their backs and they wore blindfolds. I pictured them being in their midtwenties, handsome and swarthy with olive skin that was now leathery and partially devoured, with neat round bullet holes through the backs of their heads. They were down there in the dim, lined up, all wearing tennis shoes, gold wedding bands and stiff blood-crusted dress shirts. There was duct tape stuck in the short hairs at the base of their necks. They waited, as I did, for Ian to finally bury them.

My God. What he had seen. I finally understood. He would never recover.

When Ian came home from his assignments he was always happy to see me and Charlie the first few days. "I have gotten better, don't you think?" Ian would say, hugging me from behind, his mouth against my hair. "We're happy, aren't we? Petal?"

I always answered yes, because we were, but it was more complicated than that. We were haunted in our happiness. That shadowy bastard of impending doom which followed Ian home from Iraq had now taken up residence in our home, cryptically leaving clues for me: an empty half gallon of vodka hidden under half a dozen crumpled Coke cans, a broken glass beside his computer, weeks' worth of cigarettes overflowing in the basement ashtrays, angry, almost illegible notes jotted down on receipts and Post-its, our overgrown yard across from Wayne's picture-perfect garden—and cobwebs. Real cobwebs down in the dark, looping and swaying and dangling like dramatic curtains all around the basement I avoided, dotted with dead bugs.

Those clues told me that impending doom was planning on impending for some time. Those clues made me fear that I was not doing everything that I could to keep my child safe. What would Ian do if I were to tell him that this was not what I wanted?

When Charlie was nine months old, Ian came home from Somalia and was so excited to see us. He and I made love within minutes of him walking in the door, and then he went and picked Charlie up out of his Little Tykes Activity Center and gave him a huge hug and a kiss. The following day Charlie started running a fever. By that night it was 101. By early the next morning, his fever was 103. We were new parents, and we didn't know what to do. Ian drove us to Children's Mercy, and Charlie was seen by a kind woman doctor whose face is a blur because I was so upset. There is nothing about the visit I can remember except Charlie's hot skin against mine and how limp his little body felt in my arms. My fear and rising hysteria made the room fade to black along with the doctor's words. "This probably sounds like a silly question, but has anyone traveled to Africa recently? We have to ask."

I remember thinking, *Ian has brought home death to our baby.*

Eventually Charlie got better, and it was nothing to do with Ian at all. But I knew. He may not have brought a tropical virus into our house, but he had brought other dangers. He still saw things he wished he didn't have to see. Ghosts. He spent more and more time in the basement. Things between us, they would get worse and then they would get better. Worse and then better. And then worse.

Until Charlie was about two, whenever Ian was home he and I walked into his little room together every night to look at him sleeping in his crib. On the bookcase was a soft pastel pyramid of pillow blocks and on the wall there was a colorful mural of a wind-rattled tree. The room smelled of baby lotion and hope, and we squeezed each other's hands. Each night we then crossed the hall and walked into the room where I slept. We kissed good-night and told each other that we loved each other, because we truly did. Then I would slip under the down comforter in the massive chilly master bedroom, tiny on the veritable continent of our enormous California King, and Ian would slowly make his way back down into the basement.

MADDIE

Eight days before

I tumble her clean bedding with a scented dryer sheet. I fold and refold her towels. Fresh flowers. Just a small bouquet, in a slim vase by the window. I place a bottle of Aquafina and a pretty glass cup on her bedside table, along with a box of tissues and the remote for the television. Out of nostalgia I place a good-quality merlot with a bottle opener, two wine-glasses and a giant Toblerone on a tray in the middle of her bed. This visit is going to change everything.

Between cleaning the house, preparing the spare room for Joanna's visit and trying to throw in some fun activities (television mostly) for Charlie, I've finally found a free moment to do my homework assignment for Cami J. I'm ready. Charlie is just down for his nap, and I probably have at least an hour.

Homework for Dr. Camilla Jones
The Bad Accident
By Madeline Wilson

My mom, dad, and my sister Julia and I had been visiting Grandfather Carl and his new wife, Vickie, at the cabin she owned on Lake Tapawingo in Missouri. Julia was nine years older than me. She was home for the summer from Brown University where she was quietly transforming from my secretive, sweet older sister into a very skinny and serious marathon-runner planning to be a doctor of infectious diseases.

Vickie collected ceramic dogs. As I pulled on my pink one-piece suit with the ruffle over my nonexistent ten-year-old chest I was surrounded by dead-eyed shih tzus, poodles and Yorkies. Her bedroom smelled of rose and menthol. An open box of Russell Stover's chocolate cherries sat on the bedside table, the whole forgotten mess turned dusty white. Outside the window, a wind chime fluttered frantically. I was the first to head barefoot down the hill into the fishy, sticky warmth hovering about the fetid lake.

Everyone else was still in the house changing into their swimsuits. I stood on the dock as my frail and defiant grandfather backed the speedboat, which with its dull gray hull looked to be his contemporary, away from the shore. It had belonged to Vickie's first husband, and I doubted that it had been used much, if ever, since his death five years earlier. My grandfather frowned darkly as he looked over his shoulder at the shuddering rear of the stubborn old boat while his knotty, spotted hands struggled with the controls.

"Come on down, the water is fine," my grandfather yelled to my parents and Julia, who were picking their way over gravel and skirting spiky blue grass on their way down to us. Rotten wooden cabins collapsed toward the water, dragging with them dream catchers, decorative yard ducks, wicker chairs, hummingbird feeders and terra-cotta turtles. Crushed Coors cans floated in the algae and weeds.

Julia was the first to ski. She skimmed across the lake with her strong legs gracefully together, her hair waving crazily in the wind and spray. I went next. I was a decent water-skier, but it took me a couple of tries to get out of the water because my grandfather's driving was choppy. I waited for him to bring the boat around to pick me up, watching the outdated propeller blades toss up lake spit like a frightening pinwheel, each eroded petal bloody brown with rust.

My mom was smiling at me from the boat, and my dad was nodding encouragingly, his chin bobbing up and down. Julia's face was tilted upward, taking in the sun. My grandfather gave me an A-okay sign with his fingers, just before he swung the boat toward me and accelerated.

He had dementia. To be honest I'm not sure he even knew my name. Why my mom let him get behind the wheel of that boat is anybody's guess and probably the main reason she never got over the accident.

He ran me over. He hit me in the shoulder and it hurt but not bad. I dropped the rope and surfaced, filled with relief. That was when I saw the outboard propeller blades churning toward me. I was being pulled toward what suddenly appeared to me as teeth in a monster's mouth, the rope being sucked in like a piece of spaghetti.

"Stop the boat!" That must have been my mom, though it sounded nothing like her.

"I did," barked my grandfather. He was wrong. What he had done was put it in reverse. That was why I was being sucked into the mouth.

My dad yelled my name. I saw terror transform his face before he jumped. My dad leaped from the back of the boat and threw himself between my body and the propeller, but he sank. He tried to exchange his life for mine, but he was too heavy and I was too light. Just as my dad's body dipped down below mine in the water, I was sucked toward the blades and jerked back and forth until I was restrained. The rope had cinched around my waist. When my dad surfaced, it was too late. I had not been cut at all, but the rope was wound many times around my body, strapping me to the propeller and the boat.

My head was only six inches under the surface. My mom was leaning out over the back of the boat, looking down. I could see her face upside down and backward. She was shouting and pointing. I still can't say whether it was the distortion of the water or really her expression, but I remember her face melting and her mouth an O as if she was that poor person in Edvard Munch's, "The Scream."

My dad was next to me by then, scrambling, choking on the lake water himself, his hands pulling at my life jacket. My sister was there, too, her eyes open underwater to watch and meet mine, her silhouette backed by the sun, rippling gold through the muck.

I waited to be rescued. I was ten. My capable and loving mom, dad and sister were there with me. Of course, I waited to be rescued.

When my desperate mom yanked my arms out of my shoulder sockets trying to pull me up out of the water—that was when I realized how bad it really was.

Twelve years later, the weekend of my grandfather's funeral, my mom and sister dredged up the memory of the boating accident. They began to talk about it, and my father took out his hearing aid and mumbled something about coyotes and a broken fence. He had a hangdog slump to his shoulders as he left the house with a tool belt in one hand and a hammer in the other, off to fix or save something.

Julia sat in the kitchen with a Diet Coke. I was twenty-two, drinking wine in the afternoon because on that day it was acceptable in front of my family. Someone had died.

Julia recounted to me in a distant, technical manner exactly how she had rescued me. "Dad couldn't get you out. I guess I assumed he would save you. But, I had water-skied first and I had the advantage of having already operated that particular life jacket, so I was able to free you."

Julia spoke clinically, but I knew she loved me. She was not indifferent, just resigned. She'd become a pathologist who sifted through human body parts daily. She was intimate with our butchered collective fate. "When we got you out I saw that you weren't eviscerated." She paused for a sip of Diet Coke. "So...that was a good thing. I hoped that you wouldn't be brain-dead."

"He never apologized," my mom said quietly, forcefully from the ground. She was preparing the house for the funeral guests, crawling around on the floor, picking up whatever had been left behind after vacuuming. "He never apologized," she said louder, wanting a response. "And never offered to help with the medical bills."

"Come on, Mom," I said. "I forgive Grandfather. You should, too. Everything is okay."

"Is that what you think?" she asked, wide-eyed, looking up at me, pinched fingers holding a tuft of auburn dog hair. "Everything is okay, Maddie? Really? You've never been the same!"

I suppose she's right. I spent two minutes kicking and flailing and another four minutes not breathing and dangling before my sister accomplished the methodical and time-consuming act of untangling the rope from the propeller. Only then could she open the life jacket to pull me out into her arms.

Something had changed down below. Something profound had happened to me just before I lost consciousness. At the exact second that I gave up all hope of surviving, my mind sparkled with unhinged, ecstatic, unbridled euphoria, a joy of such magnitude that I was instantly captive to it, and of a replete and searing sensuousness so irresistible that I opened my mouth to take it all in more deeply. I knew with utmost certainty, as if it were as simple as two plus two or the sky is blue, that there was nothing at all to fear.

Then came the rescue. When I woke up on the dock, my pink ruffled suit was in tatters around me. I saw the anguished faces of my family, and the gape-jawed stare of half a dozen gray-haired gawkers in Tommy Bahama shirts. My dad stopped pounding on my chest, his face a mixture of wonder and disbelief. There were sirens. I was naked and in shock. As I vomited the lake out of me I remember a strange recurring thought. I'm free. A horrible taste in my mouth, grit and sludge on my tongue. I'm free.

Then there was the hospital, the whispering doctors and the drip of sedatives followed by a sensation eerily familiar to the bliss I had felt underneath the water. Finally there was the long sleep to the quiet whirr of the rhythmic metal machines. I spent six days in the intensive-care unit with a tube inserted in my neck, winding down into my lungs where filthy water from Lake Tapawingo pooled.

My mom was right. Of course she was right. I changed, and it was only then that my eccentric grandmother began to take such a keen interest in me. From my recovery on, I wanted to suck in the world, the whole world, with the same gasping desperation as the moment I gave in and sucked in that miserable crap-filled lake. I wanted to live. I wanted to live as if I had invented the word and it meant ten times more than it does. LIVE.

To be fair, I admit that I felt invincible after my accident. If there existed out in the unknowable beyond some sort of cosmic ledger keeping tabs, I had been crossed off, released. I'm free. Free to leap, free to fly close to the flame, free to gamble, free to make mistakes, free to go recklessly to places from which others had not returned.

I wanted to live so badly. I had to live! I had to run in the dark. That's what I was doing, running away in the dark at the campground. I had to escape. If I didn't, what would happen to Charlie?

So that's it then. That's it, Cami J. Oh my God. I was being chased. And maybe I didn't fall.

I finish with a gasp and a shiver. It takes me a second to realize that Charlie has already woken from his nap. He is half-way down the stairs, holding on to the rail and taking one stair at a time, rubbing his sleepy eyes. "Mommy? Mommy?"

"Here I am, Charlie." I am trying to breathe and allow my racing heart to slow. I've done it, I think. I've done it now. I've written the most important part.

"Can I have a snack?"

With shaking hands, I make him his favorite meal of Kraft macaroni and cheese with two round hot-dog eyes and a sliced hot-dog mouth. I give him apple slices and green beans, too, knowing he probably won't eat them. I turn on *Jack's Big Music Show* because now I need to call Wayne about the sump pump.

Just as I am dialing, our doorbell rings. My trusty neighbor.

I open the door and slap on my suburban mom expression. Bright eyes and an apple-cheeked smile. "Yay," I say, clapping. "Wayne to the rescue."

"I knew you were home. I saw you drive in." Wayne politely takes off his shoes as he enters and waves to Charlie. "Cheerio, young man!"

Charlie waves, but says, "Cheerio is goodbye," before popping a hot-dog slice into his mouth.

"You need to come over and see what I'm building in my garage!"

Charlie nods, mouth full.

Wayne turns to me with an exaggerated look of excitement, clapping his gnarly hands. He is such a hackneyed, funny old man. "I bet he'd like to help me build a birdhouse. Wouldn't that be fun?"

"That would be so fun," I say. "What a neat idea. I really appreciate this, you know. Thank you, Wayne."

"Ah, it's nothing, Maddie. Now, the sump pump is going to be in your basement."

"Charlie," I call across the room. "Eat your dinner and watch your show and don't answer the door for anybody, okay? I'm going to be downstairs with Wayne for a little bit."

Charlie looks worried. Wayne looks thrilled.

We walk down the stairs to the finished part of the basement, with Ian's computers, the pool table and the bar. I lead Wayne to the door in the back corner. "I'm not positive, but I think the sump pump is in here."

"Correctamundo. This is where it would be," Wayne answers, starting to open the door.

It's locked.

"That's weird," I say. "I didn't think it would be locked. I don't come down here much."

Wayne goes, "Hmphh," while he puts his hands on his hips and contemplates this new impediment with his bottom lip stuck out. Then he stands on tiptoe, reaches above the door frame and retrieves a key that is hidden there. Wayne looks pleased with himself. "It's something us guys do."

"Well, thank God for you."

The key works in the door and Wayne opens it. The bad part of the basement is dark. Wayne finds the light switch and then we can see.

The sump pump is at the back in the middle of the concrete floor. It's actually a little flooded, but fine. Two feet to the left of the sump pump is a black hefty bag. Falling out of the black mouth of the gaping bag are a dozen empty half-gallon Stolichnaya vodka bottles. Wayne looks at me to see if I have seen what he has seen; to see if I understand what this means. I stare back. My eyes are so wide that I can feel my scar stretching and pulling my skin.

"J-j-just before Ian left," Wayne stammers, spitting all over the place, "he came over to help me cut down that honey locust and he told me..." Wayne chokes up. "He told me that he had stopped drinking vodka a year ago. That he wanted to be a better dad."

I look at the pile of bottles. I cover my face with my hands to hide my shame.

"Maddie," he says, aghast.

"He told me the same thing, Wayne."

I raise my beseeching eyes but he's not looking at me. He is sidestepping fearfully around me to see something on the far wall of the bad part of the basement, his jaw hanging open, pointing with a knotty finger.

I look up, and there's the wall of water and the barrels of doomsday food. Ian's weapons are artfully hung behind the

278 | ANNIE WARD

shelving: knives, swords from around the world, an axe and a pick. Three gas masks. One is child-sized. To the other side is a massive double-doored gun cabinet. Lying on his work-table are three bows and hundreds of arrows. It's truly a sinister display.

Wayne wheels on me. He's shocked to the core. "Maddie," he exclaims again, and this time it's an accusation as well as a question. "What in God's name? We have to do something about this! He's out of control! You're not safe! And Charlie! What about Charlie?"

"Oh my God," I manage, struggling to hold back the tears. "Tell me! What should I do? Help me! Please!"

Please, Wayne. Please.

Wayne puts one skinny arm around my shoulders and pulls me close. I can smell lawn fertilizer and chewing tobacco and that indescribable something that seems to emanate from the elderly—a whiff of mortality. The faintest scent of stale breath and our impending death.

DAY OF THE KILLING

Diane sounded nothing like herself. Again she yelled toward the disheveled shadow in the doorway, this time more urgently. "Put the weapon down!" The baseball bat remained raised, poised to strike. Diane's grip tightened on her pistol, her finger just starting to squeeze the trigger. "Put it down! Now!"

The figure took another step closer. It was a woman. One side of her face was a disjointed mess like a jigsaw puzzle made of pieces that barely fit. The effect was ghastly. It was a walking corpse.

And then Diane saw the fear in the woman's good eye. Fear and exhaustion and relief. The woman dropped the bat and fell to her knees.

"Thank God," she said in a trembling voice. "We knew you were here. We heard the doorbell but we were afraid to come out. We were hiding but then I had to go find Charlie. He ran off. Do you know where Charlie is?"

Charlie, Diane thought. *I never asked him his name.* Charlie was a good name for him. Charlie with the chocolate eyes. Diane said gently, "Are you Charlie's mom?"

"Yes. I'm Maddie."

"Charlie's good, Maddie. He's safe. He's with one of our officers."

The woman laced her hands together as if in prayer and mumbled into them.

At that moment Shipps appeared in the bedroom door, gun drawn.

"It's okay, Shipps."

He switched on the light in the bedroom and took in the wild-eyed, injured women with alarm. He lowered his gun and said, "Sweet Jesus."

"We need to get medical attention for her," Diane said, gesturing at the woman who was still cowering in the corner.

Maddie, the one with the sickening eye, said, "That's my friend Joanna."

Diane's mouth dropped open. "This is your friend?" she asked. "This is the friend that you 'had over when Daddy came home'?"

Shipps saw Diane's expression of confusion. He said to Maddie, "There's a man in the basement. His driver's license says he's Ian Wilson. Is that your husband?"

Maddie tried to speak.

"Is Ian Wilson your husband?" Shipps asked again.

"Y-yes," she stammered. "Is he? Is he…" It was not clear if she was pleading with him or just petrified.

"No longer a threat," Shipps answered, doing a grim scan of the room.

"What happened?" Diane asked, turning to Maddie.

"My husband went crazy. He—he—" Maddie couldn't continue. The tears streamed down her face. She tried again. "He—he—" She could only gasp for breath repeatedly.

The woman was in shock. Diane supposed the answer to her own question was fairly obvious. "Try to calm down. We'll get to the bottom of all this shortly." She addressed Joanna. "Are you able to walk? We can call the medics to come get you, but it's much better when we don't have people stomping around the scene."

Jo winced and nodded. Then she reached up a hand for assistance.

As Diane helped Joanna down the stairs, Shipps's cell phone rang. "It's the coroner. You go ahead."

Diane, Maddie and Joanna exited the front of the house to pandemonium. The whole neighborhood was lit up like the carnival rides at the county fair. Two additional police cars had arrived and were parked, flashers on, just down the street. The new officers on the scene were walking around the perimeter of the residence, keeping up a constant chatter on their phones and radios. An ambulance, its own red top light sweeping in great arcs around the street, was parked in the drive.

As Diane escorted Maddie and Joanna to the ambulance, she noticed that in the back of Bill's squad car there was an elderly man in a John Deere baseball cap staring out the window toward the Wilson home with blatant apprehension. She met his eyes briefly and recognized him as the runner in the backyard.

Maddie didn't see him. She was busy looking for Charlie. She found him in the back of the ambulance and stumbled trying to climb in to reach him. He jumped at her so hard he nearly knocked her over. "Baby!" she said, hugging him. "You're okay! Oh my God. You're okay. We're going to be okay." She kissed the top of his head and held him tight. His arms encircled her waist.

One of the medics smiled. "You've got a nice kid there." He patted a blue padded fold-out bench. "You want to come back here and have a seat so I can check you out?"

"Yes," she said, extricating herself from Charlie and moving into the back of the vehicle. "But I'm fine. He threw me down and I hit my head, but I'm not hurt. My friend's the one who got the worst of it."

Diane helped Joanna into the ambulance, and the second young male medic motioned her to a reclining seat.

Maddie said, "Charlie, there's room over here. Come sit next to me." She darted a quick glance at the medic making notes. "Is that all right?"

"It's fine," he answered.

Charlie joined his mom and leaned into her body, head down. Maddie's fingers went straight to his curly mop of hair and started combing through it. Diane saw that she, like Joanna, painted her nails an unusual color. They were the same icy gray as her eyes but they were incredibly short, cut down past the tips of her fingers.

"Would it be okay for me to take some photos?" Diane asked, climbing in across from Maddie. "Did I hear you say you were thrown down?"

Maddie nodded.

"Could you pull your hair back? Maddie? You said your name is Maddie upstairs, didn't you?"

"Yes," she answered, pulling her hair back to reveal her eye and the scar.

Diane cleared her throat. "I'd actually like to see the other side. You'll probably have a nasty bruise there tomorrow. I take it that's where you hit the floor?"

Another tear slipped down Maddie's face as she tucked the hair behind her ear on the good side of her face. Charlie said, "Don't cry, Mommy," and that made Maddie's shoulders heave in silence with the effort to stop. Everyone was being so nice.

"Officer?" the medic with the beard said. "Can I have a quick word?"

Diane joined him. He nodded toward Joanna and said softly, "She has three broken nails. Probably defensive wounds."

"Right." Into her mic Diane said, "Detective Shipps? You'll want to bring an evidence kit to the ambulance. We need a nail scrape when you get a minute."

"Also," the medic went on, "the capillaries in her eyes have burst. Her neck is bad already, but the bruising won't get colorful until tomorrow. The red marks are consistent with strangulation."

She sure can scream, though, thought Diane, remembering with a shiver the moment the woman had opened those fiery eyes and lunged for her hand. "Thanks. I'll take over for a sec now, if you don't mind."

Diane gave Jo a sympathetic smile. "Upstairs Maddie said that you're her friend Joanna."

Jo tried to nod and cringed.

"I'm not going to ask you any questions right now. Rest your voice. Let me just get some pictures, okay?"

Jo's eyes stayed fixed on the ceiling of the ambulance. Her lower lip trembled as Diane photographed her neck and her eyes. When Diane asked her to lift her hair up so she could photograph behind her ears, Jo let out a sharp cry with the pain of lowering her chin.

"I'm sorry," Diane said. "That's enough for now. I'll need more tomorrow once the bruising sets in."

"Are we going to the hospital?" Maddie asked. "Or the police station?"

"Both. I'm afraid we'll need to separate you. First you'll see a doctor, and then a bit later once we're done here, you'll see my boss, Detective Shipps. There's a certain way it needs to be done. Joanna, being the more badly hurt, will go with these nice young men to the county Med Center." The EMTs both grinned. "You and your son will be driven over by one of the other officers behind the ambulance."

"Not you?" Maddie said, looking up with something like disappointment.

Diane felt strangely flattered. "Probably not. I was the first responder, so I'll likely be asked to stay until crime lab arrives. The detective, who is very nice also, by the way, will ask you some questions back at the station."

"And then do we come back here?"

"Not right away. First we have to do our job and have a look at everything. Detective Shipps will determine when he feels the house has been sufficiently processed. Sometimes it's a couple of days. Sometimes it can be weeks, but I wouldn't be too worried about that. I have a feeling they'll clear the house soon. And then when that's done..." Diane glanced at Charlie, tucked under Maddie's arm. His eyes were closed. Diane lowered her voice. "You'll need to arrange to have things cleaned up. One of the officers here probably has a card for a service you can use. I'll ask around. You won't want him to come home to—" she searched for another way to put it but couldn't come up with anything more compassionate "—a mess."

Maddie breathed in sharply and wiped her nose on the back of her sleeve. "I have two little dogs. Skopie and Sophie. Sophie gets nervous and scratches at the door whenever Ian yells, so I let them out when he started getting angry. I never let them back in."

"I saw them. They're fine, but I'm afraid we can't let two dogs have the run of a crime scene."

Maddie nodded helplessly and hugged Charlie closer. "I'll call my mom and dad to come get them."

"I'm sorry," Diane said, and she was.

Shipps showed up at the back of the ambulance. "I believe I've got a nail scrape to do?"

It took no time at all. Once Shipps had bagged his wooden stick and Q-tip, he said to the medics, "I'm done. How about you guys?"

They both nodded.

"All right then. Can I escort one of you into the house to get an official declaration?"

The medic with the bushy beard said, "Absolutely, sir," and jumped down to the pavement.

Shipps leaned in to speak with Diane. "You stay with the ladies until I'm done, and then we'll all meet just there on the lawn."

Shipps and the medic disappeared through the front door. A few minutes later CJ and Bill, the short, muscular, baby-faced cop who had tackled the intruder in the backyard, joined Diane at the back of the ambulance.

CJ whistled. "Every man and his dog came out for the show tonight, right?"

Bill nodded. "And Shipps said the chief is on his way."

"Well, not to cuss us out for once, I hope," Diane said. "I think tonight could've gone worse."

Shipps and the medic returned from the house. "Okay," Shipps said, motioning the officers to huddle around him a few yards from the ambulance. "The medic declared type black at—" he checked his watch "—twenty-two fifty hours. Bill, bring us up to speed on the party in your vehicle?"

Bill took a small notebook out of his pocket. "Wayne Randall, white male, five foot eleven, approximately 165 pounds, born on—"

Shipps interrupted. "I appreciate your attention to detail but it's late and there's lots to do, so let's cut to the chase."

Bill closed his notebook. "He's the neighbor across the street. Claims he saw Diane arrive. He was worried because he's always thought that the husband was a jerk who might be a threat to his wife and child. He came over to see if he could help, saw the gate to the backyard was open and then decided to peek in the back window."

Shipps crossed his arms over his chest. "Why'd he run?"

Bill laughed and then caught himself. He became very serious again. "He's got a number of unpaid traffic tickets."

"You're kidding," Diane said. "He could've gotten shot!"

Shipps pointed at Bill. "Did you put him through the system?"

"Yes. It's true," Bill answered. "He's not lying about the tickets."

"Hold on," Shipps said. "Stay right here."

He walked over to the ambulance. After a second, he helped Maddie out. He gestured toward Bill's police car. The old man in the John Deere cap was easy to see, his face bathed in flashing light. After a second, Shipps returned to the officers. "She confirmed it's the neighbor. Says he had nothing to do with what happened in the house. Bill, you're still going to take him in for questioning."

"So," Diane said, "what's the final story? I know the wife said the husband went crazy. He threw her down. He choked her friend. Then what?"

Shipps clapped his hands together and said, "Right. Let me go find out. I'm leaving for the station to prepare for the interviews. Bill, you take the neighbor with the very poor judgment to the station. CJ, you take the wife and kid and follow the ambulance with the injured lady to county Med. Diane, I'd like you to wait for crime lab. Take some photos for us, too."

As her colleagues scattered in different directions Diane shivered in the night wind even though it was warm and humid. One by one the vehicles pulled away, off to their various destinations. The officer who'd been assigned crime scene duty had not yet arrived, and Diane's car was dark. The house looked almost the same as it had when she'd arrived. Safe. She even heard a cricket start to chirp. Or was it a toad? She wasn't sure. But she knew about fireflies, and there they were, returning after having been scared away, many cheerful little sparks in the night.

The vocal of the two dogs in the backyard suddenly resumed its outraged barking. A page had been turned.

Life went on.

DAY OF THE KILLING

Diane went to her squad car to retrieve a pair of latex gloves. She took a deep breath as she entered the house for the third time that night, steeling herself for the photos and videos she now had to take. She could handle it. She had not had to find the worst; the thing she had feared the most after seeing the water table and sandbox. Someone was dead, yes. But not a child.

She decided she would start in the basement.

As she started down, there hung on the wall a beautiful red-and-yellow African batik, with a black canopy tree like an elegant umbrella over a landscape of elephants and giraffes. One just like it had hung in the living room of her childhood home. Her dad had brought it home from Liberia when she was little. This house brought back memories. The African mask on the first floor and the tall military combat boots by the front door. Soldiers liked their souvenirs. The batik painting made her miss her dad. She was now fairly sure that this was a soldier's home.

The basement stairs, similar to the ones leading to the upper floor of the house, were winding and carpeted. The bloody handprints looked like something out of a Halloween haunted house. She photographed them and continued to follow the blood, feeling increasingly nervous. There was no valid reason for it. The assailant was dead. No, she thought, correcting herself. The man was dead. He may have been an assailant, but he was also quite obviously a victim. She reminded herself that she still didn't know what had happened.

She saw his legs first and felt her heart flutter with sympathy. He was sitting up, and for an electric second Diane thought perhaps he was not dead at all. It looked as if he had slid down to a sitting position to rest his head in the corner. His back was against the wall, his legs straight out and splayed, and there was blood pooled in the carpet underneath him. One arm had fallen to the side, and there was a broken unlit cigarette between his fingers.

He wore a short-sleeved T-shirt, and his arms were attractively muscled and tan. They were, however, covered in a thorny bramble of red scratch marks. Defensive wounds inflicted by his victim. His face, too, looked as if it had been scratched. Long slivers had been carved from his cheeks.

Diane took a video and a number of photos and noticed that the menacing man had bitten his fingernails like a nervous schoolboy, evenly and to the quick. Diane imagined him taking the cigarette out, realizing he had no lighter and failing to finish that last intuitive action when his life ebbed away.

Diane finished photographing him and began her inspection of the basement. A few feet from the man's body was a desk, a swivel chair and two computers. On one computer screen there were rows of brightly colored candy. At some point earlier on the day that he died, someone had been playing Candy Crush. On the other computer, a screen saver cycled through photos. The man holding Charlie. The man lying on the couch and laughing while the two Boston terriers licked his face. The man and Maddie dressed as Vikings, wearing giant horned hats, maybe on Halloween.

Diane turned back to him. He simply appeared to have chosen a bad place to fall asleep. She leaned closer to get a better look at his face and allowed that he was more handsome than what you usually find around Meadowlark; attractively carved features and very frank, dark, sad eyes. The boy's eyes. He was a big man. Not just big, but powerful. Solid. Diane supposed that he could be very intimidating. However, as the whimsical whistling Candy Crush song played softly in the background of his death, he did not look like the bad guy.

Suddenly the door upstairs slammed, and Diane's stomach flipped. *It's okay*, she thought. It's Seth. Seth the indie rocker from the Kansas Bureau of Investigation Crime Lab. She'd only run into him a couple of times at crime scenes, but if she ever went to The Crooked Crow on a sunny Sunday afternoon he was certainly there, wearing a Beck or Sonic Youth T-shirt, drinking a pint of beer on the patio.

Instead of going up to greet Seth, she decided to stay down in the basement just a little longer. The nervousness had passed, and she rather liked the quiet. A momentary restful respite from the police banter and her daily dose of little disappointments. Though the blood was revolting, she found that in the man's dusky vault it was not so hard to just look away. Look beyond. Maybe even close her eyes to it all. There was something about the privacy and the security of the man cave that was soothing and reassuring. She wished suddenly and wholeheartedly that this house had been a safe one for this man and his family.

But, no. Not a vault. A crypt.

Diane followed the direction of Ian's last gaze. The partially open door to a secluded part of the basement leaked a thin trail of light out into the otherwise darkened room. She adjusted the flash on her camera and went to have a look.

The time ticked by, and Seth, unrecognizable in his coveralls, face mask, gloves and booties, moved quietly around the Wilson home. Diane had finished taking her photos. She'd even taken some more videos and walked around the house a third and fourth time. She'd gone outside and spent some time talking to Mark Harrison, the patrol officer who'd finally arrived on crime scene duty. He would be spending the night at the house. Someone would be required to stay there continually until Shipps had decided that all the evidence had been collected and the family was free to return.

The coroner had stayed only a few minutes. He was an unpleasant man, and Diane was relieved that he didn't engage her in conversation. Once he left, she knew it wouldn't be long before "the crew" arrived. They would go into the house, bag the body, tag it, take photos and carry it out to their van. Then the man now slumped against the wall in the basement would officially cease to exist. He would never come home again.

Diane yawned and realized that she was famished, drained and very sad. She wasn't needed here anymore. It was time to go home. The main floor was dotted with little numbered placards, and Seth paced restlessly with his enormous camera and massive flash. She walked up next to him and said, "How's it going?"

He pulled off his mask. "Good, thanks." He was scrawny with ridiculously unkempt patches of scraggly facial hair, but he had nice green eyes, a button nose and ears that looked a bit like an elf's.

"I'm about to take off," she said.

"Yeah. That's fine." He gestured around the house. "I

haven't even finished the ground floor. I'll be here another four or five hours."

"That's a long night," she said.

He grinned. "I do longer nights when I'm not working."

She laughed. "I bet you do. Anything you might be able to tell me now?"

"Yeah, for sure. But you know, I'm the evidence tech and Matt's the lab tech, so officially I just collect and he analyzes. But if you want to know my opinion, that's cool."

"Yes," Diane. "That would be great."

Seth seemed legitimately excited to share his thoughts. Though he was obviously intelligent, he expressed himself like a teenage skateboarder. *Which*, Diane thought, *is probably exactly what he had been about ten years previous.*

She smiled at him as he waved her over enthusiastically and started pointing things out. "So here we have a big, bloody knife. That's the one that did the nasty. And over here, what do we have? A clean little baby knife. Big bloody's little bro. I can't see anything on it, but that doesn't mean there isn't anything there. Underneath the fridge? We have a cut-off ballpoint pen with the ink removed. People use those to sniff all kinds of dope, everything from OxyContin to coke, so we'll have that tested and see what sort of freaky party was going down. There were lots of adult beverages being had, and glasses being broken and what have you. Looks like there was certainly a pretty big brawl. I'm no blood guy, but I can tell you that our dude was killed here in the kitchen, and then Mr. Drippy walked over to the middle of the living room where he fell down in his own blood and then he was like, 'Oh no, I've fallen and I can't get up!' He kind of squirmed around like a beetle on its back for a while. But then he did get up because he continued on drippy-dripping over to the basement stairs. That's where I'll be hanging out next. The bloody basement." He winked and gave her a thumbs-up.

"Well, okay then," Diane said, nodding and amused. "Very helpful." She supposed that one might need an odd sense of humor in his line of work. "Thank you so much. Good night, Seth."

"Good night, Diane. Hope to see you at The Crooked Crow some weekend."

"Me, too," she called pleasantly as she walked out.

The sky was gray at the east and feathery with the first morning clouds as Diane pulled into her apartment parking lot. Inside, she filled a water bottle, took off her clothes and slipped into bed. Before turning out the light, she made a quick call to Shipps.

"You home yet?" she asked.

"Just now."

"Where did they go?"

"Madeline Wilson's parents' house. Farm out on Ridgeview Road."

"And so how were the interviews?"

Shipps laughed and said, "Oh my goodness. Interesting, to say the least. Joanna Jasinski was apparently a sailor in a previous life. I kind of wanted to say, 'You kiss your momma with that mouth?' but then I thought, you know, she doesn't seem the type to kiss her momma at all."

"What's the upshot?"

"They both said that they were a hundred percent certain Mr. Wilson was going to kill Ms. Jasinski."

"So we've got Jasinski claiming she killed Wilson in self-defense."

"Nope! What we have is Madeline Wilson stabbing her husband to save her friend."

"What?" Diane nearly dropped the phone. "You're shitting me. She looked like a quivering fawn in the headlights of a freight train."

"I know. I was shocked myself."

"Granted, I didn't get to speak with the ladies as long as I wanted between the uncontrollable tears, the boy being present and the need for medical attention. I can tell you, though, I didn't see that coming."

"Yeah. The interviews are, I cringe to say, pretty entertaining. You spoke with the women more at the scene than I did. Can you watch the interviews and let me know if you see anything that rubs you the wrong way? Keep an eye out for discrepancies?"

"Of course, Shipps."

"But now go to bed."

"Okay. You, too."

"Get a few hours, Di."

"I'll try."

Instead of going to sleep, Diane got up, pulled on a robe and walked into her little living room. She opened up her Facebook account and did a search for Madeline Wilson. She was in luck, and Madeline's account was public. The profile picture was a sweet one of Maddie kissing Charlie on the cheek, and the banner was Maddie and Ian in hiking gear, standing atop a mountain with their arms raised in triumph. Both photos were pre-scar.

She scrolled down and saw that the most recent post was six days earlier. It was a selfie of Maddie and Joanna. It looked like it had been taken outside the Kansas City Airport. The women were both wearing big sunglasses obscured by tons of tangled, brown, windswept hair. Their smiles were huge and happy. One of Maddie's hands was hooked over Joanna's shoulder squeezing, long pointed gray nails like talons. The caption said, "Look who's come to visit! The woman who speaks eight languages and doesn't know how to say no in any of them! Let the wild rumpus start!"

Diane wondered about these women and their past. It made her uneasy. She scrolled down, and the next photo was from a couple of months earlier. It was Ian at sunset, kneeling on a rock with one arm around Charlie and the other pointing up at the constellations that were just barely visible in the lavender sky. Charlie was looking up with innocent, wide-mouthed wonder, and Ian's arm was wrapped around him so protectively that Diane suddenly felt like she was a horrible voyeur, attempting to find something morbid in what appeared to be intensely beautiful.

She slept too long, and when she woke the sun was already up, the day sure to be uncomfortably hot. She was disastrously late to work, and then she remembered. Today wasn't like the others. A man had died. His wife had killed him.

DAY AFTER THE
KILLING

Sweet Water Creek was on Diane's way from her apartment back to the police station. She turned into the subdivision and was surprised to find it fairly lively. A young lady was out pushing a stroller, a few construction workers were gathered around a hole in the ground and a man in a track suit was running with his German shepherd. She drove past Ian and Maddie's house and checked to make sure the yellow police tape she'd stretched across the front door was intact. She waved at Lacey Freemont, Meadowlark's only other female officer. She had replaced the night officer and was now sitting outside the Wilson house in her car. Lacey didn't wave back. She was staring intently at her phone.

Diane pulled up in Wayne Randall's driveway. Before she could even unlock her door to get out, she could see him trotting toward her from his side yard on his spindly legs.

She stood up next to her squad car and gave him her friendliest smile. "Hello there!"

Wayne was out of breath by the time he reached her, and his face was covered in grayish dust. He was holding a hand trowel, and the knees of his jeans were muddy. He must have been weeding. "What happened to them?" he demanded. "Nobody told me nothing. What happened?"

Diane nodded reassuringly. "I'll be happy to bring you up to speed, Mr. Randall. It's Randall, isn't it?"

"Yes. Wayne Randall. I live here." He took a quick sip of air and cleared his throat. "Is she all right? And Charlie?" His face scrunched up in a little knot when he said the boy's name. A tiny snort of emotion escaped. "And Charlie?"

"Madeline and Charlie Wilson are both okay."

Wayne looked up, his old eyes watery and red. "I saw them come out last night, so I knew he didn't kill them. I just wanted to know what he'd done to them in there."

"Is that why you were in their backyard? Because you wanted to know what had happened?"

"Yes, ma'am. I was worried about her and the boy."

Diane studied Wayne carefully. "Did you think Ian Wilson was a dangerous man? Someone who might hurt his family?"

"Have you been in the back of that basement?"

"Yes."

"That man has an arsenal down there."

"There are a lot of apoca-people around."

"The vodka? What about all those bottles of vodka? You should have seen her face. I was with her when she found it."

"It doesn't look good. You're right. But drinking a lot and being lazy about taking out the trash in and of itself is not a crime."

"Well, a crime has been committed, hasn't it? For you to be here all night and again today. What's he done?" Wayne stomped his foot on the ground. Some strands of gray hair came loose from his comb-over and started dancing crazily in the breeze. "Huh? Well? He told me...more importantly he told her. He said that he was done with the vodka. Poor Charlie! What did he do to them? Tell me! What did that good-for-nothing son of a bitch do?"

A half hour later, Diane was standing in front of the refrigerated soft drink aisle at the gas station, staring at the selection. Her hands were in her pockets, and she rocked back and forth from heel to toe, toe to heel. Eventually the teenaged cashier walked over and said, "Hey, Officer."

Diane snapped out of it. "Oh hey there, Emily."

"A lot to choose from. I like Dr Pepper myself."

"What?" Diane had not even been seeing the drinks. She had been somewhere else, thinking about that photo of Maddie and Joanna that had been posted on Facebook. It was nagging at her, and she couldn't figure out why. "Oh right," she said, laughing. "God. I barely slept. How long have I been standing here?"

"Kind of a long time."

Diane smiled at the girl and said, "And you know what's the worst part? I came in for a candy bar!"

Back at the station, Diane sat down at her desk in front of her computer. She'd accessed the shared file with the videos and had Shipps's interview with Maddie up and ready to go. She broke off half of a KitKat bar and pressed Play. Shipps was cautioning Maddie. "This interview is being recorded. You have the right to—" Diane pressed Pause.

The camera was mounted in the upper right corner of the tiny interrogation room, so Diane found herself looking at Maddie and Shipps from above. She could see their faces, but only in partials, and it was hard to read their expressions. She fast-forwarded ahead a few minutes and pressed Play.

Maddie was giving Shipps her personal information. "Madeline Elaine Wilson, maiden name Brandt. My date of birth is December first—"

Diane fast-forwarded again. Maddie was still talking. "… dad was in the air force but became a CPA. My mom sold residential real estate. They're both retired—"

Diane searched ahead again. The next time she stopped, it looked like Maddie was crying. Diane broke off another piece of KitKat and turned the volume up.

Shipps said, "It's okay. You're doing fine."

Maddie wiped her nose with the back of her hand. "So, Joanna got here last weekend. Yesterday, I guess that was Friday, I got a call from Ian's cell phone asking what I was doing, which was weird because usually we Skype. We'd been to the swimming pool earlier, I remember. But when he called, Jo and I had taken Charlie and the dogs to the dog run at Heritage Park. I didn't tell him I was with Jo or that she was visiting or anything. I just told him where I was and that I would be heading home soon. Also he seemed, like, unusually happy? And excited? And he said to me, 'Hurry home, babe, and Skype me,' because he had a surprise." Maddie hunched over in her fold-out chair. She mumbled, "Oh my God."

"You're all right," Shipps said. "Take a deep breath."

Maddie sat back up and gnawed on the side of her thumb. "And umm. When we got to the house, he was there. He was home. That was the surprise. I was like, fuck! This is bad. Well, so, he and Jo were very shocked to see each other. Obviously. Very shocked. It was tense and so uncomfortable, and I was worried."

"What was your primary concern?" Shipps asked.

"Just the two of them. Together. Their history."

"What history?"

Maddie spoke very quietly. "They don't like each other."

"Why not?"

"I don't know if there's a reasonable explanation," Maddie

said with a futile wave of the hand. "Some people just don't get on."

"Okay. What happened next?"

"Ian made small talk with us and played with Charlie for about twenty minutes, and then he went down into the basement. You know, the basement. Where he goes. So."

Shipps wrote something down. "What's in the basement?"

"His stuff. His computers and stuff."

"Look, Maddie," Shipps said. "I've been in that basement."

"Well, then you know what I was dealing with!" she answered, in a voice more shrill than Diane would have expected.

"What was he preparing for?"

"I don't know. I can't answer that question. I'm not sure what he was doing. I'm not even sure I know who he was anymore."

"And what did you and Ms. Jasinski do while he was in the basement?"

"What did we do?" Maddie asked, looking lost. "We stayed in the kitchen. We stayed in the kitchen, and I made a corn dog for Charlie, and I started to make the grown-up dinner. Ian came up and said, 'I'm going to pop into town,' and he left. He was gone a long time. I fed Charlie, and then finally when Ian never showed up, Joanna and I ate, and I put Charlie to bed early. Later he came back with wine and vodka and some, like, cheese and stuff. It was weird but that's Ian. Kind of unpredictable. I was happy, though. Like, wow, maybe he's going to be nice."

Shipps waited for her to go on, and when she didn't, he prompted her. "Uh-huh. And then?"

"He asked me to put something together. A cheese-board thing. He said, 'We have a guest and I made it home in one piece from Nigeria and we're going to celebrate!' I kind of sensed he was being sarcastic, but I didn't want to rock the boat. I just put out the cheese and crackers hoping he would keep calm. He and I have had some bad arguments the last couple of years and sometimes he scares me, and that's what was happening. I was starting to feel scared."

"Scared of what, exactly?"

"That he would get angry and start yelling."

Shipps reached out and put a tentative hand on her wrist. "Has he ever hurt you, Maddie?"

"No." She paused. "Not that I know of."

They sat in silence.

"What happened to your eye?"

"I fell. On a camping trip. It was an accident. That's what Ian said happened, but I can't remember it. I got a concussion. There were two police officers there when I was getting my stitches who said my injury was inconsistent with a fall. But I always believed Ian when he said that I fell. Recently I started to have some questions about that night, but I never, I never... Let's just say that I have always, umm, maintained that I fell."

"Right. And where were you treated?"

"Glen Haven Hospital. Close to Estes Park."

Shipps was writing. "Glen. Haven."

"Yes."

"Okay. So you set out some food and then what?"

"And then we all sat down at the kitchen table. Ian drank vodka, and he wanted us to drink vodka, too, but we didn't. We drank wine. For a while, it seemed like it was going to be okay because we just talked about Ohrid and the Irish Pub. Hillbilly Buck and Milosevic and Macedonia. We were even laughing about Club Lipstick and the boys of Vengeant. But we'd been drinking for a while by then, and Joanna can be, well, sort of mouthy. She mentioned the fact that Ian thought she'd tried to get him fired back then when we all first met. She said something like, 'I can't believe you thought it was me,' and he said, 'It was you. You were lying then and you're lying now.' That was what did it."

Diane pressed Stop. She got up and walked over to the door to Shipps's office. She gave a perfunctory knock on the glass door, and he responded by waving at her to enter.

She leaned inside. "What're all those strange words she keeps using?"

Shipps laughed. "Are you enjoying the interview? It's some Eastern European language. The pair of them, they're what you call multilinguals."

"You make it sound kind of dirty. Wink wink."

"Wait until you meet Wayne," said Shipps with a huge smile.

"Oh I met him! Wayne. Wayne Randall. Wayne Randall sure thinks that horrible man got exactly what he deserved."

"Told me the same thing. Called him a disgrace, a nut, a liar and a loser."

"Oh that's nothing. I was told Ian was a good-for-nothing son of bitch, as if this whole thing is a 1920s western."

"Ha! Wayne is not a fan of Ian Wilson."

Diane made a face. "Hmm. Might be that Wayne Randall is a very big fan of Maddie."

"Bit old, isn't he? To have a crush?" Shipps chuckled and sighed. "She's a striking woman, all right. Back in the day? I wouldn't have kicked her out of bed for eating cookies."

"Please. I've got enough gory shit to wade through here without any more from you."

"Sorry."

"Her eyes, though," Diane suggested. "They're strange, aren't they?"

"Very. Shame about the…" He gestured to the left side of his face with disgust.

"Do you think he did that to her?"

"I know the police in Glen Haven, Colorado, think he did that to her."

Diane gave this some thought. "Okay. I'm going to go finish." She walked back to her desk, sat down at her computer and pressed Play.

On the screen, Shipps was leaning forward toward Maddie. "What do you mean, that was what did it?"

"That really pissed him off. Ian laughed out loud and drained his glass of vodka and then he smashed it on the floor. He yelled at Jo, 'I can't believe you're still lying about everything.' And then she was yelling and saying he was the liar and she was going to tell me—"

"Tell you what?"

"They had, like, an affair. A long time ago. And Ian laughed again and said, 'I already told her about hate-fucking you.' That's when Jo stood up and slapped him."

"Ms. Jasinski slapped him?" Shipps asked, leaning back as if stunned by this news.

"Yes." Maddie started crying violently, and it took her some time to regain control. "And he went wild. He knocked stuff over. I finally decided I better do something. I picked up the house phone and was going to call 911. But then I heard Charlie say, 'Mommy?' Oh God, it was terrible. Charlie was coming down the stairs. The noise had woken him. Ian yelled at him. 'Go back to bed! Go back to bed, or I am going to fucking murder you!' I ran over to Charlie. I caught him at the bottom of the stairs, and I told him to run back upstairs, to run away fast and go get back in bed. I think I must have pressed Talk on the phone because someone was on the line, but just then I looked back over into the kitchen, and Joanna was on the floor. Ian was on top of her. I asked the operator to hurry, to please help us. Then I dropped the phone. That's when I went back to the kitchen to help her. I didn't know what to do. There was a knife in the sink." Even though the camera was mounted high, Diane could see that Maddie was shaking. Visibly.

"Take your time," Shipps said, sounding concerned.

It was hard for Diane to make out everything Maddie said after that because she was talking through tears, but it sounded like, "I stabbed him in the back. I did! Oh God, I did it. I stabbed Ian and then, and then… He didn't stop strangling her after that, so I did it again. And then he finally let go. He rolled off her and I helped her up. He looked at us and said the same thing he'd said to Charlie which was, 'I'm going to fucking murder you.' Umm. So we ran. Jo was very weak, so I had to help her. We had to go find Charlie. And once we were upstairs we decided to hide. Joanna was barely functioning and I had Charlie with me and I thought Ian was still coming after us. What was I going to do? Try to get a hurt woman and a toddler out of the house? We hid. And then soon after, the lady officer was there."

"All right, Madeline. I think that's enough for now. Do you have anything further you would like to say?" Shipps asked.

"No. Except that I'm sorry." Maddie dropped her head onto her arms. "I didn't want to kill him, I just wanted to stop him from hurting her. I loved him. Oh my God, I loved him so much. I didn't mean to. God forgive me."

"Hey, Diane."

Diane jumped out of her skin. CJ was standing beside her and she hadn't even noticed, she'd been so focused on thoughts of Madeline Wilson.

"You scared the shit out of me, CJ!"

He laughed and set a can of Budweiser on the desk next to her mouse pad. "Shipps told me to bring this to you."

"What?" Diane said. "It's not even three o'clock."

"Are you watching his interview with Joanna Jasinski?"

"I'm about to."

"He said you might need a drink."

Diane leaned back, belly laughing. "All right then. Thank you!"

She pressed Play. Shipps was cautioning Joanna. "It's my re-

304 | ANNIE WARD

sponsibility to let you know this interview is being recorded. Anything you say can and will—"

Fast forward. Play.

Joanna was speaking in a monotone. "Joanna Marie Jasinski, Richmond, Virginia."

Diane fast-forwarded again. Joanna was ticking things off on her fingers. "Amnesty International, a brief stint at Doctors Without Borders, several refugee relief organizations. Women and children mostly. I was the project manager for Focus on Family, which operates under the umbrella of—"

Diane pressed Fast Forward again.

Shipps appeared to be looking for something he'd written in his notebook. "If you would just give me one second—"

"One second!" Joanna said loudly, looking outraged. "One second? We've been beating around the bush for an hour. Can we get to the fucking details already?"

Diane popped the tab on her Budweiser.

Shipps sighed loudly enough that Diane could hear his exasperation. "It's required information, Ms. Jasinski. I understand that you're frustrated."

"Do you? Do you really? Ian Wilson almost killed me. This has been what I call a really, really shitty night."

"Why do you think he did that?"

"Because he was an alcoholic shit stain with PTSD who was spiraling into psychosis."

Diane slugged some beer and wiped her chin.

Shipps played with his pen. "Did you slap him?"

"Yes, I fucking slapped him."

"Why?"

Joanna leaned back in her chair and crossed her arms over her chest. "He said something I found to be offensive."

"What was it?" Shipps waited a long time, but no answer was forthcoming. He went on, "You two had a complicated relationship? Yeah? No?" Again he waited and got nothing. "You had a sexual relationship, right? Way back?"

Joanna gave in. "Ugh. Yes. A few times. Until I figured out that he stabbed me in the back."

Shipps gaped at her for a second and then said, "Care to rephrase?"

Joanna considered this and then burst into laughter. "No. Oh! Oh fuck. Sorry. Until he stabbed me in the—" She literally could not stop laughing. At one point she was hugging her stomach and her mouth was open, but no noise was coming out. Eventually she recovered. "Oh my God," she said, wiping her eyes. "Yeah, that was bad. That was totally unintended."

Shipps tried to move on. "All right. So what do you mean by that?"

"When we all first met I was working in a part of the world where you sometimes have to bend the rules a little to get things accomplished. I was trying to get supplies delivered to some refugee camps, and I paid some people to help me achieve that end. Ian knew about it. He thought I'd tried to get him fired from his job, so he tried to get me fired from mine. He told people I was involved in some illegal stuff, and it worked. I was let go. He was a dick. I told Maddie to forget him. I certainly warned her against dating him, God forbid marrying him and having a child with him. I always knew— and let's be honest—I think everyone always knew that this is the way that relationship would turn out."

"With him stabbed to death in his own home?" Shipps asked deadpan.

"With one of them dead. Better him than her. He's a monster! Did you see what he did to her face?"

"You're sure Ian Wilson did that to her?"

"News at eleven! What the fuck? She doesn't know what happened for sure because her head was bashed in, and now she can't remember that night, but Ian, ever so helpful Ian, he helped her piece it all together. You're buying that? She fell, poor baby, she fell in such a way that two cops in Colorado detained her all night trying to get her to admit that her husband bludgeoned her with a tree branch! But Maddie's all, 'No, he wouldn't. No, he didn't.' Bull fucking horse shit."

"I'm going to check that out."

Joanna rolled her eyes like a teenager. "Really! Well, good for you. You want a trophy? You are a police officer."

Shipps said calmly, "You're off the charts angry. That makes me wonder."

"That makes you 'wonder'? What are you, a six-year-old? I'm angry because I was nearly murdered earlier tonight, my throat is killing me and I'm still sitting here talking to you when I want some ibuprofen, a whiskey and my bed."

"I get it. Just walk me through your version, and I'll get you all home, okay?"

Joanna bent toward him. "We came home from the doggie playground, and Ian was there. He was not excited to see me, okay? He started drinking. Maddie was scared and nervous. He left the house for a while and came back with bags of booze and some cheese and crackers and said, 'Okay let's play nice. Let's all be friends.' That didn't last. He starts making Maddie cry with stories about how he and I used to get together. Awesome, right? Super cool. He was being an asshole, and I told him so. He started shouting at me and wagging his finger in my face. Okay, no. I don't take that bullshit from anyone. I slapped him. Then he went for me, and we were like, wrestling. Maddie grabbed the phone and I was glad. It was time to call 911 on him. But then we heard Charlie crying. The poor kid had woken up and was standing at the bottom of the stairs. Maddie went over to him. Ian was yelling at him. I think Charlie was saying 'Daddy, I'm sorry,' and Ian answered, 'I'll make you sorry.' It was horrible, seriously. The next thing I know, I'm down, I'm on my back. He takes a comfy seat on my stomach and wraps his hands around my neck and starts squeezing. I'm pretty sure at that point it would have been over for me if not for Maddie. He weighs probably two hundred pounds. I started to pass out." Joanna started crying, and Diane was momentarily shocked. The woman seemed untouchable. "I thought I was going to die."

"Are you okay?" Shipps asked. He sounded sincere.

And then Joanna started laughing again. Diane took several large gulps of her beer. "Hell yeah!" she said, waving one arm wildly. "I'm okay. I'm way better than okay. I'm alive! Thanks to Maddie. Because instead of him finishing up the job, he, like, just stopped. Then he let go. But then he grabbed my throat again. He was squeezing and clenching his teeth and looking right in my eyes. And then he let go again. I didn't even know she had a knife. He fell to the side, and I saw Maddie. God she was like a ghost, she'd gone so white. She helped me stand, and he looked up at us and said, I'm going to kill you or murder you, something like that. Maddie had to practically drag me across the room. I couldn't have made it up the stairs on my own. I think she was holding me up. I don't know how she did it, but she managed to get me upstairs and get Charlie, and we all went and hid from Ian. And that's that. You know the rest."

Shipps looked relieved and closed his notebook. "Okay. I guess we're done. Nothing more to say?"

Joanna pretended to think about it, her hand curled girlishly under her chin. "Oh no, sorry. I wasn't really paying attention. Can we please go over it all one more time?"

After reviewing both the interviews a couple of times while she finished her beer, Diane went back to Shipps's office and knocked.

He waved her in, winked and said, "Have you been drinking, ma'am?"

Diane blushed despite herself. "So Joanna Jasinski is a piece of work."

"A live one," Shipps said. "Oh yeah."

"So," Diane said, looking confused. "Where are we? What are we thinking?"

Shipps swiveled in his chair, turning away from his computer to face her. "Bill's been speaking with the family in England. I'm just waiting to hear back from the Criminal Records Department in Liverpool and I've got a three o'clock call with two homicide detectives from Kansas City who may come out for tomorrow's interviews with the women. After the interviews we'll have a debriefing."

Diane nodded but didn't move. She looked at Shipps with a sheepish expression. Shipps gave her a fatherly smile with a tilted head. "Are you asking me what I'm thinking?"

"Yes."

"I'm thinking it was defense of another. Which, like self-defense, is justifiable homicide and not a crime. No crime, no arrest. Nothing further."

Diane looked troubled. "Really?"

"Really," Shipps answered. "Were there any discrepancies in their stories? Anything you were told at the house that didn't match up with what you just heard in the interviews?"

"No, but—"

"But what?"

"I've got a feeling. I'm just not sure."

"Well, nobody's sure yet," Shipps said, going back to his computer. "And that's why we're busy dotting our *i*'s and crossing our *t*'s. Right? No rest for the weary."

The next morning Diane applied a bit of makeup and wore earrings. This was a deviation from her routine. The earrings were little silver studs; the only nice jewelry she owned. She was not allowed much jewelry on the job. Studs and a wedding band, which was non-applicable in her case. With a hint of blush and lip gloss, Diane felt a tad more confident. Shipps had called early and asked if Diane could sit in on the interviews between Maddie and Jo and the Kansas City homicide detectives. For some reason she was feeling unsure of herself.

When she arrived at the station the only person there was Bill. He did a double take. "You look nice today," he said, staring. He realized he was gawking and abruptly looked away, thrusting his hands into his pockets like a seventh grader.

Diane sat down at her desk and started typing a list of questions for the interview.

1. Why was a broken ballpoint found on the floor of the kitchen?

2. Same question. Small paring knife found in the same place. Why?

3. Why was there a bloodstained baby blanket on the stairs when no one upstairs was injured? (Follow-up question: Assuming it was used to wipe blood from Madeline's face, why would a woman fearing for her life and the life of her child stop running from a threat in order to clean up?)

4. You hurted me. Who hurt Charlie? When, where and why? No one mentioned Ian hurting Charlie.

Diane hadn't gotten to the sudden transformation of Maddie's fingernails and was still typing when Leslie, the very young, sweet blonde office administrative assistant, tapped her on the shoulder.

"Officer Varga?" she said, obviously a little bit excited. "The lady murderers are here."

Diane stood up and took a deep breath. "And the homicide detectives from Kansas City? Are they here as well?"

"They're not coming," Leslie said, her face falling. "Didn't you get my email? They looked everything over, and they're not interested. They're not coming."

"Not interested? So it's just me and Detective Shipps?"

"Detective Shipps is on an important call with the district attorney. He'd like you to start without him."

"Oh," Diane said, ashamed of how afraid she sounded. She was a patrol officer. She was not supposed to conduct this type of interview.

"Don't worry. He'll be joining you right away."

"Okay," Diane said, picking up her notes and smoothing her hair back in its bun. "No problem."

She walked rather stiffly to the front of the station, where Maddie and Jo were waiting. Charlie was not there. Diane stood up very straight. Why were these women so intimidating? They filled up rooms with their worldliness, their big words and their general aura of disdain. They made Diane feel even smaller than she was.

Jo wore a bright, bohemian, fringed scarf around her neck. Diane paused, looking at Maddie's hand brushing back the dark hair at her temple. There was something about those very short metal-gray nails, almost bitten in appearance, but straight and neat.

Maddie noticed Diane's fixed stare and folded her hands into fists. Diane forced her eyes away and said efficiently, "Okay then. Shall we get started?"

Jo laughed, her voice hoarser even than the day before. "Go on, Mads. I brought a book."

"I'd actually like to start with you, Joanna. May I call you Joanna?"

"Just call me Jo."

"All right. You and I will chat first, if that's okay?"

The two women glanced at one another, and Jo shrugged. "No problem."

"Maddie, I'll be with you shortly. Jo? If you would just follow me?"

Diane led Jo past the coffeemaker and the bathroom to the tiny interview room.

"The same lovely accommodations as last night?" Jo said unhappily. "The eensy-weensy room. Can't we talk somewhere we can actually breathe?"

Diane said, "Sorry," as she used a remote control to turn on the camera. "This is where we do our recordings."

Inside was a card table, two folding chairs and a fan on the floor in a corner whirring softly on low. Diane switched the fan to medium and said, "Summer in Kansas. Sorry."

Jo shrugged.

"My superior usually runs these interviews. He'll be in shortly."

"You call him that? 'My superior'?"

"Sometimes I do. I suppose. So, you're being recorded now, and it's my duty to tell you that you have the right to remain silent—"

Joanna said, "Yeah, yeah yeah."

"So," Diane went on. "I know you've been an aid worker most of your life. That's really admirable."

"Well, thank you, Officer."

"But you're unemployed now, though?"

Joanna glared at Diane with the intensity of an insulted adolescent. "At the moment."

"And where do you live, Joanna?"

"I go back and forth between the States and Europe. Right now I'm in Virginia."

"That sounds nice. I always wanted to travel. I always wanted to go to Italy and just eat my way around."

Jo looked tickled and stifled a laugh. "Awesome, you should do that. You look like you'd love it."

"You like it, going back and forth?"

"Not always, but yeah, it's okay."

"First time in Kansas?"

"No, I have a vacation time-share in Wichita."

"What? You're joking!"

"Who the fuck has a time-share in Wichita? Of course I'm joking. I have been here, though. Probably five times in the early nineties, visiting Maddie and her family."

"That's nice."

Joanna laughed and looked incredulous.

"Well. Okay. First things first," Diane said, "Let's get another look at your bruising."

As Jo began loosening the scarf, Diane said, "The reason, really, that I wanted to talk to you first is because you hadn't seen Maddie in a long time, and then you got a pretty intimate, long visit with her just prior to what happened. Did you notice anything off? Did she say or do anything in the last week that might have given you reason to believe that Maddie was angry at Ian?"

"Yeah. He promised her the world and then stuck her in a suburb in the middle of nowhere, got her pregnant and then when there was a screaming baby to make shit worse, he took off."

"Did she say that or is that your take?"

"That's my take."

"Do you think that could have made her angry enough to want to kill him?"

Joanna paused, her fingers still hooked in her scarf. She stared Diane down with disgust and disbelief. "Maddie loved Ian. She loved him from the minute she met him. It was like a disease. Do I have any reason to believe that Maddie was angry enough at Ian to want to kill him? I'll give you a good reason why Maddie might have been angry at Ian."

Jo pulled off the scarf, revealing a neck mottled with red and brownish marks. A few dark purple impressions dimpled the skin at the rear of her neck, where the force had been the greatest. "Why don't you write this down? *According to Joanna Jasinski, Madeline Wilson was very fucking angry at her husband Ian. For trying to kill her best friend. Got it?*"

Diane swallowed and nodded. Then she raised the digital camera and took the photos in complete silence. Finally she said, "You can put your scarf back on now if you wish."

Jo moved slowly, deep in thought. "You know something?"

Diane looked up. "What?"

"Maddie called you. She called 911 before anyone got hurt. She tried to stop what was happening. You should be ashamed of yourself, going after her. She called you for help, and you didn't get there in time. This, Officer Varga, is on you."

Behind Diane, the door opened. It was Shipps. "Ms. Jasinski," he said amiably, "we're done for the day. You're free to go."

Diane whirled around, her mouth agape. "What?"

"Yeah. Sorry, Diane, I'll bring you up to speed shortly, but these ladies can go. Both of them."

Joanna stood up and continued tying her scarf back in place. As she walked past Diane she gave her a sidelong look of triumph.

When she was gone, Diane looked at Shipps with helpless disappointment. "I had my list!" she said. "I didn't even get to my list."

Shipps patted her on the back. "Come into the lunchroom for the debriefing. I think you'll understand."

Diane followed Shipps to the lunchroom, the only room in the station large enough to host a team meeting. CJ, Bill and Leslie were already seated and waiting. Shipps pulled out Diane's chair for her and she sat. He paced.

"Okay," he said, going over a printout in his hands. "This

is what I got from criminal records in Liverpool. When Ian Wilson was a military policeman in Germany he was investigated for grievous bodily harm when he ran over a soldier with his police car during an arrest. He did tours in Rwanda, Bosnia, Iraq and Northern Ireland just to name a few. At least one army psychologist thought he was dangerous enough to deny him clearance. He was arrested in Chester, England, five years ago for punching his fist through a car window and grabbing the driver around the throat. CJ, tell everyone what you told me. Everything you gathered from the family."

CJ stood up like a high-school debate student giving a speech. "Ian Wilson had nine brothers and sisters, seven still living. Mother and father passed away. His sister Lynn was not surprised. Said he was a 'lovely boy' but had a ton of problems including alcoholism and PTSD. His brother John was devastated. He confirmed the PTSD and a fondness for vodka. All the others said pretty much the same. A good man destroyed by war and liquor."

Shipps put a hand on Bill's shoulder. "Son? Let's hear what you shared with me on Madeline Wilson and Joanna Jasinski, please."

Bill had only a Post-it, stuck between his finger and thumb. "Nothing on Madeline. Joanna has a misdemeanor for using a false ID."

"That's it?" Shipps asked.

Leslie tittered and then went silent. "Nothing else," Bill said again. "Nothing more than that."

Shipps pointed at Diane. "Neighbors?"

Diane wiped her suddenly sweaty hands on her pants as if trying to figure out how to proceed. "He's not a popular guy. That much is clear but..."

"Not a popular guy doesn't quite cut it, Diane. His own family admitted he was bad news. The neighbor told Bill last night that Ian was sarcastic, rude and antisocial. He also said he was a psychotic alcoholic doomsday prepper who seemed the type who might hurt his family."

"I'm not sure that Wayne Randall is actually a credible—"

"And finally," Shipps said, interrupting. "Matt at KBI Crime Lab was kind enough to offer some early, unofficial reactions. Blood splatter looks consistent with Ian Wilson being stabbed in the back while hunching over Joanna Jasinski's body. The knife used is the one Madeline says she used. The home phone smashed at the base of the stairs is consistent with the 911 call we believe was intended to stop the escalation of violence. The scrapings from under Joanna's nails are skin. We're waiting on DNA, but given that Ian Wilson's face and arms are torn up, we can reasonably conclude that the skin under her nails will turn out to be his. Joanna Jasinski was strangled nearly to death. That's confirmed. We've all seen the basement. The wife was seeing a therapist who corroborates the narrative that the deceased was a broken, secretive, delusional and dangerous man."

Diane leaned over and put her head in her hands.

"Diane?" Shipps said.

"Nothing," she said. "I've got nothing."

"We also have a number of things Madeline Wilson wrote for her psychologist that, in my opinion, seal the deal."

"And how'd you get stuff from her psychologist?" Diane asked, not bothering to hide her skepticism.

"I didn't. When I asked, Ms. Wilson volunteered copies of the documents. I'm telling you, this guy was scary. He was like a character out of a Guy Ritchie movie. He was a fucking time bomb."

"Then why didn't she just leave him?"

"Many women don't, Diane. It doesn't make them liars. And I want you to know that the reason I stopped your interview is that I've already spoken with the district attorney. She agrees with me that we're looking at justifiable homicide.

She won't sign off until the labs are back, but we both agree that this is a no-brainer."

Shipps was right, Diane realized. The local prosecutor, Elizabeth Monroe, had started her career in St. Louis volunteering at shelters and prosecuting domestic violence charges. "So no arrest," she said, trying to wrap her mind around the speed and finality of the decision.

"No crime."

"Right."

"No crime, no arrest. Justifiable homicide." Shipps stood up and stretched, signifying the end of the team meeting. As CJ, Bill and Leslie walked out of the lunchroom, Shipps offered Diane a sympathetic smile. "The most obvious example of my career."

Diane tried sadly to crack a joke, trying to realign with him. "Or the only?"

"I have seen a body before."

"Your wife's, you mean."

"I'm going to tell Megan you said that," Shipps said, touching her shoulder. "Oh and, Diane?"

She looked at him, expecting another joke.

His expression was an unexpected blow, a mask of controlled rage. "If you ever enter an active crime scene on your own again, child involved or not, I will not keep your fucking secret. Understand? I will report you to the chief. I'm not happy with you right now."

Diane's shame rushed over her body like she'd been doused with warm water. She bit her lip and walked away as fast as she could, so that Shipps would never know that he'd made her cry.

When Diane arrived back at her desk, she was shaking and entertaining thoughts of quitting her job and moving to Alaska. Or Costa Rica. Anywhere. She hated Shipps. No, she didn't hate Shipps, she hated being reprimanded. But she'd known what would happen, and she'd done it anyway. And she'd do it again.

Waiting for her, like a slap in the face, were the photocopies of Maddie Wilson's writing therapy. She resisted the urge to sweep them off her desk along with her phone, stapler and files in progress. She squinted and leaned down to read the Post-it Leslie had stuck to the top of the pile. Dammit, on top of everything else now she needed to get some reading glasses.

No luck getting anything from the hippie psychologist, the note said, *but it turns out Madeline Wilson had photocopies of all their work. Shipps asked me to leave these on your desk. Here they are. (What a basket case! ☺)*

Diane started to read through the photocopied pages. Her eyes skimmed over the heartbreaking confessions.

When Charlie cries. Anything bad happening to Charlie.

When Ian drinks vodka in the basement. Or when he won't wake up.

When Ian gets angry at Charlie.

When I have to leave Charlie with Ian.

Jo, this hurts. I hope you still don't think I chose him over you. I didn't. I swear to God that's not what it was. It was just a mistake is all. I made a mistake and I'm sorry. I would love to see you again.

I wanted to live so badly. I had to live! I had to run in the dark. That's what I was doing, running

318 | ANNIE WARD

away in the dark at the campground. I had to escape. If I didn't, what would happen to Charlie?

So that's it then. That's it, Cami J. Oh my God. I was being chased. And maybe I didn't fall.

Diane made a face and then felt ashamed. Why? Why, somewhere deep in her gut, did she still have doubts about this timid, anxious, fearful, loving mother? Was her doubt (and, yes, that little bit of righteous indignation) all because Ian was a soldier like her dad? Probably.

She needed to learn to be more objective. It was clear. The journal entries helped confirm everything Detective Shipps believed; Maddie had lived in terror of a man who was bottoming out, binge-drinking and doomsday-prepping. He'd been to all the worst, most evil places in the world, seen plenty of murder and had become either numb enough or damaged enough to become capable of trying to commit it himself.

Diane felt troubled by the fact that while both women claimed Ian Wilson had threatened the child, neither one had said that he'd actually physically harmed him. And yet the child had been in shock, repeating, "You hurted me," when Diane found him. She was also bothered by the bloodstained baby blanket, those bizarre fingernails, the baby knife and the ballpoint pen. Emotionally she couldn't stop brooding over Candy Crush and the happy family photos on the computer screens, the backyard abundant with toys for both dogs and kids, and those two little Boston terriers that seemed very eager to return to life with such a horrible man. Such a horrible man with those half-closed, kind, sad eyes, searching for someone or something in the dark corners.

Nevertheless. Case. Closed.

IAN

Day of the killing

Ian caught a glimpse of himself in the rearview mirror, along with the curious eyes of his young Uber driver who appeared to be working up the courage to start a conversation. What will Maddie say? he wondered. Not only was he tanned from the Nigerian sun to the color of a toasted nut, but he'd been sick and lost some weight as well. Optimistically, he imagined the combination probably made him look a bit younger and fitter, and she might quite like that. In any case, even his George Hamilton tan couldn't be any more amusing than when he'd shown up in New York with his hair dyed like a hyena. He laughed out loud.

The kid smiled in the rearview mirror. "You seem to be in a good mood."

"I'm forty minutes from home, and I haven't seen my wife or my son in three months. I'm in a fucking great mood. If only I could get the smell of soot and ash out of my nose everything would be perfect."

"Sorry?"

"Nothing, mate. Don't worry about it. Just get me home."

"I'll do that, sir."

Ian rubbed his nose and began to wonder if he really was going to be stuck with the smell of the massive fire in the Nigerian oil field forever. Eh, it didn't matter right now. In a short time he'd be on the couch tickling Charlie and fussing over the dogs, and Maddie would be most likely cooking him his favorite, a big pot of steak chili.

He smiled out the window. The flat countryside sped by the highway as they drove south from the airport. It was a dry summer, and the fields were yellow and stunted, but Ian still felt comforted by the simple beauty of the quiet home he'd found.

He got out his phone and called Maddie.

"Ian?"

"Hiya, Petal! What're you doing, baby?"

"I'm at the dog park." Pause. "With Charlie. Where are you? This isn't Skype."

"I'm almost home. Get your arse back to the house so I can take you in my loving arms!"

"There's been a misunderstanding, Ian."

"What do you mean?"

"I thought you weren't going to be home until next week."

"I'm sure I said this week."

"You didn't!"

"Well, no worries, hon. It's not as if I'm going to be cross with you if the house isn't tidy, for heaven's sakes! I just want to see you and Charlie. We can order pizza if there's no food in. Actually I quite fancy the idea of that jalapeño special from Sarpinos. We can do that."

"Ian?"

"Yes?"

"I'll see you at the house, okay? Try not to be mad when I see you. Please. There's nothing I can do about it now."

"Come on, Maddie. What in bloody hell is going on?"

"I'm going to get Charlie and the dogs and go home now, okay? I'll see you there shortly."

"Maddie, you're winding me up!"

"I know. I'm sorry, I know. I'll see you at home."

"Fine." Ian hung up and smacked his fist down on the car seat.

Having noticed that Ian's mood had taken a severe turn for the worse after his phone call, the young Uber driver remained silent as they skirted Kansas City and headed for the southern suburbs. Ian was scowling now, wondering what bullshit he was going to find at home. Maddie had been acting differently this summer. The Skype calls he had made from the oil compound had been met with a frostier reception than in years previous. He suspected she was upset about her injury, but he had seen all sorts of uglier accidents over the years, and her disfigurement wasn't anything a good plastic surgeon and a decent budget couldn't fix.

What worried him more was how furious she had been about their argument the night of the accident. Did she actually believe that he planned to leave her and Charlie stranded in Kansas for the rest of her "good years" while he bounced around from Azerbaijan to Tunisia to Yemen? If only he could trade places with her! If only she could spend all that time in third-world airport lounges and secure compounds; all that time she thought was so precious and lovely and all to oneself, and he could be the one to stay home and watch cartoons and eat chips and cookies with Charlie.

How would she like it? To her, travel was chardonnay on the terrace, and to him it was body odor and bombs. However, a little voice whispered. However. She had put up with quite a lot over the years. As he had once confessed to her, he knew he was glum and angry and paranoid. And still, she'd scratched his head and tickled his face while he lay on her lap watching the horror movies that he preferred to her comedies and dramas. God knows she'd been a devoted mom to Charlie. Best of all, Ian still liked getting drunk with her and rehashing all the same stories about the Balkans—the horseshit heavy-metal band, the crotchless panties on the waitress from the pizza place, the throat-and-crap dinner and the night the mountain burned.

The last couple of years had been hard. Ian had known he was not going to be some star student when it came to learning how to be a new dad with a tiny baby. He had warned her. And then there had been all that shit with Ebola! Seriously? Fucking health-care workers, who should bloody well know better, were getting on airplanes with fevers. And Maddie wanted to take the baby to Spain? Right. Like that was going to happen!

I'm not sure what she was expecting, he thought, somewhat miserably. He had changed a few diapers, administered the occasional bottle and supervised one or two baths. But if she could just wait. Just be patient with him. Boys get big, and then they play video games and sports and go camping. They learn to use weapons and talk about famous battles and history, and he would be fine then, wouldn't he? Yes.

So he hadn't earned any medals when it came to helping out with an infant. So he hadn't wanted to travel on a hot and crowded airplane with her and Charlie to some ridiculous destination that screaming Charlie would never remember, the whole trip torture and Ian in a nasty, defensive mood. Why subject any of them to that horror? He didn't like to snap at Maddie. It was just better now to keep things simple. Simple. Not her desire for a vacation in Bulgaria. Or Thailand. Or New Zealand. Good God, why couldn't she just relax for a bit and enjoy not working and being at home while Charlie was little? Did she even know how many times they would have to change planes to get to New Zealand? Charlie would go mad. But she wanted more than camping. Understandable, really. She was a bloody woman after all.

He'd decided not to accept another assignment for at least six weeks. He'd take Maddie and Charlie somewhere easy, like an all-inclusive holiday retreat with childcare. In Mexico. It was foreign and they spoke another language, and that would appease Maddie. He knew you could fly there direct from Kansas City. Doable. Play with Charlie half the day, give him over to the nursery the other half and drink wine and lie together in bed or next to the pool. He would tell Maddie when he got home, and hopefully it would make her happy.

Ian used his key to enter the front door. Sophie and Skopie leaped off the couch and raced toward him, so excited that they lost their footing on the shiny hardwood floor, sending them crashing into his shins. He dropped down to one knee and let them jump on him and whine, relishing the taste of his fingers as their stubby tails wagged back and forth as if powered by motors.

After a bit, he stood back up and looked around. This was strange. He waited. Usually Maddie and Charlie came running to him together from the kitchen or the stairs.

Maddie slipped quietly out from the bathroom at the other end of the great room and stood still, looking at him.

Ian dropped his bag and walked toward her, arms open for a hug. Her eyes looked glassy, as if she had a fever. "Hi," she said, giving him a weak embrace. Then she inclined her head toward the chair in the corner.

Ian looked. Joanna was slumped there motionless, her hands plunged in her pockets, her wild hair hanging everywhere. Ian's jaw dropped. He hadn't even noticed her, and now his adrenaline was making him see spots.

"Hey there," Joanna said. "Surprise."

"Holy. Fucking. Hell. You've got to be kidding. I thought I was uncomfortable in the middle of a Nigerian oil inferno. That was nothing. Right! I'm off!" He turned his back on them and started heading back to the front door.

Maddie ran and stood in front of him. If he'd lost weight, she'd lost more. She was very pale, and her eyes were puffy as if she'd been crying. Also, it became suddenly clear to him that she was absolutely terrified and shaking, almost as if she were about to faint. "I was lonely, Ian," she said. "I missed her. I made a mistake about when you were coming back. I've been making a lot of mistakes since the accident. I saw a new doctor, and he said I may have some sort of brain injury. I'm sorry. I'm so, so sorry."

"What kind of brain injury? Why didn't you tell me?"

"I don't know. I didn't want to worry you. I know how stressful your assignments are, and I didn't want to make it any worse for you. You hate being away from me and Charlie, and if you knew I might be…sick…you would probably just have quit and come home. I didn't want to mess up your job."

"Oh, Maddie. The job wouldn't have mattered." He turned and looked at Joanna with helpless hatred.

"My psychologist thought it was a good idea to get back in touch with Jo. And she was right. We've worked everything out. She's been so helpful this last week. I really have been feeling better, and it's thanks to her. Please, let's all try to be adults about this?"

Ian rubbed his chin as he and Joanna stared at one another. She stood up and walked over ever so sweetly. He looked back at Maddie, seeing naive hopefulness and that horrible scarred eye. "Okay, Petal," he said.

He extended his hand. "Truce?"

Joanna regarded him darkly from under her curtain of hair and shook the hand he offered with a fake smile. The awkward moment was interrupted when, from the staircase, Charlie cried, "Daddy!"

Charlie clambered down the stairs and then across the house excitedly. Ian picked him up, and he slung his little legs around his waist. *My God, he's gotten so big*, thought Ian, beaming at him. Charlie ate it up and squealed as Ian bounced around the room for a minute singing a song from his childhood in England. "So I went to my granny's but my granny wasn't in, so I sat on the chair and the chair fell in!" Each time the chair fell, Ian whooshed Charlie down to the ground and back up again in his arms. Charlie was laughing in a delirium of happiness. Skopie and Sophie saw that it was playtime and began circling them, barking and jumping up on Ian's legs.

"More, Daddy. More! More!" This was the first time Ian had heard 'Daddy, more, more,' and loved it. His son had gone from a baby to a boy while he was gone.

"I went to my granny's but my granny wasn't in, so I sat on the chair and the chair fell in!"

Joanna walked past Maddie. She whispered, "I'm going to my room. Call me when this show is over."

"What's that?" Ian said, looking at the two of them. "Is everything all right?"

"Joanna's going upstairs for a bit," Maddie answered, her eyes crawling the floor.

"She doesn't have to. She's perfectly welcome to stay down here."

Joanna trotted up the stairs without another word.

Ian approached Maddie with Charlie still clinging on to him like a baby monkey. "It's okay, Maddie. I'm not angry. I'm not going to say a word. Except…"

Maddie perked up. She cocked her head to the side. It was a challenge. "Except?"

"Since yesterday morning," he said in a low, warning voice, "I've only had to pass through three shitty airports."

Maddie reached out and gently took Charlie. "Baby, you know those drawings you did for Daddy? The ones up in the playroom? Go get them so you can show Daddy!"

Charlie ran off, and Maddie turned her eyes back to Ian, who was waiting. "Three shitty airports," she prompted, making the boo-hoo face she usually saved for Charlie.

Ian breathed through his nose while he took this in and then leaned very close to her, his face almost touching hers. "Yes. Full of transport workers that can't be trusted and people who don't have the slightest idea how to queue. Several men were dragged out of the crowd and hit with a baton. In two out of the three airports I was in today, half the crowd was staring at me because I'm white, of which a good percent probably were hoping I was going to get pulled out of line and get my head lopped off. It would have been awesome of you to have the decency to inform me that I was going to be ambushed at home as well."

Maddie looked away in an unfocused manner and mumbled, "I haven't been myself. I mixed up the days. I'm sorry."

Ian didn't know what to say. What he wanted, in the worst way, was for Joanna to disappear, to order pizza, and for him and Maddie to play with Charlie and the dogs. There was no way that was going to happen. Suddenly Ian very much wanted to have a cigarette in his basement. "I'm going downstairs."

"Charlie's gone to get some drawings to show you. I'll send him down, is that okay?"

"No! I don't want him down there when I'm smoking. Tell him I'll be up shortly."

Ian planted himself in front of his computers, lit a cigarette and started to play Candy Crush instead of one of his strategic war games. He wanted something mindless. The time slipped by and he felt better. He should go up and see Charlie. See the drawings. Tickle some more. But Joanna was up there. He'd heard her come down a half hour earlier.

Fuck it. He trudged up the stairs and stood, a stranger in his own house, looking across the open living room to the kitchen. Charlie was sitting in front of the television with some sort of snack on a paper plate, Maddie was cleaning out the dishwasher behind the bar and Joanna was drinking wine and looking at her phone.

He took a deep breath and marched over to the women, skirting Charlie's toys littered across the hardwood floor. His conciliatory smile was a surrender flag. "Okay," he said, nodding first to Joanna and then to Maddie. "I won't pretend this is not a little awkward, but what the hell? I just got home, and I'm in the mood for a laugh seeing as how the bastards failed to kill me yet again. I'm starving and I need a drink. Anyone else need a drink?"

Joanna pointedly took a sip of her wine.

"Joanna, I see you have a drink. That's good. I'm going to just go out and get some cheese and crackers and more wine—you ladies do like wine, right? Just kidding. We'll make it a nice night like we used to, back in Skopje. Maddie, do you need anything from the store? Anything to make dinner?"

"I've got leftovers for later if that's okay. Chicken and rice?"

Ian had been living on a diet of mostly rice and stringy meat, and it was literally the last thing he fancied. "Awesome, Mads. I'll be back shortly with some tidbits and wine. Joanna. We're really in need of a catch-up!"

After careening out of the driveway as if he had just looted the joint, Ian hit the steering wheel of the car several times. Ninety days in the goddamn sun and then home to this bullshit. It took less than a second for him to decide that he was driving out of the way to Gambino's for one drink before he went to Walmart.

It ended up being two glasses of white wine, his reluctant drink of choice ever since he'd sworn off the vodka that had made him a surly insomniac and nearly ruined his marriage.

He didn't look up from the bar except to order and pay, and the pretty girl serving him leaned over on her elbows in front of him. "Having a rough day?"

"You've got no idea." He left and drove to the store. He rolled through the giant aisles at a fast clip. His detour to Gambino's meant he had been gone a long time. He grabbed a French baguette. A soft cheese. A hard cheese. Salami. Olives. Grapes. Check out.

The Nigerian assignment had been a dry one, and after three months of not drinking, he noticed the effect of the wine. He squinted as he negotiated the small-town streets from Walmart to Premium Stock. He picked up two nice bottles of chardonnay for the women and then found himself staring longingly at his favorite vodka, Stoli Elit. After a wistful second he walked away, picked up a bottle of the pinot grigio, which was his inoffensive alternative to vodka, and paid for it along with the chardonnay. He had a pit in his stomach as he drove home.

He marched into the kitchen with his bags and a yell. "The party has arrived!"

Maddie stepped out of the downstairs bathroom with her finger to her lips. "Let's keep it down for twenty minutes. I've only just now gotten Charlie to bed."

Ian nodded. "I'm going to go up and give him a kiss goodnight."

"You'll wake him," Maddie said.

Ian considered this and answered, "I haven't seen him in ages. I'm going to give him a kiss good-night. Without you complaining, preferably."

Ian went into Charlie's room, the room where he and Maddie used to hold hands and watch him in his crib, and sat on the bed. On Charlie's nightstand was a small plastic cup with water and the home phone from the charging station in the master bedroom. Charlie had never had sippy cups. When Maddie first brought one home, Ian had told her to throw it away—he couldn't stand the sight of it. Ian knew he was damaged, and many times he'd thought to himself that he should never have had a child.

But he was so happy that he had.

Charlie was asleep, making soft noises as he breathed in and out. Ian smiled. Despite his early doubts, Charlie was the best thing that had ever happened to Ian. He pulled a green-and-black paracord bracelet out of his pocket. He slipped it over Charlie's wrist and pulled it snug. "I made you a new one while I was away, matey. This one's called a viper."

He brushed Charlie's hair back and kissed his forehead. As it occasionally happened, he was knocked over sideways with affection for the boy and an even stronger need to protect him. It was a wounded world, to be sure, and Ian no longer cared for it. Back in Iraq he'd had those daydreams about one day living in a cabin in the woods with Maddie. Now he wanted it even more, but for Charlie. The three of them together, safe, off the grid, cozy and warm with a nice big satellite dish for internet and movies. Ideally he'd have an underground bunker in the backyard in the event of a "worst-case scenario." If the world was to be terrorized by savages and run by brutes, then they would just leave it behind.

"I love you," Ian whispered, and for a second Charlie's eyelids fluttered open, and he saw his dad.

He held out the new stuffed Minecraft cow that Ian hadn't seen before and said, "Kiss Moo Moo." Ian obliged. Charlie smiled and snuggled down into his pillow, asleep again and content.

"I do love you," Ian said again. "And I always will."

Three, maybe four more years of savings, that was all Ian needed. There was still time to leave the world behind.

Ian picked up the phone from the table and returned it to the charging station in the bedroom. He didn't want it ringing and waking Charlie.

★ ★ ★

Downstairs, Maddie and Joanna seemed to have come around. There was even a bottle of Stoli Elit sitting on the granite bar that separated the kitchen from the rest of the great room. "What's going on?" he asked, gaily picking it up and turning to Maddie with a smile.

"I bought that a few weeks ago," she answered. "I thought that when you got back you might like a real drink."

"What about our deal?"

"One night, a little splurge. No biggie."

"Just tonight?" he asked.

Maddie nodded. "Just tonight." Joanna laughed out loud at this and then continued scrolling through her phone.

Ian joined Joanna at the breakfast table with a friendly, if slightly forced, smile. He drummed his fingers on the glass top as Maddie made the drinks.

"So you're just back from Nigeria," said Joanna, finally putting her phone away.

"Yes. Port Harcourt. I was looking after a group of firefighters from Boots & Coots who had been sent down to try to put out a fire in a government-owned oil field."

Maddie brought over Ian's vodka rocks and wine for herself and Joanna. Ian patted the chair closest to him, and she sat.

"And it took three months?" Joanna asked.

"Don't get me started. It took forever. What with the preparations and then removing all the melted machinery from this gaping bloody pit where the ground had collapsed. And the smell! Anyway. I'm not complaining."

"Yes, you are," Maddie said with a laugh.

"Of course I am."

"At least the money is good in your line of work," Joanna said before biting into an olive.

"Not as good as it was back in the early days of the Iraq war."

"I heard you were very successful."

"In the end, Joanna, none of us were very successful. Look how things have turned out. The coalition was a bloody joke. No one would share information. Unable to find the fucking weapons of mass destruction."

"Speaking of weapons of mass destruction..." Joanna stared at him, nibbling at a piece of cheese. "I've seen your apocalypse arsenal downstairs. Impressive."

"Ah, you've seen that? Well done, Mads, you've given her the royal tour of the place. Including the basement! Nice."

Maddie looked down and slowly folded and unfolded her paper napkin.

"Oh yeah," Joanna went on. "Looks like you're ready to take over the unfinished work of the Unabomber."

Ian leaned back and laughed heartily. "Oh my! I've been traveling for two days and I'm sure that I look as if I've been dragged through a bush backward, but the Unabomber, Jo? Come on. Ted had way better facial hair."

The three of them sat in an uncomfortable silence for a second. Maddie stared into her wine.

"And you?" Ian said eventually. "No longer delivering nappies and Tampax to the needy?"

"Ian!" Maddie said sharply.

"It's okay, Maddie," Joanna said, holding up a hand. "Nope. No longer." She gazed at him intensely.

Ian played with his Zippo lighter, flipping it back and forth through his fingers. "Then what have you been up to?"

"Figuring out my next move."

"Well. That's very deep and cool."

"I'm trying so hard to impress you, so thanks for that."

Ian took an enormous swallow of his very large vodka and clapped his hands together with a fake upbeat smile at Maddie. "I'm going to go downstairs and have a cigarette. I'll be back in a flash."

"Take your time," Joanna said, drawing her wineglass closer to her with both hands.

Ian looked at Maddie before he left and noticed how sweaty her face looked, as if the conversation were causing her to be sick. He put a hand on her shoulder before leaving and said, "It's okay, Petal. Relax."

She looked up at him with one startled, wide animal eye. The other, the ruined one, drooped in a way that made him sad. "It's okay," he said again, a bit uncomfortably. She nodded, swallowed and looked down into her wine.

Ian breathed a sigh of relief as he descended into his favorite place. He clicked back on Candy Crush and lit a cigarette. He'd brought his vodka down with him, and he was quite content.

Until he glanced over at the pool table and saw the computer case for his gaming laptop. It was lying open in the middle of the table, and it was empty. He always put his laptop in the case and stashed it underneath his desk when he went away.

Ian felt a crushing, sickening dread. Then there was a gut-wrenching déjà vu back to a night in Cyprus years before when he had also realized that his personal emails had been read. Back then Fiona had seen old drafts of weird letters he had never sent to Maddie. Now his wife had likely seen the photos Fiona had sent to him. Why Maddie had even allowed him to walk in the door was a mystery. He would have been furious. Then again, he had pass code protected the computer, and he didn't think Maddie would have been able to remember his army number. Maybe she hadn't seen them after all.

The situation with Fiona had been escalating for three years, and it was now totally out of control. It was a constant burden. He'd had no idea how to handle it. He didn't want to tell Maddie the whole story because, just like the day in the hospital when the square glass vase filled with black roses had arrived, he hadn't wanted her to worry. That afternoon after

Charlie had been born, Ian had pounced on the nurse who was sashaying in with the unusual bouquet and said, "Whoa, whoa, whoa!"

The roses had been fake, made out of polyester or some such fabric. The blackish-purplish hue was not intended to brighten anyone's day. He'd been sent a black rose once before—from Fiona. She loved to be gothic and macabre and mean. He'd snatched at the card and then the damn thing had fallen to the floor. The nurse managed to retrieve it before him, looked and then gasped.

"Don't get too attached, Maddie. You stole what I loved most. Maybe I'll do the same to you."

It took an afternoon of chasing down old military contacts to find out that Fiona had manipulated a Facebook friend of theirs from the army into giving her his new phone number and address in the States. That same friend had also told Fiona that Ian and Maddie were expecting a child.

Ian's first instinct had been to call and berate her and threaten to have her arrested. The more he thought about the situation, and the vicious swings of Fiona's bipolar personality, the more he worried about the potential fallout from such a knee-jerk reaction. Instead, he decided upon damage control. Keep tabs on her. Though he doubted Fiona would get on a plane to Kansas, he did not put it completely past her. She had a history of showing up unannounced in places she was not wanted.

Ultimately, he called her and apologized for how things had turned out between them. He said he understood how angry and hurt she was. He'd treated her with respect and had hoped that by killing her with kindness he could lessen her pain and hatred. All he'd wanted to do was make sure she had no sudden hateful inclination to show up at his door one day.

It had backfired. In the last couple of years his occasional Christmas and birthday missives wishing her well had been misinterpreted. Six months ago, she'd started sending him the photos and explicit messages. He'd saved all her emails in case he needed evidence to get a restraining order. He kept the whole big nasty bunch of them in a folder he'd named "Bunny Boiler." It didn't seem very funny now.

He'd wanted to call her up and explain in lengthy detail how much he hated her. That, however, would have made it impossible to sleep at night when he was in Pakistan and Maddie and Charlie were at home in Meadowlark alone. Fiona knew where he lived.

He wished he'd told Maddie the whole truth long ago, but he hadn't. He'd told her it was nothing. He hadn't wanted to worry her. He thought about it now and was filled with regret. I didn't want to worry her. It sounded so stupid. Now Maddie had taken his X-rated laptop somewhere, and he was the one who was worried.

Suddenly upstairs a racket had begun. The girls appeared to be arguing, and he couldn't help but feel vindicated. He wondered if Maddie had told Joanna off for her snotty attitude and general bitchiness. He hoped so. He enjoyed the sounds of a scuffle until it seemed that it had gone on far too long. And why weren't either of the girls yelling obscenities at each other like back in the days when they fought in Skopje? He was starting to get curious. Then he heard what sounded like the smashing of a glass.

"What's going on?" he yelled up, craning his neck around for a response. No one answered, but he heard a chair being dragged across the floor, and then a crash as if it had been knocked over. He put out his cigarette and marched up the stairs. "I said, what's going—"

Maddie met him at the top of the basement stairs, eyes wet and feverish, stammering. "She ate the cheese you got! It had walnuts in it! She's in shock! Tree-nut allergy, remember? Anaphylactic shock! She can't breathe!"

Ian's first drunken thought was that he wouldn't have bought cheese with walnuts in it; that sounded absolutely disgusting. His second thought was that he must have done it unknowingly, and now he had to solve the problem.

Joanna lay between the refrigerator door and the sink, on her back, clutching her neck. Her face was splotchy and red. She wasn't breathing. If Maddie was right and it was anaphylactic shock, there was no use pounding on her back or trying the Heimlich maneuver.

"Ian," Maddie said, tears streaming down her face. "We don't have an EpiPen. You've done it before. You told me. You did it for a soldier in Cyprus who was allergic to shellfish."

"I know I did."

"Can you help her? Please? Please do that thing. Save her, Ian."

To the right of the refrigerator was the phone, the calendar and a ballpoint pen. He grabbed the pen, pulled the end out with his teeth and shook out the ink tube. He reached for the Cuisinart knife block on the left side of the refrigerator and grabbed the small paring knife. He intended to access Joanna's trachea below the swelling in her throat and insert the pen tube in the hole to allow her lungs some oxygen until the medics arrived. He straddled her with his knees over her stomach. Hunching over her body, he touched her throat, finding the right spot.

Bizarrely, Joanna suddenly reached out with both hands and raked her fingernails down his arms. "Calm down, woman!" he bellowed. "I'm trying to help you!"

She responded to this by scratching his face. "For fuck's sake, Joanna! Stop it!"

She stopped. Ian took a deep breath. As he was just about to make an incision in the hollow of her throat to perform the emergency tracheotomy, she inexplicably pulled him down into a tight hug. Joanna wrapped her arms around the back of his neck and held him there. In a voice muffled against her shoulder he said, "Let go! What's wrong with you? Let go of me!"

Joanna kept her arms locked around his neck, and he felt an extreme, blinding pain in his back followed by a spreading cold through his body. A split second later he was overwhelmed with nausea. He dropped the tube and the paring knife. Something came loose in his lungs. He tried to pull away, but Joanna's arms were strong and tight around his neck. With each attempt to sit up he was pulling up the entire weight of her body. It was too much. She was able to hold him down, close and tight.

There was a moment of relief as the deep pain lessened and then it came at him again, sharper and stronger, and it was ten times worse than having the wind knocked out of him. His whole body felt incapacitated, as if he'd been drugged. He was starting to go weak. Finally she let go and he fell to the side of her body.

Joanna lay there, breathing in great frenzied gulps.

"Maddie?" he asked, looking for her. "What's just happened?" It didn't make sense. Maddie crept into the edge of his tunnel vision, blurry and fading, but he could see she was scared, more scared than he had ever seen her before. There was a light spray of blood on her, on the refrigerator, everywhere he looked. "Help me, baby," he meant to say, but this time it wasn't words that came out.

Oh she was freaked out all right, completely freaked out. What had happened? Heart attack? No, there was blood everywhere. He reached out a hand toward her, to comfort her that he was still here. Just like her eye, he could be fixed. She recoiled and took a step back. She was mad at him. She had seen his emails. Or maybe it was that he hadn't had the chance to tell her he was going to take her away, get her out of Kansas for a nice holiday. She'd never stayed mad at him before. She couldn't. He felt himself shrinking, smaller and smaller.

Maddie picked up the home phone from its charging station on the kitchen counter. "Now?"

"Not yet," Joanna responded, standing up. "Wait a few more minutes to be safe."

Ian moved about a little on the floor, making a gurgling noise. Blood ran from his mouth.

The women stood there in silence. After a minute Joanna said, "Yeah. Let's go. We're good."

MADDIE

Day of the killing

We ran side by side to the foyer. Standing at the bottom of the stairs, I raised the phone over my head and then dropped it to the floor, where it broke into several pieces. The batteries went rolling.

"Quickly now," Joanna said, and we started up the stairs. One of Charlie's blankets was there, waiting to be carried up to the laundry room. I grabbed it and wiped my face. There was blood in my eyes. I dropped it back on the step.

We entered Charlie's room, where he was sleeping. Joanna whispered, "Where's the phone?"

I whispered back, "It was here!"

"Maddie, come on, don't fuck around. We don't have time!"

"It was here!"

"Well, it's not here now! Go find it!"

Ten seconds later I returned with the phone. "Call now?"

"Yes."

I dialed 911.

At that exact moment, Joanna woke Charlie up with a vicious pinch on the arm.

While Charlie howled, I whispered into the phone, "Go back upstairs, baby, please." My voice sounded urgent. Good. "Please! Go! Go now!" And then suddenly I shouted, "Oh my God! Hurry! Please help us! Hurry! No!" My heart was pounding as if it was all happening, as if it was all real.

Then I took the phone, banged it once against the wooden bed frame and turned it off.

I stared at Charlie. His eyes were tightly shut and his mouth an open oval as the tears rolled down his red cheeks. He was hysterical. I reached out to him, and Joanna said, "Go, put the phone back on charge in the bedroom like we talked about."

"Okay." But I didn't move. I couldn't tear my eyes away. I couldn't speak.

"He's fine, Maddie," Jo said. "He had a nightmare, that's all. Right, Charlie? It was just a nightmare."

"You hurted me!" he sputtered between sobs.

"I'm sorry, baby," I said, sounding desperate and hysterical. "Mommy shouldn't have let—"

"Give me the phone," Joanna snapped. "I'll put it back. Take him and go hide! We came upstairs to get Charlie. We thought we heard Ian, and we decided to hide rather than go back downstairs with a drunk madman loose in the house. You remember what to say, right?"

I could only gawk like a catatonic mute at my son. What was wrong with me? His nose was running, and snot was smeared across his upper lip. My chest was heaving. I could hear myself breathing. Gasping.

"Can you handle this?" Jo demanded.

"Yes," I answered, blinking and shaking my head. "I'm okay now. Come on, Charlie. I want you to come with me."

Charlie was wearing his nighttime Easy Ups and a Thomas the Tank Engine T-shirt. He took my hand and, still inconsolable and wiping his nose, followed me out of the bedroom and down the dark hall.

IAN

Day of the killing

When Ian opened his eyes, he could see the night sky. The fiery star came sailing in, landed and rocked the desert. Behind the hangars, he saw a swelling red sphere, followed by a heart-stopping explosion. Graceful arcs of multi-colored light trailed this way and that in the murky distance, and Ian suddenly knew where he was. He was in Iraq, at that godforsaken airport in Kirkuk.

"Okay," he said, finally lurching awkwardly to legs that could barely hold him. He took one heavy, struggling step after another, pausing often, to make it through the field. Though it was dark, he thought he could find the abandoned jeep he remembered seeing earlier. As he crossed his own living room to the stairs, explosions sent plumes of red, yellow and orange dirt up around him. The ceiling was the sky. He was a world away.

Down he went, intuitively, to escape.

He fell against something solid and was relieved he'd found

the jeep. He slid down to a seat on the cracked mud, and it was more comfortable than he'd expected. He felt relatively safe, though it was dawning on him that he'd taken a hit to the back and he needed help. The sound of a droning siren wheeled in and out of his ears, and suddenly he was as heart-broken and hopeless as he'd ever been. Something bad was happening. Something really fucking bad.

This was battle shock, he told himself. He looked around and it was so damn dark, except for the bizarre light show. None of this made sense.

"I'm okay," he mumbled. Just tired, he told himself. He'd been tired in Cyprus in a way that made him not want to wake up, and now he remembered what that felt like. Bloody hell. He hadn't had a decent night's sleep since Rwanda and the meadow of bones. He'd never been able to walk out of it. Never been able to walk away.

He heard footsteps. Heavy, like boots on the ground. Some-one was running toward him. There, in the moonless dark, were orange explosions behind an approaching figure.

He tried to lean forward because his back was soaking wet. The fucking desert heat and all the drenching sweat. It was a bad idea. The movement caused him to spit blood, and now the front of his shirt was wet, too. He reached for the familiar pistol grip of his rifle and found that it was not there.

Yes, someone was approaching. Someone silhouetted against an orange glow. Then a flare in the sky burst the night open into sparks of brilliant white sparkling light and everything was visible, including Peter. Oh Peter, fucking Peter. He'd never been the sharpest tool in the shed but seriously? Run-ning across that field?

Ian winced and curled in, bracing himself, knowing what happened next, but when he opened his eyes, he saw Peter was fine and standing in front of him. Peter, who was sup-posed to get hit by the luckiest fucking sniper the world has ever seen. Ian made a feeble gesture for him to get down, take cover, and then he closed his eyes. He didn't want to see what happened to Peter again.

Nothing happened. Ian opened his eyes, and Peter was turning around and sinking down to a sitting position next to Ian. He was smiling. He looked way better than Ian remembered. Blond curls and round blue laughing eyes. A manchild. A character in a fairy tale. Ian laughed with unhinged joy, but his laughter never made it out of his body.

"Pete, you're okay?"

"I'm good, mate! Aces." Peter reached into his shirt pocket. "Remember that last cigarette I told you I was saving? It's for you."

Ian tried to reply. Nothing came out of his mouth but bubbly blood, all over his shirt. "I have." He vomited more blood. "To call." It happened again. "For help, Pete." His hands wandered over his own body, applying useless pressure. "I don't want to die yet." Ian fumbled in his pockets for his radio, found it and pushed the pressel switch. "Alpha?"

"That's not your radio." Ian looked at the cell phone in his hand. Again, Peter held out that last cigarette. He waved it enticingly. "Come on. You know you want it."

It seemed so final, and Ian wasn't ready to take it. He burst into a hacking cough. He felt like he was drowning and tried to spit it out and there were more frothing bubbles and he now realized that at least one of his lungs was done.

"Pete," he managed to say. "I have. I have."

"What's that, Ian? What're you trying to say?"

"A chest seal. It's in my first-aid kit. It was here," he said, touching his leg. "Can you help me find it?" They both used their hands to search the dark ground around them, but the first-aid kit was nowhere to be found. Where the fuck was it, and why was he wearing jeans? It was way too bloody hot to be wearing jeans.

"You're going to be all right," Peter said. For the first time, Ian's mind had decided to protect someone new. Himself. Ian wasn't a crier, but he felt a sob well up in his chest and burst out his mouth.

"Lying bastard," Ian whispered, trying to smile through tears. "I've got shrapnel in my lungs."

"Think about your family. That's what you said to me. And you, Ian, you won the lottery, mate! You have a wife and a lovely little boy who thought the world of you."

Ian looked at him, confused. "I don't have a family. You have the family."

"I had Ashley and Polly and another on the way. You've got Maddie and Charlie."

"Was that real?"

"Don't be daft, Ian. Of course it was!"

"Charlie? Oh God, Charlie and Maddie? Oh thank God for that!" Ian looked at the phone in his hand and started trying to call Maddie. The numbers swam in his eyes, and his fingers fumbled. "One time," he mumbled, imagining he was talking. Not much was coming out. It was mostly in his head. "One time in Iraq I tried to call her from the TV control. John was so mad. My brother. You know him. I was drunk. One time I... This isn't working either." He couldn't do anything. "I fucked up, Pete."

Peter's cherubic face suddenly changed to anger. "You did not fuck up. You did not fuck up, Ian. You set them up for life. There will be no wars for your son. And you loved Maddie, right?"

"Always. Still do."

"Just hold on to that."

"Can I say goodbye to them?"

"No, mate. I'm afraid not." Peter brightened. "But you kissed Charlie good-night and told him you loved him. That's even better than goodbye."

"I did! Yes, I did. So, I'm not in Kirkuk, am I?"

"No."

"I'm dying and I'm in my basement?"

"That's the situation, I'm afraid."

"How did I get here?"

Peter laughed. "You staggered, mate. Just like back in our drinking days." He offered the cigarette again, and this time Ian took it. Peter then helped him up to his feet and said, "Let's get ourselves to the safe zone, what do you say?"

Ian nodded.

They walked, Peter's arm around Ian, past his beloved computers. He tried to go to them because they were full of cycling photos: Ian in a ball cap nodding off in an armchair with newborn Charlie in his arms, he and Maddie on her parents' back porch the day they got married, and a gorgeous shot of all three of them and the dogs against the Rocky Mountains at the campsite the afternoon before Maddie hurt herself.

With a gentle tug from Peter, Ian moved away from those images and made it past the home movie theater where he would never watch his *Star Wars* marathon with his son. Then, that was all. Ian rested his eyes and the darkness became whole except for the sliver of light shining on the concrete floor like the moon on water. He and Peter followed where it led, through the wooden door, into the shelter and his final, secure bastion of safety.

MADDIE

Five months later

My mom was right. I was never the same after the boat-ing accident. While I lay in the ICU, sleeping and deep dreaming, I went around in my head. It felt like I was search-ing an endless maze of a mansion. I found a room where I could rest, located the lights, and like an efficient maid, switched them off one by one. It became a cave-like place. There I found a soft spot, burrowed like a dog in blankets, and I made myself comfortable. I hunkered down, animal and ready, and looked out at the world with shining eyes, from the darkness into the light. I was safe. I was hidden.

It was easy to move to Spain or Bulgaria or jump on a plane to Croatia. It was no problem to cross dirty Balkan borders by bus in the deepest night, and it was not an issue at all to sleep with strangers from The Corner Bistro, nor to befriend drug dealers, drunks and mercenaries.

Ian would not have cared for me as much as he did if I'd never had my accident. He knew I was damaged and he liked it. He needed someone to save. He appreciated my fascination with danger, because that was the root of my fascination with him. My near-death experience under the boat led me to seek out others who knew that moment of blissful survival, and Ian knew it better than anyone I ever met. I did love him. I still do love the Ian that once was.

Many times I have woken up in the one-room apartment I share with Charlie in San Juan del Sur, thinking I'm back in my studio in New York, waiting for Ian to call me, write me, show up, let me know he's alive. Then I smell the lush frangipani blossoms floating in on the breeze through the screened window. I remember where I am and I can't bear it. I have to think about anything else. What will we have for breakfast? Where will we play today? When I look down at Charlie sleeping beside me, I know I made the only choice I could. It feels like I can't bear it but I can. I have to, for Charlie. The sadness is manageable. I have evolved beyond anguish. The best I can do is to muster regret and comfort myself with the truth. He got what he wanted. Me, Charlie and finally peace.

I wish things had gone differently. I wish that Ian had not caved under the weight of his experiences and that he had not painted me a picture of a future that he likely knew he was incapable of living. But what I wish more than anything right now, is that Ian's brother John would fuck off and leave me and Charlie alone.

Leo's Cyber Café is halfway between our apartment and the beach. Charlie and I usually come here once or twice a week, in the mornings. I have a cappuccino and he plays Crossy Road on his new iPad (money no longer being such a huge issue) while I check my email. Two weeks ago, I received a message from John Wilson. I'd only met him the one time in Bosnia when I threw his phone at him, but I'd heard plenty about him over the years. I knew that he was as intelligent—if not more so—

than Ian. Also, he loved Ian. I knew that it was John who held the Wilson family memorial for Ian at his house in England.

From: John Wilson
To: Madeline Wilson
Sent: Friday, 5 January 2018
Subject: Hello

Dear Madeline & Charlie,

I am writing on behalf of our family. I should have written sooner but it's very hard to convey our thoughts and feelings about Ian's death. Most importantly, we care deeply about you and Charlie.

We were aware that Ian had some issues, but we never ever thought that it would come to this. Had we known the depth of Ian's troubles, perhaps we could have done something, and things would have ended differently. I, for one, believed him when he told me he was done with the vodka. We had some arguments of our own on the same subject over the years.

We (my brothers, sisters and I) would like to reach out to you and make it clear that you and Charlie have a big, loving family in England who are eager to meet you both.

I understand why you have not been in touch. Perhaps you were expecting a cold reception, given what happened, but that's not the case.

I have six weeks of free time before I'm due back in Afghanistan. I would very much like to come to Kansas as soon as possible with my family so my wife, Monica, and I can meet you and our nephew. Our son, Sam, is eager to meet his cousin. It's long overdue.

We don't want the tragedy that occurred to result in any further anger or alienation. Please consider how much it would mean to all of us to have you and Charlie in our lives.

All our love to you both,
John

I didn't answer him and hoped that he would bugger off back to Afghanistan. He didn't. Last week the email he sent took a somewhat different tone.

From: John Wilson
To: Madeline Wilson
Sent: Friday, 12 January 2018
Subject: Hello again

Dear Madeline,

It's not my intention to harass you. I am fully aware that you and Charlie are going through a lot right now. I only have a short time before I must return to Afghanistan for the fore-seeable future. In the event that you're willing to see me, I would like to make my travel arrangements. I will not be bringing Monica and Sam. I realize that was probably far too much to ask given the delicate circumstances.

I wasn't going to mention this until I saw you, but Ian and I were co-owners of a rather large estate in Caldy of which fifty percent now belongs to you and Charlie. Though my desire to meet with you is fully about solidifying family ties, I do have some documents for you to sign as well. I can arrive in Kansas City as early as Wednesday. Please do write me back this time.

Sincerely,
John

He doesn't know me. He doesn't know I'm smart enough to realize when I'm being baited.

And now today. Charlie and I have only just arrived at Leo's Cyber Café. My cappuccino is still too hot to drink. Charlie's little chocolate-chip pastry remains untouched. We have been here less than five minutes, and in that time my entire world has lurched onto its side. I can barely see the screen in front of me. My heart is pounding out of my chest, so loud that I look around to see if anyone else in the café can hear it. Yes, they are all staring at me. My ears are ringing, and my throat feels like it has been stuffed with algae. I can't swallow. I can't even breathe. I put my head down between my legs and count to twenty. It feels like I'm on a boat, lurching over waves.

"Mommy, what's wrong?" Charlie asks, tilting his head thoughtfully to the side, putting his hand on my shoulder like a grown-up.

The floor is filthy with crumpled sugar packets, cigarette ash and dust bunnies. I gag and mumble, "I dropped something, baby."

The overly friendly owner with the muttonchop sideburns is suddenly rubbing my back. *"Señora? Señora? Estas bien? Estas enferma?"*

I have to pull it together. I sit up with a big sigh and smile. "I'm fine. *Estoy bien!*"

He smiles and walks away. I hit Print the seven times that it takes to print my seven fucking emails and shut down. After retrieving my papers from the printer I pay our bill, wrap Charlie's pastry in a napkin and put it all in my big beach bag. I take Charlie's hand, and we walk out into the blazing sun and down to Paseo Del Rey. I realize that I have forgotten to cover my scar with my sunglasses. People are staring at me. I stop and pull myself together. Hat, glasses, smile. Nice pretty lady.

Charlie starts to head out toward the water, but I say, "Wait, honey. Come with me." Just up the street is the Iguana Bar. It's the kind of place where no one is going to think twice about a mom with her son ordering a Macuá at ten in the morning. Such a thing exists. Thank God we're not in Kansas anymore.

There's no server behind the bar. Two old men are playing chess on the patio, and a couple of drunk American boys in fraternity T-shirts are swaying on their bar stools and watching *fútbol* on the television, but there's no server in sight. Charlie spies a rack of chips and *chicharrones* hanging behind the bar. He suddenly looks like a starving adorable puppy. I brought him to Nicaragua, and now he loves pigskin fried to a bubbly crisp.

"Mommy, I want *chicharrones!*"

"Okay," I say, looking around for the goddamned server. I smack my hand down on the bar. "Hello?"

A woman walks out from the kitchen and past me without meeting my eyes. She grabs some cleaning products and a rag. She leaves silently. "Excuse me," I yell at her back. *"Perdón!"*
Nothing.

Charlie climbs up on the bar stool and stares at the *chicharrones*, then at me, then back at the *chicharrones*. Finally a young, bearded, very handsome man with his hair pulled back in a bun comes whistling through the front door, packing his new cigarettes. *"Que quiere, Señora?"* he asks cheerfully.

"Una chingada bebida," I answer irritably, immediately regretting it. Be sweet, I say to myself. No need to demand a fucking drink.

He raises an eyebrow, and as he goes behind the bar he says in perfect English, "You talk that way around your kid?"

"He doesn't speak Spanish."

Charlie says, "I do, too."

"Can I have a Macuá, please?" I say politely.

The bartender is slow, probably stoned, and his jeans hang low on his hips. I can see his underwear and the hair under his armpits as he mixes my drink. His earlobes are gauged with giant rings. I am about to apologize when Charlie, still on the bar stool and with his arm outstretched toward the *chicharrones*, topples over.

I leap to his assistance, but he is fine, sprawled on the dirty floor giggling. "My God, Charlie! What's wrong with you?"

The bartender is annoyed with me. "Here's your drink."

As I'm digging through the beach bag with Charlie's napkin-wrapped pastry, pages of printed emails, an iPad, flip-flops, trash and bottles of water, he says, "On the house."

I put on my sad, kind, messed-up face and finally locate some money. "I'm sorry. I really, really am. We received some bad news this morning. Can I get that package of *chicharrones* for him, please? Charlie, I shouldn't have yelled at you. I'm getting your snack, sweetie."

The bartender rethinks me and hands over a bag of the *chicharrones*. Charlie is elated, practically giggling in anticipation. "We all have bad days," he says. His eyes travel over me. "Come back and see us again when you're in a better mood."

We walk across the sand. Charlie shovels a fistful of *chicharrones* into his tiny mouth. I can hear him chewing. My hand is shaking, leaving little droplets of alcohol behind me like a bread-crumb trail. "Okay, this is good," I say when we reach an umbrella with two chairs for rent by the water.

I squelch my drink into the sand and dig through the bag, throwing sand toys this way and that. I sink into my chair.

I feel numb with fear and nerves. I stare forward at Charlie with his trio of plastic toy trucks, hauling sand and making puddles at the water's edge.

I have done what's best for Charlie. With so much violence and horror in the world every single day—shootings, bombings, beheadings, massacres—what's the big deal about sacrificing the father to save the son? If Ian wanted to believe God was dead so we better go hide, I thought the opposite. Anything was possible, anything was permissible, if you were smart and strong enough. Had Ian wanted to live? He'd be alive.

I'd started thinking about how our lives were going to go, Charlie's and mine, almost immediately after my fall. I sat on that patient table wearing a blood-soaked T-shirt from Target and my pajama pants and went over and over the argument Ian and I'd been having.

Charlie was in the tent asleep with the dogs, and Ian and I were about twenty feet away at the picnic table next to a campfire drinking boxed wine.

"I think we should take Charlie to see your family in Liverpool soon," I said. "He can get to know all his crazy aunties and uncles and play with his cousins."

"I'll think about it," he'd answered.

"What's to think about? Let's start planning. We've been married for over four years now, and I've only met John and Jimmy. I want to go to England and meet the rest of your family."

"Charlie's too little. I get sick of airports, Maddie. When I'm off I just want to be with you and Charlie and relax. Away from everyone and everything. Like we are now."

"You're sick of traveling, but I haven't been anywhere other than a campsite and our house since I got pregnant with Charlie."

"It's a nice house. Nothing wrong with that. Better than sweating your arse off in Yemen, like me."

"You said, 'If we move to Kansas we will save so much money that we'll have more for taking trips.' You said that."

"And we will! When he's older. I'm not fucking flying around the world with a bloody three-year-old, Maddie. You know how I feel about it."

"If you and John really do have a ton of money in that bank account that you're both so cagey about, we could hire a nanny to stay with him and go somewhere ourselves!"

"Oh so now you want to hire a stranger to raise Charlie for us. Who the fuck did I marry?"

I stared at him, furious. I played my best card. "Well, I married someone who is keeping a very big secret from me."

He was probably worried I'd found out about his gross Fiona fetish porn stash.

"I know about the place in Montana, Ian." I had his attention. "You got a letter from Survival Shelters and I opened it. It thanked you for your inquiry. It said that it would cost sixty-five thousand dollars to build the survival shelter you want, with oxygen generators, on your land in Montana. Since when do we have land in Montana?"

"Maddie—"

"Oxygen generators?"

"I was waiting for the right time to tell you about it."

"Before or after you had a bunker built and locked me and Charlie up inside?"

"That's ridiculous. I would never do that."

"You didn't let me leave the Hudson Hotel! Remember that first winter? You told me, 'Keep your arse right here in this hotel room with me! I don't want you to go out there! Why would you want to go out there when we can stay right here and order everything we need?' Maybe you want me and Charlie locked up, too. That's something we've found out that men do, right? Build little prisons in their backyards and keep women and children in them?"

"Maddie, please."

"Explain."

"The way I behaved at the Hudson Hotel was terrible. I'd just gotten out of Iraq. I know that was crazy. Look. I don't want to lock you up. I was hoping one day to build us a cabin."

He took in the look on my face. "Not just a cabin. A really beautiful house! I figured if I work a few more years our savings will be enough that I can actually retire early and we could just…just…escape."

"Okay. You want to know who the fuck you married? I'll tell you who. Someone who doesn't want to escape. I never asked for *A River Runs Through It*, Ian. You told me that if I agreed—against my wishes—to settle down in Kansas that we would travel to the places I like to go. Spain or Bulgaria. Portugal or Croatia. Not eventually move to an even more isolated ranch where Charlie can get home-schooled by his bitter, alcoholic mom and turn into some freak who's into taxidermy and making his own butter. Who did you fucking marry? Someone who is not going to stand for this shit anymore!"

"Oh your life is so hard. You really are a spoiled little bitch. Stop drinking and go to bed."

I stood up and stormed off toward the brick bathroom up the road. I hated him. With every pounding step I thought, *I hate him. I hate him. I hate him.*

Let's not beat about the bush. I was wasted. Then, out of nowhere, the ground came flying up to meet me, and my hands were useless and the blow to my face was staggering. Smack. Down. Staggering. Darkness and stars. Down. I was out. I drowned again, and I swum in my murky death. Inky comfort. Swirling silence.

When I woke up, it was just that. Gasp. Like coming out of a dream, except the dream was my life. Stars and dust descended around me. A wrecking ball had just hit my house and broken down the wall to my safe hideaway. My room with the lights turned off wasn't a room anymore. It was flattened. There was smoke and emptiness. And corridors. New corridors that I'd never known existed. Secret doors and passageways that had been closed. I imagined black ink bleeding into my eyes, it felt so much like a curtain falling. My mind was like a paper towel. The feeling, seeping through and taking over, felt for thirty luxurious seconds like tripping balls on the world's best Ecstasy. And then, just like with the near drowning, there was the beauty of what came after. The realization, so obvious that I couldn't believe I hadn't seen it before.

Charlie needed to live. I needed to get away from Ian before he reached out, grabbed our hands and pulled us down into the grave he was digging. He was going to imprison us in his bunker made of misery and anger under dirt.

What if I just left him? a small voice, the old me, asked. *Leave him! It's what's right.*

And another voice answered, *Yes. And lose. Lose everything.* And Charlie would still have to spend half his time with a man who brings home deadly viruses from Africa and sits his little boy in front of horror films and feeds him limitless butterscotch candies and will one day take him to England and talk up getting pissed with your mates and then on to a discussion of which tattoos to get and where. I should have thought about the son when choosing the father, but I wasn't just in love, I was conquered. And I was not who I am now. Now my desire is for my son.

Suddenly, Ian was the enemy. He was my spoils of our war. If he had almost enough money to retire, then it would be enough for me and Charlie to have a sparkling future. Without him.

As soon as those two police officers came in and sat down across from me and started asking questions about Ian, I knew that I was the good one and he was the bad one. It was evident that no one would ever blame me for anything that happened. I had no criminal record. I'd never even had a parking ticket. Ian? Fuck. Those policemen distrusted him from the moment I said *British*. From the moment I said military. Security. Private contractor. Iraq. Aggressive. Angry. PTSD. One arrest that I knew about. They were frothing, I tell you. They hated him even more when I told them how successful he had been.

What could I do about Ian? He wasn't going to travel with me. He wasn't going to stop drinking all night. He wasn't going to start mowing the lawn. He wasn't going to take Charlie to England or even to Chuck E. Cheese for that matter. No, what Ian was going to do was collect dusty old power cords in boxes all over the basement. He was going to shop online for antiviral masks, hunting knives and fishing kits. He was going to amass more and more survivalist bullshit, take us to the wilderness and make me and Charlie track scat, eat edible weeds and kill animals. He was going to remain broken, and do so mostly in his disgusting hoarder's basement. We were not eventually moving to a beach bungalow in Marbella, we were eventually moving to an underground metal box with an oxygen generator in Montana.

And guess what? That part of me that always before, every single time, ended up feeling badly for him? It was gone. It had escaped when the wall came down. Like bats, my pity had gathered, black and beating, and scattered in the sky. The poor soldier, he's seen so many terrible things that he really needs to sit and smoke and mull it all over instead of getting off his ass and taking out the fucking trash. No. Not anymore. Ian and I, we put up the good fight. And we lost to the world. But I would not go down, not with Charlie. We would cut our losses and move on. Charlie and I had a world to experience, and it wasn't going to happen in Kansas, and it wasn't going to happen with Ian.

I knew what had to happen. I'd already decided what I was doing and how I was going to do it when Dr. Roberts, out of the blue, unknowingly and ever so nicely, explained to me the one thing I didn't know. Why? Why was I suddenly able to maneuver my mind in ways that previously would have been unimaginable? That day in Dr. Roberts's office, he told me that it's not uncommon for a traumatic brain injury to alter a person's personality. That didn't surprise me, but I was very interested when he told me that in one case, a man hit his head, went into a coma and came out able to play the piano. I, too, had gained a new ability. The ability to proactively defend my future and Charlie's future from a potential source of harm. I was lucky, I decided, that I'd been altered in such an advantageous way. I was given new eyes. I could see ahead, and ahead, so far, so clear.

A single injury rarely results in an irreversible transformation. But the more times you suffer a head injury, as in the cases of football players and boxers, the more you run the risk of finding yourself a changed person. I told Dr. Roberts that I'd never had a head injury before, but that was incorrect. Strapped to my grandfather's boat, parts of my brain had been without oxygen long enough for the electricity to flicker and fade away. Ironically, that experience of bondage was what left me untethered to the human leash.

In a way, my grandfather is responsible for Ian's death. Had it not been for the transformation underneath, I wouldn't have gone looking for a man like Ian, and even if we had met, he would have found the normal me unpalatable. Ian was a damage junkie, and I was out of order in a way that got him off. So in a way, it's Ian's fault, too. Grandfather Carl and Ian. Not me. That's what I tell myself when I wake up screaming, after the recurring dream in which my grandmother Audrey is hissing at me, "People like us? We don't play by the rules."

It's her fault, too.

Charlie calls to me. "Mommy, look!"

He's incredibly proud of his hole in the ground. I give him a thumbs-up and take a giant drink of my Macuá. More than anything, I wish I could share this new development with Joanna. I know that she'd be able to calm me down because she'd already succeeded in calming me down a dozen times. In Meadowlark, before we were sure it was over, we huddled upstairs in the bedroom and she told me, "Don't worry. Are you kidding? No one will ever think it was you that strangled me."

I whispered back, "The woman officer was staring at my nails in the station."

Joanna said, in a voice that sounded a lot like the one I use for explaining something to Charlie, "Yes, you cut your nails. But if you hadn't there may have been nail marks against my neck. With a choice between real evidence and a curious lack of evidence, we've taken the right route. She can't do anything with nothing."

"And the vodka bottles?" I asked, needing all the answers to be on our side.

"Stop it about the bottles," she said. "You don't fingerprint bottles when no crime has been committed. No one will ever know that you poured the vodka down the drain. Seriously, Mad. They have better stuff to do than think about a closed case. They won't bother."

A few weeks later, once we had the house up for sale and had already checked into the Holiday Inn Express in Raleigh, we sat drinking wine in our little living room while we watched Charlie playing in the tub through the open bathroom door. I got the dry heaves a couple of times, and she demanded to know what was wrong.

"I'm afraid," I said. "I'm afraid someone will put the ballpoint pen together with the knife and know something about medical emergencies. They'll figure out how we got him into the right position." I panicked. "Why didn't I pick them up? I left them there, the pen and the little knife. Why didn't I pick them up and put them away? Why didn't I? It was part of the plan! Jo! Listen to me."

"Maddie," she said, her eyes wide almonds of pity. "If an emergency tracheotomy was a stretch of the imagination for me to come up with, and I have an IQ of a hundred and sixty, no one will ever put it together. No one. Ever."

Once we left the States, we swept through Frankfurt and onward to a lovely Flip Key on the beach in Bulgaria with an infinity pool overlooking the Black Sea. There, we really finally celebrated the fact that we were free.

"It's over," Joanna said, clinking her glass of Bulgariana Cabernet against mine.

But for me, it was never over. I thought about my plan obsessively, looking for places where I may have gone wrong. I

360 | ANNIE WARD

couldn't share everything with Joanna because the plan started long before she arrived. There were always tiny details taunting me, telling me that I should be looking over my shoulder. "Jo," I said. "What if they ever go back to the 911 recording and there's a problem with our timing? We took too long to call because I had to go search for the phone."

Sometimes when I look in Charlie's big brown eyes I see it all over again—him, sweetly asleep in his bed and waking to find Joanna's dark form hunched over him, her fingers on his arm. Squeezing. Twisting.

"Forget it. Listen, Maddie. Ian got what he deserved. Do not look back. It's done."

Of course she'd think he got what he deserved. Not only did I tell her that he did this to my face, I also said, "I know about the baby."

It was the night she arrived in Kansas City, before I'd confided in her about my plans. My mom and dad were babysitting Charlie and I had taken her to Louie's Wine Dive for dinner. We were drinking martinis, and she nearly knocked hers over in her shaky haste to set it down.

"Ian told you?"

I nodded solemnly. "I'm so sorry."

She started plaiting her hair nervously, and she looked just the same to me as she had back in Lake Ohrid at the fish tavern. The night everything changed. "That was such a bad time for me. I hate even thinking about it."

I caught her hand and her eyes and I held them. "Why didn't you tell me?"

"I wanted to. That moment of peeing on that stick and seeing the double lines? Oh my God. Holy shit. But first of all, I felt stupid. I mean, I speak eight languages. You would think I could switch brands of birth control without getting pregnant. And then, I wasn't sure at first what I was going to do. I mean, it's not like I could have kept my job and been a single mom. I didn't want to tell you until I knew what my plan was. And by the time I had decided that I just wanted to quit my job and go home and, I don't know, become a dog walker, you and I were fighting all the time. And then what happened happened and I didn't want to talk about it. And then you were gone."

Was that a tear? No. Maybe.

I nodded sympathetically and waited a beat before going on. "And was Ian the father?"

She looked up sharply, that pointed chin of hers jutting out and her eyes flashing. The vein in her forehead. It was like a beating heart. "What?"

"I know about you two." For once she was speechless. "I don't understand, Jo. Why would you not tell me about that? You knew everything about me, and I thought you told me everything, too. Why keep that from me?"

She drew in a quick breath and looked up, trying not to cry. "I wasn't going to keep it from you. It started right after we all met, and you had gone back to Sofia. I was going to tell you on your next visit but then—then—"

"What?"

"You came to visit, and before I could tell you, he started flirting with you." There it was. A single tear rolled down her cheek, and she whisked it away quickly. Adept at hiding her pain. "And it was humiliating. So I didn't tell you after all. What would I have said? 'Oh guess what, I've been shagging this guy for a month and look at that, it turns out he likes you better.' I couldn't bring myself to do it. I even tried. In the bathroom at Club Lipstick? He and I were already finished, and I took you in there to tell you the whole story, and then I lied. It just came out. And so you never knew any of it. And you left."

"I'm so sorry, Joanna. I really truly am. He was the father, wasn't he?"

I sat quietly. I needed to know where this suggestion would

lead. After a second she semi-collapsed and said, "He came to see me afterward. He brought me some medicine and soup. I didn't even tell him anything about whose it was. He couldn't have known. It's not as if you and I ever pretended to be pure as the driven snow. I suppose he thought I'd been with everyone."

"But you hadn't."

"That spring? No. Only with the guy from Vengeant and that was after."

"But you knew it was Ian's," I pressed, just to confirm. Before I said the rest.

"Yes, I knew."

"Jo, Ian did know. He told me he was sure it was his. He told me how relieved he was when you lost it. Because after you lost it, he thought it would be all right to pursue me. 'Not so awkward,' I think he said. Oh God, Jo. It's horrible."

"Not so awkward?" she repeated, losing color in her face. She dug her hands into her hair and her eyes were blinking so fast her lashes looked to me, for a fleeting moment, like the flapping black wings of a dying moth.

"He only just told me before he left this time. He was drunk. Had I known, I never would have…" I trailed off sadly.

At last she let out an inhuman sound. She grabbed the sides of our little two-top and lowered her head. She said, "I want to murder him."

"Me, too."

Good old Jo.

Of course Ian didn't know he was the father, and he never said any of those disgusting things about being happy she lost a baby.

I made it up.

He had slept with her. And he'd gotten back together with Fiona. Joanna was hurt and angry and went on to have a miscarriage, but for all Ian knew she'd slept with the entire Balkan Peninsula along with the Albanian king of black market tampons and each of his underlings. I imagine a man like him would have at least considered the possibility that he might have been the father, and it didn't surprise me much to know that he'd shown her some kindness in the aftermath. He felt sorry for her. He took her some painkillers and soup and he carried away some kittens. End of story. Except...

I needed it to be much worse than that.

It's important to recognize one's limitations, and I quite simply could not have done it without Joanna. I required her old but loyal black market contacts in Albania, and I needed a witness. I'd done my research and the truth is, most women who kill their husbands go to jail whether they've been abused or not. If a woman has been getting beaten up for two years she's supposed to divorce the prick, not kill him. In that scenario she probably loses half of her time with her kids. I considered faking a history of abuse, but my research made me change my mind. That would give me motive for murder, and I would be arrested. I needed there to be little to no history of abuse—aside from one very vague incident on a camping trip that poor little wifey can't even remember. It worked in my favor to have signs that he was spiraling out of control and losing his mind before—out of nowhere—he attacked me and my best friend. No premeditation. That would be a clear-cut act of defense.

Even then, our idea was tricky. A woman is only able to defend herself or another until the attacker stops being a threat. I wasn't able to stab him ten times to be sure. Just the two. Just the two, well done and deep. With the blade pointed downward, as Ian had taught me that night at Club Lipstick after the fight with the dunce who didn't know how to use his knife. "You've got to hold it like this," he'd explained, "if you want to hurt someone, if you want to get the blade between their ribs and puncture the lungs."

That's not a conversation you forget.

Joanna and I argued as we planned. I hadn't wanted her to pinch Charlie. I said, "We'll call 911 after Ian's dead. No need for Charlie to cry."

She was adamant. "No. We need to pretend the call was before. Hurry! Help! Before something bad happens! Please help! Whoops. You took too long. We were forced to do what we did and forced to go and hide. He's dead. Your fault."

We were both frankly astonished to learn that Ian's body was found in the basement. We had assumed that he would die then and there in the kitchen. It was a lucky, lovely thing that he'd walked all the way across the house and down into his man cave. It gave credence to our claim that we'd stayed upstairs for fear of the man staggering about down below. I still can't believe he walked across the whole house bleeding like a stuck pig. Physically he was so strong. Mentally so weak. To look at him you would never have guessed that the sight of an ordinary child's sippy cup could send him into a spiraling depression that could last a week.

It was, of course, necessary to create a valid reason for Joanna to show back up in my life within a week of Ian's death, hence all those sappy letters to her in Cami J's office. "Dear Jo, I've been through something very traumatic, and it has made me question my choices. I want you back in my life. I miss you so much. Blah blah blah. I was so wrong to let you go."

I knew from the moment that I came up with the idea of working with a writing therapist that it was the best way to spin my tale. Once I found Cami Toe, the world's most unprofessional psychologist, I had to be very self-aware during my assignments. I needed to come across as helpless and fretful, while portraying Ian as a frightening figure as opposed to just tragic. Thank God I remembered, just in the nick of time, not to write about Ian's bunker in the basement for her when I had not yet staged my grand reveal for Wayne with the sump-pump honey trap. And of course, there was that outright lie about me being chased the night I fell.

Oh Joanna. She was perfect. Without Joanna's Albanian "friends," I wouldn't have been able to get the new travel documents for me and Charlie or make Ian's money vanish using a Hawala transfer through Dubai.

Now I don't have her to talk me down with the voice of reason, and my fears are spiraling out of control. What if Cami Toe decides it just might be worth calling the police to tell them I came in two weeks after Ian's death and told her I was finished because I didn't need her anymore?

"Finished! Don't need me anymore? But this, this is your greatest time of need," she said, pleading, holding my hand. "We were making progress."

I snatched my hand away and left. Such a stupid thing to do, I admit, but so liberating to be rid of her and her ridiculous, touchy-feely belief in basket-weaving and fish-fostering for the soul. All those assignments to get in touch with my emotions, to grow and to really and truly feel. What makes you mad? What makes you sad? What makes you scared? Good God, Charlie could have come up with that shit. It's true that I liked her at times. She was so easy and useful. And even more predictable than Wayne.

A teenage boy is here to collect payment for the beach umbrella and chairs. As he tucks my money into his belt bag I look up to see that Charlie has enlisted a cute, tubby-tummied, half-naked girl in braids in the construction of his castle. I glance toward the public bathroom, and tell myself no. I can't leave him, though I feel like I'm going to vomit. I force myself to swallow down the taste of lake water and the rising terror of what they could discover. I fold in on my pain, slug the Macuá and wipe the sweat from my brow.

Things back home, they're not looking good. I wonder, has anyone spoken to the woman at the gym who I hurt in that Cardio Kickboxing class? I imagine her face looks something like mine right now. I'd also be interested to know if there is any CCTV footage of the tussle I had with the security guard down at the Plaza, after I ripped up the black peasant dress at Anthropologie and told the rude salesgirl to use it to wipe her ass?

My anxiety was and still is real, but I used my terror as an impetus to do what was necessary to live more and live now. Before the inevitable. I wanted to give Charlie a remarkable existence every single day, knowing that any day could be the last. Any day can be a sunny family outing to the lake that goes horribly wrong. I just wanted to be alive and be with Charlie, the one good thing that had come of all this mess. Sometimes it feels like that is all I've ever wanted.

Look at him. Oh I want to eat him up. He's tan now, a caramel color to complement his chocolate eyes. He looks like Ian, but with my wild hair. I ache with love as I watch him abandon his plastic trucks to build turrets for his sand castle with two torn clear plastic cups, refuse from the Iguana Bar.

The little girl is called back to her beach towel by a mother offering a banana, and Charlie comes to me.

"Mommy," he says brightly. "Help me find seashells to make the walls pretty!"

"Yes, baby," I answer. "Two minutes. Let me finish my drink."

He doesn't ask very often about Ian. I've thrown his superhero bracelets in the garbage and told him sadly that they're lost. Ian was gone more than half his life anyway. I get a lot of questions about when we might get to visit Gramma and Papa, and just last night he asked what happened to Joanna.

"She never came back from her swim," I said.

"Why?" he asked.

"She swam too far away from the boat," I answered. "She shouldn't have done that, should she have?"

"No, she was bad." His expression went stormy and thoughtful for a second, and I knew he remembered that pinch.

And he was right. She'd been bad. The amount of money that Ian thought he could retire on was laughable. How were we supposed to live the next thirty to forty years on a few million dollars? Oh yeah, we were going to grow our own vegetables and stew them with the bunnies we killed in Montana.

It was never about the money for Jo. She didn't do it because her career had gone sideways and she was broke. She did it because I told her Ian hurt us and because of the lie I told her about Ian being glad she lost her baby.

Though it hadn't been the reason she agreed to help me, Jo didn't mind luxury. Once we'd been cleared and it was over, once we had our new identities and our rental on the coast of San Juan del Sur in Nicaragua. She got greedy. She wanted to stay.

But she did something worse. She did something even more unforgivable than forcing me to watch her pinch my child. She became worried about me.

"Maddie," she would say, when she found me in the bathroom staring in the streaked mirror. "Are you okay? You're clenching and unclenching your fists, and your eyes look weird."

"Maddie," she would say, when she found me with the sink full of water and me with my face plunged into it, trying to remember what it felt like to take it into my lungs. "Let's get you some help, okay?"

She started to wonder if maybe she should spend more time with Charlie. So I could rest.

She started trying to be his mom. "Let me give you a

break, Maddie. I'll take him down to the beach for a little. Why don't you have a nap, and Charlie and I will go see if his friend Pedro is at the playground? Pedro's dad is a hottie! Would it be okay if I buy a soccer ball and start teaching Charlie to kick it around?"

No fucking way. Besides, the savings we had were for me and Charlie, not for Joanna's Nicaraguan fantasy holiday, which required a daily allowance for costly wet suits, swim goggles and scuba gear, aromatherapy massages, new rock-climbing paraphernalia and "salsa lessons with Enrique." I guess she thought it was blood money.

Wrong, bitch. My money. My kid. You don't get to swoop in at the last minute and have it all. I know what you want after all this time. Ian's baby. The one you lost.

She was an excellent swimmer and always had been. Charlie and I were accustomed to her disappearing into the ocean for long stretches of time. One day we rented a little fishing boat to take Charlie out for some fun. When Jo left for her swim I gave Charlie a dose of Benadryl and made him comfy in a pile of life jackets and towels. It turns out it is almost impossible for someone in the water to board a small fishing boat if you don't throw down the ladder. It's even harder to get out of the ocean if someone on the boat has an oar they can use to just keep pushing that swimmer away. It gets easier and easier to nudge a person back into the water when they start yelling and calling you a bitch. That makes you want to give them whacks on the head, which bloodies the water. Are there sharks off the coast of Nicaragua? If so that would be convenient. The hardest part is at the end when they reach out, crying and begging, blood and hair everywhere. I did it, though. Charlie needed me to do it and my good boy, my sweet little sugar booger? He slept through it all.

I watch him. He is serious and particular as he searches for the rare exquisite little rippled shell-fans to adorn the facade of his fairyland castle.

He's in his own little world. He and I are so much alike.

Everything I have done is for Charlie, which is why the seven emails that were waiting for me this morning are so infuriating that I can't see straight. My dad's emails were the first I saw.

From: Jack Brandt
To: Madeline Wilson
Sent: Tuesday, January 16, 2018
Subject: Hi from Dad

Maddie, listen, Ian's brother John has just left the house and your mom is very upset. He's here in Meadowlark looking for you. He had no idea you and Charlie are in Bulgaria. Can you please call me and mom as soon as you get this?

From: Jack Brandt
To: Madeline Wilson
Sent: Wednesday, January 17, 2018
Subject: Trying again

Maddie. John's here at the house again. We are all waiting to hear from you.

Then there were more from John himself.

From: John Wilson
To: Madeline Wilson
Sent: Wednesday, 17 January 2018
Subject: Urgent message from John

Hello. It's John. I need to speak with you. Please get back to me as soon as possible.

★ ★ ★

Of course my mom had to get involved.

From: Judy Brandt
To: Madeline Wilson
Sent: Thursday, January 18, 2018
Subject: This is Mom, write or call ASAP

Your dad and I are starting to get very worried. Ian's brother is asking us all kinds of questions. Why is there no answer when we call the number you gave us? I have called you twenty times! I spoke with the rental lady in Bulgaria. They said you left ages ago. Are you even in Bulgaria? Why aren't you answering our emails? Ian's brother John is getting very angry and he's scaring me and I think scaring Dad. We want to talk to Charlie. I want a phone call. Get back to us the second you get this message.

From: Jack Brandt
To: Madeline Wilson
Sent: Friday, January 19, 2018
Subject: Serious trouble

Well, guess what? Ian's brother John has been to the police station. Mom's friend Kathy from book club whose husband owns Prime Liquor says Diane Varga has been down there asking if an Englishman was around last spring buying giant amounts of vodka. When Kathy's husband said no she showed him your photo. He said he knows you. I want to know what the hell is going on. If you don't get back to me TODAY you are going to be in BIG trouble.

From: Judy Brandt
To: Madeline Wilson
Sent: Friday, January 19, 2018
Subject: Where are you? Where is Charlie?

Maddie, what's going on? I'm at my wit's end. I can't eat. I can't sleep. Where are you and are you okay? My heart is breaking. I need to know you and Charlie are all right. I can't take this. Please call or write one word. This is so painful. I love you, honey, whatever has happened can be fixed. I don't know where you are or if you're hurt or if you're in danger. I will help you whatever it is. Please let me know what's going on. You have always run off but you've never taken my precious grandbaby with you. Think of how we feel. We are so scared, Maddie. Please sweetheart, please. I'm waiting by the phone.

From: John Wilson
To: Madeline Wilson
Sent: Saturday, 20 January 2018
Subject: Last message

Madeline, this is the last message I'm going to send you. I want to know the whereabouts of my nephew. I'm now officially concerned for his safety. You need to bring him home to his grandparents. Do what's best for Charlie. If I don't hear back from you, the next time we communicate will be in person. That will not work out well for you. You can take this as a warning.

How could they doubt me? Of course I will do what's best for Charlie. I would never hurt him.

I stand up and walk over to my little boy. I take him in my arms and hug him tight. So John's after me now. And the pretty dark-eyed police officer has found a few of the holes in my story. It's only a short amount of time before she moves on from the vodka bottles to the fingernails and the phone, the pen, the knife. Fingernails, pen, knife, phone, boat, murder. Murders.

That's why we're here after all, isn't it? In hiding. Just in case.

Should I see a therapist?

I sometimes feel like my mind is possessed by another person or creature.

That quiz seems like such a long time ago.

So it's just us now. Forever. That's okay. I'll show Charlie the whole world and teach him all the languages, and no one from home will ever see either of us again. This is the life I wanted for us anyway.

Don't worry about Charlie.

We're fine.

★ ★ ★ ★ ★

ACKNOWLEDGMENTS

A special thanks to my agent, Madeleine Milburn. Her surprise entrance into my world was a miraculous and life-changing moment. Thank you also to Anna, Alice, Hayley and Giles at the Madeleine Milburn Agency for believing in this project and working so hard to make it happen.

To Erika Kahn Imranyi, please know how incredibly grateful I am to you for holding the torch as I tried to find my way. Your encouragement and advice were truly invaluable. Stefanie Bierwerth and Jennifer Lambert, I am so lucky to have found a home with you. Thank you for your kindness and support.

Mom and Dad. Everything I have ever accomplished is quite simply due to the two of you and your boundless capacity to offer love and support. Russ, Wendy, Laura and your families: thank you for never giving up on me. You are the best. Thank you also to the close circle of friends who have been there for me through thick and thin, triumph and failure and a few very dark days along the way. You know you are family as well, and to all my family I say, "Is there a word bigger than *love*?"

To the local police officers who patiently sat and answered all my questions, I owe you so much. You were such gentlemen, so forthcoming and charming. Thank you for your time and sincerity in helping me find ways to make the impossible possible.

Caidan and Jude. You gave me the happiness and hugs that I needed when writing alone was too hard. Everything I do is for the two of you.

Finally, for Jos... No one else besides you read the book as many times as me. You stayed up countless nights helping me with dialogue, coming up with ideas for plot, editing new pages and doing much of my research. You ended up being not just my life partner but my writing partner. There would be no *Beautiful Bad* without you.

1. In *Beautiful Bad*, it's not so clear-cut who can be trusted. Who is the villain and why?

2. A recurring theme in the book is the fine line between rational fear and obsessive overprotection. In what ways do Joanna, Ian and Maddie all cross that line for those they love?

3. *Beautiful Bad* takes you on a journey to Bulgaria, Macedonia, Croatia, Greece, Cyprus, Iraq, New York and Kansas. Which location did you enjoy reading about most and why? Did the book make you want to visit any of these places?

4. The first draft of this book was a memoir. Later it was heavily fictionalized. If you had to guess, which parts of the story are true and which are purely from the writer's imagination?

5. More than one character suffers from PTSD. Who do you think is the most badly scarred? Do you think damaged people gravitate toward one another? Does PTSD and the behavior that can accompany it have anything to do with the obsessive attraction between Maddie, Ian and Joanna?

6. The writer has said she wanted to write about imperfect real people, at the risk of them being unlikable at times. In what ways are Maddie, Joanna and Ian deeply flawed, and what are their redeeming qualities? Assuming this worked for some readers and not for others, where do you stand?

7. The book tries to question stereotypes; the innocent likable stay-at-home mom pitted against the rough, uneducated soldier who has returned from war broken and abusive. How do stereotypes like these affect the way we live our lives? How do they affect who we love? Who are our heroes? Have you ever misjudged someone you wish you had not?

8. If, like Maddie, you were asked to make a list of things that made you scared, what would be a few of your answers?

9. Maddie's childhood boating accident supposedly changes her forever. What do you think happened under that boat? An actual spiritual near-death experience? Significant brain damage? Terror that would result in uncontrollable, dangerous PTSD? Was she born with a predilection for reckless and immoral behavior, as her grandmother suggests? Or is it a combination of all of the above?

10. It's suggested that Ian might be an atheist, because he had seen too much pain, cruelty and horror to believe in a benevolent God. And yet, as he is dying, he feels his good friend "Peter" has shown up in his basement to comfort him, help him up and walk him to the light spilling through the door. What does this scene suggest? Was it religious, spiritual or purely shock? How did it make you feel about Ian, after all is said and done?

11. At the end of the book, Maddie is under scrutiny. Detective Varga has reopened the case and Ian's brother, John, a force to be reckoned with, has threatened that he is going to come looking for her. Do you think Maddie and Charlie are going to live happily-ever-after?

THE STORY BEHIND
BEAUTIFUL BAD

Quite a bit of *Beautiful Bad* was inspired by my own experiences. I was still in my twenties when I first set foot in the Balkans, a cluster of small Eastern European countries where *Beautiful Bad*'s three main characters—Maddie, Ian and Joanna—originally meet.

Full disclosure: I went to the Balkans for the man I loved at the time. He took a job in Sofia, Bulgaria, and we moved there from Los Angeles together. The Balkans, and particularly Bulgaria, instantly held a dark fascination for me. Having been raised by sensible parents in a very safe small town in Kansas, I was enthralled by the lawlessness of the Balkans. People were raw, candid, mostly poor and unapologetically scrappy. Brutal regional wars were still a fresh memory, as was communism, and that atmosphere of "living on the edge" made me feel alive, young and ready to learn about and experience the world.

As an aspiring writer, there was one thing about Eastern Europe at that time that was particularly alluring. It was cheap. The apartment we rented was one hundred dollars a month, and I knew plenty of Americans living in Sofia who paid even less. Yes, our washing machine drained into our kitchen sink and our bathroom was a small tiled room in which you sat on the toilet while you showered, but it didn't bother us in the least. Once you walked out into the city, you could have anything you wanted, and we wanted it all.

Most of us hung out with locals and ate and drank in Bulgarian kurtchmas or taverns. We feasted nightly on salads made from tomatoes so luscious I felt as if I'd never tasted one before. The food was amazing: peppers stuffed with aromatic spices and lamb, fried zucchini in yogurt sauce, spinach and feta pastries wrapped in buttery layers of phyllo dough—just to name a few of my favorites. The wine was excellent and inexpensive. We could dine as a huge group in a garden under the stars and pay next to nothing. I have to admit in retrospect I am ashamed of our excess, but at the time we thought we had discovered a secret paradise.

As the country careened ever closer to a revolution that would ultimately (and temporarily) overthrow the corrupt Soviet aligned and mafia-connected government, the man I moved to Bulgaria with decided it was best to go home.

Suffice it to say, I stayed. On my own. I was able to find lots of time to write in Sofia on a balcony overlooking the red rooftops of the city villas. I traveled across much of the Balkans—Turkey, Greece, Macedonia, Romania, Kosovo and Croatia—and was absolutely stunned by the physical beauty of the area and the unusual collision of culture that resulted where Europe bled into the Middle East.

I wasn't the only one fascinated by that often-maligned

little corner of Europe. The Balkans was teeming with intriguing people: writers, artists, arms dealers, aid workers, soldiers, teachers, filmmakers, you name it. I stayed in Bulgaria nearly four years and did something that would have been far more difficult to do anywhere else. I actually made a living as a writer, and enjoyed a nice quality of life. I took assignments from Fodor's travel guides and wrote screenplays for an American/Israeli film production company. I reported for an English-language newspaper and taught at the University of Sofia. I made a best friend there and met and fell in love with my husband.

Eventually that chapter in my life came to a close and I moved home to the States. A few years later I found myself back in Kansas starting a family. It was time to accept the fact that though I missed that place and time terribly, there was no going back.

But I could write about it.

Beautiful Bad was born out of that unique experience of meeting others who were also living recklessly, joyfully and somewhat dangerously in "the wild east." In the book, Maddie's best friend is Joanna Jasinski. I based Jo's character on an American woman I met by chance on New Year's Eve in a remote Bulgarian mountain village, dancing at midnight in the snow. We shared an obsession with language, travel and writing, and it was like finding a sibling who'd been separated at birth. We became close friends and she introduced me to a British soldier in Macedonia who would become the basis for *Beautiful Bad*'s charismatic bad boy, Ian. (He would also become my husband and the father of my two little boys.)

A lifetime fan of psychological thriller films and books, I knew I wanted to challenge assumptions about the domestic genre, about who is trustworthy and what makes a monster. I also knew I wanted to write an international thriller about those fascinating and unique characters I'd encountered in the

Balkans all those years ago. I wanted to explore their deep and immediate connection and loyalty as they orbited one another throughout their lives, dealing with tragedy, jealousy, failure, fear and trauma. The love triangle that develops between Maddie, Ian and Jo in the book is a major departure into complete fiction, but there was a period of time in real life when we were nearly inseparable. I think it's fair to say that the three of us truly loved one another, and I couldn't help but imagine the many different ways our intense friendship could have easily played out over the years.

The relationship between Maddie, Joanna and Ian evolves in a barbaric way, partially because of the twisted and dangerous lives they've led, but also because their feelings for one another are so ferocious. When one is wronged, there is literally hell to pay. *Beautiful Bad* is a story about human beings who have seen the worst the world has to offer and would do anything for the people they love. Even if it's terribly bad.